—A Cam O'Brien Novel—

HIS BROTHER'S KEEPER

KIMBERLY BLAIR

First Edition

PAGE PUBLISHING, INC.
New York, NY

First originally published by Page Publishing, Inc. 2015

ISBN 978-1-68139-859-4 (pbk)
ISBN 978-1-68139-860-0 (digital)

Printed in the United States of America

To my sister Sasha, my best friend, my other half.
Words cannot express how
much you mean to me and how grateful I am
that you have always been by my side in everything
I have ever done. This book wouldn't have
happened without your faith in me and the numerous
kicks in the ass that you have given to me during this
process. I love you to the moon and back, Sushi!

And to my husband, my soul mate, my best friend Josh.
Your unwavering faith in me gives me the courage
to be myself and it gave me the courage to reach my
dream. And now to give you something back, "You
were right." There now it is in print for the whole world
to see. You were absolutely right and I did it!
I love you more than words!

PROLOGUE

She fought back with everything in her. His fists beat her, breaking bone, tearing her skin. She struggled, trying to focus, knowing her life depended on it.

"Please." She struggled. "Please stop." Her voice was silenced, his fist slamming into her jaw. She felt and heard the crack as her jaw broke. Fear and panic fueled her struggle. Ignoring the pain, she fought with all she had.

Her stomach rolled as he leaned his face, his mouth closer to her. She could feel his hot, sweet breath crawling across her skin, unaware the more she struggled, the more he became excited. He struggled to maintain his control, desperately fighting to keep himself from an early climax.

She sobbed as her dress was torn from her body. Her panties cut her as he ripped them from her body. She tried to empty her mind as his hands painfully groped her breast. His fingers left a trail of bruises down her belly. Even though her jaw was broken, she screamed as he jammed his fingers deep inside her. "Why?" she mumbled. *Why?* Her mind screamed, *God why?*

She never expected an answer, but was shocked when he stopped long enough to. "Why not?" His voice chilled her. Dead calm. Emotionless, cold, hard.

"Please. Please," she whispered. He stilled, giving her hope. Silent tears ran down her cheeks. Her pleas shimmering in her eyes. For a moment she had hope. For a moment she let herself believe.

Just one moment.

Cat watched his eyes go dead. Dead and cold. Cold and hard. And in that one moment she knew she was going to die.

But still she fought, still she struggled. She clawed and bit. Struggled and squirmed. Pain exploded in her stomach when he forced himself into her. Her vision began to waver; dots danced in her eyes.

As she slowly faded, her last thought was for the one person who had shown her love. The one person who loved her no matter what. *Finn, I'm sorry, I'm so sorry,* and she faded away.

* * * *

Detective Garda Finn MacDougal stood beside Mary Catherine Donnelly's bed holding her hand. He looked over her broken and bruised body. The fiery little faery girl was nowhere to be found in this black-and-blue mess of a body. He looked at his card, crumpled and bloody on the bedside table. The hospital had gotten his name and number from it. It was the only thing that was on her body, tucked in a pocket of her torn dress.

He remembered the day he handed it to her. Cat had promised him, his card in her small hand, she was done with the prostitution. But six months later, she was still selling herself. Finn had met her when he caught her during an undercover sting. Underage prostitution was a huge problem in that part of Dublin, and her pimp was the main trafficker. He had tried to get her to flip on him, but her loyalty was fierce, a quality he admired. Finn had spoken to her every week since, trying to get her off the streets.

The beeping of the machines brought him back, and the bright and smiling girl was lost in a stark and sterile bed. Tubes snaked in and out of her body, her smile was gone, replaced with a jagged cut that split her bottom lip in two.

"Damnit, Cat! You're supposed to be done with this. You're only fifteen. Why the hell are you out on the streets selling your body like wares?" Finn's voice caught on the lump in his throat that threatened to choke him. Cat had no family. That's how she ended up on the streets, selling her body and doing damn near anything to support herself. But that had changed when Finn met her. He took her under his wing, trying to better her life. The fiery redhead, with the quick smile and blue eyes, captured his heart in the same way his little sister had, in some ways he saw her as his child. But now the blue eyes were closed and bruised, and the quick smile would never dazzle again.

Finn glanced behind him as Dr. Malloy walked in, and with one look he knew he would never hear Cat laugh again. He swallowed the tears that suddenly clogged his throat, and tried to switch back on the cop mode. It was one of the first things taught to police. If not the horrors of the job would eat your soul alive.

Dr. Malloy placed his hand on Finn's shoulder. "Are you the detective?"

"Yes, sir." He swallowed again before he continued, "She has no family. I'm all she has." He glanced at the doctor again. "Or had." He amended.

"Unfortunately, the victim suffered a brutal attack. Leaving her with severe head trauma resulting in permanent and total brain damage. That's not including the numerous other injuries and internal damage inflicted as well." He paused, looking down at his notes. He didn't need to consult his chart; there was only two options left for the poor girl. "Due to the injuries, the victim—"

"Her name is Mary Catherine Donnelly. Or Cat," Finn interrupted. "She has a name." He squeezed her hand to calm himself. "She has a name."

Dr. Malloy nodded his head. "I'm sorry, Detective. I meant no disrespect." At Finn's nod he continued. "Ms. Donnelly has suffered severe brain damage and, as a result, has been placed on life support to keep her body alive. Detective, there is no easy way to tell you this but there is a decision that has to be made."

Finn nodded. He knew the decision. He had talked to many families who had to make the same one. He just never thought he would be here making it himself.

An hour later Finn held Cat's hand as she breathed for the last time.

CHAPTER 1

Every day she deals with death.

The cruel and unfair part of life. But it is the only constant that life has. It doesn't discriminate. You cannot stand in line and pay for an extension. You can't bitch and whine your way out of it. Everyone faces it.

Death is unavoidable.

She sees the evil side of humanity and what it can do to another life. Every day she faces an unspeakable amount of horror and she questions, *Is this what the gods wanted for this world?* But every day, no matter the horror, she gets up and does her job.

Her name is Camille O'Brien and every day she deals with death.

She gets up every morning and puts on her badge and weapon. She walks into someone's death and stands for them. She looks at and faces what evil can do to us, what evil can do to a family. A father. A mother. A child. But still every day she puts on her badge and stands for them.

But she also sees them. She feels them and understands them. Because, unlike her partners, she lives with them, the dead. But with this "gift" comes a curse, because when they come so does their murder. Her team thinks that she has an uncanny ability to visualize the murder, to reach inside of the scene, see the evidence and picture it as it happened. If only that were it. If only she could have that little of a connection, but no, the gods have "blessed" her with an eye for the dead.

She has another word for it—cursed. But if this is her curse, her burden, she will do with it what she can.

So she gets up every morning and stands for them.

Only her partner, family, and best friend know her secret. Only they know why, when the dead come, she completely loses herself to them. Why work can't stay at work. When the dead come, she relives their final moments. Seeing the murder as it happened and on very rare occasions, she feels it. The fear, the agony of knowing, and sometimes the pain. This is her gift. This is her curse.

* * * *

Cam woke with a feeling that she couldn't completely explain or understand. Her legs felt heavy, as did her body. Pulling herself from bed, she dragged herself to the bathroom, catching a glimpse in the mirror. She stopped and stared. It looked like she'd been in a fight. A war actually. Her eyes were swollen, bruised an ugly purplish black. Her lips, already full, were swollen. Her red hair stood out from her head as if she was full of electricity.

Her gaze moved down from her face, taking stock of the rest of her naked body. The bruises didn't stop at her face, her entire body was covered in them. Scrapes and scratches only added to the weary and confused state she found herself in.

"What the fuck happened?" she asked herself. Her gaze wandered wildly over every inch of her body. Her heart was racing and her breathing was starting to hitch. She had to calm down or she was going to have a panic attack—that's the last thing she needed right now.

Staring in the mirror, Cam frantically thought back through her night.

She came home and locked up. She was alone. "How could I not remember?" she asked herself. No. *No*, she thought, *this is something else.* She had never lost time or blacked out in her life. Never.

Looking at her wild-eyed, wild-haired reflection, Cam ordered herself to calm down. Desperately fighting to regulate her breathing, she took a deep breath in and let it out. Again, she willed herself. Until finally she calmed down and regained her focus.

"Okay," she told herself. "Remember, damn it, remember."

Cam began to think back, her mind racing through everything she could remember. She froze when she caught movement out of the corner of her eye. All traces of her previous panic vanished and training kicked in. Accessing the situation, Cam realized two things: first, she was butt-assed naked, and second, she had no weapon.

Great, she thought. What the hell was she going to do? Flash them into submission? She wasn't overly blessed in the booby department, but at least she wasn't the president of the *Itty Bitty Titty Committee*. Her body was in very good shape, but she still doubted that flashing the perp would work. And she was damn sure not going to die butt ass naked and give her precinct a good show when they found her body.

As she looked around for anything to use as a weapon, she took stock of her counter. A flat iron, hairspray, toothbrush, toothpaste, etc. So she could do their hair and get rid of plaque and bad breath. This morning was getting better and better by the minute.

Grabbing the flat iron, at the very least she could hit them with it, Cam readied herself for attack. *Okay, well, here goes nothing*, she told herself.

On a battle cry, Cam ran out of the bathroom and stopped short. Sitting on the bench at the foot of her bed was a young woman in her mid-twenties. Dark red hair surrounded a pale, heart-shaped face, with ice blue, almond-shaped eyes. She had a small perky nose, turned up at the end and pouty, bold red lips. Her body was small and curvy, and it was showcased in a skinny red dress that stopped about an inch short of her end zone. Her legs were bare and ended in skinny, stiletto heels, the same siren red as the dress.

Cam stared, deciding on whether she could pull off a dress like that, when she realized she was still standing butt ass naked. Rushing to her closet, she grabbed her robe, and the reason for the perky little red head, currently parked on her bench, became clear.

Clearing her throat, Cam asked, "Who the hell are you and why are you here?"

Red dress woman looked irritated and put out at the question, but she answered anyway. "Nina. Nina Petrelli. Who the hell are you and where the hell am I?" A New York accent was dripping through every word. "And what the hell happened to you? It looks like you pissed off the wrong bitch and she took it out on your face."

Jesus, Cam thought, *this was not going to be a good morning. First the bruises, and now this.* Cam walked back to the bathroom to put away the flat iron. She knew ignoring her would not make her go away, but she wasn't dealing with the New York witch without coffee. She walked back out and headed for the kitchen. Nina followed her, all the while whining and talking non-stop.

Walking down the hallway of her beloved downtown condo, Cam thought about what happened last night. Of course Nina hadn't shut up, but Cam was well practiced at tuning out annoying people, including dead ones. But what Cam couldn't understand was why she looked the way she did. Not only Nina, but herself included. Cam had always been able to speak to the dead, always able to see them. But they always came in clear, not fuzzy. And Nina was fuzzy. Kind of like out of focus, but her voice was not affected. And that was a damn shame, Cam thought as they walked into her kitchen, with its pale yellow walls, natural wood cabinets and wall of windows that overlooked the harbor on her breakfast nook side and Fells Point on the other. The appliances were stainless steel and a chef's wet dream, and Cam used and loved every one of them. This was her favorite room.

Nina looked around, her eyes scanning every inch of space. "Why do you have a TV in here? I think that's tasteless," she said, rolling her eyes and head. She leaned against the counter, looking put out and bored, twirling a piece of hair around her long fingers.

Cam took a deep breath, filled her favorite mug with coffee, and turned and faced Nina. "The TV is there because I want it there. I like to be able to keep up with the Ravens or Orioles even if I'm in the kitchen. Not that it's any of your business."

Nina just stood there twirling her hair and, of all things, pouted.

Cam chuckled. This was getting better and better. She put down her cup and started to rub her temples. *Why? Why does this shit have to happen to me?* she thought. Finally, she asked Nina, "Do you know why you are here?"

"NO!" Nina screamed. "Damn it! Haven't you listened? No wonder you got your ass kicked, you're rude and…and like- stupid!"

Like-stupid? What? Was this high school? Cam thought.

Cam had to steel her body before she jumped Nina and bitch-slapped her. "Breathe. Just breathe," she said under her breath. She finally had enough control to look up at Nina. "Nina, this may come as a shock you, and I really don't care at this point, but you're dead." And even though she knew it was mean and spiteful, she smiled and walked out of the kitchen. The look on Nina's face was priceless, and Cam thought, *Worth it.* She knew it was mean and she should have been nicer about it, but damn, the girl was a bitch, a whiner, and a total pain in the ass. There was no other way for her to put it. Her voice dripped disdain every time she opened her mouth. So even though she knew she should be nice and explain the situation, she left Nina standing in the kitchen, her mouth open in shock, and went to get ready for work.

In her bedroom, all of the weariness and heaviness from the previous night came back. She still was sure what exactly happened and that only added to the stress. She finished drying off and started applying her moisturizer. She looked over her body again. It did look like she got her ass kicked. Bruises littered her body, face, arms, legs, stomach, and back. Luckily, it seemed as if it was all just superficial, no internal damage. Well, none she could feel anyway.

"At least its fall," she told her reflection, "and I can cover up most of this mess." Cam thought of her partner Jimmy and how he would react to this. Yes, thank God it's fall, and she set to work on her face.

* * * *

When she walked into the precinct, Jimmy took one look at her, and his face went from red to white to red again. Cam guessed her attempt at concealing everything sucked, or it could be because he knew her as well as he knew his own daughter, which made sense since she was Cam's best friend since the womb. Jimmy Aaron, and his daughter Brooks, had been a part of Cam's life for as long as she could remember. Cam's father, Jack, and Jimmy had been childhood best friends and the same tradition was implemented with their daughters. Cam was grateful that she had Jimmy and even Jimmy's eccentric wife Evelyn. Who was the only mother figure Cam had ever known. Her own mother had run out on her and her father when Cam was four, and it had just been the two of them since.

Before Jimmy could say a word, a call came in of a possible homicide. But once in the car, he let loose. "What in God's name happened to you?" he yelled.

Cam shrugged and pulled the passenger visor down to look in the mirror. "I don't think I did too bad a job at covering it up. You are the only one who said anything," she said, looking at her face at every angle.

"They didn't say anything because they knew I would. And not to mention you scare the shit out of most of them in there. The little bitches."

Before he could continue on, Cam took that opening and ran with it. "So they are scared of me. I knew it. What is it that they're scared of, huh? Does the big bad woman with a gun make the little men shake in their boots?" She said mockingly, turning to smile at Jimmy only to see that her little ploy hadn't worked.

She huffed, slamming the visor back into place and flopping back in the seat. "OK. Fine. I woke up like this this morning. I'm not sure what happened but I woke up with a feeling like I was drugged. I was really drowsy and my head was fuzzy. Then I walked in to the bathroom and saw this in the mirror," she said, pointing to her face, pausing before she continued. "Trust me you don't want to see the rest of my body, which looks like I got the shit seriously beat out of me. The thing is, I'm not sore. It's like it's just superficial—no pain, no discomfort."

Jimmy stopped at a light and turned to look at her. "Just superficial!" he said incredulously. "How in the hell can that be superficial? Jesus Cam, it looks like someone took a two-by-four to your face."

"Light's green," she said pointing. "Look," she said as she fiddled with her coat buttons, "I understand it looks bad, but I promise it doesn't hurt. And please, please, pl-e-ase don't tell Dad. I know that he is going to notice but it will be worse if you make a big scene out of it too."

He looked pissed, clenching and unclenching his jaw, but she knew the minute she had him. And of course so did he. "Fine. For your dad. He has enough stress with you doing this job. But what bothers me still is how. How did this happen?"

Cam just shrugged. "I have no fucking idea." And, damn, if that wasn't what pissed her off the most. The not knowing.

As they pulled up to the scene, they saw an ambulance pull away. "That must be the vic now," Cam said to Jimmy as they walked toward the crime scene. "Severely beaten and possibly raped. Damn, this day just keeps getting better and better."

First on the scene was a young, fresh-faced cop who looked like he just graduated the ninth grade. He stood there eagerly awaiting their acknowledgment, ready to give the run-down of the call and scene.

It must be his first "big" scene, Cam thought. She couldn't fault his eagerness. Hell that was her a few years ago, but today it just irritated the shit out of her. She moved toward the alley where the victim was found, and noticed the neighborhood for the first time. She was in Highlandtown, a neighborhood in downtown Baltimore, not far from her father's pub, O'Brien's. The row houses are narrow and tall, brick and stoned front. Every four houses there is an alley squashed in between. The alleys in this part of the city are narrow and long. About three to three and a half feet wide and long, thirty or so feet, and very dank and dark. They empty out into a shared back alley that run behind the rows of homes. A drug dealer's haven. Plenty of places to get in and out and not be seen. Not to mention in this part of town it is hard to find witnesses willing to testify. Most inner city residents, all over the country, live by the motto "Snitches end up in ditches." So it is always a challenge to work a scene here. Not to mention there is no telling who has trampled all over the damn scene before the cops arrived. Cam glanced around again, the crowd had already doubled. Gathering on stoops, steps and street corners, many wondering if they can gain any turf if it is a rival dealer that is dead. She just shook her head and called the rookie over.

As soon as Cam and Jimmy moved in the alley, the temperature dropped five degrees and the smells slammed into them. *God,* Cam thought, the urine and feces smell overwhelmed the dank, mildewed trash smell normally found in these places. The darkness covered about twenty feet into the alley, perfect for a murder. About halfway down, behind a couple of trash cans she saw the blood and markers.

"Okay, Officer…" Cam started, looking down to catch his name on his tag.

"Crabtree, ma'am. Jonah Crabtree," Officer Crabtree said. He looked like he was going to bounce out of his boots.

"All right. Officer Crabtree, what happened when you arrived on scene?" she asked, trying to ignore the eagerness wafting off of him.

"Yes, ma'am. I received the call at oh-nine hundred of a possible homicide. As I arrived on scene, a witness pointed down the alley stating that he discovered the body while taking his garbage out. The witness stated he did not touch the body, but he did move closer to make sure that it was an actual body that he was seeing. Upon realizing it was a body he immediately dialed nine-one-one—"

"Stop!" Cam snapped. She looked Jonah Crabtree up and down. He was good-looking. Tall, blonde hair, and blue eyes—a pretty boy, she thought. Looking all official and snappy in his pressed uniform. More than likely top of his class at the academy. He probably kept his nose shoved firmly up the ass of every instructor. *Jesus,* she thought, *so damn eager to please.* She took a deep breath, trying to bank her pissiness that had followed her throughout the morning. It's not his fault, she thought, remembering her first scene. She was probably just as eager.

Taking a deep breath, she continued. "Look, we don't need the damn narrative of your report. You're not on the witness stand, just tell us as quickly and concisely as you can, what you saw when you got here."

Officer Crabtree, a little redder in the face at being chastised, began again. "Okay, when I arrived I went down the alley and cleared it. I noticed the body of young woman—and I say woman loosely. She may have been dressed like a woman but in my opinion she can't be older than fifteen. She had the shit beat out of her, her dress—if you can call it that—was torn and shoved up around her waist. I noticed she looked like she was still breathing so I called the EMT's into the alley and they found a pulse. Within minutes they had her in the back of the ambulance and off to Johns Hopkins."

Jimmy looked down the alley to the area where the girl's body was laying. He saw something red and as he approached he noticed a stiletto heel. "Have the crime scene techs already photographed the area?" He looked toward Crabtree.

Jonah cleared his throat. "I'm not sure, sir. I'll go check for you."

As he moved toward the techs, Cam went over to Jimmy. As she got a good look at what he was holding, her breath caught in her throat and she went white. "Cam, what's wrong?" Jimmy asked.

She shook her head. "Nothing. I thought I had seen those shoes before." She cleared her throat and moved on. "Those shoes seem to be a little much for a young girl to wear, don't they? They look like working girl shoes." Cam looked up as Jonah came back.

"I spoke with the techs and they have all the photos they need and all the evidence is marked," he said. He stood there looking at Jimmy, nervously glancing out of the corner of his eyes at Cam.

Noticing the glances Cam started chuckling. "Seriously? Do I scare you that bad? How long have you been on the job?"

Officer Crabtree started turning pinkish again from his neck up. "I graduated top of my class one month ago. I immediately began on road patrol. So one month," He said this with as much arrogance as he could muster. He knew about Camille O'Brien. Star child of the Homicide squad. The stories about her were legendary, how she could vividly picture the murder in her head. How she could completely immerse herself in the victim, connecting with them as if they were standing right there next to her. Even at the academy, her name was heard everywhere. She broke and set many records. And Jonah had tried to break every one of them. And now here she was, and damn, if she didn't live up to some of the hype. She was a common topic for the locker room chatter; the male officers fantasizing about how she would be in bed. And standing here face-to-face with her he couldn't blame them. Cam was all legs and had a slim body to go with them. Her breasts were small and her ass was perky and showcased very well in the jeans she wore. Her face wasn't bad either. Slender, with high cheekbones, splattered with freckles. Her nose was slightly crooked, like it had been broken once, and her lips were full with a dark freckle perched on her bottom lip. Her eyes were deep green and could make a man's mouth water. Her hair was bright red, long and curly, currently wrangled into a tail that ended in the middle of her back. She dressed to intimidate, in snug jeans and high brown boots, the same chocolate brown as her suede jacket that she wore over a cream turtleneck sweater. She wore very little makeup, just mascara and lip gloss that highlighted the freckle that some of the officers wanted to lick. But it was her attitude that caught him off guard. At the academy, he thought of her often. He wondered what she would be like. He expected the ballbuster attitude, but he didn't expect his reaction to it. He knew he should be pissed, but just hearing his name on her lips set off bells and whistles in his head and sent a long, slow burn deep in his belly and he struggled to regain control. He wasn't used to women being pissy with him. All it took was a flash of his smile and dimples and the women just fell at his feet, but not Cam. She was a hard ass. He glanced over her slim body one more time. He was wearing shades, so he was sure the flash of heat and longing was well hidden.

The fact that he was immensely proud of his achievement smoothed some of Cam's irritation. She remembered that feeling. How she had to be better than everybody. She didn't want the other officers to question her promotions and her awards. More than once a female had slept her way up the chain and she was damn well not going to do that or have others think that. She earned every one of her promotions and assignments.

As she thought about this, she filed away the rest of the irritation from this morning and turned to Jonah. "Look, I think we got off on the wrong foot here. I'm sorry I snapped at you. I woke up pissy this morning and I carried it with me. I think you did a damn good job of securing the scene and working it so far. So truce?" And she held out her hand.

Jonah looked at it and shrugged. "Truce," he said as he took her hand. He wondered if she felt it. That sizzle that flashed in his palm when he finally felt her skin.

Unaware of the effect her presence was causing, Cam nodded and turned to Jimmy. "How about we let the rookie here go and take some witness statements?" Jimmy nodded, and she turned back to Officer Crabtree. "All right, rook, go and canvas the crowd. Don't dismiss anything, no matter how minute it may seem at the time. It all adds up to something. Ready?"

Jonah, annoyed by the rookie comment, but eager to help and to stay near her, nodded. "Yes, ma'am."

He turned to leave, but Cam caught his sleeve. "Oh, and one more thing, I'm not a ma'am," she said with a cocky grin. Jonah, perplexed, nodded and walked off.

She turned back to Jimmy. She saw that he had heard the whole exchange. "What?" she grinned. "I liked him. He reminds me of me."

Jimmy grinned and shook his head. Turnning back to the shoe, he asked what she knew he was waiting to ask. "So you recognized the shoe? Does this have anything to do with your face and your bad mood?"

Cam just looked at him and scowled. His quick grin had her grinning back and she told him of her visitor this morning.

He listened to her and believed every word. "Well, it can't be the same girl. Our victim here is not dead. And from the last time I checked, you only see the dead right? Right?"

Cam huffed. "Yeah, that's all it's ever been, but this one was different. She was fuzzy. Like her signal wasn't clear. But I don't think her appearing and us finding this red shoe, that looks exactly like the ones she was wearing by the way, is a coincidence." Cam stood up and paced. Her nerves were beginning to fray. They didn't have to worry about being overheard. All of the tech and other detectives knew not to come near them when they were assessing a scene. It was a way they could guarantee that her secret would stay just that. A secret.

* * * *

The ride to the hospital was silent. When they pulled up, Cam realized that it was probably the first time that they had not said word to each other. She knew Jimmy was worried about her, about what her father Jack would say when he found out what was going on. Those two never kept secrets. Friends since the womb, their families were just as close then as they are today.

James "Jimmy" Aaron was as close to a brother that Jack had. They both were only children and that just made the two closer. Best man at each other's weddings, their wives became just as close. So when Cams's mom, Joannie, had run out those many years ago, she shattered not just her own family but theirs as well. But they all had picked up the pieces and moved on. But deep down Cam knew that they all believed the same thing—something had happened to Joannie, no way would she ever leave her family. But Cam had always thought that her mother had left because of what her daughter could do—what she was. That she somehow thought she was defective. And never good enough. Because of that deep fear, Cam decided that no matter what she did she would be the best. So she set records at her high school and the academy. Graduating both at the top of her class. When she was on patrol, her cases were always cleared the fastest, she had the highest arrest record, and now, even in Homicide, she and Jimmy were legendary. But no matter what she did, she still wasn't good enough. Her mother never came back.

Shoving the memories back down, deep down, she followed Jimmy inside. Johns Hopkins Hospital is internationally known for its brilliant doctors and cutting edge technology. An impressive building, and God forbid, if you ever got wounded on the job, this is where you would want to be, but she hoped she never had to test that theory.

At the Information Desk, a sturdy, no-nonsense middle-age woman guarded the patient's whereabouts like a guard at Ft. Knox. Cam and Jimmy both approached and took out their badges. "Detective Aaron and Detective O'Brien here to see a victim brought in to the Trauma Unit from Highlandtown."

"Name?" the clerk asked in a clipped voice. She reminded Cam of some of the nuns from high school. Cam evened straightened and squared her shoulders, remembering all too well the nuns' disapproval for improper posture.

"Jane Doe, ma'am," Cam said politely. It was a struggle not to get snippy back. "She was found severely beaten this morning, no identification on her. Is it possible to see if she is still in the Trauma Unit or she has been moved?" Even though Cam knew her name, they still had to follow protocol and have it verified first.

They received a curt nod, but the clerk got to work. Within a few minutes they were told that Jane Doe was in ICU on the tenth floor, and that the staff would help them further.

At the nurse's station in ICU, Cam and Jimmy met with Dr. Horton. A middle-aged, plump man who fit snuggly into a pair of green surgical scrubs and white lab coat that couldn't possibly button over his belly. He had a kind face and a balding head. With glasses perched on the end of his nose, he peered at Nina's chart. "Your victim is in very bad shape," he told them as he led them into a glass-walled room directly across the hall from the nurse's station. Machines beeped and hummed as they provided life for their frail recipient, who lay still as death on a bed that seemed too big for such a small girl. Tubes snaked in and out of her body, a body that was almost completely black and purple. "She took a severe beating. One of the worst I have seen in almost twenty-five years of medicine. The beating caused severe trauma to her internal organs, both kidneys are basically dead. One lung is collapsed, her spleen had to be removed, and she has internal bleeding that we tried to stop. Not to mention she was brutally raped." He stopped, took a breath, and looking down at her, he took her hand in his. "She is brain dead. Whoever did this killed this little girl. Her heart may still be beating, but she is essentially dead laying here. Do you have a name for her? Does she have any family we can contact?"

Cam looked to the person standing on the other side of the girl lying so small and broken in that bed. "Yeah. Her name is Nina Petrelli. I'll have dispatch find out how we can contact her parents." Cam looked back down at the broken little girl. "We'll find the son-of-a-bitch who did this, I promise." He nodded and looked one more time at Nina before leaving. "I'll hold you to that Detective." And then he left.

Cam glanced back up at Nina. She saw the fear in her eyes, and the disbelief. Cam assumed that seeing yourself laid out in bed would shock anyone, even a ghost. "How old are you?"

"Twenty-one," she said, not looking up. She was still in her red dress and stiletto heels. Now that Cam saw what she looked like lying there, she realized how young this girl was. And she knew this was no twenty-one-year-old. She looked back up at Nina. "Tell me the truth. There is no way in hell you are twenty-one. Maybe your fake ID says that and you might pass for it in the dark with the inch of makeup you're wearing, but you and I both know that is bullshit." Cam saw Jimmy move to block the door. She also knew that he was on the phone running Nina's name through NCIC and the DMV databases.

Nina finally looked up at Cam. "Am I really dead?"

Jesus, Cam thought, she hated it when they were kids. "Basically, yes, or I wouldn't see you. I was trying to figure it out earlier. How you came to me, but in reality you weren't exactly 'dead.' When I recognized your shoe at the scene, it freaked me out. This is a first for me. I mean, you're not my first dead person, but you're the first who has come to me while your body is still alive." Cam sighed, then continued, "But I guess since you're brain dead, that's why I can see you. There is no coming back from that."

As Nina dealt with this, Jimmy came back over. "I found her. She is fifteen years old. She ran away eight months ago. Her parents are on their way here." He stopped and scrubbed his hands over his face. Cam knew he was trying to get his thoughts together. "Jesus, Cam. Her mother was hysterical. Apparently the last things they ever said to each other was hateful. She ran away after they had a fight."

Cam looked back at Nina, "What was the fight about?"

Nina, rolled her eyes, and Cam could all but see the attitude wrapping around her like the little red dress she was wearing. "They said I couldn't see my boyfriend anymore. That he wasn't good for me." She started pacing back and forth, gesturing outlandishly with her hands. "Like, I would know if he wasn't good for me. What the hell do they know. They're all old and shit." Nina swung toward Cam. "I love him. He is my everything, my soul mate. He takes care of me. And he loves me." Standing there, with her arms crossed and her left hip thrust out, Cam thought she looked more like the child she was than the woman she pretended to be.

Cam gestured to the broken girl in the bed. "This is how he takes care of you? Leaves you bloody and broken in an alley? Thrown out with yesterday's garbage?"

Nina glanced toward the bed. "Brad wouldn't do this. He protects me. He wouldn't do this." She looked less and less sure, with each glance at the bed.

But she slipped up, Cam thought. *She gave me his first name.* Now she just had to get his last name. "Where was he last night? It doesn't seem like he did a good job protecting you."

After a few tense moments Nina's shoulders deflated. Gone was the attitude that had fueled her for the past eight months, and here was a scared little girl who looked lost and alone. "Morris. Brad Morris." She turned back to Cam, tears running down her cheeks. "He didn't do this. Couldn't do this. Besides he's in jail." She paused, and Cam just waited. If there was one thing she had learned, it was to shut up and wait. Suspects and witnesses will talk if you just sat back and waited.

The beeps and hums of the machines echoed in the quiet room. Nina watched her chest rise and fall, as the ventilator pushed air into her damaged lungs. She all but shrank in her too small dress and working girl shoes. Overwhelmed she sat down on the edge of the bed. Looking back toward Cam, her eyes filled. "Am I really dead?"

Cam's irritation dissolved. Looking into those big blue eyes, Cam's heart broke for the scared girl. Not trusting her voice, she just nodded.

Nina looked down, her tears falling, splattering dots on her red dress. After a few moments, she looked back up and continued her story. "Brad's in jail for weed. Can you believe that?" She laughed. "Weed. God, he's a dumbass." She scrubbed her hands across her face. "When we first ran away together we did okay. We had a couple hundred bucks between the two of us, but the money ran out fast." She choked out a laugh. "I can't believe that I thought we were flush. I guess I am the dumbass."

Cam started to make an excuse for her, but Nina just waved it away.

Picking at the hem of her dress, she went on. "So Brad came up with the idea of me selling my body for some quick cash. At first I was pissed. Why in the hell should I have to do that? He promised that he would take care of me. But here he was suggesting that I do this." Unable to sit any longer she stood up to pace. "Of course I said yes. I didn't want to go home. I wanted to stay with him, so I made myself believe that this was the only way. Besides, to make sure I was safe, he said he would be my body guard. No one would touch me. At first I was scared and nervous. And believe it or not that made the guys want me more and so we decided that would be my thing." She paused, smiling at some memory.

It took all Cam had not to interrupt her. But damn it was hard. She knew as soon as she told Jimmy, they both would be thinking the same thing. That this Brad, Nina's reason for leaving her family, pimped out his young girlfriend so he could collect. Cam had seen this before, and it was always the same. Some sick SOB who likes little girls will pay big money to screw one. And Brad, realizing he had a gold mine, got into the game. Yeah, Cam thought, they were going to have a chat with this Brad Morris guy. And Cam would bet her next check, Nina wasn't the first girl to run away with Brad. But if she had anything to do about it, Nina would be his last.

Still smiling some, Nina continued. "Brad and I came up with a gimmick. I would play the meek and scared young girl, selling my body because I'm afraid of my boyfriend. And the Johns would swoop in, my white knight, there to rescue me. And God, they fell for it. Even the ones who didn't still paid big money because they all knew I was young. And that was what they all were interested in. The sick bastards. Some may have used the excuse of 'Oh, I want to rescue you, baby. Keep you safe. He'll never touch you again.' But what they really wanted was a young girl to fuck. And I gave it to them. It was a great ploy and a successful one." She turned to look at Cam. "Do you know how much they pay if you're 'young and innocent'?"

Cam nodded. "They pay big for the young ones." Cam had to swallow her disgust. There are some really sick bastards out there. She had locked up many of them, but they still went right back to it when they got out. But Cam had never run across one who beat the girl to the point of death. She hated these cases. Hated them to her very core. As far as she was concerned, the system should castrate every person who sexually assaulted a child. But they didn't ask her for her opinion. It was her job to catch them. And she would catch this one.

She knew Nina couldn't tell her who did it. No, that would be too easy. Unfortunately when the dead made it to Cam, they couldn't just point to a person and say "It was them." Nope, they don't have that memory. Apparently, the powers-that-be thought that would be too easy. But she did have the opportunity to get into the victims head, and that helped the cases tremendously.

But she was having a hard time with this case. Children were the worst; it was unfair and wrong to die so young. But Nina literally put herself at risk and did so without a thought of worry or care of the repercussions. And here she was, talking to the girl, who still didn't understand that she was gone. In her childish way, she didn't realize that this was permanent. There was no coming back from this. Her choices landed her in this bed and there was no getting out of it.

Cam jumped when Jimmy laid a hand on her shoulder. "I guess I was lost in what she was telling me. Are her parents here?" Jimmy nodded. Cam took one last look at the broken girl on the bed and the lost one sitting next to her. At least her parents won't see what she had become.

Nina's mother, Eve Petrelli, came flying into the room, followed closely by her husband, Mike. Mrs. Petrelli's sobs became louder and more hysterical as she saw her daughter for the first time in eight months. She all but threw herself on the bed, screaming and begging for her baby to wake up. Mr. Petrelli, uncertain of what to do, stood there staring at his wife. He watched as she pleaded and begged the doctor, and God, to fix their baby. Begging them to take her instead. And yet he never moved. He seemed frozen, afraid if he moved, she would be ripped away.

Jimmy walked over and placed a hand on Mr. Petrelli's shoulder. "My name is Detective Aaron and this is Detective O'Brien. We are assigned to work your daughter's case." He paused and glanced at Dr. Horton. He stood off to the side, struggling to keep his face void of emotion, but Jimmy saw the rage and pity swimming in his eyes. "Has Dr. Horton had a chance to explain your daughter's condition?"

Mr. Petrelli nodded his head. He closed his eyes and swallowed. "Um, yes. He stopped us before, um, before…um…before we were allowed to come in." He paused and swallowed again, fighting to keep control of his emotions. "Ah-I…I," he stammered. "I'm not sure what I'm supposed to do." He looked at Jimmy and Cam, the tears he had willed back spilling down his cheeks. "Please tell me what I am supposed to do." He looked back at his wife, who was rocking his child back and forth in her arms, sobbing her name over and over. Looking back at the detectives, a sob ripped from his throat, and Jimmy did the first thing that came to him and wrapped this grown and broken man in his arms and held him while his heart broke. Looking at Cam, Jimmy blinked back his own tears. What would he do if it was his child in that bed? Or Cam? A girl who was as much his as his own daughter. So Jimmy just went with his gut and held this man as he cried for his baby to come back.

Cam had to turn away for a moment to shove her emotions down. Her throat burned hot with the tears she fought against. She had down this a hundred times, but never had a case hit her so hard. Swallowing one last time, she turned and walked over to try and comfort Mrs. Petrelli as best as she could. This was the worst part of the job. They don't teach you how to deal with grieving parents at the academy. It's just something you have to figure out. And "I'm sorry" seems so fucking insignificant and cold. And after so many notifications and grieving family members, it still is lost to Cam on what she is supposed to do.

She couldn't imagine the fear and the grief these parents have had to endure for the past eight months. Not knowing where your child is or whether she is alive or dead. And then, as if fate decided to play some sick and twisted joke, you receive a call that she has been found, but she is severely injured, unsure if she will survive.

But Cam had another thing on her mind, as she looked over to where Nina had shoved herself into a corner. She looked scared and upset, unsure how to take in the overwhelming grief and anguish pouring from her parents. Cam finally caught her eye and motioned for her to come closer. Nina just shook her head and was gone. So Cam sat there, holding Nina's mother. She was unsure of many things, but she knew she had to get this monster off the streets. No mother should have to go through this. She just had to figure out how.

But somewhere in the back of her mind, she wondered would her own mother have grieved for her if it was Cam in this bed.

CHAPTER 2

It was a quiet ride back to the scene. Both Jimmy and Cam seemed lost in thought, neither wanting to discuss what happened in the hospital room. It never gets easier, Cam thought. That was the part of her job she hated the most. She could deal with the dead and the details, but dealing with a mother's agony? A family's? No thanks. She could do without that.

They didn't get any other information from Nina's parents. They hadn't seen nor heard from her in months. *God*, she thought, *I hope Jonah got lucky*. They needed something from this canvas, as of right now they had shit to go on.

Finally Cam spoke. "What do you think, Jimmy?" She didn't have to elaborate; they had been partners since she became a detective at twenty-four, the youngest in Homicide.

"I have no fucking idea," Jimmy huffed. This one was eating him alive. All he wanted to do since the hospital is grab up his daughter and never let go, but that would have to wait. At least he could keep Cam safe. Hell, she might as well be his too. He'd helped raise her from the time her worthless mother walked out on her and Jack. And he knew damn well Jack felt the same about Brooks.

"This one just sucks Cam. It just fucking sucks." Jimmy was quiet the rest of the ride. Cam knew when "fuck" came out of his mouth so many times to just leave him the hell alone. And she couldn't blame him, she could still feel Mrs. Petrelli's arms holding on, tightening. Her body rocking with each sob. She scrubbed her hands over her face, willing the emotion back down. *Jesus Christ,* she thought, *to get your daughter back, just to let her go again. This time for good. And to make that decision. God, it just wasn't fair.*

"Jimmy," she said after a moment, "we're going to Dad's for a drink after work." Cam knew that even if he didn't want to go, he would for her. Just as she knew his wife wouldn't say a word about it.

Ten minutes later, they were back in the alley. Nina's red shoe was still there, an evidence marker beside it. The crime scene techs were still all over the place scouring for any clue. And standing at the end of the alley was Nina. Cam was still pretty pissed about her just leaving earlier, so she ignored her and went to work.

They interviewed every person standing on a stoop. And of course, no one saw a thing. "You know," Cam started, "someone could get shot, right here in broad daylight, every freaking person in the neighborhood could be out on their stoops, *and* still no one would see a goddamn thing."

Jimmy just chuckled. "You know, when I was younger—"

"STOP! Just stop," Cam yelled. Facing Jimmy, her hands up to stop the onslaught. "Okay, you win. I will stop bitching, just for the love of God and all that is holy, please don't tell me a story that starts with 'When I was younger…blah, blah, blah." Cam laughed.

Jimmy just watched her smile, then reached up to grab her ponytail, a gesture he had done her whole life. Cam turned to him, "You know when you start a story like that, it means you're getting old."

"Bite me," was all Jimmy said.

As they both turned back toward their car, Jonah came rushing up, "Hey, Detectives wait up!"Cam looked at his flushed face and knew what he was going to say.

"Let me guess, someone saw something," Cam was impressed.

Jonah immediately looked deflated. "You already know?"

Cam had to swallow a chuckle. "No, but I can tell from your face. And plus I was thinking you would have some luck considering your boyish good looks and considerable charm," She said, her voice lathered with sarcasm. "I figured some girl would open up to impress you. Spilling all over her secrets and dreams." Cam couldn't tell if he was blushing now or if she pissed him off. She knew she was being a smartass, but she needed to release the tension that had been building since the hospital. And pretty boy was the first one to cross her path.

Jonah swallowed. "So you knew someone would talk?"

Jimmy had to walk away before he laughed in this boy's face.

Cam just stood there as serious as ever, all the sarcasm had left. The hurt and anger on Jonah's face was beginning to piss her off. "No," she said. "I didn't know exactly, but I figured, what with your specific charm and good looks, maybe one of these girls would open up to you. You know try to impress you." She finished with a smile. She was struggling to keep the bite from her voice.

Jonah just stood there. "So you used me," he said flatly.

"Yes," Cam said. There wasn't even a hint of remorse or apology in her voice at being found out. "Listen, rookie. Sometimes there is no room for hand holding and sweet talking. Sometimes you just need to put your big boy panties on and suck it up. Yes, I took advantage of you. I saw a bunch of the girls watching you when we pulled up, so I took a gamble that they would talk to you. Deal with it. I will use whatever means I deem necessary in order to get this sonofabitch. In this case it was you. If that hurts your feelings then too bad. You don't like it, go asked to be put on Harbor Patrol or directing traffic and get your sensitive ass off my crime scene. Now if you're done whining about my miss-use of your skills and my lack of etiquette, then maybe you could tell me what was so important that you came running your ass over here for." She was so intent on chewing him out that she didn't notice her captain over. Cam wondered what brought him out here. Normally he'd wait back at the precinct to hear the rundown of the case. Apparently this one had all of them on the edge.

She turned away from Jonah and began to address her captain. "Officer Crabtree here was just about to fill us in on his canvas as you walked up."

Captain Thems looked over towards the red-faced officer currently boring holes in the back of Cam's head. He could understand the boy's frustration at being dressed down in public, especially by a female, but in this case Cam was right, the boy needed to get over it. Especially if he wanted to make it in this profession.

He glanced at Jonah and nodded. Jonah puffed out his chest and straightened out his hat and nodded back. "Yes, sir. Uh, um, I mean Captain. Um, well you see, sir."

"Jesus," Cam swore under her breath. "At this rate we'll be here all damn day."

That apparently worked because Jonah, his face getting redder, breathed out and began again. "On my canvas, sir, I noticed a few women standing off to the side and I approached them. After explaining who I was, sir, and the nature of my questions, two of them confirmed that they had seen something the previous night." He paused and took out his notebook. "According to the witnesses they noticed a tall man coming out of the alleyway alone at about 3:00 a.m. They didn't notice if he was white or black, only that he was tall. They thought it strange, because he was wearing a suit. But they figured he was just some desk jockey buying some crack. That's all they had, sir." Jonah finished, straightened, and looked at the captain for approval.

The captain nodded, dismissing Jonah, and turned toward Cam and Jimmy. Not one to mince words he got straight to the point. "Anything new that you two can add?"

Sensing Cam's frustration, Jimmy spoke up, "We spoke to Nina's parents at the hospital. They report neither of them have had any contact with Nina in at least six months. They were shocked to learn what she had been doing, but not surprised to learn that this Brad was involved." Jimmy had to stop and scrub his hands over his face. He took a deep breath before he continued. "Dammit Captain, the son of a bitch beat her to the point of death. It's like he left her knocking on deaths door on purpose. Her parents are now left with the choice to keep her on life support or pull the plug."

Captain Thems looked equally as sickened by this. They had seen a lot of murder, but something about this one just left a sick feeling in one's stomach. What none of them could understand was whether she was meant to die before she was found, or if the son of a bitch intentionally left her, as close to death as possible, for her family to decide to end her life or keep her on machines. Jimmy took a deep breath and glanced at Cam. Could he decide her fate, or his daughters? Could Jack? As he wiped his face, he silently said a prayer, asking God to never lay that decision at his feet.

* * * *

Back at the precinct, Cam and Jimmy set up the murder board. An old-school tactic, she knew, but one that Jimmy had instilled in her from day one. Something about having everything laid out, all at once, helped make connections you might miss going through it one piece at a time. Cam sat and studied the board. The first picture was a current one of Nina that Jimmy had gotten from her parents. She looked so innocent and young. It was hard to imagine that this girl willingly ran away from the family who surrounded her in the photo. Both parents, still together and still in love, a rarity in today's times, and a younger brother. A brother who will have to grow up without his older sister and who will always question whether he played a role in her leaving. It's a lot to have on young shoulders. Cam had to get off that train of thought fast—too many memories of her own would cloud that thought fast.

Jimmy stood up to brief the team. Before he started he turned and took Nina's picture down. He stood there and looked at her, he let the emotion take hold one more time, and then he filed it away. Emotion was good for one thing; you fought harder for things that mattered. And even though none of them knew Nina, he knew they all had emotion for the young girl killed too soon, and he would exploit and use that to drive them to find the son of a bitch who did this. "This is Nina. Nina Petrelli. She was fifteen years old. She ran away from home eight months ago because of a boy. A fucking boy who turned her into a whore so he could buy his weed." Cam watched as Jimmy clenched his fists and jaw, willing the emotion back down. "Unfortunately, he is off the suspect list because he is in the city lockup for drug possession. But trust me, his ass will pay for taking this girl and pimping her out." He paused and looked at every member of his team. Emotions were simmering, because they all knew the ass clown would get little time for it. Jimmy wanted to find a way to pin part of the murder on Nina's boyfriend Brad, but he knew it was a long shot. He hoped Nina would slip up and tell Cam something that would make that possible, but glancing at Cam, he knew he'd have to keep that tidbit between them. Only the two of them knew of Cam's "spidey sense."

Jimmy looked back down at Nina's face and continued. "According to her parents they had no clue that their daughter was a prostitute. They had not spoken to her since she left home months earlier. Based on eyewitness accounts sometime around 3:00 a.m., a tall man in a suit was seen leaving the alley where Nina was later found. According to the doc, Nina received her injuries around that time. So it's looking good that this man in a suit is our perp or at least a person of interest. And before anyone asks, yes, that it the only description we have to go on. To tell you the truth, in the neighborhood where she was found, I'm amazed we got anything." Jimmy looked straight at Cam and couldn't suppress the grin, before he continued, "Officer Jonah Crabtree, is the one who was able to get a witness to talk to him. So"—Jimmy looked around at his team before continuing"—before any of you ugly pricks go back to follow up on the canvass, call down to dispatch and request the rookie to assist." He paused as one of the detectives on his team started to laugh, and he quickly turned toward Cam, and Jimmy knew this was going to end badly.

Detective Edwards turned to Cam. "So O'Brien, how sexy and fine is this rookie? Did you promise him a good time for his help?" He began to laugh, slapping his partner on the shoulder, unaware of the uncomfortable looks being shot his way. "Or did you promise him some late-night tutoring on how to make detective in two years? We know how talented you are in that area." He stood there, still laughing at his own joke, still unaware he was the only one.

Cam rolled her eyes and stood there letting him believe he'd gotten to her. She knew one of the team believed she had slept her way into this spot and now Edwards, an overweight and greasy-haired asshole, had just solved that mystery for her. She knew he had purposefully said it loud enough for the rest of the squad room to hear it. So she wasn't shocked to notice how quiet it became. The only noise was Edward's snorting chuckle. She quickly glanced Jimmy's way before she said or did anything. His quick grin gave her the all clear signal she wanted. She moved so fast Edwards didn't see her coming and he found himself flat on his face, his right arm twisted and pinned behind his back.

He struggled, trying to free his arm. His shoulder was burning and his wrist hurt like a sonofabitch. "Goddammit, Jimmy, get the fuck off of me! What your girlfriend can't take a fucking joke?"

Cam had the pleasure of watching his face turn a reddish purple when he realized it wasn't Jimmy holding him down. She leaned down and whispered in his ear. "Would it be easier for you to take if it was Jimmy holding your fat and nasty ass down? Too bad motherfucker, it was a woman who took you down. But I can see how you would get it wrong. You probably haven't had a woman touch you in a long fucking time. Now you listen to me, you have something to say to me then you say it to me, not the entire squad. I don't really give a flying fuck what you 'believe' I did to get here, but you will keep your goddamn opinion to yourself. But just so you know, I got here because dried up, old fat fuckers like you don't know the difference between their ass and a hole in the ground so they had to get someone in here to do your job. So how about your shut your goddamn mouth and let me do my job—and yours. Actually I think maybe I will take your advice and teach that fine rookie how to be a detective, then maybe your partner will have a real man to work with instead of some fat, drunk, lazy asshole, who needs his bifocals to find his dick in the morning."

Finished, she let go of his arm and stood up. And looked straight into Captain Them's face. *Shit,* she thought, that's just great. Just fucking great. She started to say something and was shocked to hear him yell, "Edwards! Get your ass off the floor and into my office."

Edwards, who was mortified and fuming, pulled himself up. He watched as the captain turned and walked towards his office. Seeing his one and only opportunity, he made a move toward Cam. Before she could react, Jimmy walked in between them and stared Edwards straight in the eye. Edwards shook his head and chuckled. "So I guess now we know who she fucked—" And Jimmy's fist stopped anything else coming out of his mouth.

* * * *

With a bag of ice taped to his knuckles, Jimmy began working the board again. Something about this case had his gut churning and pulling at the back of his brain. He knew if he kept on it, it would just bury itself deeper and deeper. Knowing it was best, he sat back at his desk and watched Cam. She was typing up the report, but he knew that what happened earlier was replaying in her mind. Just like he knew she was berating herself for losing control in front of the squad. Especially the captain. She prided herself on her ability to control her emotions. It was hard for her, being only one of two women in the squad. Just like it was hard for her to ignore the rumors about how she became the youngest detective to make Homicide. He also knew she would be pissed if she knew he was sitting here worrying about her. But he didn't care, let her be pissed. He was worried. She had struggled with the gossip her entire career, but she had always handled it. Jimmy thought back to the night she found out she was getting her chance at a gold shield.

Cam burst through the back door of her dad's house. Jimmy was over having a beer and watching the O's take on the Yankee's. The last time Jimmy or Jack saw Cam this excited was when she was accepted into the academy. Jack glanced at Jimmy, but he just shrugged his shoulders. He knew but wasn't going to ruin it for either of them. Cam hurdled the coffee table and landed in between them. She grabbed her dad's beer and placed the paper she was flapping in his now-empty hand. She just stay there grinning like a loon chugging on his beer. Jimmy caught Jack's eye and grinned. All the while Cam sat there watching the exchange. She knew the two of them could have a whole conversation without a word being said. They had been friends that long. Cam knew what that was like; she had called her longtime BFF on the way, to her dad's, just bursting with the news.

Cam couldn't take Jimmy and Jack's silence any longer. "Did you read it?! I made it! I freaking made the detective list! I have to still take my test, but I just know that this is happening. I am going to be a detective! Two years of busting my ass and it is finally paying off." She paused and looked at Jimmy.

Damn, he thought, *she is fucking wired.* Well, the rest of what he knew would have to wait. Let her get through the test and then he would tell her where she will be if she passes. It was a bittersweet moment for him. His longtime partner had put in for retirement just yesterday, and when he saw the list of detective candidates, he did something Jimmy had never seen. He walked up to the captain and gave his recommendation for his replacement. Seeing as how his partner, Charles Ruley, had trained both Jimmy and Captain Thems, Jimmy knew that Ruley's recommendation would be granted. So as he watched his goddaughter dance around the room waving her letter, he looked at her father, the man who was had been his brother in every way but blood his entire life, and tried to figure out how to tell him that, when she put on her gold shield for the first time, her partner would be him.

Jimmy chuckled at the memory. He looked over at his goddaughter, and partner, and smiled. She was the first detective that he knew that went straight to Homicide from patrol. In his mind, it was a blessing, and a curse, to be her partner. On one hand he wouldn't have any other person by his side while working on a case, but on the other hand, he wished she wasn't there when the guns came out. He swung around when he heard his name called.

Cam glanced up too. "Uh-oh, captain's calling. Damn it. Don't you dare fall on the sword for me." Cam snapped to get his eyes on her, "Jimmy promise me. I can take my licks myself."

Jimmy smiled. "Sure, kid. Trust me, I'm not standing in the line of fire for you." No matter what that prick Edwards said, none of this was coming down on Cam. He didn't care if she got pissed or not.

Captain Richard "Dickie" Thems, pronounced "Tims"—he got pissed because everyone mispronounced it, had gone through the academy with Jimmy. They both entered Homicide at the same time as well and learned their trade from one of the best Homicide detectives in the history of the Baltimore City Police Department. He watched his classmate close the door behind him and shut the blinds. He leaned back against the door and started laughing like a loon. Thems leaned against his desk and joined him. He wiped his eyes and tried to catch his breath. "Goddamn boy! You don't know how hard it was to hold that in. There he was blowing off at the mouth and the next thing I saw was his fat ass on the floor." He started to laugh again. "Jesus! I think my mouth hit the floor!"

Jimmy walked over wiping his eyes as well; he was trying his best to stop laughing. "I knew someone, and I figured it was him, had been running their mouth about how Cam made it to detective so fast, but I didn't think Edwards would have ever had the balls to say it to her face! The next thing I knew she had him laid out in an arm lock and his mouth is moving like a fish out of water." Jimmy knew the next part was coming so he jumped right to it. "So how much trouble am I in for punching him?"

Captain Thems shrugged and had a blank look on his face. "I never saw a punch." He held up a hand before Jimmy could say anything. "And as far as anyone else, they saw Edwards walk into a pole. And that is how it is going in the report too. Look, Edwards knows he fucked up and overstepped, worse than usual. Just like he knows that no one will back him." He watched Jimmy's shoulder sag. And knowing his old friend felt pity for Edwards', he put his hand on Jimmy's shoulder and gave it a friendly squeeze. "Jimmy, I know what you are going to say and just stuff it. This is how it is going down, and there will be no issues what so ever. Edwards fucked himself as soon as he opened his mouth, and I think this time even he knows it. What both of you did was justified. And trust me, he doesn't want it getting out that he got his ass handed to him by a hundred-and-thirty–pound woman. But on top of that, she handed it to him in front of the entire squad, and not a single one of them stepped in, including his partner."

Jimmy thought about that last statement. Damn, he couldn't imagine what it took for your own partner to not even have your back. "OK, can I make a suggestion though?" The captain raised an eyebrow. "Have you had any thoughts about moving him to another team?"

Captain Thems stared down at his shoes, making Jimmy wonder if he was overstepping his bounds. The two had known each other for thirty years, but when it came down to it, this was still the captain's squad. "Edwards accepted the suggestion of looking at a transfer out of homicide or starting his retirement six months early. He is supposed to let me know of his decision at the end of his two-week vacation." Jimmy nodded. He knew that the vacation was a polite way to say that Edwards had received a two-week suspension for his comments. Jimmy smiled. He's lucky he walked out of here at all. It had taken all he had not to beat the shit out of that man when he insinuated that Jimmy and Cam are sleeping together.

When he turned around to leave, Captain Thems cleared his throat. "Jimmy, I've known you what, thirty years? Let me make a suggestion, leave it alone. Don't go looking for trouble. He is just a hack detective who hung on to the team's coattails. His comments aren't taken seriously anyway. And everyone in this department knows that Cam is more like your daughter than someone you are sleeping with."

Jimmy shook his head. He paused as he was walking out. "That's not why I hit him." He watched the confusion spread across his captain's face. "I hit him because he made the insinuation that Cam slept her way to that gold badge."

Captain Thems shook his head. Sometimes the human race baffled him. He walked over to his door and watched his squad work. They were a wild mix of personalities. But one thing that they all had in common was dedication. Dedication to the job. To the victim. To the families left behind. And one of the most important to him, they were dedicated to each other.

But he wasn't just watching them work. Wasn't just admiring their skills and unity. He was watching them for a more personal reason. His eyes went to the only female in his squad room. The first thing he always noticed, as he was sure every other man with a pulse noticed, was how she looked with a gun on her hip and the badge glinting beside it. The gun and badge were clipped to a pair of jeans. Jeans that hugged every curve and displayed her fine ass in exquisite detail, and ended in a pair of sexy, kick-ass, leather boots. He was so fixated on the way her ass moved in those jeans, he didn't notice his wife walk in.

CHAPTER 3

The next morning, Cam woke stiff and sore. She had worked off her mad at the gym, picturing Edwards's face on the punching bag. Now on her way into the office she let her mind go back to yesterday's incident. She knew she should let it go but it burned her ass that someone in the squad, let alone her team, thought she slept her way to her badge. At least she knew the rest of her team knew the truth. Hell, Edwards's partner, Rodriguez, didn't even help his ass up.

She let her mind drift as she worked her way through traffic in downtown. She thought about what direction the case needed to go, when she suddenly remembered something unusual on her desk yesterday. A telephone message from a detective in Dublin, Ireland. With everything that happened yesterday, she had completely forgot about it.

She remembered the message had been urgent, something to do with the case. What Cam thought odd was that he would call about a case that happened three thousand miles from his jurisdiction.

At least one bright spot in her morning was Nina hadn't made another appearance. Nina was another conundrum altogether. How did she get through? she wondered. Cam never understood why she could see the dead. Why she could talk to them. It was something that was just always there. She thought back to the first time her parents had realized their little girl had a secret. Her dad just accepted it and so had his parents. In their home country, she was considered blessed. But of course the Irish lore gave considerable room for those who were bestowed with "blessings." Her mother and her family were not so accepting, and Cam often wondered if that was the reason she left. One night she even gained the courage to tell her grandfather her worries.

She smiled at the memory of her grandfather's explanation. "Cam," he said, "the faeries and elves loved you so, that they left their marks on you inside and out." He brushed a finger over her freckled cheeks. "On the outside, all their kisses show, and on the inside, they blessed you with their magic. It is up to you to decide how to use it. But always remember they saw something special in you, so make them proud. If there are those who don't understand, then the hell with them! As long as you remain true to who you are, that's all that matters."

And Cam took that to heart. That night at six years old, she set aside her fears and embraced who she was. And at seven she helped her uncle Jimmy solve her first murder. And from that day on she knew what her purpose was in life.

As she got older, it was hard sometimes to remain true to who she was. When her first love found out about her ability, he ran. And for the first time she felt cursed rather than blessed. She still remembered his parting words: "Who in the hell would want to deal with this shit day in and day out. You're a crazy bitch. No one would want you knowing what you really are." He slammed the door, walking out two weeks before their wedding. After that night, Cam slammed the door on her heart.

She walked into the bullpen, earphones in, trying to get the morning's memories out of her brain. Unaware of what was going on in front of her, she damn near sat on the person currently occupying her desk. Jimmy, jumping up, caught her arm before she fell and squealed like a little girl.

Knowing her like he did, he kept his hand on her arm until she looked up. He noticed the earbuds for the first time and knew that something was up. Cam never wore them walking in. She always needed to hear and feel what was going on in the bullpen when she first arrived. She said it set her mood for the day. Pumped her up. So he knew something was wrong before he even saw her face. Jimmy knew of one thing that could mess her up like this, and if that motherfucker was coming back around, he had to pause and take a breath. He realized that he had started to squeeze her arm so he let go.

Cam's heart was going a million beats a minute. She reached up and yanked the earbuds out of her ears and spun around to see who was at her desk. "What the fuck—" She was expecting one of the detectives in her squad, so when she saw him standing there, her mind froze.

Jimmy, taking pity on his partner, gestured to the man in front of him. "Cam, this is Detective Guarda Finn McDougal. He is with the National Police of Ireland. Detective, this is my partner, Detective Cam O'Brien."

Holy Mother of God, he is gorgeous, screeched through her head as soon as her brain caught up with the rest of her. She prayed her mouth had closed and she wasn't standing there gaping like a damn fish. *Jesus, Cam*, she scolded herself, when she realized she was doing just that.

She held out her hand. "Good morning, Detective," she said smoothly. "Sorry for the weird look. I was just wondering what brings you to Baltimore."

Cam cut her eyes to Jimmy when she heard him mutter. "Sure you were…" Ignoring his sheepish grin, she smoothly looked back up to the detective from Ireland. "So what can we do for you, Detective Garda—"

Still holding her hand, Finn politely interrupted her, "Finn. Just Finn is fine." He released her hand and gestured for her to sit in the seat he had just vacated. He swiped a seat from a nearby desk and sat down to take in the beautiful Camille O'Brien.

Her reputation was known to many, even across the pond. Smart and cunning, ruthlessly fighting for the dead. But he realized the moment he saw her, that her reputation could never live up to the flesh and blood woman seated before him. Tall and slim, with athletic curves. Her green eyes immediately captivated him. Clear and bright, he found himself staring and falling. The spatter of freckles only added to the allure of her. He noticed a dark one on her lower lip and found himself struggling to ignore the low burn settling deep in his belly.

Cam was just as captivated. His stormy blue-gray eyes betrayed his swirling emotions, and Cam found herself wanting to help erase the hurt that brewed there. His face was chiseled from stone, with sharp angles and a strong jaw line. His hair was wild and a little long, and black as a raven, it curled just above his collar. She found herself thinking of the stories of the Celtic warrior-gods her grandfather would tell her. When her eyes settled on his mouth, she knew she was in trouble, as she wondered what it would feel like on hers.

Jimmy watched the two of them, amused to see Cam so lost for words. He wondered if either of them knew how long it had been quiet. When he saw Finn's eyes slowly start to make their way down from Cam's face, he loudly cleared his throat, chuckling when they both jumped.

Jimmy looked at Finn, although he was amused to see him squirm, he got right to the point. "What can we do to help you?"

Finn nodded and began his story. "A year ago there was an especially brutal murder on a CI of mine named Mary CatherineDonnelly, a.k.a. Cat. She was a teenage runaway who often prostituted herself out in order to make money. I busted her about a year before her murder and she started helping me with the local underage sex trade. Now prostitution is legal to a point in Ireland, but underage prostitution carries heavy fines and jail time." He paused and reached into his bag and pulled out a folder. He placed a mug shot of Cat on Cam's desk. "This was the first time I busted her. She was fifteen years old. And after a while I had convinced her to get out of this lifestyle and get back in school. I hadn't meant to get attached to her, but she just had a way about her that I couldn't help it." He had to pause to control the rage and grief that was starting to build. Finn was aware that both Cam and Jimmy noticed his internal war and he was grateful that they both just sat back quietly, waiting for him to continue.

After a few moments, Finn looked back up. The rage was mostly reined in, but it simmered in his stormy blue eyes. "A year ago I was called to the hospital to see about a possible murder victim. When I arrived I was stopped by my captain. He knew that Cat and I had developed a friendship. He told me how she had been found by a couple of tourists who were out walking after dinner. They were out in the shipping docks walking along a pier when they came across her body. They had thought she was dead, but when they had approached her they realized she was alive, but barely." Finn took a haggard breath; it was startling to him that he still held this amount of emotion in him after year. He was so wrapped up in his memories that he didn't notice Cam start to pale.

"When the doctors got their hands on her, there was nothing that they could do. She was raped and beaten. The bastard beat her to death. Or so he thought. Somehow her body was still breathing, but her brain shut down about an hour after she arrived at the hospital. When my captain was called in, he realized who it was and contacted me. He knew I would want to say good-bye before they turned off the machines. God, when I saw her I wanted to kill the bastard with my own two hands." He looked down at his hands, amazed the fury he felt that night still shook them. He took a shaky breath and swallowed. The cyclone of emotions brought the burn of bile to his throat. Forcing it all down, he resumed his story. "He left nothing of her. It was as if an animal had gotten a hold of her. I must have sat there and held her hands for hours. It seemed so unfair. She was changing her life. Taking back her independence and she was going to rebuild her life. She was talking about going back to school to be a counselor for teens." After a deep breath, Finn finally looked back at Cam. "She died while I held her hand. At least she didn't die alone. I don't know if she knew, but at least I knew. She wasn't alone."

"She knew," Cam whispered before she caught herself. Jimmy snapped his eyes to Cam. He noticed the pale face and shaky voice. They were going to have a long talk, but not in front of the detective.

Finn just smiled. "Thanks. Anyway, the reason why I am here is the tourist who found her was Captain Richard Thems and his wife—"

"What? What do you mean the captain and his wife?" Cam swung toward Captain Thems's office.

When in the hell was he going to inform them off his link with the case? Not only that, but he never informed them that their case was an exact match to a case in Ireland. Cam was seething as she threw open the door to his office.

"When were you going to inform Jimmy and I of your link to the Ireland case? You should have told us that you had seen this before. I don't care if it is in another country, or another planet! If you had seen another murder that has the same MO as this new murder, that should have been immediately disclosed to us. Not only that but you call and inform another detective from three thousand miles away before you can call and inform your own damn detectives?"

Captain Dickie Thems was used to his detective having a quick temper and a sharp tongue, but he was damned if she was going to come in here and dress him down like he was rookie. And she damn well wasn't going to do it in front of a visiting detective. Cam just stood there pulsing with frustration and betrayal, while Captain Thems quietly and quickly rose to close his door and his shades. He moved quite nimbly on his large frame, all two hundred and fifty pounds. He was solid, a fact he was proud of, at fifty-two years old. He took care of the body that had given him a full scholarship, playing football, for the University of Maryland. His office boasted of his accomplishments, his degree proudly displayed behind a large wooden desk. Commendations and medals, all earned during his thirty years on the force, were all over the walls, displayed in frames and shadow boxes. Photos of his family covered his desk. While others with actors, the mayor and the chief sat proudly looking back at him on the shelves facing his desk. And that's where he stood, looking at all of those faces, trying to keep his temper in check.

Cam stood there, watching his back trying to force her temper and emotions back down. What Finn had told them of Cat's death shook Cam to her core, because that's whose death she had dreamt about two nights ago. When she awoke with the bruises that still littered her face. Why she felt betrayed by her captain, she couldn't explain. But she and Jimmy would do anything for the man standing before her, and the thought of him keeping this from them and turning first to another detective, sliced Cam deeply. Had she not stood in front of him just sixteen hours before giving her report? And still he didn't tell them of this connection.

She cut off her internal debate when he turned and faced her. He appeared calm, but there was a storm in his gray eyes. It was hard to break his calm façade. No matter the situation his face always remained smooth and gentle. But Cam learned long ago to watch his eyes. They could be a calm gray or stormy and dark, that was his one tell and why he no longer played poker with her.

He looked her over and his anger eased some at the hurt in her eyes. Like a tempest in a storm was his detective, such passion and drive. If she could control the temper that betrayed her, she could be chief of this department one day. But by God she had to learn to control that damn temper. He chuckled at the thought and Cam just looked like he had lost his mind. "Jesus Christ," he breathed. "Detective, sit down." He strode to his chair and sat.

Cam sat, and immediately the guilt came in one wave. This man was her mentor. He took a chance on her when no one else would. And she came in here like an ass. "Captain, I'm sorry."

Captain Them's eyebrows shot up. "The great Cam O'Brien sorry? Wow, hell must have frozen over." Seeing her smile, he continued. "Cam, I apologize too. I should have come to you both before, but my immediate thought was for Finn. We stayed in touch since that night and this case has all but consumed him."

"He told us the details of the case."

"Ah, but did he tell you all of it?" When she raised her eyebrows, he continued. "Cat was a likeable girl. Sweet, generous, funny, and beautiful. When Finn first busted her, she about talked the cuffs right back off. She was that charming. So he started helping her and she did the same. She would give him tips about the underage sex trade and he would give her money and he tried his damnedest to get her off the streets. After a year, his constant badgering seemed to sink in, because the day before she was killed, she told him she was done. She had made enough to get into school. And starting tomorrow she was going to be her own woman. Finn was ecstatic. He and Cat had become almost like family. So he felt as if he could finally breathe. She would be off those streets and doing something for herself." He looked down at his hands. God, whenever he thought of Cat he wondered if he and his wife had been faster would she still be alive?

After a deep breath, he continued. "When she died, I think it broke something in him. He became consumed with her case, nothing mattered but finding her killer. He paid for her to be buried, and from what his captain said, he goes to her grave every week. He brings flowers and sits there and talks to her."

When her captain looked back up at her, Cam knew this incident weighed heavily on him. "Are you sure it is a good idea letting him in on this investigation?"

He shrugged his shoulders and looked at one of the best detectives he had ever groomed. She had the uncanny ability to connect with the victim. Sometimes he wondered, was there something more to her, something that you couldn't teach. "What would you do? Would you want me to bench you if you were in his shoes?" He knew her answer before she spoke.

Thinking of Brooks, her best friend, her sister in every way but blood. "No. There wouldn't be a damn thing you could do that would keep me away from this case." And Cam knew what she had to do.

She stood and looked at the door. "Do you want to yell and throw me out so the guys don't think you're a pushover and a wimp?"

He was laughing as he stood up. "Nope. They know that you're the one who actually runs this department so they might kick my ass if they see me throwing you out."

When she got to the door, she paused and turned around. Captain Thems stood there with the weight of the department on his shoulders and all those faces staring at him. He was wrong. He ran this department and there wasn't a damn thing any of his detectives wouldn't do for him. "Thanks, Captain. I'll go tell Finny boy out there he can play with us big kids."

CHAPTER 4

At the morgue, she paused at the autopsy suite. Inside lay Nina Petrelli. Her parents had made the choice to take her off life support early this morning. Cam couldn't fathom the agony in making that decision. How do you put the emotion aside and make a rational choice to take your child's life? Cam understood probably better than most that Nina wasn't there. Hell, for two days she had been with Cam, but it still broke her heart to know that Mr. and Mrs. Petrelli would always live with this on their hearts and minds. She hoped it didn't break them. And before she got any deeper in this, she had to switch it off. You couldn't do this job if you didn't know how to switch off your emotions. It would eat away at your sanity before you made it to lunch.

But she paused at the door for another reason. Looking at Finn, she asked, "Are you sure you want to do this? From the report you gave me her injuries mirror Cat's." She almost said victim, but realized Finn needed to keep it personal. And maybe so did she.

"Yes," he answered.

His blue eyes betrayed the storm of emotions battling his will to stay calm. He was dressed in his everyday work attire, jeans, a T-shirt, an open long-sleeved button-up shirt, and his trusty leather jacket. The jacket was almost as scarred as the boots on his feet. His cheeks and chin carried the scruff of a two-day old shave and his dark hair was in desperate need of a trim. He shoved his emotions down and raised his eyes to meet Cam's.

"Sorry, I just wanted to be sure." Cam pushed the buzzer and waited silently beside him.

The autopsy suite was just like the one in Ireland. Sterile, white, and smelling strongly of cleaner and bleach. Stainless steel tables, scales, and instruments were neatly arranged and in their proper places. The harsh florescent lights glared down, revealing every miniscule detail in the room and its occupants, which for this department was a necessity. The one and only bright and colorful spot in the sea of white and steel was currently bouncing her ass to the music roaring out of her docked MP3 player. Her choice for today seemed to be a mix ranging from Five Finger Death Punch to Pitbull.

Finn grinned and wondered who this marvelous, little petite bunch of energy was. Although he felt like he was in the twilight zone. The medical autopsy rooms in Ireland were white and sterile, like this one, but it was silent. All business. All the time.

Cam caught his smile. "What?"

"I was thinking my medical examiner at home would stroke out if he saw this."

"Then he apparently is entirely too serious and I have pity on his soul." Chief Medical Examiner Brooks Aaron turned around and raised her eyebrows. The man standing in between her father and her best friend was gorgeous. Drop dead gorgeous. So this is the Irishman who had her best friend in a tit last night. She gave Cam a wink now that she had seen him with her own eyes, completely understanding her friend's plight.

Cam rolled her eyes. "Detective Finn McDougal, meet Chief Medical Examiner Brooks Aaron."

He glanced at Jimmy with an eyebrow raised. "Is this little wonder yours?"

"Yes, she is. My pride and joy." Jimmy grinned at his daughter. The differences between her and Cam were glaring. Cam's tall and willowy frame versus Brooks's small and petite one. Cam was subtle and muted clothes were drowned out in the color and vibrancy his daughter wrapped around her. But they were two peas in a pod. They always had been. He guessed their differences were just some reasons the two had lasted as long as they had. Cam anchored Brooks where Brooks pushed Cam to fly.

Jimmy always knew his daughter would be a doctor. It was her one constant in her life. But what shocked him was when his colorful and vibrant daughter took the job as chief medical examiner. Her reason was simple. There are thousands of doctors who fought for the living and she was proud to be one of them, but the dead needed someone to fight for them too. And she was the person to do it.

Jimmy's heart swelled at the memory. Call him crazy but he was happy when Brooks got the job. Now he got to work with both of his girls, who could ask for anything better?

Brooks caught Cam's quick look at Finn. Anyone else would just have thought that she was being polite and watching and waiting for this conversation to steer back to the case. But to her, who knew Cam, sometimes better than Cam did, she noticed both a wistfulness and worry. Yes, she thought, this case is going to be interesting on many levels.

Knowing she was being stared at, Cam sent a smoldering look at Brooks. Someone else would wither under that glare, but Brooks just smiled and got back to the point at hand.

"Okay, now that everyone in this little party is acquainted, let's get back to the dead." Brooks stroked a hand down Nina's hair. "Nina Petrelli. Age, fifteen years, seven months and two days. Cause of death is blunt force trauma to the head and multiple internal injuries causing massive bleeding throughout. The trauma was inflicted by blows all over the body. The instrument used…" She held up her balled fists. "Not only was she brutally and savagely beaten, she was raped with such a force that it cause massive bruising and swelling to her vagina and uterus. If she would have lived, she would have needed a hysterectomy. The damage was so severe." She had to pause a moment. She had seen a lot of death and brutality in her career, but something about this made her heart bleed for this poor girl.

Finn stood quietly and watched Brooks. She was struggling to contain her emotions. It was the first time in his career that he had witnessed open compassion from an ME. He wasn't sure if she was aware, but throughout her entire report, she had been stroking the girl's hair. Looking at Cam, the compassion continued. And for the first time since Cat died, Finn felt hope. If anyone could catch this monster, this was the team to do it. And he'd be damned if he sat on the sidelines and watched.

He focused back on Brooks. He nodded to the unspoken question he saw in her eyes. "After reviewing the autopsy reported provided by Detective McDougal—"

"Finn," he interrupted.

"Finn," she said with a quick grin. "The two deaths, professional opinion, were committed in the same manner. I would also conclude, without a doubt, that they were committed by the same individual."

"What makes you so certain?" Jimmy asked.

"Well, for one I'm awesome. As I have told you before, I am the best there is, and I know you would agree, and not just because you are biased." She grinned when he rolled his eyes. "Also I have found an identical marking on both victims."

Cam's eyes sharpened. "Where?"

Brooks motioned to the right side of the body. Midway down Nina's torso, on her third rib from the bottom, a small geometrical shape was barely visible in the bruising. It wasn't complete, but two horizontal lines were connected to two vertical ones.

"Here, let me magnify it. Look toward the monitor." She pointed to a flat screen positioned near the top of the table. It was attached to an arm that allowed her to move the screen in any position needed. One half of the screen was occupied with a picture of a bruise from Cat's body and the other half was the magnified bruise from Nina's body.

When the image focused, Finn gasped. "Holy Mary Mother of God!"

Cam all but pressed her face to the monitor. "Holy fuck." Her eyes widened.

Jimmy's mouth gaped open in shock. Both girls had the unmistakable image of a cross bruised into their skin. *Is this a holy mission some sick fuck had decided to wage?* he wondered.

He finally tore his eyes from the screen and he saw Cam with her head buried in the case file from Ireland.

"Nowhere in here does the ME make note of this. And I believe if he would have made the connection, he would have noted it." Cam looked at Finn for conformation.

"I agree. So it must have either been missed or he overlooked it and didn't see the shape." Finn was already pulling his phone out to call the ME to verify.

Cam looked at Brooks. "Have you put this in your report yet?"

"Nope. I figured I would wait to see what you wanted to do with it."

Finn wondered where Cam was going with this. He guessed Brooks seemed to be wondering the same thing considering her confused look.

Cam thought back to another case. A consistency, a mark on both bodies, was noted in a file and somehow the information was leaked and the killer changed his MO. They almost lost the son of a bitch. No way in hell that was going to happen again. She looked at Finn. Could they trust him? Cam had an instinctive nature not to trust people. Call it mommy issues, but it had saved her ass on more than one occasion. But something in her gut instinctively trusted him. So she'd go with it.

Cam looked at Brooks and mouthed, "Recording?" When she shook her head, Cam nodded.

"Okay. As of right now, this piece of evidence goes no further than the four of us. No reports, word of mouth, nothing. We still need to document it so we make a hard copy file only. We will keep it in a safe place. I will take that responsibility. Everything else gets put into the department file and turned into their respective places." She paused and looked at Jimmy.

"Agreed. We have to guarantee this leaks to no one. This could be the one piece of evidence that nails this son of a bitch. We can't afford for him to realize he made a mistake."

Finn nodded. This was something he wasn't used to, but he trusted these three. "I agree, on one condition." He looked all of them in the eyes. "I am not left out of anything."

Cam just grinned. "Finny boy, if you were going to be left out, we never would have brought you here. And you can be damn sure that you wouldn't have heard about any of this."

Getting back to the rest of the autopsy, Cam, Jimmy, and Finn listened as Brooks filled them in on her tox screen. "Only drugs in her system were the ones administered by the hospital. Also there was no semen in the rape kit from the hospital. So the bastard used protection. There was also no skin found under her nails. So he either tied her up first, which in my professional opinion is a big fat no, or he damn near knocked her unconscious." She opened her mouth and then closed it again.

"What?" Cam demanded. "What is it?"

Brooks took a deep breath in and let it out. Cam had rarely seen her unsure of saying something, so her ears and mind stayed open as Brooks finally told her theory.

"Rarely does a person successfully render a person unconscious with one blow, so I am perplexed. I went through her medical records from the hospital, and in the pictures taken there, her hands are clean. Which is unusual considering she was found in a dingy alley. Every day people gather little bits of dirt and grime under their nails and around the nail beds, but in this case her hands are clean. Including under her nails and around her nail beds. So I am inclined to believe that her hands were cleaned, by her killer."

"So he cleans up after himself. Protects himself in more ways than one. He not only wears a condom, but he cleans the victim's hands." Cam paused and looked at the screen that still highlighted the vertical and horizontal lines on Nina's side. "So if we believe that he is this careful, then we can probably conclude that he is unaware that he left any evidence, including this, on her body." She pointed to the screen. Which made keeping this discovery a secret all the more important. She struggled with the thought that she would essentially be keeping this from even her captain. But the less that knew the better the chance of it not being accidentally released to the public.

Jimmy spoke up, "Okay, so this evidence stays out of the official report. When we catch this son of a bitch, I'll take the hit for not informing the brass." He held up his hand to cut of Cam. "I know what you're going to say and you can just suck it up, buttercup." Her eyes narrowed to slits. "I'm lead on this team so I will take responsibility. Make one copy for our hard file. We will put it in a safe place, outside of this building." He looked at Finn and hoped his gut was right about trusting him. And continued, "Jack's safe should work."

Cam smiled. "Yup, no one would look for a file there. Jack's place would work just fine."

Finn raised his hand. "Who's Jack?"

CHAPTER 5

Fell's Point sat along Baltimore's harbor. In the nineteenth century, the area was primarily industrial warehouses, but during the past thirty or so years, the industrial warehouses became high-end condos and lofts, and the area became a mecca for the yuppies and business executives. Young successful family's moved in and the area became a trendy place to live and experience. Although the area had recently become popular, there were many families who had lived in there for generations.

On the water's edge sat on old Irish pub called *O'Brien's*. It was cramped and loud. Dark wood graced every inch of the place. Old barstools lined the bar, their seats a rich burgundy leather. Worn and creased by the countless bodies that slid across them over the years. Tall tables scattered the floor surrounded by two and three long-legged chairs. Even at the early hour, pints were pulled and slid across the bar and the smell of lunch wafted out the open doors. Out back, a deck extended over the harbor, and umbrella tables were placed around the old, worn wood planks.

O'Brien's had stood for over sixty years in this spot. Built by an Irishman who fled a war-scarred Europe for the wonders of America. He arrived with a wife and a one-year-old boy. He built the bar with his own two hands and poured the best Guinness in the area. His wife cooked in the back and treated you like family. She would also throttle you if the occasion called for it.

Jack Sr. and Fionna O'Brien had built a home for themselves in this marvelous city. They took an empty and vacant shell and turned it into a home and business they could pass on to their only child, Jack Jr. O'Brien's sat on the ground floor and they lived in the apartment above it.

To this day, it is still the same, just a few improvements here and there. The deck was added by Jack Jr. and the building next to it now belonged to the O'Brien family as well. Fionna still lives above the pub. Jack tried to move her to his house next door, but she steadfastly refused. She wanted to stay where she and her husband had lived for sixty years. Jack Sr. succumbed to a heart attack two years before and Fionna refused to leave. And Jack had the sense not to argue.

So Jack lived next door and turned the third floor into a condo for his daughter. It was her gift when she graduated the police academy. And his childhood best friend lived on the other side, with O'Brien's sandwiched in between, where he had lived every day of his life.

When Finn got out of the car, he momentarily forgot he wasn't at home. The wonderful smells and laughter brought him back to his neighborhood pub at home. Cam smiled as she watched the warmth flood his face.

He looked at the name above the doors. "Yours?"

She nodded. "My da's. And his da's before him. My pop built it when they came here after the war. My nana still lives upstairs. My dad bought this building, when he married my mother." She pointed to the building on the right. "And Jimmy and his wife live on the other side. When I graduated the academy, my dad redesigned the top floor to give me my own space. I wanted to stay close so I could still help out when needed and plus my nana still cooks in the back and I grew up on her food. Free food and free beer. I've got it made."

Just then a voice boomed out the open doors. "Camille Fionna! My baby is home for lunch!"

Finn laughed when a blush flushed her cheeks, but to his surprise she didn't seem embarrassed. She shouted back, "Aye to that and I've brought you two more!" Finn was surprised to hear a faint Irish lilt in her beautiful voice. What an amazing and complex woman. This was the first time he'd met this side of Camille O'Brien. Opposite of the rugged and tough cop was a loving daughter and an apparent pub favorite by the sounds of the greetings being shouted around. He followed Jimmy in and sat down next to him on a stool that was surprisingly comfortable, and he whimpered when the kitchen door opened and the smell of lamb stew billowed out.

Jack saw his look of longing and smiled. "You must be the Irishman my daughter told me about." Jack's voice was large and carried a bit of Ireland in it, easing some of the homesickness that had plagued Finn.

"Aye. And you'd be the famous Jack O'Brien. The one who created the beautiful Camille Fionna." This time the blush on Cam's cheeks was from embarrassment.

Jack watched the Irishman's eyes follow his daughter as she moved through the back of the bar and into the kitchen. He knew that look well. He had given it a time or three. Jack thought of his daughter and wondered if she looked at him the way he looked at her. Swallowing the clutch of fear, worry, and madness that came with having a daughter, Jack held his hand out to this boy from Ireland and gave a silent prayer when Finn smiled and shook it.

When Cam came back through, with lunch in her hands, the sight stopped Finn short. Her head was thrown back in laughter, and following her was a woman who, even in her eighties, was beautiful. He saw Cam's green eyes and red hair. The smile was the same and the confidence matched. Jack caught his stare and smiled. "There is where Cam comes from. My mother, Fionna." Jack paused. It still stopped him short to see the two of them together. It was like looking at two generations of the same woman. Cam had the beauty and the strength of his mother. And the kindness and love as well.

Jack often thanked God that his mother and father were there to help him raise Cam. A strong-willed child, scarred by the loss of her mother. Even if she wouldn't admit it. But his mother had filled that void and the woman Cam was today was proof of it.

Turning back to Finn he saw the wonder, and want, in the lad's eyes. Jack smiled. "I have heard stories from my father where he said he had to fight all the boys to win her hand. They loved each other their whole lives, and still to this day she wears his ring. He's been gone for two years now and she turns everyman down who asks her for a drink. 'I'm a married woman,' she tells them."

Finn thought of his parents. Loving and kind, but would they still say that when the other was gone? And he looked at Cam when she set his food in front of him. Standing next to her grandmother, their beauty was staggering, and in his stomach he knew his life would never be the same.

"Thank you, ladies." He turned his smile on Fionna. Cam just rolled her eyes.

Fionna turned to Cam. "I'd say he's more handsome than you let on." Finn raised his eyes to Cam.

"Shut up, Finny boy."

Fionna turned back to Finn. "So Mr.—?"

"McDougal. Finnegan McDougal. My family is from the County Clare."

"Is your grandfather Finnegan as well?"

Finn's eyes drew together. "Yes, ma'am. I am the oldest of his oldest. So I was named Finnegan as well. My grandmother is named—"

"Camille." Fionna smiled. God works in mysterious ways.

"What?" Cam turned to her grandmother. The look in her face was wonderment. What the hell was this? "You know his family?"

"Fionna?" Finn said to himself.

A memory of sitting at his grandmother's feet came flooding back. He had just had a fight with one of his best friends and his nine-year-old world was shattered. And his grandmother had told him of her childhood best friend and of the dreams and fights they had shared over their twenty years together. And of her heartbreak when she waved to her from the dock as her ship sailed to America.

"Finnegan," she had said, "a true friend you will never lose to a fight. Nor to three thousand miles."

And she had shown him a box filled with letters and keepsakes. And on top was the photograph of two young girls standing hand in hand. And another of the same two girls, grown and hugging at a dock. Even through the tears they smiled and looked hopeful. Finn asked his grandmother why they were crying.

She looked at him and said, "Her husband was taking her and their child to America for a new start after the war. So the tears were for the parting, but the smiles were for the friendship that parting would never break."

Smiling at the memory, he looked at the woman who had been hugging and crying with his grandmother on that dock. "You're Fionna Callaghan?" Finn's voice was full of wonder. "My grandmother would always tell us stories about you and her growing up. She always spoke fondly of you. You were her best friend when you were children."

Fionna's eyes misted. "Yes, she was my best friend when we were children. When the war ended, my husband moved us here. I still write to your grandmother every month." Fionna turned to Cam. "Small world, huh? When I was pregnant with your father I was going to name him Camille. So knowing I loved that name, he named you for me."

Cam didn't know whether to be surprised or not. From her grandmother's stories she knew the village she grew up in was small and close. So it wasn't uncommon for her to know or know of a few of the tourists who came by. But looking at Finn, Cam wondered how small the world really was. What were the odds?

Glancing at Jimmy, Cam was expecting him to be enjoying the stories as well, only to find him huddled with her father and the file. She walked up and laid a hand on her father's shoulder. "Don't keep it at home, keep the file here. Put it in the safe in your office. We don't think anyone will find out about it, but we just don't want any of it getting out. So, sorry—What?" He had dropped his fork and was staring intently at her face.

Crap! she thought. "No, don't look at Jimmy," she said when he swung back toward his best friend. "He wasn't there when this happened." She turned and saw that Finn was still laughing with her grandmother.

She turned back toward her father. "Look I had a nightmare and I woke up with a few bruises. I guess I must have hit myself a few good times in the thrashing. It was a rough dream," she half-lied. Knowing full well that he knew she was lying. But they both chose to drop it for now, mainly because he knew it was pointless to try to get anything out of her know. Especially with Finn sitting in the same room.

He stroked a hand down her face. "It worries me, no scares me, knowing you do what you do." He led up a hand before she could speak. "I know it's what you are supposed to do, but I have the right to worry. Hell, I'd worry if you stayed at home. It's my job. But this"—he gestured to her black eye—"is not a settled matter."

She leaned in and kissed his cheek. "I know." Turning she caught Finn's eyes on her. "But this is for later."

Her father nodded. He walked over and saw Finn take out his wallet. "Nope. It's on the house. I feed those two 'most every day. You are treated to the same." He looked over at Cam who was gathering her stuff. "Take care of her, or Jimmy won't be the only one who gets his ass handed to him." He caught the look that passed over Finn's face.

"Yes, sir," and with that he turned to Fionna. "Thank you, ma'am, for the wonderful meal and company."

"You be safe out there." Fionna smiled. She looked at her son when they left. "Cam doesn't see it, does she?"

"See what, Mother?" Making Fionna smile, just like his daughter, absolutely clueless.

Back at the precinct, Cam, Finn, and Jimmy sat in the captain's office updating him on the case so far.

Captain Thems sat back in his chair. His tall and muscular frame was clothed in a charcoal gray suit with a slate blue tie. Subdued and calming. He always wore gray suits and monochromatic ties. Never flashy, he always had a calming and peaceful presence about him.

This case, though, had him rattled. Hell it had them all rattled. "Are you saying that we have a serial rapist and murderer who has now killed on two continents?" He looked absolutely aghast. A rare sight for the captain. "Are there any other cases?"

"We are currently looking into that. As of right now, we know of only the two," Jimmy answered.

"Are you absolutely sure these two are connected?"

"Our ME reviewed the case file from Dublin and found that the two are almost identical. Same MO. There was no DNA left on either body. But the bruising pattern is similar as well as the fist size. Both girls were violently raped and beaten severely."

"What about the victims?"

Finn spoke first. "Cat—the first victim—was a teenage female who was a known prostitute. She was also a runaway. As of right now we believe he is targeting young prostitutes. We are unsure if he knew that either were runways, or if that was a coincidence."

Captain Thems folded his hands on his desk. "Well, generally speaking, if you have a young prostitute, it would be most likely that she was a runaway. Don't you think, Detective?"

"Well yes, sir, but in some cases we have found that the daughter can go out by a learned behavior from the mother, or father. Especially in Dublin where some forms of prostitution are legal. Some girls are even pimped out by their families."

Captain Thems looked disgusted at the thought. "Why on earth would a parent do that? It always sickens me when the parents are involved."

Finn agreed. As did every other cop and reasonable person on the planet.

CHAPTER 6

Later that night at his hotel, Finn found himself thinking of Cam. What an enigma she was! Tough and rash, but at the same time soft and whimsy. He had a feeling if he shared his latest thought he would see more of the tough than the whimsy. Her eyes could seduce a man and her mouth could throttle him back. Her body enticed a feeling from him he wasn't sure he had ever felt. He had plenty of experience with woman, but he closed his heart when Cat died.

He truly believed part of his heart died with her. From the moment they met, that fateful day two years ago, he felt an instant connection with the fiery sprite of a girl. She awoke a need in him he thought he never would feel. He had always had an instinct to protect, but never had he felt a need to parent until Cat. God, the sleepless nights he had fearing for her on the streets.

He had finally gotten through to her though. He promised if she quit he would pay for her to go to university. Hell, she had the brains for anything and everything. Except for herself. And finally, she had agreed. She decided to quit and go to school. He had even convinced her to stay in his spare room. His sister, Morgan, came to town, and along with Cat, redecorated the room.

It all changed that night when he got that call, and after, he shut that door and it hadn't opened since that night. He failed. He failed her was all he could think. All he could feel. He thought he had gotten past the most of it, but seeing that poor girl on the table, it all came rushing back. Slamming into him with such force it had knocked him back. And damned if he didn't feel that failure again. He had failed to catch the bastard, so he had come to America and he killed again. What kind of cop was he that he couldn't find one fucking guy? What kind of father was he that he couldn't protect the one thing he loved the most?

The thought stopped him cold. That was the question, wasn't it? What kind of father would he be if he couldn't protect his child? And that's what she was to him, his child.

He was unaware he had left his hotel and had begun to wander the city streets, until he heard a ballad, floating through in the night. It was so full of longing and love he almost thought he was back at home. As he walked toward the song, he realized he had wandered in the direction of O'Brien's.

He froze in the doorway when the source of the siren's song became clear. Cam O'Brien sat on an old man's knee, singing him to geriatric bliss, a song of her lost lover. And the enigma of Camille O'Brien grows.

Her hair was down, swinging full and curly down near to her waist. *Where did she hide all of that during the day?* he wondered. Her cheeks were flush with warmth and merriment. Her body was showcased in a low-cut T-shirt that hugged in all of the right places and her hips and ass were molded in perfectly cut jeans. The gods bless him, he was done for. This was the woman of his dreams, even if she didn't know it. If he left now, his mama would throttle him from here to the end of days.

So he did what any true Irishman would do. He walked in and began to sing.

Cam's voice faltered, but she quickly recovered. She thought about an escape but her nana had blocked the door. Noticing the look on her face alone was worth the embarrassment of the lover's duet. Cam hadn't seen that look since her grandfather had died.

So she swallowed her pride and most of her embarrassment and finished the song. She was unaware she had ended up in Finn's arms, until the catcalls began. She looked up into his eyes and it dawned on her. She was in trouble. Big trouble.

She glanced over at the woman who had laid a hand on both of them. "Nana, are you okay?" Her wonder turned to alarm at the sight of tears on her grandmother's cheeks.

"Aye, I just haven't heard a voice like his since your grandfather passed. It does this old heart good to hear a song of home."

Finn smiled down at her. He let go of Cam and turned toward her grandmother. He drew her in and began to sing another ballad of love and home. Within a few words the pub hushed and a fiddle picked up the tune.

As Cam watched, Finn danced and sung to her grandmother. She was unaware of the tears running down her face until her father came to stand behind her. She leaned back into the arms of the only man who had ever truly loved her and watched the happiness flush her Nan's cheeks.

After the calls for an encore quieted and the pub was back in full swing, Cam pulled two Guinness and sat down beside Finn. "That was some voice, Finny boy. Do you sing often?"

Finn, who had never really been embarrassed of singing in a pub, felt heat rise some in his cheeks. "Aye, most every time I go to the pub at home. But of course, most all of us Irishmen sing a song or two when the pints are flowing." He glanced at the beautiful woman sitting at the end of the bar singing along with the fiddle. "But none has touched me so as the look in your nana's eyes as I sung to her tonight." He looked back at Cam. "You're blessed beyond measure. I hope you know that. Never take that for granted."

Cam followed his gaze. "Never. I am blessed beyond words. I have a good family and great friends. But most important, I have a solid foundation. Something that will carry me farther than anything. What about you? Do you have a solid base?"

"Aye, that I do. I have family as numerous as the stars in the sky. My ma and da raised six of us. I have five sisters who ruled the house, even though I was older. I learned long ago the power of a woman." His eyes twinkled at the memory.

"Six of you!" Cam exclaimed. "There was just me and Brooks. Raised next door the same way our fathers were. They had enough trouble with just two of us I couldn't imagined if there was six." She laughed. No, she and Brooks had drove their fathers crazy; two was plenty.

"So what brought you our way this evening?" Before he could answer there was a commotion at the front of the pub.

Both of them turned and watched three drunk boys stumbled into the doors. "Hey! Bar guy, how 'bout a free beer for my boy here? Just turned twenty-one today." He slapped the friend's shoulder and almost put him face first to the floor.

Jack shook his head. "I think he's had enough, and so have you. How about I call you a cab?"

The friend looked hopeful. It seemed he was ready for the cab. But his friend disagreed. "I didn't ask for a cab. I asked for a fucking beer, so how about you just shut your fucking mouth and do your job, asshole. Pour the fucking beer." He tried to sound bad, but it was hard to take him seriously when he was swaying and slurring.

"I said no. Now get out," Jack said through clenched teeth. He slapped a hand on Finn's shoulder as he started to get up.

The kid was apparently dumber than he looked. He squared off and started toward Jack and the bar. "How 'bout I teach you a lesson about minding your fucking business and doing what you're told, old man. I said I wanted a beer now. Give me a fuc—" His yelp cut off his tirade.

He found himself staring at Cam's boots and his arm up and behind his back in a wrist lock. "Now you have two options. One, I let go, you apologize to my father, and you walk out of here with your dignity. Or two, I throw you out on your ass, you still apologize, and your dumbass goes for a ride in the back of my car to the precinct. So what is going to be?" She took his grunt for option one. And let him up.

His face was glowing, from embarrassment and drinking. It got brighter when he realized he was held down by the chick he was trying to impress. His buddy noticed her when they walked in. He and his friend had made a bet on who could fuck her first. "You're a cop?" He snorted. "My buddy and I thought you were a whore. You're not worth the fifty bucks to fuck. I bet you're a dike too."

It's not very often someone's temper beats Cam's but for the second time in two minute the idiot ended up on his face. This time with blood pouring out of his broken nose. "Goddamn, cunt bitch!" he screamed.

"It wasn't the cunt bitch, asshole." Finn's voice was dangerously low. "And unless you want your jaw wired shut, I suggest you apologize to both the lady and her father."

His head bobbled and Finn set him back on his feet. His friend, on the other hand, grew his balls at the wrong time and he found himself up against the bar, his nose bloody as well. "Seriously? Do you two share the same brain?"

Cam, in a rare instance, stood there mouth open and speechless. Her voice finally came back as the two uniforms came walking in. "Hey, Jack, Cam," The officer stopped short. "What the hell is going on?" He took in the two obviously drunk kids, and a very pissed off man holding both of them by their collars.

Cam spoke first, "This is Detective McDougal, from the Irish National Police, and these are two idiots who tried to assault my father and I."

The two uniforms gaped at Finn. It was a rare sight to see when someone was faster than Cam O'Brien. Adams, who had spoken up first, looked from Finn to Jack. "Um, Jack would you like to press charges?"

Finn who still had the two jack wagons by the collars turned them to face Jack and raised his eyebrows. "No, Derrick. I think they have learned their lesson. Just as long as they pay for the spilled beer and broken stool."

Officer Adams turned to the ring leader. "Are in going to pay? Or do I need to have the detective haul your sorry asses down town. And just to make it clear, the woman you tried to assault is the owner's daughter, but she also is a favorite of the chief of police. Not to mention, you dumb fucks tried to assault a cop in a cop bar."

Cam nodded to Finn and he let them go. Lead dumbass reached back to his pocket. Cam reacted on instinct. "Hey!" he yelled as his arm was jerked behind him once more.

"Are you a fucking idiot?" Cam said from behind him. "You are surrounded by police. You never reach into your pockets unless you are told to. Jesus, what pocket is it?"

"The left." he grunted. His cheeks were as a bright as the traffic light outside. He wished with everything he could pay this bitch back for this. Goddamn cunt had no right to treat him like this. She'd be sorry. He spun around when she let go, pulling his jacket into place.

"You don't have the right to go through that." He objected when she opened his wallet.

She just ignored him. "How much, Dad? And don't low ball, this asshole doesn't deserve it."

"A hundred and fifty should do it." His clenched jaw had Cam swallowing the snort. She took a hundred from idiot number one's wallet and turned to idiot number two.

Apparently smarter than his friend he held up his hands. "It's in my right back pocket."

Cam grinned. "I guess you have the brain between the two of you." She dug fifty dollars out and handed him back his wallet.

Officer Adams cleared his throat. "You both are on trespass notice for this establishment. You are not allowed to come within two hundred and fifty yards of these doors or these two people. If either one of you violated this, you will be immediately arrested. Understood?"

"Yes, sir."

"Good now get your asses out of here before I let the detective remove your asses from the property." Officer Adams watched the two of them stumble out, and at his partners "all clear" nod, turned toward Jack, Cam, and Finn.

"So Irish cop, huh? What brings you here?" Adams said with a grin.

Jack laughed heartily. "First round's on the house! On the account of the Irishman with a fist of stone and voice of a god!"

Finn accepted the slaps on the back and handshakes all around. The laughter and recounts grew louder and more heroic as the beer flowed.

By the time Finn found a place to lay his head he was drunker than he could remember and happier than he had been in a long time.

When he woke the next morning, his head was screaming and he found himself momentarily lost. He struggled to remember where he was and what in God's name had happened to him. He remembered the rounds of beer that had kept coming in a never-ending cycle. The bar, he learned was full of cops, off duty and retired. A few were regulars who had been coming as long as O'Brien's had been pouring pints. So his actions, to protect one of their own and Jack's daughter to boot, had earned Finn the respect of every one of them.

And man had they showed it. Finn lost count, but he didn't remember paying for a single pint.

His brain struggled to think where the hell was he. And then her scent hit him. Cam. He looked around and realized, with a twinge of both sadness and relief, that he was on her couch. Well, most of him was. One foot dangled over the edge and his left arm was numb from hanging over the cushion for who knows how long. He was a little embarrassed to realize he had to be put to bed, but he was good with it. For the first time, in a long time, he had good time.

Laying there for another few minute, Finn took in his surroundings. Cam, he noticed, liked warm, calming colors. Deep, rich fabrics and comfort led the charge with her furnishings. A massive TV hung on an exposed brick wall. And he noticed recessed speakers in her ceiling. *So she likes her toys*, he thought. He would bet that she was a sports fanatic. Her slim athletic build hinted at a strong will for staying fit.

Once he felt sure that his stomach wouldn't heave, he stood up slowly. He started his search for her bathroom down a hallway lined with photographs done in black and white. When he was coming out of the bathroom, one photograph stopped him in his tracks.

A woman in a flowy dress stood on the Cliffs of Moor. Her hair floated in the wind around a face caught in profile. A ghost of a smile touched her lips and her eyes were closed. Her arms were raised up, as if trying to hug the wind. The sheer beauty of her was only amplified by the beauty of the cliffs. Never in his life had he seen the cliffs overpowered by another's beauty until now.

Cam noticed the couch empty and came through the hallway and stopped. Her breath caught on the sight of the shirtless man before her. *Jesus*, she thought. Never in her life had she seen a man who was so beautiful. And never to be one at a loss for words, this was the third time he had struck her dumb.

Sensing eyes on him, Finn turned. "Is this you?" he said, pointing to the photo.

"Um, yes." *Wow, that was smooth. Idiot*, she thought. She shifted her weight and glanced at the photo. "Brooks's hobby. That was about two years ago. My nana wanted to spread some of my pops ashes there. It seemed as if the wind and sea picked up as soon as we let him go. I just wanted to hug him one last time." She felt stupid as soon as she said it. She had never told anyone that, so why it popped out was beyond her. She swore this man was making her brain cells just roll over and play dead any time he turned those eyes on her.

He just smiled. "It is said the faeries live at the cliffs. And the sea roars and the wind blows when one of their own comes home." He was surprised when she smiled.

"You sound just like him." She looked up into his eyes. "It was a very sweet thing you did for my nana last night. We haven't seen her smile like that since pop died. Thank you." She smiled. "And thank you for your help with those two idiots last night as well."

Laughing he replied. "I don't think you needed my help, but you are welcome." He paused and looked around. "I will just gather up my stuff and get out of your way. You probably want out of your running shoes." He pointed to her feet. She had just run three miles. The perfect cure for a hangover.

"Actually why don't you grab a shower and then I am to take you down to dad's where Nana has cooked you a breakfast that should remind you of home. Her cure for a hangover. Do you want a coffee?"

Leaving him no room to decline, she turned toward the kitchen.

CHAPTER 7

Monday morning dawned cold and clear. No new victims had turned up and Cam didn't know whether to be grateful or irritated. She couldn't get much done over the weekend, due her thoughts straying back to a half-naked Irishman standing in her hallway. It didn't help that he was a complete gentleman. Swooning over her nana's cooking and bringing that glow back to her cheeks. So she couldn't understand why her mood had soured on the way into work.

"Spending entirely too much time thinking about something I can't have. That's why." She crumbled to herself. She was so completely wrapped up in herself she almost missed dispatch coming over the radio.

"Five eight two three, be advised there is a 10-42 at 2358 West Pratt Street. Victim has been taken to Johns Hopkins. Responding Officers are still on scene waiting for your team."

"Shit!" She slapped her wheel. She picks up her radio. "Ten-four Dispatch. Show 5823 as 10-50." Snapping the radio back in place she hit her lights and did a U-turn. "Goddammit!"

She grabbed her phone and called Finn. He picked up on the first ring. She told him the address and as much as she knew. "Can you find it?"

"Yes, I'll meet you there." He hung up and Cam floored it.

Cam screeched to a stop outside the yellow tape. Officer Crabtree came over and lifted the tape as she ducked under. "Detective, it appears to be the same as the other victim."

"Have you briefed the others?"

"No, ma'am, you're the first to arrive." He stopped and turned at the sound of more screeching tires. The man who jumped out was not familiar to Jonah, so he started to stop him as he ducked under the tape. "Sir! You can't—" He stopped at the withering stare Finn gave him.

Finn grabbed his badge and shoved it in Jonah's face. "Yes, I bloody well can."

Cam laid a hand on Officer Crabtree's arm. "Officer Jonah Crabtree, meet Detective Finn McDougal, Irish National Police. He is here helping with our investigation. The guy hit in Dublin first."

Jonah's cheeks flushed. "Sorry, sir. I was unaware."

Finn had a rare flash of guilt. "No, I apologize. I should have introduced myself."

Jonah was taken aback. He wasn't expecting an apology. He took in the man before him. Tall, dark, and handsome. Jonah felt a pang of jealousy at the way Cam looked at him. Jonah squared his shoulders. "Thank you, sir. I was first on the scene and was about to give my report to Cam—I mean Detective O'Brien." He ignored the narrowed look Cam shot at him at his use of her first name.

Finn grinned and thought the boy was lucky there was a witness. But if he needed to puff his chest in front of her, he'd let him. And true to form, Cam was oblivious to his pathetic attempt at claiming her as his territory. "Well, now that Detective Aaron's here, let's start." Finn held his hand toward Jimmy. "Morning, Jimmy."

"Morning." Jimmy looked toward the alley and the crime scene techs. "Well, I thought it was a good morning." Turning toward Jonah, he said, "Officer. Were you first on scene again?"

"Again?" Finn asked.

"Yes, sir," Jonah started. "When Officer Michaels and I arrived on scene, one of the homeowners directed us to the back of the alley. Like the last one he found her as he was taking out his trash. He was afraid to touch her but he did call it in. We arrived and I noticed shallow breathing, so I called for the ambulance to high tail it. We taped off the scene and called it in to dispatch to alert you and Detective O'Brien." He paused to look back at his notes.

"Did you start a canvass for witnesses yet?" Cam asked.

Jonah looked up and smiled, ignoring the cold tone in her voice. "Yes, ma'am. I had Michaels keep going when I noticed your arrival. My last interview yielded a witness who thinks they may have noticed something." He paused. Cam's impatient look must have been very evident because he quickly continued. "Just like the other night, one of the witnesses swears he saw a tall man, in a dark suit, walk away from the alley between oh three hundred and oh four hundred."

Cam turned to Finn. "Was there any mention of a man in a dark suit in your case?"

Finn, who knew every word of the case file, didn't need to look at his notes. "We actually had one person say they noticed a man in a suit around the area, but he couldn't be sure of the time. So I'm going to venture and say yes. It appears our guy not only favors teenage prostitutes, but also fine suits."

Cam nodded. Glancing back at Jonah, she asked, "Did you run her?"

Looking back down, Jonah flipped a page in his book. "According to ID found on the victim she is Beverly Ann Goodall. Born November 16, 1997. Hair is red. Eyes are—"

"Blue," Cam finished for him.

"Yes, ma'am." Jonah's forehead creased. "Am I missing something?" he asked.

Cam took a deep breath in. "This asshole is targeting teenage prostitutes. Red hair and blue eyes. Jesus Christ." She breathed, rubbing her hands over her face. She asked a question she already knew the answer for. "Is she a runaway?"

Jonah looked down again and looked back at Cam. He only nodded.

"Shit!" Looking over at Jonah's notebook, Cam wrote down her parent's information and went to do the part of the job she hated most.

Jimmy caught Finn's eye and jerked his head after Cam. "You go with her. I will finish here and meet you both there."

Finn nodded and jogged to catch up with Cam.

An hour and a half later, they entered the ICU at Johns Hopkins. Cam wished for a bottle of Ibuprofen and a shot of whiskey. Nothing can prepare you for shattering someone's world. She could do it a million times and she would never become numb to it. This morning was no different.

What made this case harder was knowing when she got here, she was leading the parents toward a decision no parent should ever have to make. Whether or not to turn off the machines that was keeping their child alive. Leaving the parents with the doctor Cam looked at the floor and said, "I swear I will fucking get this guy. And he will pay for every life that he has shattered. And I don't even think hell would want this guy."

"That's if I don't rip his balls off and choke him with them first." Cam didn't know if Finn was joking or not. And Jimmy, standing stiff with his arms crossed over his chest and jaw clenched tight, nodded his head in agreement.

"Well," Jimmy said. "The report from the doctor is almost the same as it was with Nina. Beverly was severely beaten all over her body. Her left cheekbone is shattered, as well as her jaw and right eye socket. Her skull is cracked around her right temple. Broken collarbone and some ribs. It appears that he grabbed her right arm and jerked it so violently behind her that he ripped her arm out of the socket." He paused to pinch the bridge of his nose between his thumb and forefinger. "Jesus Christ. He even punched and pummeled her vagina area." He broke off and started pacing.

Cam voiced what they all were thinking, but none wanted to say aloud. "The bastard is escalating. How in the hell that poor girl survived is beyond me."

Cam thought they would have more time to catch this guy before he started again. There was a year between his attack in Ireland and Baltimore. Why in the hell was he killing again already? It had been three days since they found Nina. Would he wait another three days? Or would he kill again tonight?

Something else bothered Cam. Where was Beverly? Why hadn't she come to me yet? Cam glanced around. Nina hadn't been back around since the day at the hospital. She guessed seeing the pain on her parents' face was too much. *Or was I too hard on her?* Cam asked herself. She caught Finn staring at her as she looked around.

"Who are you looking for?" Finn asked.

Cams shrugged her shoulders. "No one. I was just thinking." She hoped she was casual enough that he would accept that and leave it alone. But if she had to guess by the look on his face, he didn't.

Finn didn't buy that for a minute. There was more to Camille O'Brien than meets the eye. Something was up and he'd damn well figure out what it was.

The doctor who had treated Nina was on duty today, and it appeared he had taken over Beverly's case as soon as he heard she had come in. Cam watched him and noticed the doctor showed Beverly's family the same compassion he had given to Nina's. Two girls in four days, Jesus they needed to catch this guy and Cam hoped the doctor may have something new that might help.

As soon as he finished with the girl's parents, he joined the detectives down the hall. Dr. Horton looked tired in his rumpled scrubs and scattered hair. His glasses were sliding down his hawk nose, which was prominently set in a pudgy face. Beverly's chart was still clutched in his hand but he didn't consult it. This was a man who knew his patients and prided himself on it.

"Detectives," he greeted. "I had hoped not to see you both again." And realizing what he had said, he quickly tried to change his words, "I mean, not that it wasn't a pleasure to meet you the other day but—"

Jimmy smiled and held up a hand. "Sir, we know what you meant. It's okay. Is there anything new you can tell us?"

Dr. Horton looked at Cam and Jimmy and sheepishly grinned. His eyes came to a rest on Finn and confusion came to his face. "I'm sorry I do not remember you from our previous meeting."

Finn held out a hand and smiled. "You wouldn't. I arrived the day after. I am Detective Gaurda Finn McDougal, Irish National Police."

Dr. Horton's Eyes widened in surprise. "So the other girl was not his only victim. God bless their souls."

Cam nodded. Grateful they didn't have to spell it out for him. Some doctors just see a body on the sheets. It seems Dr. Horton saw more than that. And she hoped he was just as astute as he seemed.

"Correct. Beverly"—Cam pointed to the girl currently hooked up to numerous machines— "is his third. That we know of at this time. Is there anything new you can tell us?"

Dr. Horton flipped through her chart. More to gather his thoughts than to review his notes. "As you can probably tell, this girl had it worse. Several broken bones in her face: eye, both cheeks, jaw, nose. He cracked her skull twice. Broke her collarbone on the left side. Wrenched her right shoulder out of its socket. Broke her left wrist. Numerous fingers on both hands." He paused. He drew his eyebrows together. He looked as if he was going to say something else but stopped.

Finn caught the doubt in his eyes. "Is there something else?"

Looking at Finn, Dr. Horton continued. "Well, it's just that her hands were different than the rest of her body. They were…they were clean. You see, when she was brought in she was covered in blood and grime. But her hands caught my attention because they were so clean. And it seemed out of place." He looked back and forth between the detectives, waiting for one of them to tell him he was overthinking it. But when they looked to each other, he knew that he hit on something.

"What? Is that important?" he asked.

Cam looked at his pudgy and friendly face, and going on instinct, she trusted him. "Yes. All of the girls have had clean hands—"

"I knew it!" he hissed. "The other girl's hands were clean too. I thought at first maybe the medics or your techs did it. But they seemed a little too clean."

Cam wondered what else the good doctor had noticed. "Was there any other similarities between the two that you can tell us about?"

"As a matter of fact, some of the bruising patterns on the two were identical. There was a pattern in some of the bruising that was on both girls." He paused and glanced around, seeing no one near he continued, lowering his voice to keep the information between the group. "It appeared to be an indentation left by a ring the attacker was wearing."

Sensing their one key piece of evidence was now out, Cam tried to stress the importance of the find to the doctor. "Dr. Horton. Please keep this to yourself. Did anyone else see this mark?" Cam prayed that it was just him and was relieved when he shook his head no.

"Good. This cannot go into either of their files. It is the one piece that we need to keep from the public. It may be the thing that brings this bastard down, and if he knows we know it, he may remove it."

Dr. Horton straightened and look appalled that she would question his discretion. "Young lady, I have been practicing medicine since before you were born. If you are implying that I would run off at the mouth—" He stopped and narrowed his eyes when she chuckled.

"I'm sorry. That was not my intention." She had to pause to compose herself. She had never been so politely told to shove it. "I know that you are very professional and well respected, what I was trying to say was you cannot even speak of this to another doctor or any colleague. Is this information in either file?"

"No, it is not. I thought that I should discuss this with the two"—he glanced at Finn—"pardon me, three of you first. And I see that I was right to do so." He glanced behind him at the glass room holding the fragile life of Beverly. "She is worse off than Ms. Nina was." He gazed back to the detectives. "Please catch this guy before he does this to another girl. Although I am afraid, if he does strike again, that girl won't be brought to me."

Cam drove back to the scene on auto pilot. The final words Dr. Horton said were replaying in her head. He was probably right. The next girl wouldn't make it to the hospital. The bastard was escalating in violence and time. How long would they have to wait for the next body? A day? Or two?

Finn watched her think. He wondered if she knew she silently spoke, her lips moving as she worked through a problem. Her face betraying every emotion and frustration as she silently worked through a case. Did she know how beautiful she was doing it? That magnificent mouth silently working toward her answer. Her marvelous brain working through all the scenarios. Those captivating eyes betraying her frustrations and fears.

But he too was dwelling on the final words of the doctor. His gut was telling him another girl would be killed tonight. This bastard was starting to enjoy the power, the absolute high that flowed through him as every hit slammed home. But what a weak bastard he was, hitting little girls. Raping the innocent. Finn hoped with every fiber in his body that he would get the chance to put his hands on this bastard, watching his eyes as he beat the life out of the sick fuck. No. He wouldn't use a gun. His bare hands were enough. The need to strangle the life out of the man shocked him. He knew the dangers of letting it get personal, but they went out the window as he watched his baby girl die. He knew if Cam learned how deep his relationship was with Cat, she would pull him off the case. So he shoved those feeling deep and blanked his face of emotion.

"Penny for your thoughts?" Finn queried.

Cam took a moment to collect her thoughts first. "I was thinking of what Dr. Horton said." She paused and glanced at him. She saw that the same fears racing through her had made their way around his brain as well. "We'll have another girl tonight. Won't we?" He nodded. She took a deep breath and tried to push it aside. The thought sickened her. She should be able to catch this guy before he took another girl. Frustration and anger surged through her veins.

Her thoughts were interrupted by her cell phone ringing. She searched her pockets and her lap. Why did she always forget where she put the damn thing? She glanced over when she heard Finn's voice. What the hell was he doing with her phone? She made a grab for it and was shocked when her hand was swatted away.

She swallowed her reply when she heard the news. Beverly was dead. Her body gave out before her parents could make a decision. The rational part of Cam's brain was thankful. At least her parents were kept from having that decision following them. Haunting them. But the other part broke silently for the child that was taken too soon.

When Finn ended the call, Cam saw the same emotions roll over him.

"God, this job can really fucking suck." She wasn't aware she spoke aloud.

"It sure as hell can," he agreed.

"You have this habit I have noticed. You talk to yourself when you think too hard. No sound, just your lips silently moving in conversation." Her glare made him laugh more. "You usually keep it silent but occasionally you speak aloud. It's cute." If looks could kill, Finn guess he'd be dead on the spot.

"I. Do. Not. Talk. To. Myself," she said through clenched teeth. "And why are you watching me anyway?"

"You fascinate me. Your face, your brain. It is a wonder to watch you, Cam."

She had to sit in the car for a minute when they stopped. Normally she would be pissed, but for some reason she found herself flattered. She needed to shake that off. She had no time to be flattered by a slick Irishman who looked damn good in his jeans and boots. She watched him stride around the front of her car to her door.

He grinned as he opened it up and held out his hand. As usual he made her body react in fifty different ways and it frustrated the hell out of her. Ignoring his hand, she jerked out of the car and left him grinning like a loon on the sidewalk.

Officer Crabtree watched Cam and Finn from behind the tape. What the hell is the sonofabitch up to? Jealousy ran rampant through his system. He hoped Cam flicked that prick off like a fly and he silently cheered when she ignored MacDougal's hand. Jonah put on what he thought of as his "sexy" grin and sauntered over to lift the caution tape for Cam. His mind cheered when she smiled back, and he dropped the tape in MacDougal's face.

Finn shrugged it off and ducked under. He had to pick up his pace to catch up to the two of them and noticed Jonah angle his body to exclude him. *All right you bastard*, he thought. He stood close enough to hear, but back a ways to take in all of Jonah's slight advances and Cam's complete oblivion to them. He grinned and shook his head. Poor kid has no idea what he's getting into. After watching his pitiful attempts to rub shoulders and his not-so-subtle attempt at peering down Cam's shirt, Finn had enough.

He walked up and grabbed Cam's elbow and started walking toward the alley. When she tried to pull away, he held firm.

"What the hell's your problem?" Cam demanded.

"For someone so astute, you certainly are oblivious to what is going on around you."

Fury had turned her face red and she finally jerked her arm free. "What the fuck does that mean?" she hissed.

"Seriously?" Finn positioned himself so Jonah stood behind him. "If that boy tried any harder, Victoria wouldn't be the only one who saw your secrets!"

"Have you lost your mind?" Cam said incredulously.

"So I must have imagined his eyes lingering on your breasts or the subtle look at your ass? Come on, Cam! I'm a man! I know a guy checking out a chick. Jesus, cut me some slack." His eyes narrowed at the grin she was failing to hide.

"Jealous?"

Christ Jesus, did she actually just flutter her damn eyes? Jealous? Jealous! She could only be so lucky!

She couldn't stop the chuckle that escaped. "Thanks, Danny boy, for defending my honor."

"Shove it," he growled. And he stalked the rest of the way to the alley. Shoving all thoughts of Cam out of his head, he focused on the scene in front of him.

The narrow alley smelled of mildew, blood, and sex. Running between two row houses, it was only seven or eight feet tall, rounded at the top, and running twenty to thirty feet in length. Two narrow doors, on either side and at the rear of the tunnel, allowed access from each house. He spread his arms out to either side of him. Maybe only three or four feet, not much room to maneuver, he thought. Running his hands along the rough wall, images flashed through his head of a terrified girl, struggling and scrapping against the wall. Her heart would be slamming against her ribs, fear choking the air from her lungs.

He had to close his eyes and breathe. His heart was racing. *Is that what she felt?* he wondered.

"If you are Beverly and a man is going after you, wouldn't you scream?" Cam had come up behind him while he was thinking of the girls.

"None of the neighbors reported hearing anything out of the ordinary." She looked around. "Of course screams, yelling, and shit is ordinary to most of these people."

Finn tried to move past her and scrapped against the wall. He paused, turned around, and tried again. He scraped again. Looking at the arm of his favorite leather jacket he noticed the elbows had scratches on them.

"Let me see you flashlight." He pushed it on and started scouring the walls.

"What are you looking for?" She stood there, waiting and watching. She was about to ask again when he stopped at one point and leaned in closer. She walked up beside him and looked over at the wall.

"Is that leather?" She glanced at his elbows. "Yours?" She barked for one of the techs to give her another flash light. And yelled for Crabtree to get his ass over there. "Didn't one of the wits say they saw a man in a dark suit?"

He flipped through his notes. "Yes, ma'am." Cam turned on her light and started on the opposite wall. If Finn's leather was on the wall, maybe, just maybe, the perp's suit was there as well. Scouring the walls, Cam and Finn would holler to one of the techs any time they came across any fibers. One of them had to be his. The violence had to have been staggering; the perpetrator would have rubbed against the alley walls.

She pulled her phone out and called Jimmy. He was over at Nina's scene re-canvassing, looking for any new leads. When she told him what Finn had thought of, he called for another tech team and started back on that alley.

After an hour, they left it in the tech's hands. They had them go back over the walls and then the floor. They'd bitch and complain, but they do it. They wanted this bastard as bad as any of them.

CHAPTER 8

Back at her desk, Cam read through the report again. Something was nagging at the back of her brain, but she couldn't find it. She slammed the report closed and twirled her chair to face the board. Five feet by three and a half, it held everything they had so far. Which, sadly, wasn't much. Nina and Beverly stared back at her.

Cam got up and walked to the board. She reached up and removed Nina's picture. Young and innocent, her blue eyes stared back at Cam. Framed by high-arched, honey blonde eyebrows, her eyes were wide and clear. The color of the sky, clear and blue. She had long eyelashes, and her cheeks were dimpled and rosy. Her mouth spread into wide and easy smile.

Cam looked to her left and compared the picture to the girl standing beside her. Nina's back was to the board and her eyes were on Finn. Cam really couldn't blame her. He definitely was good to look at. She watched Nina study him, wondering if she saw the man or dollar bills.

Nina sensed that she was being watched. "What?" Nina demanded. Cam just shook her head. Nina assumed it was because of Finn. "Is he yours?" Cam looked around the bullpen and shook her head again. Finally she clued in.

"Seriously?" She swept her arm around. "They don't know?" She turned to face Cam and put her finger up and tsked. She knew Cam wouldn't do shit about it while there were witnesses. "So I am not the only one with secrets. Hmm, what would they say if they knew the real you?"

She started circling Cam. Tapping her finger against her chin she continued to bait her. "Straight-laced and hard-assed Cam can see *and* talk to dead people. Would they consider that cheating? Even though you can't see our killers? Would they believe you? Or would they persecute you as a freak?"

Cam refused to rise to her baiting. She turned back toward the board and put Nina's picture back.

Moving on to Beverly's photo, she took it down to study it. Much like Nina's, Beverly's showed a fresh-faced beauty. Cam hadn't seen her without the broken and bruised face. Unlike Nina's eyes, Beverly's were deep and dark. Like a rich sapphire. Her cheeks were smooth and untouched. Her smile more reserved and shy. Cam sensed that the young girl was unsure of herself, lacking confidence in her beauty. Completely opposite of Nina. Cam wondered how she ended up a prostitute. She searched for her again. Why she wasn't coming through? She asked herself for the umpteenth time since they found her. Normally she caught sight of every one she stood for.

Turning back to the board, she hung Beverly's picture back up. She stepped back to see the board as a whole again. Both of the girls were pictured in life and death.

Cam turned to Finn. He was looking through a file, but he had stopped on a photo. His face broke out in a grin, but his eyes held both sorrow and love. The smiling girl was standing in front of a fountain, which in turn was in front of a large stone castle. Her red hair cascaded all the way down her back, falling in ringlets and large curls. Her cheeks were rosy and deeply dimpled. Her mouth was stretched wide, laughing at the person behind the camera. Her eyes danced and gleamed. They were a striking shade of blue, unlike anything Cam had ever seen. A striking and deep cornflower blue. She had a smattering of freckles across her nose and cheeks and they dotted here and there on her forehead. She seemed like she was on top of the world. Her arms were thrown above her head; the photographer had caught her in mid dance. Her smile was infectious and Cam caught herself smiling at the beautiful and carefree girl.

"Is that Cat?" Cam asked Finn.

Finn cleared his throat. "Yeah. I took this when she made the decision to get off the streets. I took her out that day to celebrate."

Looking over his shoulder, she realized he had Cat's file. "Was Brooks done with that?"

Finn shook his head. "This is my copy." He held up his hand, stopping her interruption. "I know it's not standard procedure, but this case is different to me." He paused, wondering how much he should tell.

Cam sighed and sat across from him. "How well did you know her?" she asked, even though she knew the answer. She was struggling with his deep personal attachment to this case. She immediately heard her nana's voice in her head—*Pot, meet Kettle. Kettle, pot.* Personal attachments came with all of her cases.

Finn looked down at the picture in his hand. And before he could change his mind, he told her.

When he finished, he looked up to see Cam with her eyes closed. And a single tear ran down her cheek. Without even thinking he reached up and ran his finger down the tiny stream.

Cam watched him as he sat back down. She wondered if she was the only one who felt the burning need down in her stomach every time they touched. God, she hoped not.

Shaking off the touch, she stood up and placed Cat's picture up in the left corner of the board. She looked at the fresh, smiling face full of life and hope. "The faeries must have loved her too," she mumbled to herself.

"Aye to that. Most of us at the Guarda too." Finn chuckled. "She had my whole team wrapped around her little finger. You couldn't help but to love her. She was so full of life and laughter. When we first arrested her, she was full of piss and vinegar, made half of my guys blush with what was coming out of her mouth. But once we got her back to interrogation, she pulled out the charm. Tried her damnedest to get out of the charge. So that's when I turned her into my CI." Finn smiled and shook his head at the memory.

"None of us had an inside girl worth a damn. And we were fighting against this huge and very impenetrable ring of under-aged prostitutes. Girls and boys. We couldn't get anyone to flip on the guy running it—well, the guy we all believed ran it. We couldn't even find out who was working for him. Cat didn't work for him but she was willing to ask around for us to try to get someone to slip up and mention something to tie this guy to these kids."

Cam's heart sped up. This might be their first lead. Hell, they had nothing but a guy in a suit so far. "Why haven't you mentioned this before?" she demanded.

Finn sat back and scrubbed his hands down his face. "Because why would this guy have anything to do with your American girls? From what we know this is only happening in Dublin. And we had nothing to tie him to Cat's murder so it didn't seem relevant."

Cam scooted off the desk and started toward the board. Marked in hand she drew a line dividing the board into two halves. The three girls on one side and she drew a "?" mark on the other. "Okay. For shits and giggles let's work this guy through and see if it's possible he is any way remotely connected to any of this. Name?"

Finn sat up and picked up Cat's file. Along with her murder, he had all of his notes about the ring included in his copy. "Sean Flannery. White. Thirty-five. Five feet and eight inches. Two hundred pounds. Green eyes, brown hair." He looked up at her neat and precise writing. He got up and stood next to her. Could this sonofabitch been the one this whole time? He was mentally kicking himself for not working him harder.

Cam noticed the internal war raging through Finn. "Detective, if you can't pull yourself together and pull your head out of your ass and stop blaming yourself, I will kick your ass back to Ireland. Trust me I know it is hard and damn near impossible but you have to let the personal go and focus on the job."

What the fuck does she know about separating the personal? Finn thought, shocked with the wash of anger and hatefulness that flooded his system.

Cam, noticing she had succeeded in pulling that anger away from himself and refocusing it on her, continued. "What do you know about this ring?"

Finn struggled to reign in the fierce emotions ragging through him. He thought of Cat and forced himself to focus. He walked back to the desk and picked up the file. He knew every word printed on those pages but he needed the physical contact of the file to keep himself focused. "We believe this Sean Flannery is the face of the organization. He is a suspected mobster in the Dublin area. His family is believed to be running the East Dublin Liberation Army. And there are numerous other families involved, but theirs is the leading one. They are listed as supporters of the IRA. They have a legitimate corporation under the name of Flannery and Sons Shipping and Distribution. But not everything they ship and distribute is legitimate."

Raising the marker to the board Cam started writing. "Let's start with the legitimate arm of the corporation."

After hauling another board to the bullpen, they had a good strong sense of the legitimate side of the business. Firmly rooted in the community, they employed a lot of the locals on the east side of Dublin. They had scholarships and foundations they sponsored, as well as many churches and youth groups.

On the legal side of the business they shipped and distributed many imports into Ireland. Cars, produce, electronics, clothes, and other freights. They also exported many of the community's small business wares. From authentic and locally made clothing, foods, and crafts. And they seemed to create a healthy income for both their workers and the local businesses.

They also made a fair wage for themselves. Part of the Flannery clan was involved in the local government and, as Finn had soon discovered, the local police. They had a person in nearly every occupation in the government that deals directly, and also indirectly with the import/export business. On the outside, this family was a true blessing to the community. Very respected and influential, and the community seemed to rally around them.

Sean Flannery is the chief executive officer and president of the company. His older brother, Patrick, is the chief financial officer. Both serve on the board of directors, along with their father, Seamus and their grandfather, Michael. Sean and Patrick's younger sister, Eileen, is the executive vice president of operations, and she is the face of the foundations and charitable organizations for the company.

Cam looked closely at the three siblings. Finn had brought pictures of each, and Cam taped those above their names. She could see why Sean was the face of the company. Slick and good-looking, he had a baby-faced complexion, and a look of innocence and trust. An expensive suit and tie draped his athletic body, and handmade Italian leather shoes adorned his feet. He had a Rolex that peeked out from his sleeve and he stood in front of the company's headquarters. His brother, Patrick, shared his coloring, but nothing else. Shorter by two inches, his face was pinched and narrow. He had a hawk nose and beady, rat-like eyes. His hair was receding which only added insult to his appearance.

Not very personable, Cam thought. No wonder the younger brother is the face of the company. She wondered if that caused any tension at the family dinner table.

The last of the siblings was Eileen. She had an entitled air to her look. All primped and polished. Her hair was a pale straw gold and definitely from a bottle. Her eyes were as blue as the sky above. She wore a sheath dress and a matching coat, the color of fresh strawberries. Five-inch stilettos, in the same color, were on her feet. Just seeing them had Cam's arches aching. Eileen's face was flawless and perfectly made up; same with her hair, done in an elegant twist. She wore pearls around a slender throat and gold on her ears.

Cam studied her picture. She looked just as soft and innocent as her older brother. But something was off, and it took Cam a moment to pin it down. Her eyes. Those cold, flat eyes sent a shiver down Cam's back.

"She's in on it," Cam said matter-of-factly.

"Really?" He almost sounded incredulous. "You are the only one, other than myself, who has said that." Finn grinned.

Cam kept looking at the board. Between all three siblings. "They all are in on it. Not just because they are part of this crime family, I think they would be crooked anyway. They chose the younger brother as the 'head' of the company because his face screams innocence and cute, but if you look it is all there. In their eyes." She looked over at Finn. "Have you talked to any of them?"

Finn thought it was time to drop the next piece of evidence. "Cat was found on one of their docks."

Cam turned back to the board. *This shit just keeps getting deeper*, she thought. "Okay. Let's move onto the other side of the family business."

Finn looked at the boards. “How many of those do you have?” Pointing to the two boards Cam had already filled.

She shook her head and hollered for Rodriguez to get more boards and went to reserve one of the conference rooms.

Finn and Cam spent the rest of the day compiling the boards on the case. What they had now was four extra boards detailing the East Dublin Liberation Army’s business and hierarchy. At least everything Finn had been able to gather in the past year and a half.

With Cat’s help, Finn had started gathering intel on one of Dublin’s most secretive mobs. They had their hands in all of the pots, from extortion to prostitution, and drugs to arms dealing. But the police didn’t have a single shred of evidence. Nothing they could link back to them. Finn took it personally, and now, because he couldn’t stop them in Ireland, now they had jumped the pond and had set up shop in Baltimore.

CHAPTER 9

Cam, Jimmy, and Finn found themselves in a briefing the following morning. After being brought up to speed, the captain decided it was time to brief some other departments and delegate a task-force if needed. So Cam found herself surrounded by a room full of detectives from five other departments—homicide, narcotics, gang-task force, vice, and under cover surveillance. They also had a representatives from the ATF. After the introductions had been made, Captain Thems turned the meeting over to the three of them.

From the front of the room, Cam took stock of the new team. There were those in attendance who had a strong dislike for women in uniform, many of whom had made their dislike personally known to her. But she'd be damned if anyone would take this case from her. So she let the glares and stares roll off her back and she got down to business.

"September 9, 2012, Dublin, Ireland. At approximately midnight to zero one hundred hours, Mary Catherine Donnelley was attacked and raped. She was severely beaten and left for dead. Approximately zero two thirty, two witnesses come upon the scene and called for help. Ms. Donnelley was then taken to Beaumont Hospital, where she was placed on life support and her next of kin is contacted. Ms. Donnelley was then taken off of life support in the early hours of the same morning.

"According to the Chief Medical Examiner in Dublin, Ms. Donnelley died as a result of blunt force trauma to her entire body. Eighty-five percent of her internal organs were either severely damaged and/or shut down." Cam paused and glanced up. Many of the faces looking back had turned the color of ripe tomatoes. Many of the men had faced death, but a cop has to have the ability to remove their emotions from the equation. If they didn't, well then you were not going to last that long on this job. Which is one of the reasons the victim is referred to as "the victim." She didn't want that right now. She wanted that emotion. That anger. And it was only going to grow as she continued.

Looking back down, she continued. "Ms. Donnelley also suffered a cracked skull, broken left eye socket, her right cheekbone was fractured and her jaw was broken." She glanced at Finn before she continued. She wanted to make sure he was handling this before she continued.

Taking a deep breath, she steeled her nerves. "According to the ME, Ms. Donnelley also suffered a broken collarbone. Broken radius to her right arm. Left shoulder dislocation. Six broken fingers. Seven broken ribs. There was also damage inflicted to her genital area. After he brutally raped her, it appears as if her attacker punched and pummeled that area." She paused. The rest needed to come from Finn.

"Mary Catherine Donnelley was sixteen years old. Known as Cat to her friends. She was a runaway who had gotten into prostitution through a former boyfriend. The night she was killed was her last night on the street. The next day she was registering for her classes at university." Finn had stayed plastered to his seat. He hadn't wanted to risk the sneer or chuckle at the mention of her leaving the streets. He worked vice long enough to know that they all said that and turned around and went right back out. But Cat was different. She was done. Finn knew and believed that with every fiber of his being.

On a long exhale he stood up and faced the room and what he saw choked him. In a room full of burly guys, many had the head in their hands. Others were pale, and the rest were red faced. And for the first time in a year Finn knew they would find the bastard who had taken Cat from him. He stood and listened as Cam filled them in on Nina and Beverly. The shock and anger grew with each injury outlined; the bastard who had committed these crimes now had a bounty on his head.

When she had finished, Cam had to stop for a minute or two. As much as she had seen in her career, and as a medium, nothing could compare with the horrors these girls had suffered. She also paused to give the team a breather. Those who were fathers struggled with the horrors this bastard had committed. Not only knowing a child suffered tremendously, but to then leave the child's parents with the decision of terminating life support only added to the torture and horror this monster inflicts.

Matt Roberts, a tall and lanky country boy, summed it up for the team. "What kind of sick fuck does this shit?" The southern rang through every syllable. He was from a small town in upstate South Carolina. He joined the ATF after returning from Afghanistan and leaving the army two years ago. The ATF sent him to this meeting because they didn't think the city had anything on this gang, or that this gang is even in the US.

Before Cam could answer, Jimmy's phone rang. He quickly looked at the readout and then walked out. She glanced up at Finn, who looked as bewildered as she did. Shrugging they got to the rest of the information they had found last night.

Finn raised his hand, and the focus went straight to him. "I know all of you are wondering who I am. Detective Finn McDougal, Irish National Guarda. Cat was in my care as my confidential informant. I busted her two years ago for under-aged prostitution in East Dublin. Certain forms of prostitution are legal in Ireland, but hers was not. So I struck a deal. We had reports of a certain gang, mafia, or mob family, whatever you call them here, who had entered into the prostitution business. Specifically setting up rich businessmen and dignitaries with young girls." He paused at the mutters going around the room. He held up his hand and again the room quieted.

"These rich men like their girls young and innocent and the Flannery Gang decided to profit off of it. The family runs Flannery and Sons Distribution out of East Dublin and we know that they have ties to the East Dublin Liberation Army. It is our belief that they are the controlling family of this mob. When the whispers started about their side business, the Guarda tried everything to tie them to it. But we had come up empty. Now when we got Cat, we saw a way in and she was willing to take the risk. We do not know if they had anything to do with her death, but with the noises of them moving an arm of the family here to set up shop, and then these two other girls' murders, our senses started clanging."

"Who is the head of the organization?" This question came from Sorrece, a detective from the city's gang unit.

Finn turned to the boards he and Cam had set up the previous night. Pulling off the sheet, he uncovered the first board. He pointed at Sean Flannery. "Sean Flannery. CEO and president of Flannery and Sons. He is the face of the company and from some intel, we believe he is the family's go-to guy for the organization as well." Pointing to his sibling's Finn gave a brief description of them.

Tom Bennett, from surveillance, was the next to weigh in. "Makes sense. Rich guy, head of the family's business. In shipping and distribution, he would deal with a lot of business heads and some military figures, as well as some government figures."

Cam noticed as they laid out their theory, more and more of the group was nodding and focusing.

Jimmy walked back in and nodded to Finn and Cam. A signal for them to let him take over. "We have just had conformation that our first Baltimore vic had an indirect tie to the new guys in town. My informant has also confirmed that there is new blood in town and prostitution is their main focus. They are dipping into arms and drugs but girls is their main money. Our first vic's boyfriend, who was also her pimp, has a brother in the lower rankings of this gang. Mid-level management put in a request for some new and fresh meat, so the older brother went asking his little brother. Now he had to have known that little brother's girlfriend had just runaway and there was his answer. We do not know if the vic had any knowledge of this, but the boyfriend paid a 'due' to this gang in order for her to work a certain section of the city."

Todd Smith, a detective from the Vice Unit raised his hand. Jimmy nodded in his direction. "If there is a new gang infiltrating the prostitution scene, we haven't heard anything." He looked around to the other members of the group before he continued. "What makes you so certain that this gang is here to start with?" Looking Finn directly in the eye he finished. "No offense to the detective, but I am starting to wonder if he is projecting, trying to find any link that it is this gang."

Cam had to slap her arm on Finn's chest to keep him from doing anything stupid. They were going to have a long talk about forcing the personal side of this down. Or he was off the team.

She looked at Smith. He was a lead detective in Vice. Standing just under five and half feet, he was popular among the prostitutes because of his boyish good looks and unimposing stature. His light brown eyes and round face gave the impression that he could easily be manipulated. And knowing this, he used it to his advantage. He had more CI's on the street than any other detective in that unit. He could work a girl with ease, generally getting them to confess to anything in under an hour. His question was valid. If there was a new gang in town, especially dealing with working girls, he would generally be the first to know. But the files they had received late last night from Ireland could explain why no one knew about it.

"You're right about one thing, you should have heard about it. But according to some reports we received last night from the Guarda, there is an explanation to why you haven't heard anything. Fear." She stopped to let Finn take over.

"According to our files, anyone who we have made contact with, who was willing to talk to save their own asses, have mysteriously ended up dead, or worse missing. They have people everywhere. Police, EMS, local government, hell, we even think they may have a few in the national government, all willing to let it slip whenever we have someone willing to turn on them. And they make a damn gruesome example of them." Finn slid the sheet off the last board. The groans coming from this harden group of detectives was justified.

Three gruesome photos were blown up to show, in detail, two men and one woman, what happened if you decided to flip on the Flannery Clan. They were found sitting side by side on a bus stop bench. Completely nude. The bodies appeared to be clean with the only signs of trauma being the wounds. There was no blood pooled at the scene as well as no blood on the bodies. All three showed signs of severe torture and mutilation.

The first man had knife wounds all over his body. Various symbols and words were carved into his skin, from his face down to his toes. His tongue had been cut out along with his eyes. Sending a clear message of "You don't see anything, and you don't say anything." Their genitals had been sliced up like a loaf of bread. And there was ice picks sticking out of each ear.

The other man and the woman were in the same state, varying only a little in the degree of words and symbols. But the rest mirrored the other man. The old proverb of "See no evil. Hear no evil. Speak no evil," was conveyed through the positioning of the bodies. The first man was placed with his hands over his eyes, they were kept in place by wire tied around his wrists and looped over his head. The woman was in the middle, her hands bound by the same wire around the ice picks coming from her ears. And the final man had his hands bound to cover his mouth.

Finn looked directly at Smith. "Do you understand why no one talks?" From the look on his face, and every other face in the room, the message was conveyed, loud and clear. Nodding to Smith, Finn continued. "The traffic cams on the surrounding buildings were all conveniently disabled, so there is no video of the person, or persons, responsible for the murders and/ or the placement of the bodies."

Joe Sorrece interrupted Finn. "So are we to assume there is nothing to tie these murders back to the Flannery Clan?" Finn nodded. "Fucking fabulous," he muttered under his breath.

"Two days before we apprehended all three of these victims, they neither denied nor confirmed that they were tied to the Flannery Clan. We offered them a deal for their testimony against the Clan, and none of them would sign. We cut them loose to think on their fate and two days later they were found." Finn paused and scrubbed his hands through his hair. Cam already knew him well enough to know that he blamed himself for all of this. She knew he questioned himself on whether he made the right call letting the suspects go, and most of all for letting Cat go undercover.

"We really only had circumstantial evidence, at best, against the three and it was for petty crimes. So really our only option was to let them go. I don't think the three of them were dumb enough to go blabbing about the deal offered to them, but you never know. My belief is that we have a mole in the Guarda." He watched the men and women around him, glance at each other. Were they wondering if one could exist here? There was only one way to find out.

Cam watched them look to each other, to her, and to Finn. How long would it take for this gang to infiltrate the department? Or had they already?

Jimmy moved to the front of the group. "Effective today, everyone in this room has been temporarily reassigned to a specialized task force, whose job is to gather information and evidence on this new gang run by the Flannery Clan. Then it is up to us to take the sons of bitches down and make them pay for these murders." Jimmy paused to let them digest their new assignment. "Captain Thems will be our brass who runs interference with the media and the rest of the brass upstairs. Detective O'Brien and I will lead the group. All data and evidence must be cleared through us, before being submitted. Agent Roberts will coordinate all interaction and resources with the ATF. Roberts, this gang is known for running weapons and drugs along with their girls. I want you to put feelers out and see if they have brought any of that with them from over the pond."

Turning to the Narcs, he continued. "Detectives Franks and Jones. We need you to put out feelers as well. Ask your CI's if there is any new faces in town. Or if any turf disputes starting. We need to know how far they have stretched their business."

The Gang-Task Force Detectives were next. "Sorrece and Johnson, do the same. We need to know what hand is in the pie, or how many. Rival gangs will probably spill first. Knock out the competition."

Catching a red flash in the back corner, Cam focused and found Nina taking it all in. She had been really distracted lately and remembering the boards, Cam wondered how much she had seen and heard. Her eyes were wide and dark, her pallor had paled. Many would expect a spirit to be in perfect form and not able to show emotion or changes in their appearance, but in reality, they were still a lot like us. Still able to feel sympathy and empathy, which is why some feel comforted when they believe a spirit is there with them. Or after talking to the dead and purging some of their emotions, they feel as if something is there with them comforting or soothing.

Seeing the look on Nina's face, Cam was certain that she had overheard most of the meeting. She saw Brad's picture up there with his brother's and the question mark linking them to the Flannery Clan. The pictures of Cat, Beverly, and herself on display for everyone in the room. Cam was curious about what she actually knew. Did she know more than she had let on? She was certain of one thing: gone was the bratty bitch who had pestered her for three days and here was the real Nina Petrelli, a scared little girl who couldn't go home. And for the first time since she had arrived, Cam's heart broke for her. She hoped Nina would know that she couldn't talk to her now. Not in front of the group. She tried to convey the message for her to come back when she was alone. And with more regret and struggle than she would have thought, Cam had to turn away from the scared girl huddled in the corner. Still dressed in her skimpy outfit, hooker heels, and dark makeup, she made Cam think of a young child playing dress up for Halloween.

CHAPTER 10

Cam, Jimmy, and Finn were joined at the table with Detective Todd Smith, from the Vice Unit and Detective Tom Bennett, who represented the Undercover Surveillance Squad. While the others were out beating feet, they discussed where they should go from there. Smith had been picking Finn's brain from the moment the task force broke, clear through lunch. They were comparing techniques and stories of their cases in Vice. Smith had even apologized for the hard knocks he had given Finn during the brief. Of course Finn had just waved it off, and said that he understood.

They had gone to her father's for lunch and were still gathered at a round table, one of many in the section that served as a dining area. The pub consisted of a large rectangular room, with the bar in the back, two rows of high topped tables were positioned in between the bar and the section known as the dining area.

Cam's grandmother had designed the area to accommodate anyone from a single guy sitting at the bar to a family enjoying a nice warm meal in the evening. Fionna and Jack Sr. had gone back and forth on whether to put up a partition wall in between the dining and bar areas, but Fionna had wanted the space to be open and inviting. And she was right. It was a warm and comforting room, even during the talk of death.

The warm wood, that covered almost every inch of the place, glowed a rich caramel in the afternoon light. The stools around the tables were padded in a rich, emerald green leather. They were low backed and wrapped around a person in a half moon shape. A must, her Grandfather had told her, for the man who comes here gets to swaying with each pint, and the chairs had to hold him in. Cam smiled at the memory and stretched back and stroked her hands across the worn and smooth wood. The bar was the main focus of the pub. The wood was the same rich caramel, but the top was a dark slab of oak, polished to a high sheen. The stools were worn smooth from the thousands of asses that had slid onto them.

Cam noticed Finn staring at her. "What?"

"You're doing it again." He grinned.

She could feel her cheeks warm. "For the last damn time, I do not talk to myself." She glared at Jimmy when he opened his mouth.

"Ah, never mind." He shut his mouth and turned back to his conversation with Jack.

Finn shook his head and smiled. Damn, she was pretty when she got riled up, he thought for the thousandth time. He had watched her as the memories veiled her eyes. He had been comparing notes and war stories with Todd, but he couldn't keep his eyes off of her. She transforms when she is here, in this place that made him think of home, and he realized that he wasn't as bothered by it as he normally would have been. Her skin warmed and softened as soon as she sat down. The stress just melted away. He knew she still thought about the case, and the girls, but here, in her home, the stress couldn't weigh her down. He thought of the picture in her hallway. Her arms stretched wide and the laughter on her face. He promised himself that one day he would see her like that. When this was over, he needed to see her like that—carefree and happy.

Tom had been sitting quietly taking everything in. He noticed the chemistry between Finn and Cam. *Hell,* he thought, *a blind man could see the sexual energy sizzling between them.*

Todd looked at Finn like he was James Bond, and Jack and Jimmy discussed everything from the case to baseball. He liked the feel of this place. Homey and inviting. "Makes me think of Cheers," he said to himself.

But his attention kept returning to Cam. Smart and sexy, with an attitude to defend both. He knew her reputation with the police department. A lot of the guys thought she slept her way to that gold badge. She was one of the youngest detectives on the force, and from what he saw earlier, one of the toughest. And if her casework was any indication, she was one of the best Baltimore PD had.

When he was first told of his assignment to this task force, he thought he had pissed his captain off. Captain Ann Morehead, was a legend in her field. She was one of only two females ever appointed as the head of the Undercover Surveillance Unit. She was as striking as she was imposing. Standing at six feet, she had a commanding presence about her, with her flaming red hair and striking green eyes. She almost looked as if she could be Cam's mother, and it wasn't just the similarities in appearance that made Tom think that. Captain Morehead ran her unit with an iron fist, but she had the respect of every detective under her.

Tom replayed their conversation the evening before. She had called him into her office a little before closing time. A shoebox of a room, it always shocked him to see her sitting in the overly feminine space. She had pictures displayed of her family, two daughters and three grandchildren. And always facing her on her desk was her husband of thirty years. She had been wearing a pair of light slacks and a cream sweater. Her feet were shoved into soft leather boots and her side arm was tucked close to her right side in a shoulder holster.

When Tom sat down, she pulled out a file and placed it in front of him. Opening the file he saw the photos of the two recent victims. The brutality of them rolled his afternoon snack around his belly. He looked to his captain for answers.

"Captain Thems placed a call to myself and the Captains of Vice, Narcotics, Gangs- and the ATF." She paused and raised an eyebrow and noticed Tom had done the same when she mentioned the ATF.

"He requested the presence of a minimum of one Detective to be present at a task force briefing at zero nine hundred tomorrow. He left the decision to us on who to send, but he stressed the importance of this case. Twenty minutes later, this file was couriered to myself and every other captain involved. He explained that the brief would fill in all the details, but he wanted each detective to have a brief summary."

Looking him in the eye, she got to the real reason she was giving him first shot at the task force. "Tom, you need to get back to a team setting. I know since Mark was killed you have preferred to work alone. But it's time. I have recommended you for this for two reasons. You need to get back out in the field and you're the best guy I have." Pointing to the pictures she struck a low, but needed blow. "These girls deserve the best."

So Tom found himself sitting at a table, in an Irish pub, with four other detectives. His stomach hadn't stopped flipping since he walked in at 9:00 a.m. and saw his new team. Half of them were around Mark's age. In their early thirties. He pushed Mark's face from his mind and focused back on the conversations around him. He guessed it was time to leave the valley he had been in for the past year and start climbing the hill in front of him.

* * * *

The conference room boasted a long, rectangular table that seated eight on each side. Against the far wall, a whiteboard covered the top half of the wall. Against the other wall, nearest the door, a projection screen displayed the files that had come in from Ireland. A packet sat in front of each chair, waiting on the rest of the team. Cam, Jimmy, Finn, Todd, and Tom poured over all of the data, attempting to narrow down the pertinent information. The rest of the team was due back at sixteen-thirty, to discuss the day's progress.

All the data that had been transferred was everything the Guarda had on the Flannery clan, their business and the East Dublin Liberation Army. And it wasn't much. The Guarda had tried numerous undercover operations, but to no avail, which strengthened the case for a mole within the department. They found every agent bloodied and severely beaten. And two they had found dead. And still there was no physical evidence to tie to the Flannery clan. They had only gotten the thugs who inflicted the injuries and they refused to turn. And Finn couldn't blame them, as frustrated as he was. He had personally seen the three bodies. They had dubbed the "Proverb Rats."

But still, the team picked through every shred of paper. There had to be something.

Three hours later, at three thirty, Matt Roberts returned from the ATF. And judging by the bounce in his step, Cam knew he had found something. He sat down across from Tom with a grin.

"Whatcha got, Junior?" Tom had discovered the boy's love of racing and his near obsession with Dale Jr. during the lull before the meeting that morning.

Matt's face lit up. He knew it was stupid but he liked his nickname. He hadn't been around the guys at the ATF long enough to pick one up. Plus, something about Tom just clicked with Matt; he really liked him.

"There is a newer club, in West Baltimore, goes by the name of Faery Hill. During a surprise DHEC inspection, the inspector notices a crate of bottled liquor, PSF Whiskey. The crate is plain and showed no markings from Customs. Curious, he approaches the bartender setting up and inquires about the bottles. The bartender is fidgety and starts to sweat. Upon further pressing, the bartender admits that this whiskey is for VIP guests personally vetted by the owner. So the DHEC inspector confiscates the crate and gives the owner a violation. The incident is written up and filed and everyone goes on their merry way."

Tom asked the question he knew the kid was waiting on someone to ask. "Who owns Faery Hill?"

"Duke Green."

"Who the fuck is Duke Green?" Cam's head was throbbing.

Matt ignored the sourness of her tone and finished his story. "That was my first question too. I almost just left it at that but the club's name kinda stuck in my head through lunch. You know what I mean?"

Finn kicked Cam under the table. He knew she was about to blow, hell they all were, but the kid worked hard. Let him have his moment. He figured he had just had his leash cut and this was his first solo project. He ignored Cam's glare and nodded to Matt.

Matt was buzzing. He knew he had something big and he knew this case was going to be huge. So he focused back at his notes, even though he knew it all by heart. He had rechecked and rechecked his information four times between his cubby and here.

"So according to my notes, Duke Green's mother is from Ireland. East Dublin, to be exact." He saw the shift in everyone's attention the moment it hit home. Just as his had. *OK*, he told himself, *calm down and focus*. "Duke Green's mother's name is Mary Margret Flannery. Seamus Flannery's little sister. She met and married an American engineer named Ed Green and moved to Bel Air, Maryland." He had to pause to pat himself on the back. He had made the connection that put the Flannery clan in Baltimore. He thought of three of his teammates back at the ATF who always called him a slow hick. *Well, take this and shove it*, he thought. He found the Flannery's Baltimore arm.

Cam walked over to the whiteboard and added Duke Green's name and the club, Faery Hill. And drew lines connected him to Sean Flannery and Sean Flannery to the club. She capped the marker and leaned against the table. Jimmy had stepped out to run a background on Duke and his parents. He also was having a contact at Customs to discretely start a check on all records they had for Flannery and Sons.

While they waited on him, the guys started discussing theories on how this club was used. Whether as a legitimate business or as front. Or both. But something was nagging her. It had been for two damn days and she knew she should let it come on its own but she was picker. So she picked and picked. And became more pissed and pissed.

Finn watched her. She was tapping the marker against her temple. He had been watching her face work through the frustrations and anger. And he didn't blame her. This case had been like a diseased tumor, attached to him and killing him slowly. He saw the same fear, anger, and exhaustion creep slowly over her. The sudden onset of anger and the need to protect her knocked him back. He had known this woman for less than a week, but he knew how to read her like a book. She talked to herself to work through problems. She carried every death like it was walking beside her. Her anger was quick to flash, but her smile could stop a man dead. And her body. Damn, her body kept him up at night.

He dropped his head to his hands. He didn't need this shit right now. He needed to stay focused for Cat. She deserved all of his attention. She deserved more than just his distracted mind because this woman wouldn't get out of his head. He steeled his resolve and looked up. And his breathed rushed out of him. Those piercing green eyes stared straight into him. And he knew then, he would never get her out of his mind.

Ten minutes later, Jimmy walked back in with the new paperwork. And the rest of the team followed right behind him. He walked to the board and put the pictures above the newest names. He turned and waited until everyone was seated, then he gave Matt the go-ahead.

He chuckled at the pumped up stance Matt had as he gave the rest of the group the information he had just learned. Jimmy had to hand it to him; he had done damn well.

"Okay, so we now have a connecting thread back to Ireland. Todd, why don't you start with what you have?"

Todd remained seated and used the laptop he had beside him. "So far there has not been much in the way of chatter about these guys and prostitutes. But I decided to look back at some of the arrests and busts made within the last two months." He paused while a spread sheet loaded to the projection board. Using a laser pointer he started linking the gang loosely to the arrests. "I checked to see if anyone had mentioned any of the players by name and got nothing. So then I looked at any common traits between the arrests. And I got a hit. Ten girls in the past two months have been arrested for solicitation in the vicinity of the club. But to take it a step further, I looked at who bailed them out and/or paid their fines. And that's where I really struck gold." Turning to the white board, he lit up Brad Morris. "Five of the girls had their bail posted by a Bradley Morris and three others had their bail posted by a Jonathan Morris. Bradley's brother."

Turning back to his laptop, he pulled up another screen. "Now, the guys running this are smart. They paid in cash, but because of paperwork they had supply identification. So we have the two idiot brothers on paper, but we have no paper linking them to the Faery Club or the Flannery's. But if they are dumb enough to give their actual names, they are dumb enough to screw up again."

Cam nodded and looked at Finn. Some of the tension that had been written all over his face had eased. They were making headway.

Narcotics reported nothing yet, but their CI's were sniffing around. It looked like the clan may be out of the drug game here.

But if there was any new blood, the other pushers would sell out their own mother to get the competition off their turf.

The Gang Task Force detectives finished the meeting. "There have been some rumors of a new force in town. Not much is known, even in the deepest circles. These guys either have top rates and complete loyalty, or they have made their handiwork known," he said, pointing to the three snitches, "and no one's talking." He said he would have a more concise update for tomorrow.

Cam jumped in picking up on one of Sorrece comments. "I will look back through any open and cold homicides going back two years. We don't know how long they have been moving over on this side of the pond, but I think two is a good start." Pointing to Finn she continued. "Finn, over here can be another set of eyes. He has firsthand knowledge of the clan's handiwork so he may catch something I won't."

Jimmy nodded and ended the meeting. "Everyone is on call until these bastards are caught. If any new body turns up, everyone turns out. We have knowledge of what to ask and what to look for. So suck it up, you will be canvassing. If there is any break in the case, let myself or Cam know. We will decide if it needs to be acted upon then or if it can wait until the next morning. If it stays quiet, we meet back here at zero ten thirty. Dismissed."

CHAPTER 11

Cam unlocked her front door and walked into the blissful quiet. For the first time in months, she had snuck up the back stairs, past her family and the pub. Her brain was fried, and for the next hour, she just wanted the quiet.

She leaned back against the door and closed her eyes. The faces of the dead swarmed her thoughts and she quickly opened her eyes. She just wanted to escape everything.

Cam looked around her condo. She had thought and mulled over every piece of furniture. Every picture, every color, and every little aspect that rested inside these walls. The warm mocha of the plush suede couch complemented the soft taupe walls in her living room.

A giant seventy-inch TV hung above her fireplace. When she had bought it, Brooks picked on her about the enormity of it, but every baseball, football, or hockey game, her smartass was the first one on the couch. To soften the sharp lines and edges, she had her dad build a boxed frame around it. And she had the ability to sync her pictures to it, so it could be an ever-changing piece of art.

On her mantle sat tall, antique silver candlesticks. The flowy and elegant lines added beauty and whimsy to the dark and heavy wood. They were two of the very few items her grandparents had brought with them from Ireland. Cam remembered the night her grandmother gave them to her. Fionna had told her that Jack Sr. had told her a fanciful story of how the leprechaun's had made the candlesticks specifically for their wedding day. They were meant to bring good luck and good fortune, and since they had so much of both, it was time for them to bring their magic to Cam.

Cam smiled at the memory and she pushed off the door and placed her keys in a crystal bowl. It sat on a tall, dark Chippendale table that she had found, by sheer luck at a small antique store in Hagerstown.

She had surmised that her love of the old had come from her gift. Every piece held a small glimmer of its previous owners and it helped to ease some of the loneliness that she often felt. Moving through her hallway, she passed the collage of photos that had captivated Finn the previous weekend. The thought of him gave her heart a little pang.

Most of her colleagues would be shocked to see her life away from the precinct. She had overheard many theorize that she lived in a harsh and stark environment, a cave of sorts, with steel and rock. No softness or femininity anywhere.

Pausing at her bedroom door, she chuckled at the thought. The walls in here were painted a soft bluish gray. A four-poster, king-sized bed sat in the center of the far wall, framed by two generous windows. There were soft cream-colored linen curtains that were draped on each post, creating a dreamy canopy. The windows were framed in the same fabric, softening the light that poured through the floor to ceiling glass.

On her bed was a down comforter covered in a duvet that was a mix of chocolate, cream, and blue. At the foot of the bed was an old chest that housed a smaller TV that could be hidden away by a flick of a button. It appeared to just be another antique chest, but her father had modified it. Large pictures adorned the walls on either side of the door. One showed a raging sea, its waves beating and slamming the coast. The magnificent cliffs were staggering in size and beauty. It was the same cliffs that were in the photo in her hallway. Unlike the one in the hallway, this photo showed just the cliffs. No people, just the shockingly green grass and the jagged rocks below. On the other wall was a picture of castle ruins. More cliffs could be seen here, but the crumbling tower was the focus. The ruins hugged the edge of the cliffs and the once magnificent tower had begun to crumble. It had belonged to the O'Brien clan for almost two hundred years starting in the fourteenth century.

The sheets on the bed were bought during her last trip to Ireland. The Irish lace trim was hand stitched by a woman her grandmother had known from the old village. There was a mountain of pillows on the neatly made bed. All of the furniture in the bedroom were antiques she had found either in Maryland or Ireland.

Cam moved to her closet and began to undress. She removed her weapon and place it in a safe that was bolted to floor. It could only be open by a code and her fingerprint. Some would say that was a bit of overkill, but when you lived above a pub, nothing was too much. Her closet was neatly organized. Her work attire lined one wall, with her personal clothes lining the other two. She had obsession with shoes. Boots and tennis shoes were her kryptonite. She had them displayed all along the bottom of her closet. Hanging her jacket on the rod, she placed the rest of her clothes in a hidden basket. She grabbed her favorite fleece pajama bottoms and a long-sleeved shirt and headed to the shower.

Cam pulled out her stack of take-out menus and tried to decide on dinner. She phoned her dad to let him know she was safe and home. She also let him know that she was staying in. She knew he was disappointed, but he would never say it. He knew if she stayed in, it was a bad day. It wasn't so much the day that had her down, but the case. And Beverly. She couldn't understand why the girl hadn't found her yet.

Cam remembered a conversation she had, with Brooks, when they were teens. They had been talking about her gift, which at that time she still hadn't decided one hundred percent that it was a gift. Brooks was trying to understand how the dead people found her. Cam explained it like this: the dead are all around us. Some go straight to heaven and stay, some go to heaven and come back to look out for their family or friends. Some forgo heaven for a bit in order to atone for the sins they may have committed in life. Cam compared that to the Catholic purgatory. Others just weren't ready to leave and go to heaven, so they wandered around. But if they sought out someone who could see and talk to them, they would look for a medium.

Mediums, Cam explained, are like beacons in the dark. The dead see them and they are drawn to them like a moth to a flame.

So Cam wondered why Beverly hadn't been able to find her. In her experience, there had only been a handful of people who had not come to her when she had their case. Some of them, she believed, were so evil, the devil immediately took them, and some went immediately to heaven. But something about Beverly had Cam's itch going. She was still here. And what Cam feared was she didn't know she was dead. And that was never good. There was a lot of craziness going on with this case. Take Nina for example, she had sought out Cam before she was even dead. That and then the fact that she was the bitchiest ghost Cam had ever had. Generally the dead lose a lot of their crankiness in death, but not all. Then there were some who ended up gaining it back, but that normally took years.

Cam set her broodiness aside long enough to choose what she wanted for dinner. As she was picking up the phone, her door burst wide open. In one motion, she jumped up and grabbed her personal weapon she kept hidden in one of the drawers of her end table.

"Jesus!" Brooks yelled, almost dropping the box loaded with food.

"Damnit, Brooks!" Cam yelled back. She yanked open the drawer and shoved the gun back in the holster. "I almost fucking shot you! Jesus Christ!"

Brooks stalked to the kitchen bar and set down the box, leaving Cam to deal with the door. "What in the hell were you doing? I knocked three fucking times. So I had to juggle the box and the beer, you're welcome by the way, and dig out my friggin keys!" She slammed her purse on the counter next to the box. "Only to find out you were sitting here on your lard ass!"

Cam looked at her best friend. She was disheveled from the wind and the struggle from the door. She walked over to her and wrapped her arms around her and, to her horror, started crying hysterically.

Brooks hugged her back and did her best to soothe. Only when she felt the cold around her ear did she realize Cam hadn't put down the gun. "Um, Cam? I hate to break this tender moment, because they are few and far between with you, but could you possibly get the gun away from my head?"

Cam froze and then put it down. Then she started crying even harder. Brooks, who was starting to panic, guided her back to the couch. But knowing her best friend, she swiped two beers from the case before she did. Settling her down in the corner of the couch, Brooks handed her a beer and then went to get a blanket. On her way back, she flipped the fireplace on and sat down on the leather ottoman at Cam's feet. She made one promise to herself before she opened her mouth—if Cam didn't stop crying in fifteen minutes she was calling her dad. She reached for the box of tissues she knew was stashed in the end table and she switched them for the beer. Like any true city girl, she had a bottle opener on her key chain. Handing Cam back the beer, Brooks tried to get to the bottom of this. "Sweetie…Come on, Cam, you're starting to really worry me. Please tell me what's going on."

Cam heard the worry in her friend's voice, and she tried her best to stop, but the tears wouldn't dry. "I-I'm, tr-trying," she stammered. She felt Brooks place the beer in her hands and she took a deep breath and then a long pull of the beer. A few more deep breaths and a lot of wiping, and Cam started to calm down. She looked at her friend's worried and pinched face and let out a choked laugh. "I'm really sorry," she said again as she scrubbed her face with her hands.

Seeing that she really was calming down, Brooks gave her a minute, to go splash water on her face. While she was in the bathroom, she really wondered whether to call Jack or not. Brooks had to take a long pull of the beer as well in order to calm her nerves down. To busy herself, as much to calm herself, she went back to the kitchen to grab some forks, napkins, and the food. She put the rest of the beer in the fridge and paused to shake her head at the state of the fridge. A block of cheese, two beers, eggs, and soured milk. OK, she knew one call she was going to make no matter what. Fionna or Brooks's mom would fix that in no time. Closing the door, she sent a quick text to her mom. She would call Fionna to decide who would replenish the fridge, and upon further inspection, the cabinets. Shaking her head, she kicked off her shoes and dropped her jacket on the nearest stool. She gathered everything up and walked back into the living room as Cam was coming back in. "Feel better?"

Cam let out a watery laugh. "Yeah, I guess I am." Noticing the relieved look that flashed across Brooks's face, she added, "I'm sorry for worrying you." Then she noticed the pile of stuff in her friend's arms. She hurried over and relieved her of half and set everything on the ottoman.

"I guess my spidey senses were tuned in because I felt the need for beer and Chinese. And you know what that means—girl time." Actually it was the call from her dad. He had called her on his way home to share his worry about Cam. He had noticed the dark circles and he could swear she had lost a few pounds. "And trust me," he said, "she can't afford to lose much." And with that Brooks ordered enough Chinese to feed an army, stopped for beer, and came right over. Hell, she was still in her scrubs.

Cam knew what was up. "Your dad called?" At her nod, she had to blink back the tears that rushed up. She blinked them away and then seemed to really notice Brooks clearly. "Your PJs are in the drawer in your room. I washed them." Brooks rolled her eyes and Cam grinned. "Okay Nana washed them the other day."

She stood up. "Okay, I am going to change. You start breaking out the boxes. And don't eat all of the fortune cookies. I counted them so I know how many are there," she said heading down the hallway to the guest room. She loved this room. Cam had let her decorate it since she was the main one who used it. It was bold, but classy. Like herself. She loved the turquoise walls, with the purple accents. The comforter was down, like Cam's, but brilliant white. She had Fionna add embroidered flowers to it. One giant turquoise lily and a giant purple orchid. She had throw pillows it all three colors and Jack had made a cabinet to match the one in Cam's room. Pictures adorned the walls, shots of their life growing up. The first time Jack took Cam and her to Ireland. And spring break in college where they spent the week in St. Croix. Her clothes were neatly folded, with a perfumed card on top. "Love to my other girl, Nana." Brooks kissed the card, while breathing in the soft musk that was Fionna. She slid it into a box in the nightstand. In it were the same cards, she had one from every week, for as long as she could remember. In her closet at home was all of the boxes that had already been filled with the notes. Every time one would fill she would take it home. And the next time she came back, she would find another box in its place. She knew Jack worked with wood and she always assumed it was he who made them.

She put her scrubs in the hamper and glanced back over the room. She thought about the room Cam had done at her place. It was done in soft muted colors that exuded peace and tranquility. She shook her head and grinned. It looked almost identical to her bedroom next door.

In the living room, Cam had placed cushions on the floor on either side of the ottoman. She had the Orioles game on low. They were winning two to zero against the Yankees. She had needed the distraction and the background noise. Brooks came in and started counting the fortune cookies. "I didn't take any!"

Brooks ignored her and finished counting. "I don't trust you when it comes to them. You horde them all of the time. Mr. Wu knows it too, which is why he gives us extra." Mr. Wu, owner of Pagoda Chinese Restaurant, had known them since they were little. In business for over forty years, he was good friends with both of their fathers.

Cam laughed and threw her chopsticks at her. She could never master those damn things, something Brooks loved to shove in her face, because she, of course, had been able to use them the very first time. "Thanks again for the pick me up, and the shoulder."

They ate and caught up a little bit on the happenings of each other's past two days. Brooks had had a triple homicide, gang-related, and a mysteriously uninjured person who was "killed in a car accident." There was an accident and she was dead, but her husband had done both.

Brooks couldn't wait any longer. "Do you want to tell me about it?" She saw the pain flash in Cam's eyes and wondered if she asked too soon.

Noticing her wince, Cam was quick to reassure her. "It's not that. I need to talk about it anyway. It's not just this case, but that's the main of it." Leaning back against the couch she took a deep breath and began. "When I first saw Nina, Jesus, just five days ago, she really irritated me. I have never had a spirit that is as bitchy as she is. But anyway, that day I woke up and was covered in bruises. I didn't know how or why it happened, but it pissed me off. Mostly because I knew our dads were going to flip, which they did."

Brooks nodded her head. That sounded about right.

"Anyway, when we got to the hospital and her parents showed up—God, that was bad. I have had to notify more people than I care to count, and a lot of them were parents. But this one, this one was bad. Not only did I have to tell them I found their daughter and she's hurt, but they have to decide if they keep her alive or not." She took a deep breath and fought her anger. "I swear I want this bastard dead for that. Then we get Finny boy from Ireland. But he hits us with another girl." She had to pause to collect herself. This is the part that started it all.

Brooks noticed her friend's internal battle. She reached across and grabbed her hand and held on. "What was it about Cat?" She had a feeling she knew, but Cam needed to work it out herself.

Cam figured she already knew, but she said it aloud for the first time. "It was her I had dreamed of that night. That has never happened before." There she said it. Emotions rolled through her like a tidal wave. Cat's screams echoed in her mind, the pain of the punches slammed back, her fear choked her throat.

Brooks just sat quietly. She knew Cam well enough to let her take her time. It was agony. She wanted so badly to gather her friend up and take the pain away, but she knew she couldn't. Just like she knew it would piss her off in the long run. Cam was a fighter. That she could take to the bank. No one knew her like she did, and no one ached for her the way she did. It was different than what Jack or her dad felt; this was as if the other half of her was hurting and she could do nothing about it. Brooks thought of something Cam's grandfather had said before he died. He held both of their hands and told them they were special. Special because they were two halves of the same soul. Soul sisters he called them. He said there was no tighter bond, no love just like the love they had for each other. It was rare to find your other half. Many people found their soul mate, whom they would spend eternity with, but it was a rare thing to find your soul sister or brother. And their family was blessed, because not only did their fathers find it, but their children did as well. He told them that their love for one another was greater than the love they have for their blood kin.

Brooks looked over at Cam, her soul sister, and finally understood, completely what he had meant. She would give anything to take just one ounce of her pain. She did the next best thing and sat there, silently, and let her sister work through it. At least, she thought, she wouldn't be alone.

"Then the next day we found Beverly." It had been quiet for so long, Brooks was startled to hear Cam speak.

Looking around her home, Cam continued. "I can't find her. Or she can't find me. I am afraid she is lost or scared. Or both. Nina has come back a couple of times. She is a little less bitchy, but she still pushes my buttons." Brooks chuckled and Cam joined in. "God, it feels good to laugh."

"Where do you think she is?"

"I have no idea. I have seen Cat some. Just a shadow of her. She always comes when Finn seems to need her." Cam got up and started to clean up. She needed something to occupy her hands. "I think they had a closer relationship than he lets on. The feeling I get was it was almost a father-daughter or much older brother to sister type deal. You can see he loved her, and still does. It breaks my heart to see the look of failure in his eyes. And there is nothing I can do to change his mind on that."

Brooks followed her into the kitchen. "What else? I know that's not it."

Cam leaned back against the cool granite. "There is a new gang in town. God Brooks, to see what these people did to three people who, in their minds, snitched on them. They butchered them."

Brooks walked over to Cam's bag. She knew the case file would be in it. "I haven't had a chance to look at what you sent. I have been swimming in bodies for the last week." She walked back to the couch and plopped down. She reached over and slid one of the leather ottomans over. She began to read through the file and to lay out the crime scene photos. When she got to the MEs report, she paled.

Seeing her face, Cam climbed over the back of the couch and flopped next to her. "What is it?"

"These were the victims in Ireland?" Brooks already knew but she just needed to hear it aloud.

"Yes." Sensing something was wrong, she went and got her laptop. And her phone.

CHAPTER 12

When Brooks saw the photos of the three snitches, her face paled and her eyes widened. Cam rushed over the back of the couch, grabbing her arm and shaking her to get her to acknowledge Cam's question. Her heart was beating out of her chest, as a million questions flew around her head. It was a rare sight to see Brooks speechless, let alone pale and frightened.

Brooks put her hand on her chest and turned to Cam. "Are these the victims in Ireland?"

"Yes." Cam turned Brooks to face her fully. "What the hell is wrong?"

Brooks looked widely around the room. "Where is your computer? Now! Cam, I need your damn computer."

Cam, startled by the outburst, ran to her bedroom for the laptop she kept there. Glancing at her nightstand she grabbed her phone and began dialing.

Jimmy showed up first, with Finn right on his heels. Hearing the panic in his partner's voice, he threw on a sweatshirt and his slippers and ran out of the house two doors down. Running past the pub, he heard Finn's voice holler after him. Jack called to Fionna and Beth, who tended bar part time, and ran after Finn, his heart in his throat.

Twenty minutes later, Todd showed up. Tom, who was having a beer with Matt, was last. The ATF rookie came along for the ride.

After reassuring her father she was fine, Jack reluctantly left, heading back to the pub. On his way out, he gave one look to Jimmy, who followed him out to the hallway.

Jimmy saw the fear and anger on his friend's face and waited for the controlled explosion. He knew if he spoke first, the control would be lost. "What is going on?" He held up a hand, cutting Jimmy's "ongoing investigation" crap off. "Don't give me that shit, Jimmy. Don't." Pausing not a foot in front of him, Jimmy saw the rage and fear were quickly winning the battle with his control.

"It's the worst case I have ever seen. Goddamn it, Jack! This bastard destroyed those girls. Their parents could barely recognize their own children in those beds!" Jimmy's control was quickly losing the battle with the rage surging through him. Just as rare a sight as his daughter losing her control. That was the one thing the Aarons prided themselves on: self-control.

Turning back to his friend, he told him the worst of it. Of the three bodies in Ireland. "It's bad, Jack. Between that and the girls, I'm starting to wonder if I can get through it." Stopping and turning back to Jack, he made one promise. "But there is one thing I do know, nothing, and I mean nothing, will touch our girls. I swear my life to it."

Jack, who normally is the one who needs the calming, placed an arm around his friend's shoulder. "I know, Jim. I know. When I saw you run past my door and head Cam's way, my heart nearly stopped. She didn't even come down. And she's been crying." He turned and glanced into the open door. He saw his strong-willed and hard-headed daughter sitting on the couch. Brooks beside her, their shoulders touching. Then he glanced at the tall and dark man who stood behind her. Watching her.

"He didn't even pause when he saw you. He just flew out the door."

Jimmy looked to his friend. "He's a good man, Jack."

"I know. I just wonder if she does." Slapping Jimmy on the back, he turned to go. "Watch my girls. Or it's your ass that'll receive the kicking."

Jimmy chuckled. He looked back to the couch. He'd die first before any harm came to the two of them. And he'd kill the bastard who tried.

Finn saw the redness in her eyes. She tried to hide it, but he knew her face. He'd come to the pub looking for her. He had tried to sleep, but her body wouldn't leave his mind. So he got up and came looking for her. The feeling of relief was still coursing through his veins. He was shocked at the intensity of his fear when he saw Jimmy running toward her place. He had been debating on coming and knocking on her door. But now here he was, and all he could think was, thank God she's fine. His second worry of the night was seeing the vivacious and charismatic Brooks pale and shaken. Now with Jimmy back in the room, he walked to the kitchen and searched until he found some brandy. He found two sniffers in the next cabinet and poured two generous fingers and gave them to them.

Brooks, who had been entrenched in the computer, seemed to just notice the living room full of men. She took a long swallow of the liquor and welcomed the blooming heat spreading across her chest and down into her belly.

When he saw the color start to work its way back into her cheeks, Finn finally took off his coat and sat down on the chair next to them. "Better?"

Nodding Brooks finished the glass. Cam knocked back hers in one long gulp and looked back to the kitchen. "Do you want another?" she asked Brooks. She had decided she needed one. Not waiting for an answer Cam got up and took both glasses for a refill. She needed a minute and the brandy was a convenient excuse. She felt him before she saw him. Turning around, she walked straight to him and wrapped her arms around his waist.

Finn, shocked for a moment, wrapped his arms tight and smoothed her hair. "Do you want to tell me about it?"

She could feel his breath across her scalp and goose bumps raise along her arms. She knew this was a bad idea, but she couldn't help herself. God, she felt safe. And for the first time, in a long time, she felt peace in a man's arms. Looking up, she was barely an inch from his lips. Before they both could stop, they closed the distance. Time stood still and the air was sucked from her lungs. Her knees struggled to support her and her head began to swim. Never has a kiss felt like this. Never has a kiss dropped all of her walls and grabbed her heart. Her soul.

Finn could barely breathe. Fire stormed through his veins, and the heat worked his broken and scarred heart. This woman, he thought, this woman was like a drug. He felt alive for the first time in over a year.

His hands moved up to frame her face. His hands left a trail of fire up her body. As they pulled apart, his hands stayed, framing her face in a way that made her heart sigh. She knew she shouldn't torture herself, but she had no choice. Her body and heart overpowered her mind. And in that moment she knew. She knew, even if it was just for a night, she needed him. She wanted him. She would deal with the repercussions later. He would leave. No matter what he would leave. They all did. Once they learned the truth, but in that moment, she didn't care. She needed him. Even if only for a night. She needed him more than she needed her next breath.

He opened his eyes. Cam still had her eyes closed. "Look at me," he whispered. Slowly, she opened them. The blue of his eyes looked like a raging storm. Emotions raged a war, fighting for control. "This isn't settled." Pausing he glanced behind him. "This isn't finished." He brushed his lips over hers like a whisper. He turned and walked back to the living room. He needed to breathe. Hell, they both needed it.

It took Cam another minute to gain control of her body. A million different sensations were wreaking havoc of her control. *Get a hold of yourself*, she scolded herself. There is a room full of cops out there. Taking a deep breath she filled another sniffer of brandy and swallowed it in one gulp. She grabbed Brooks's glass and made her way back into the living room.

Brooks could see the color in her friend's cheeks and knew instantly what that meant. But that was for later. Now they had death.

Looking to the room full of men, she noticed the broody one in the recliner. When he turned his eyes to hers, she felt warmth rise to her cheeks. *Uh-oh*, she thought and turned back to the rest of the group.

She knew some of them, but a few were new to her. So she decided to start with the formalities. "Hi, I'm Brooks Aaron, chief

ME, for the city. I am the ME for the three cases you all are working on."

When she paused Cam jumped in. She introduced Matt and Todd. She also resupplied Tom's name and Brooks was grateful. "Cam and I were reviewing the case and she was catching me up on the international side of it. During this I came across the photos of the three Proverbial Rats. I am told this is how you all refer to them. Anyway, as soon as I saw them I had my episode that freaked the hell out of Cam, and my father, which brought the rest of you down."

Tom flicked his glance to Jimmy. Father? He knew one of the ME's was Jimmy's daughter, but the fucking chief ME? Jesus, he had a moment of pause thinking of what she looked like under those pajamas, but that information slammed on the breaks. There was no way in hell he was getting into that boat. Jimmy would rip his balls out and shove them down his throat. He caught the end of what she was saying.

"What?" He wasn't sure he heard her correctly.

Brooks took a deep breath and turned on the TV. Cam had her computer linked to her TV so Brooks transferred the photos to the larger screen.

The pictures showed three bodies. All in various stages of decomp. There were numerous injuries inflicted and something was familiar about them. Todd noticed the genitals and exhaled sharply. "Jesus Christ."

Brooks took back over. "These three males came into the morgue at various times last week. Due to the high-profile cases with the girls, I got a little behind. I just finished the last one before I came over. So when Cam showed me the report from Ireland, I immediately made the connection."

Finn moved to stand directly in front of the screen. All three men had suffered. And suffered terribly. The wounds were similar to the wounds of the others. "What was the condition of the bodies when they were found?"

Brooks pulled up the file and began to read. "Victim number one was found near the docks in the harbor. The victim was nude from the waist down. He had a tattered and bloodied T-shirt, one sock, and one black work boot. The witness states he came in to work and a foul smell in the area. He went to investigate and found the victim. There were traces of vomit on the shoes but the witness states he vomited when he saw the body. I have traces of that being compared to the witness to see if the DNA matches." Glancing up, she concluded, "I am certain it is going to be a match." Nods came from around the room.

Finn stared at the screen, tuning out the rest of the conversation behind him. A sick twisting was starting in his stomach, and before he knew it, he was standing back on that street corner in Dublin.

Holy Mary Mother of God, Finn. Who the fuck would do that to someone? Davey Green was hunched at the waist puking in the trash can.

Finn, struggled with his own stomach, but he be damned if he would give in and puke on the street like some pansy. These fuckers have done it again. He knew exactly who these three were. He had just spoken to each of them during the previous two days.

He turned around and scanned the streets. And with his stomach knotting more he scanned the officers at the scene. Someone here was a rat. A filthy, fucking, flea-ridden rat. And he would damn sure find out who.

Finn shoved it down and turned back to the three on the bench. They were positioned like the See, Hear, and Speak No Evil monkeys. All three had been tortured and mutilated. Two men and one woman. And not a damn trace of their killer anywhere.

Finn closed his eyes against the horrific scene. He had had too much horror in the past three months. First Cat, and now these three. Not to mention the undercover agent they had sent in six months ago. His body was similarly mutilated. It was hard for him to maintain his professionalism when every fiber in his being wanted to tear the Flannery clan apart limb by limb. Fuck the system. So far it hadn't done dick for him or anyone else on the force.

Finn sucked in a ragged breath and opened his eyes on the scene again. And his eyes opened right on it. Someone was feeling cocky. And Finn was going to shove it down his throat.

Cam watched him stand there. His eyes were closed, and his face hard as stone. But she had spent a great deal of time on that face this past week, so she saw the little minute flexes of his jaw and eyes. He had something going on. She would just have to wait to see what that something was.

She caught a flash of red out of the corner of her eye. Her eyes sharpened and she saw the whisper of her. Cam knew every inch of her face, so her memory filled in what was only faintly there. The first thing she noticed was the sadness and the love in her eyes. The emotion poured through the brightest. She had seen wisps of her before. Here and there, but this was the first time she saw the whole of her. She was very beautiful. The picture did little justice to her. It couldn't capture the true essence of her. Her presence was very strong. Cam had felt her many times before, but this was the first time she had seen Cat face-to-face.

Her attention was broken when Finn suddenly spun around and grabbed the photos from Brooks.

"Hey! What the hell, Finn!"

He dropped to the floor and spread every photo out of the victims in Dublin. "Can you zoom in on those photos?" he asked, pointing to the screen.

Cam took back the computer and worked her fingers over the key board. "How much?"

When he started rifling through her drawers in her desk, she thought he had lost his mind. "If you tell me what it is you're looking for, I can help you get it faster."

Finn turned around, and for the first time in a week, Cam saw determination and fight in his eyes. "Magnifying glass."

"Top drawer, right side." She laughed at his stupid grin and thumbs up. *What in the hell?* she thought.

He scooted back to the photos on the floor. "Okay. Zoom in to the left chest area." Looking up at the screen he watched the photo enlarge and center on that area. Looking back down, he rechecked all three bodies. "Once someone is brought into the clan, they are given a mark to show their absolute trust and faith to the family." He paused and grabbed a pen from the desk and a notepad from the table. He drew the Celtic symbol for unity or trinity. Then he drew a circle within the three points. He held it up. "This is the sign for family. In this circle somewhere would be place an F and a C. Only high-ranking members are allowed to get this mark."

Tom stood up and walked to the TV. "There is no mark on these bodies other than gang tattoos. But hell all of the fucking bangers have them."

Finn stood up and held up the photos from Dublin. He held the magnifying glass to the area around the left nipple on the first victim.

Cam saw it first. "An X. Whoever did this marked an X over the symbol." But even then she had to squint to see the symbol in the first place. How in the hell did he catch that?

She got up and came to the TV. "There is an X over the same area on all three victims." She turned and glanced at Brooks. "Weren't these gang related? As in not related to this case?"

Brooks flipped back through the file. "According to the detectives this was over turf. Two are from the Eastside Heights Mafia and the other is from the rival Crypts gang. The bodies were found…" She paused, flipping through more pages. She paled as she found the answer. "The docks. They were found in the shipping yard. No one thought anything of it because that has been disputed turf for years. No one has been able to lay claim to it."

Cam glanced to Jimmy, but he was already pulling out his phone. "Got it. Finish this," he said pointing to the screen. "I'll call Joe."

Looking at Finn, Cam asked her next question, even though she thought she knew the answer. "So you guys thought this was a symbol to erase them from the clan?"

He nodded. They had had nothing else to make them believe otherwise. "But I think it also is the signature of the…" he struggled with the appropriate term. "Sick fuck" didn't seem appropriate. Although it rang true.

It was Matt who supplied it. "Artist."

He shrugged when all eyes turned to him. "Why else would he sign it? If he didn't think himself an artist?"

Cam couldn't argue with that logic. "Fine, it's better than 'sick fuck', as I'm sure that's what the rest of us were thinking."

Looking at her watch she realized this "meeting" had eaten up most of the night. "We all need some sleep. And some time to think. So let's meet back at the conference room at zero nine thirty. Maybe we will have more to go on by then."

Everyone closed up and packed it in. She knew they were all drained and this case was sucking the life out of them, but these girls and now these men deserved everything they had to give. And damn it, she was going to make sure they got it.

She noticed Brooks slipping on shoes. "I thought you were going to crash here?"

Brooks shook her head in pity and wondered how her friend could be one of the best detectives in the city and not notice what was going on right in front of her. Finn had been hanging back, dragging his ass so he would be alone with Cam, and she was completely blind to it. "Honey, I am going to my dad's." Glancing at Finn, then back to Cam, she rolled her eyes. "Trust me you won't need me tonight." She kissed her friend's cheek and dragged her father out of the apartment.

Cam turned and faced the only person left in the room.

CHAPTER 13

He had his arms and legs crossed as he leaned back against the counter. His face was blank, so blank she wondered if she imagined the kiss earlier. His jeans hung low and loose on his long, lean frame and his shirt clung to his chest and arms.

She remembered the feel of his lips on hers and for a moment sheer panic went through her as she thought of the words he spoke to her in the kitchen. Did I remember to shave? Great, she thought. She couldn't remember. The next thought was what underwear she had on. *Please, please don't be granny panties! Damnit!* Why couldn't she think straight?

The sound of laughing brought her out of her internal argument. She narrowed her eyes at the gorgeous face in front of her. "Are you done?"

"Are you?" he replied.

And for the second time in a few short hours she felt the flush and heat steel up her cheeks. "I was not talking to myself."

The heat turned to utter mortification when he replied. "What are granny panties? And why shouldn't you be wearing them?"

She wished the floor would open up and swallow her. *Please God. Take me now,* was her only thought. And then she remembered the last time she shaved and defeat was ensured.

Following him into the kitchen she watched him move. His long, lean body moved with a slight swagger. Most men tried to have that and failed miserably. Cam was sure this was his normal gait. Confident and sure. Without being aware of the immense pleasure women took watching him move. He opened her fridge and pulled out two beers.

"How is it you live above a pub and you have neither food nor other drink?"

She rolled her eyes. "I live above my pub. So if I want food or beer I go down to my pub and get it."

"Touché, my friend. Touché."

Sighing, she twisted off the cap and took a long pull. "I haven't had time. And Brooks was in here earlier so I suspect by tomorrow afternoon my fridge and cupboards will be restocked." She explained further when his eyes brows arched. "Nana or Mom will go get me food."

"Mom?"

"Jimmy's wife. Brooks's mom. She's the only one I have ever had. Mine left when I was four. Just took off. I guess she couldn't handle me. She stopped. *Fuck!* she thought.

Finn noticed her pale. So he'd leave that for another conversation. But his heart broke for that little girl and the woman who stood before him. He thought of his own ma and couldn't fathom not having her there.

"So…um…how's the hotel?" Jesus, she felt like a dud.

He nodded his head. "Good. It's good." He was enjoying watching her squirm. Beautiful and confident. Sexy yet so unaware. She fiddled with the label on the bottle. Even in an oversized shirt and pajama pants, he couldn't help but want her. It was a need that kept him awake at night. He wanted to feel her skin come alive under his hands, to hear her whimper with pleasure. To whisper his name.

And damnit he was done stalling. He set his bottle aside and in one move she was in his arms. Her legs wrapped around his waist. His hands tangled in her glorious hair. Her mouth hot and heavy on his. He carried her out of the kitchen and pinned her against the wall. Her body pressed deeply into his and he felt the heat building from that glorious center. His mouth teased and nipped at her lips. His need pouring into every nip and lick.

She met him nip for nip and lick for lick. Tasting and exploring every inch. She could feel him pressing against her. God, she was going to explode. Never had she had so many sensations going off at one time. She moaned as he pressed against her harder. Her control was gone. She had lain awake many nights wondering and fantasizing about this very moment. Soft and slow. Exploring each other. Slow and soft were out the window. Fast and hot swiftly took over.

He pulled back just for a moment. Her eyes were heavy. Her fingers digging into his back. "You sure?" he asked. Praying to God she was. He didn't know if he could stop.

"Yes," she breathed. *Yes, God yes*, her mind screamed. She dove back into the kiss. Nipping his bottom lip.

He worked her shirt up and over her head and it fell to the floor. He had to find a bed or he was going to take her here and now. "Which way?" he stuttered, although he knew. Just at this moment his brain wasn't quite putting it together.

She threw her arm up and pointed. "That way." He had set her down and her heart skipped when he scooped her back up. She had never been carried like this by a man. Her need ebbed some and passion took over. She wanted to enjoy this. Savor him.

He set her on the bed and framed her face. He slowly leaned in and started a slow, deep kiss. She felt herself fall gently backward, his weight pinning the length of her. She ran her hands up his back taking his shirt with them. As it landed on the floor her hands ran along his skin. His muscles reacting to every touch. Hard and sleek.

His mouth left hers and began to search and explore her neck. His hands tracing fiery paths down her skin. His lips soon followed that same path, down her neck to her collarbone. Her shoulders to her breasts. She arched as his teeth bit her nipple. The sensation shocked a gasp from her lips and he quickly moved to the other one. Her hips arched against his stomach as he tore the bra from her. His mouth began its assault again, this time skin to skin. She fisted her hands in his dark hair and rode the wave of heat his mouth created. His lips began to pick back up the trail of his hands, moving slowly, achingly slow, down the quivering muscle of her stomach.

Cam swore her head was going to explode. Every time his lips touched her skin fire began to dance across the path. She fingers dug into his shoulders, trying to explore and to her shock he pinned them above her head. So she was left to squirm and moan. She was certain she was going to come before he even reached the heat between her legs.

She felt her pants slide down her legs and forgot all about shaving and granny panties. She could have sworn they would have burned off before he even got there. She arched as he kissed the dip between her stomach and leg. A moan choking from her throat.

Finn watched as she twisted and arched. His strong and smart-assed Cam turned to putty with a kiss. The power from that drove his need. Strong and almost uncontrollable. He watched her eyes glaze and go blank as his mouth found her. She came instantly. All of her strength and control lost in that instant. He felt her go limp. Her body softened and warm. He began his way back up, ready to take her again. The satisfaction of watching her eyes glaze steeled his will and he was ready to watch her lose that control again. To his surprise he found himself on his back, her legs wrapped around him, her lips on his.

She watched the surprise in his eyes as his back hit the bed. Still shaking from the complete assault on her sense, she began to attack his. She pinned his arms above his head and traced his jaw with her tongue. She nearly moaned when she heard the moan in his throat. *Good*, she thought, *two can play this game.*

She looked him in the eye. "Arms stay there. Got it?" She didn't wait for his answer. And she began her journey. And what a glorious one it was. She followed the hard lines of his jaw, to the stubble on his neck. She kissed the beat she felt pumping, lingering for just a breath.

Something about that got to him. Never had a woman done that, and he had a fleeting thought, never did he want another woman to.

She smiled when his breath caught in his throat. She felt empowered and she rode that high. Moving down she traced her tongue over his nipples and delighted in his moan. *A man enjoys it too*, she thought. His chest was hard. Each muscle standing out. A perfect body. She found a scar and remembered the one on his back. *So he's a fighter*, she thought.

He felt her lips press to the scar below his lower left rib. He remembered the bullet that ripped through him, but that thought quickly vanished as her fingers lingered after the kiss. So many mysteries his Cam has, he thought. Never would he have expected the softness from this woman. A softness he had never felt before. His mind quickly jumbled as he felt his pants slid down his legs. And all thoughts vanished completely as her mouth closed around him. Before he lost himself, he reached to her and flipped her back under him.

He watched the surprise in her eyes and just laid a moment. So much emotion flooded him, it shocked him to his core. He brushed the hair from her face and leaned in to kiss her. Slowly he slipped inside her and the two moved together. Slowly and achingly, he kept the same pace. Building the pleasure and need in them both. His eyes stayed on hers and still slowly he moved. Her legs came around him, locking him to her and she matched him, movement to movement, thrust to thrust. He saw the moment her control was lost and the orgasm took over. Her eyes deepened a dark stormy green and he felt himself go with her. His lips found hers and on a whispered "A'Ghra'," he fell with her.

Cam's mind registered his body weight a few minutes later. Finn still lay across half of her body, his arms still around her, her legs still locked around him.

Jesus Christ, she thought. The man was a godsend in bed. He awoke sensations in her that she didn't know existed. She had had knock-your-socks-off sex before, but compared to this, it was a wham-bam-thank-you-ma'am.

Finn's mind was equally blown. He felt her hands making lazy circles along his back and then he realized he was probably crushing her. He started to roll off, and he smiled and stilled when her legs locked tighter around his waist.

"No, not yet," she whispered into his neck.

Well, apparently it was good for her as well, he thought smugly. He had never had an experience quite like this one. His body was still humming.

He propped up on one elbow and watched her eyes open lazily. Her mouth spread into a slow grin and he found himself hardening in her. Jesus, he thought, she was going to be the death of him. The thought didn't bother him. He would die a happy man.

Feeling him come alive again, Cam tightened her legs around him and in one motion flipped him to his back. Arching her back, she took him in deeper. A purr let low in her throat as his hands encircled her hips, moving up her sides to cup her breasts. Her hips began a slow rocking, sliding him deeper and deeper.

Finn edged up to take one of her breasts in his mouth. His tongue worked it to a sharp point and he almost lost control at her cry of pleasure as he lightly nipped with his teeth.

Her hands framed his face and tilted his mouth up so she could plunder it with her own. Fire and need began to consume her, her control slipping away. Their first love making was slow and simmering, this was slipping into fast and hot.

He fell back as she pushed him to the bed. Her hips grinding harder and faster. His hands closed over those powerful and slender hips, urging her releasing the control she barely had a hold of. Here was his Cam. Strong, quick, and fast-tempered. He watched her arch as the orgasm took her. Her hips starting to slow.

"No, keep going," he urged. He wanted her to lose control. Lose control with him. He wanted to drive her beyond her senses, need and fire battling with her will.

His fingers dug into her flesh. She felt him urge her on. To lose all control. Her hips rocked faster, taking him deeper and deeper. Her fingers bit into his chest. Holding on to him, driving him with her.

She knew the instant his control was lost, his muscles hard, his fingers tightening. The power made her drunk, the thought that he was just as lost as she. She rocked faster and faster, until both cried out. Losing the battle, the fire exploded sending them both over that blissful peak.

Finn was the first to move. She had collapsed onto him, her breathing ragged against his chest. His arms encircled her, sealing her to him. His mind was beginning to clear.

He noticed they had torn her bed apart. Pillows and blankets scattered the room. There was a trail of clothes from the kitchen to the bed. He felt her breathing regulate and slow; she had fallen asleep on his chest. Not wanting to let her go, he slid them both up and into the bed. Finding one pillow he kept her encircled in his arms and slid his head to it. He kicked a blanket up and worked up over both of them. And still holding on, he slipped into sleep with her.

* * * *

Cam awoke at first light. She panicked when she couldn't move. Her heart slowed when the previous night flooded back. She realized he was half on top of her, his arms holding tight. A slow and satisfied smile spread on her face and she quietly enjoyed the weight of his body next to hers. The warmth of his arms around her, holding her to him. Memories of the night before began to build a slow heat, and she found herself wanting this man again. She was rolling over to take him again when her phone rang beside her.

"Goddammit." She slid one arm out and snatched it off the nightstand.

"O'Brien," she answered. A bit tersely as this call had ended any warm thoughts of round three.

Dispatch relayed the information of a body found at the docks. A male, possible homicide.

As she snapped the phone closed, Finn spoke. "Do you think it's related?"

She turned to face him. "It's at the docks. Only one way to find out." She rolled reluctantly out of the bed and sent a quick text to Jimmy and Brooks.

She walked quickly to the shower and jumped in before it had even warmed up. "Holy Christ!" she breathed. A ritual she used to shock her senses awake, she huddled until the hot water came through.

The warm water loosened her muscles and she began to move around. Finn had waited until she moved and he guessed the warm water had finally kicked in. He opened the door and slid in behind her.

Twenty minutes and one quickie later, they were on their way to the docks. Coffee's sweet aroma swamped her SUV, as her butt was warmed by the seat heater. They were in her personal car, her department-issued one was dead on her street. She called maintenance on the way to the docks threatening them with bodily harm if it wasn't fixed by the end of the day.

Seeing the set of wheels they were taking, Finn snatched the keys from her hand and jumped in the driver's seat. He was lucky she was in such a relaxed mood or she would have shot him and left him on the road. No one, save Brooks one drunken night, had ever driven her baby.

A Range Rover, a year old. It was a birthday present from her father and Nana. She had dreamt of one her whole life and it was a thirtieth birthday gift. Most women fall apart at thirty; Cam embraced it. She'd made it in one piece, she had a career, and a wonderful family. She had a job she loved and the best partner she could have asked for.

Glancing over at the grinning goon next to her, she was beginning to really enjoy her thirtieth year.

"You're lucky you're sexy and great in bed," she told him.

Finn grinned from the driver's seat. "You cops in America must make great money." He fondly rubbed the steering wheel.

"We do OK. This however was a present." She laughed when his eyes cut over to her. "My dad and Nana, you damn pervert." Checking the navigation, she sat back and enjoyed the ride. "It was my thirtieth birthday present. I have always dreamed of this car. I would bore them to death with the different options, colors, blah blah."

She rubbed her hand over the two-toned rich leather. Chocolate mocha and warm sand. It set off the blue green of the exterior. "I woke up that morning to the smell of coffee and frying bacon. Brooks and I had our annual sleepover. We've done that since we were kids. Always stayed with the other on their birthday." She smiled warmly. Remembering the many nights spent dreaming of their life. What they would do, who they would marry. The piles and piles of cash.

"Anyway, I woke up as Brooks was carrying in my breakfast on a tray. Whoever's birthday it is the other has to make coffee and breakfast. And serve it in bed."

"Sounds like you two really mean a lot to the other."

"It's always been the two of us. We don't come from very big families. So we were always it. 'Soul sisters' is what they always called us. Got the tattoo to prove it." She rubbed two fingers over the symbol inked below her hairline. It was their eighteenth birthday present to each other. A variation of a Celtic knot, the symbol for sisterhood.

Finn remembered the symbol. He had just had a close up of it less than an hour prior. "So breakfast in bed?" Steering the conversation back.

Cam picked up where she had left off. "So she brings me my tray and goes and grabs hers. We are piled in the comforter eating our breakfast and a car alarm goes off. We ignored it, thinking a neighbor down the street had tripped the alarm. But after three minutes the damn thing was still going. Needless to say, it's my birthday I don't want to hear a damn alarm all morning. So I climb out of bed, Brooks following, and I go to the front window, raise the blinds, to see my baby with a giant red bow on the roof. My dad, Nana, Jimmy, and Evelyn standing there waving up at me. I started to scream and jump up and down like an idiot, and I turn around and there is Brooks, jumping right along with me, holding the key in her hand."

Finn watched her face light up and laugh with the memory. He had never seen her so animated before. It was a whole new side, and he liked it.

"So there we were jumping and laughing and screaming. I grabbed the keys, slid on my Crocs and ran out the front door and down the stairs in my pajamas." Cam was laughing, her hands waving wildly in the air. Reliving that moment. "I couldn't believe it. Brooks and I jumped in and went for a spin, pajamas and all."

Finn found himself laughing at the thought. He could see the two of them, in the car, bouncing up and down, pajamas and slippers not stopping them from a dream come true. "It sounds great. It drives like a dream." He, himself, had coveted one of these. He had even set up a change jar in is flat in Dublin. He figured by the time he was ninety he should have it.

And then it hit him. What they were doing. Driving along, talking about dreams and great memories. Sharing the drive into work. Coffee filling the mugs in the console, Cam completely at ease and relaxed. It was all so normal. So domestic. So right. He looked down and saw their hands were even joined. Resting on the console, completely at ease. His heart stuttered.

Cam sat quietly, enjoying the ride. She was peaceful and content, sitting here, holding his hand, reliving fond memories. Laughing and talking on the ride into work. She glanced over and studied the profile of the gorgeous man beside her. Watching him coolly and confidently handle the car she loved. And her heart slid, deeply and effortlessly. How had this man, whom she'd known for only a week, captured her heart so completely? She knew she should be scared, more apprehensive at the thought, but for once in her life, she just let it be. Looking at their joined hands, she decided to live in this fantasy for a moment or two longer.

Glancing in the rear view mirror, she noticed a flash of red. Life, and death, would break the spell. It always did.

CHAPTER 14

They arrived at the scene ten minutes later. At her request, Officer Jonah Crabtree was called in. Standing at the tape that encircled the scene, he watched them get out of the car, together. He immediately wondered how the man got such a fancy ride. The slow burn of jealousy settled in his gut. What the hell was he doing driving her here anyway? And didn't they look perky and well rested.

Jonah lifted the tape and Cam ducked under. Over her head, he snarled at Finn. He childishly dropped the tape before Finn could duck under.

Finn had come to expect these pitiful gestures from the rookie, although the childish behavior was beginning to wear on his nerves.

Jonah pasted a lopsided grin on his face. "Good morning, Detective. You look rested this morning."

Cam smiled back. "Morning, Officer. How was your night?"

Finn rolled his eyes when hope flashed across the young man's face. "It was great. Just great." Edging closer to Cam, he began to fill her in on the scene.

"We've got a white male. Early twenties. Blonde hair, hazel eyes. Found shot." Pausing he glanced at his notes. "Appears to be once. Entry wound is to the base of the skull, exit wound through the left eye."

Cam held up a hand to stop the rundown. Brooks was squatted near the body, and Jimmy stood behind her. He watched them approach and saw when Cam recognized the victim. She looked from the victim's face to Jimmy, then to Finn. He saw it too. Brad Morris' disfigured face stared up at them from the ground.

"Goddammit," Finn breathed.

Brooks looked at Cam. "Dad said this was Nina's boyfriend. And pimp," she added with disgust.

Cam nodded her head. "Yup. And he was our only tangible link to the club. And therefore to the Flannery's."

She put on a pair of gloves and knelt beside Brooks. Lifting up the corner of his coat, she began to look through his pockets.

Jonah stepped forward. "According to the doc here, the vic had a cell phone and a wallet on him. Doesn't look like robbery was a motive."

Brooks's eyes flashed hot. "Brilliant observation." Sarcasm and disdain dripped like ice in her voice. Just like Finn, she had noticed the puppy-love looks that Jonah had been flashing at Cam. But she didn't trust him. Something in her gut was telling her that he was bad news. That there was something not right about the way he looked at her friend.

Finn coughed to muffle the laughter that slipped out. Jonah, completely unaware, beamed at Brooks.

She rolled her eyes and shook her head. *Idiot*, she thought. "The position of the entry wound suggests execution. I will confirm back at the morgue. From what I can see, there is no other injuries on him. Again, I will confirm when I have him on the table."

Looking over at Cam, she asked, "Why did you bring that?" Pointing to Cam's SUV.

Jonah glanced behind him. So it wasn't the Irishman's, he thought. "If you need me to, I can give you a lift back to the station."

Cam stood and stretched her legs. "I'm good." Looking back at Brooks, she said, "When we came outside, my duty car was dead. Not to mention, it had two flat tires. Maintenance takes forever to respond so we hopped in my personal car and came here." Answering her unspoken question, she added. "Finny boy here swiped my keys and commandeered the driver's seat. And seeing how I was in such an agreeable mood, I didn't shoot him." She shot a grin at Finn.

He smiled back, "She drives like a dream." And to Cam's complete horror added, "So does the car."

Brooks snorted and dared to steal a glance at Jonah, whose face had gone completely red. He stiffly turned on his heel and began to canvas the crowd.

Looking back at Finn, she grinned. "That was mean and low. And completely childish. I liked it."

Cam, who for once was completely lost, looked between the two. "What was that for?"

Brooks turned toward her friend. "Are you blind? The boy is following you around like a puppy. Lapping up any crumbs you throw at him. Not to mention he is a complete ass to Finn." Bewildered by her friend's complete oblivion, she just shook her head. "For someone so astute, you are so freaking blind to men."

Walking off she hollered for her assistant to start loading the body. Cam watched her for a moment before turning back to Finn. "I am not 'blind to men.' You two are just reading way too much into this. He is just eager to learn."

Finn shrugged and wisely changed the subject. He knew women. He had grown up with five of them. "Do you think we will be able to link this to the case?"

Cam looked around the area. They were standing in between two large warehouses. All red brick and steel doors, they were the two largest buildings surrounding the docks. Windows lined up along the top of the buildings, just below the roof lines fifty feet up. The asphalt was cracked and bleached. The sun baked this part of the lot late in the afternoon. The rest of the day, these areas were hidden in the shadows. The only light post in the area was broken out, the glass littered the ground around it. And Cam guessed that it was recent.

The breeze circling the empty lot carried the ting of salt and seagulls circled overhead. Fences enclosed the asphalt lot, the owners foolishly thinking it would provide enough security and deterrence. But the broken chains and locks that hung limply against the bent gates said otherwise. Graffiti decorated the buildings, adding color and breaking up the monotony of the red brick and steel. Judging by the tags, they were deep into Crypt territory and Cam made a note to get Detective Sorrece to confirm. She knew they had nothing to do with this, but maybe one of them had seen something. It was a long shot, but maybe one of them would talk. Hell, it would be a simple way to get your competition off the streets.

Cam's back was to the body, and Finn, when she saw Nina appear. Before she could stop her, Nina ran past her and straight for Brad's body on the ground. Before she could stop herself, she opened her mouth to stop her. "Nina stop!" she hissed.

Cam saw Finn's startled look, but quickly turned away. She would lose it if she saw any look of horror or disgust. She moved to crouch by Brad's body and a wailing Nina.

"Brad! Brad, baby, please. Baby, wake up!" Nina sobbed. She turned on Cam and began to yell. "Why aren't you doing anything? Help him! Goddammit help him!"

Cam's heart broke. Keeping her voice low, she tried to explain to her that he was gone. "Nina. Nina, please sweetie, we can't do this here."

Nina turned on Cam, fury lining her face. "This is your fault! You did this to him!" And then, as if it just occurred to her, she began to frantically look around. "Where is he? If you can see me, you have to be able to see him!"

Cam's heart broke at the hope in her voice. No one understands. Not even the dead. She couldn't see everyone. And it was extremely rare she saw someone like Brad. Someone who had no regard for the human spirit, when they were alive. Why would the gods grant him the chance to have any regard for them in death? There were a few who managed to make it through, but Cam believed they were never human to start with. An evil so pure, their spirit withered and died long before their body did.

Cam, reaching out, trying to comfort the girl, tried to explain. "Nina, I can't see everyone. I can't see Brad."

Nina jumped up, nearly knocking Cam on her ass. Finn reached out, on pure instinct, and caught her arm. He was completely bewildered on what just happened. "You bitch! You're lying! You're lying! Brad! Brad!" She ran off hollering for the boy she thought she loved.

Finn still had a hold of Cam. His mind was trying to process what was happening. He watched Cam talk to someone who only she could see, at least he hoped it was to someone, and then she fell back as if someone pushed her. But there was no one there, his brain screamed.

Cam was scared to look up. He was completely still, completely cold. She couldn't take it. To her horror, she felt a knot of tears well in her throat. She tried to jerk her arm free. "Look, I'm sorry. I don't have anything to explain to you. Let me go."

"Oh, hell no," Finn snapped. She wasn't going to dump this on him and then walk away. Tugging her around, he stood face-to-face with her. And his words caught in his throat. The tears in her eyes began to spill. Immediately he let go and began to rub her arms. "Ah, come on. Not that. Don't cry. Please don't cry." He gathered her to him and held for a minute. His mind was completely jumbled. He was shocked and mad, but the sight of her tears, crumbled the wall he threw up and made him feel like an ass.

Cam just stood still. Not moving, not breathing. She was afraid if she moved or breathed she would completely mortify herself and sob.

He rubbed his hands up her back. "Come on, Cam. I'm sorry." He pulled her back to face him. "You still have some explaining to do." He gathered her back. "But please don't cry."

Cam took a ragged breath and pushed him back. "I know. I know, I have to explain, but please…" She paused looking around, noticing that no one was looking their way. "Please, just give me a few. I'm sorry. I'm so sorry."

Finn, who was shocked and confused, stood and looked at this woman who had become so important to him. He didn't know what the hell was going on. He had an inkling, but he'd give her time. But he would have an answer before the end of the day. He nodded to her and then cussed under his breath, "Shit."

Cam quickly wiped her face, just in time to turn and come face-to-face to the one person, who would see right through her.

Brooks took one look at the hard line of Finn's jaw and the slightly red tint to her friend's eyes and immediately went into ass-kicking mode. Jumping between the two of them, all five feet, six inches of her went toe to toe with Finn's six plus feet. Poking a finger into his chest she rose up on her toes. "What did *you* do?" she growled.

Finn didn't know whether to laugh or be scared. He found himself doing a little of both, and with both hands in the air, he pleaded with this fiery sprite of a woman. "I didn't do a damn thing! I swear!"

Cam, who had begun to chuckle at the sight, grabbed Brooks and tried to reel her in. "He didn't do anything! Brooks, stop!" She was on the verge of hysteria. "Stop, you dumbass! It was Nina!"

That stopped Brooks in her tracks. "Oh." She turned a sweet smile to Finn, then swung toward Cam. "So he knows?" she asked.

Cam glanced up at Finn. "Well, he does now. She came flying in here and before I realized it, I tried to stop her." She couldn't look at him. She didn't want to see the look of rejection in his face. She wouldn't be able to handle it.

"Oh," she said again. She whirled back to him again. "I still got my eye on you!" She pointed to her eyes then to his. "Don't judge her, or I'll kick your hot, Irish ass." With one more glare, she turned on her heel and yelled to her assistant, "What in the hell are you gawking at? There is nothing to see here! Get your ass in the truck. It is time to go!"

"She's like a damn bulldog."

"You don't know the half of it."

* * * *

Two hours later, the team had reconvened in the conference room. Brad Morris's picture had been added to the "dead" side of the board. Everyone was talking among themselves, waiting on Joe Sorrece to finish a call.

Cam kept quiet, still reeling from earlier. He had kept his word; he was giving her time. It had been a quiet ride back to the station. None of the morning's conversation or laughter accompanied them. Finn had kept both hands on the steering wheel, leaving Cam to wonder if she would ever feel his hands on her again. It wouldn't surprise her if she never did.

The last man who found out about her left in a tirade of anger, accusations, and insults. Chad had broken her heart when he walked out four years ago. The rejection sliced deep, all because of who she was. "It's bad enough I have to tell people you deal with criminals and murderers all day," he yelled at her. "You look and touch dead bodies. But now this! Now, you're telling me you see and talk to them?" The disgust was plain on his face. "You freak!" She had tried to go to him. To let him see she was still the same person. He slapped her hands away and pushed her. "Don't touch me! You fucking disgust me! Don't you ever touch me again, you goddamn freak!" He slammed the door and walked out, leaving her broken and crushed. Huddled and sobbing on the floor. And in that moment she wasn't sure who hated her more—Chad or herself.

She swore from that day forward, no man would ever hurt her again. And she had been doing well, until this morning.

She risked a glance in his direction. It still baffled her that he had become so much to her in just a few short days. She chastised herself for allowing her heart to feel again. To hope. The sadness and hurt she was feeling was her own damn fault.

Cam turned her eyes when he glanced her way. She couldn't do it. She knew if he looked at her with an ounce of the disgust Chad had she would never recover.

And that's when she realized it.

She was in love with him. She had gone and fallen in love with Finnegan McDougal.

Cam pushed it all from her mind. The dead needed her and she would stand for them like she always did. So she shoved it all down and focused back on the case when Joe came back in.

Joe Sorrece, a ten-year veteran with the Gang Task Force, strode to the front of the room. He had confidence and swagger, two things that he prided himself on. His skin was the color of latte, and his eyes were a striking blue. His father was a first generation Italian-American, and his mother came from a long line of New Orleans Cajun. Most saw his eyes and assumed it was from his Italian father, but they actually came from his mother, whose coloring was identical. Short and stocky, he was built like a battering ram, which helped him on the streets.

In his line of work, the crazier they believed you to be, the less likely these damn gang bangers would try to do anything to you. Which is why he always told new detectives, "The key to survival in this job is to make these guys believe that you are absolutely fucking crazy. If they believe that you are crazy than they are, you will have fewer issues on the streets." It was a motto he lived and breathed, and after the phone call he just received, he counted himself lucky that everyone believed it.

"Okay," he started and paused while the room quieted. "I just received a call from one of my CIs. Demarcus Johnson. A mid-level Crip, who is pretty high up in the hierarchy. He says the word on the street is, if you want to run anything on the east side of the city, you have to go through the new bosses in town whom they call the Irish Kings.'"

Walking to the white board he began to chart the hierarchy. "Now let me explain the standings on the streets. At the bottom, you have the different street gangs. Crips, Bloods, Latin Kings, etc. Going a step up, you have the kingpins. The guys who supply the drugs to the gangs for distribution in the local areas. Going into the prostitution game, you would have what we call a king pimp. Most of the high-ranking positions are held by members of local mafia or mob arms. The street gangs feel that they are running the show, and at the street level they are, but if you want to get to the people that run those people, you have to work through this hierarchy."

Cam flipped out a pad and began to diagram out the same model. She listed the players as she knew them for this case. Brad Morris's name was written at the lower street level. Cam put his brother, Jonathan, between street and the next level, the go-between's. Those who were information and supply curriers. In most cases they are considered still at the lowest levels, but to Cam they hover in between the levels. They have face-to-face contact with the higher ups, so they have slightly more power than the street hustlers.

Joe kept on. "Anyway, back to it. According to Demarcus, this new gang is running the whole show. They moved in within the past year and began to methodically take over the top tier. They did this by money, fear, and a lot of persuasion, and by the looks of the three bangers on the board, their style of persuasion is very aggressive and very brutal. Some of the gangs lead members they paid off, or brought them into the fold. The ones that did not want to take either of the previous options, they 'persuaded' them to comply." He paused to cap his marker; he knew that the other's understood what exactly the clan did with their version of persuasion so he did not have to elaborate on how many times it took for the other gang members to figure out that they just needed to comply.

Turning to face the room, he got to the point. "Demarcus says that these new 'kings,' which is how they are referred as, are a bunch of white dudes that talk funny."

Chad Franks, with Narcotics, threw his pen down. "Fuck me, we got 'em."

Blake Rogers, Joe's partner, laughed at Chad. "No one's going to fuck you, so quit asking."

Chad flipped him off, laughing with the rest of them. It did no good to have thin skin in this line of work. Most people view police as crass and aloof; they also find that a cop's sense of humor is the same. If they didn't have these qualities, most of them would go crazy in under three years.

"All we need now is a link." Blake bounced his leg, a sign his adrenaline is up. "So Detective McDougal—"

"Finn."

Nodding he continued. "Finn. Are you sure these are the people responsible for your girls' death?"

"Ninety percent. No one else gained anything from it. No other murders, like hers, happened after that. Plus her body was found on their docks. She worked for them. She was helping us gather information on them. Then the gang moves here, and bodies start popping up again. Only logical conclusion I can come to."

Blake shrugged his shoulders. "It's just something doesn't add up for me." He noticed Finn's jaw tighten severely. "Just saying. Something just feels a little too...convenient. For instance, the girls. If you want to get into the business of young girls, why would you start killing them? Plus, what was the point of killing one of your boys, who, even though, he is probably not worth much, brought you young girls?" He paused and looked around the room. "Just saying."

Finn glanced around at the nodding heads. Forcing his instant rebuke down, he took a moment and mentally stepped back. He had to break the personal ties, and what had become a personal vendetta against the Flannery clan, in order to see this the way these detectives were.

He looked over at Sean Flannery's picture. The cocky bastard smiled back. Looking spiffy in his three thousand dollars suit and handmade Italian shoes, he stood like a man who owned the world. And in his eyes he probably did. Cam's initial suspicion of Sean had fueled the fire in Finn. The burning need to destroy this man and his family, and all the shit they had brought down on the people of East Dublin. And now the shit they were bringing to this city. This need had consumed him the past few days. But now he had to step back and reevaluate. They all did. Detective Blake Rogers was right. Could he have been focusing on the wrong guy? If he could take out Sean Flannery and his family a lot of the crime in Dublin would mostly disappear.

Blake was the quietest of the whole team. Standing at an imposing six and half feet, he was a solid wall of muscle. He carried himself like a man who was sure of himself, but one who didn't want to have to prove it. Brown shaggy hair framed his face. His cheeks and chin were covered in the same brown hair, a beard that needed a desperate grooming. Finn thought of a sleepy brown bear when he moved. Lazy gait and not one to rush, for such an imposing man, he had an easy presence about him.

And apparently he missed nothing. Finn cleared his throat and acknowledged the statement. "I can see your point. As much as it frustrates me and pisses me off, I can see how a man could use this to his advantage. Assuming he knows we are focusing on the Flannery Clan."

"That or he just thinks we are dumbass cops, sitting around eating our doughnuts and having a dick-measuring contest." Glancing at Cam, Matt Roberts, quickly flushed. "Sorry, ma'am, I mean—um… well—"

Deciding he had floundered enough, Cam cracked a smile. "It's okay, Roberts. We all know I am bigger than you." She laughed for the first time since that morning. Matt's mouth opened and closed like a fish out of water while the guys ragged him.

She sat quiet for a moment, letting the noise drown out in the back ground. Blake's theory ran through her head. She was just as guilty as Finn, zeroing in on the Flannery's right away. Focusing on them completely. She still had a feeling that they were somehow involved, but she didn't just couldn't figure it out.

"So," she started. Bringing the group back to the task at hand. "If we surmise that the clan is not involved. Where does that leave us?"

Chad's partner, Donnie Jones, a short bulldog of a man, with skin the color of dark coco, spoke up for the first time. "You have multiple witnesses who reported seeing a tall, white man in a dark suit at every scene, right?"

Cam nodded. "Every scene had at least one witness who could place a man fitting that description in the vicinity of the crime scene."

Donnie sat forward, a habit of his when he found a lead he wanted to chew on. "Are there any witnesses who could elaborate on anything else about the man? Or anything else that jumped out at them?"

"According to Officer Crabtree, whom we have had at every scene, the only common piece of witness testimony is a tall white man in a dark suit." Jimmy saw the question, before Donnie could ask it.

"We have called in Crabtree, because he was the only one to get a witness to come forward at the first scene. And then again at the next scene, he was one of the responding officers, and he was able to ascertain basically the same description from another of the witnesses. So at the last scene, we called him in."

Donnie nodded. Some officers just have that way about them. Witnesses just opened up. "Do we have his reports? Maybe he thought of something we haven't been told yet."

Jimmy went one step further, and thirty minutes later, Officer Jonah Crabtree was sitting at the conference room table. He sat down across from Cam and puffed out his chest, recalling the earlier conversation with his partner.

When Jonah received the call he had bragged to his partner. "The task force has called me in to help."

His partner rolled his eyes. "Why the fuck do they need your help?" Not that he cared.

All Jonah had been talking about since that first scene was Cam. Oh, she's a bitch and the next day it was that she was so fucking hot. Then a few days later she was a slut because she was screwing the Irish guy, and then the next day Jonah said that he was doing an undercover operation, because the department believed that the Irish guy forced himself on her. And since Jonah was so great at getting info from people, they put him as the lead on the undercover assignment to get the bastard to confess to the rape.

Officer Mike Carroll, Jonah's partner of the last year, was ready for the break. He knew everything Jonah said was bullshit and why he thought anyone with common sense would believe the shit that came out of his mouth, was beyond him. It amazed him, this crazy world Jonah lived in. *How in the hell did this guy get on the force?* Mike thought. So when Jonah got the call to come in and brief the team, Mike was relived. Hopefully they would "need" him for the next month and Mike could finally start to enjoy his job again.

Mike had thought about bringing up Jonah's behavior to their shift sergeant, but he didn't think the guy was harmless. Crazy, definitely, but dangerous, well Mike didn't think Jonah had the balls for that.

Cam introduced Jonah to the detectives around the table. He couldn't believe he was here. He memorized their names and then he worked on calming himself down. Jonah had always known he was more than a street cop. He was destined for the gold badge and the fancy suits. He felt a little uncomfortable, sitting in his uniform, surrounded by all these plain-clothed detectives, but he quickly shoved that down. Why should he be embarrassed? he scolded himself. *They called* you *in*, he chided. *They need* your *help*. So he focused and waited for them to ask their questions.

Jimmy was the first to speak. "Thank you, Officer, for coming in so quickly. We need you to go over your witness statements. And maybe you could give us your opinion on whether you feel we could possibly get more from the witness."

Finn watched the boy's chest puff out. Something about the officer sat wrong with him. He couldn't put his finger on it, but it was there. Or maybe, he thought, it was because the boy openly drooled on and mentally undressed Cam every time he was in her presence. Anyway, he wasn't going to let his guard down.

Jonah debated on whether to stand up or address them from his seat. He settled on his seat. He had noticed no one else had stood, so he wouldn't either. He was one of them, he thought. He wasn't addressing his superiors. He stole a quick glance at Cam, and his heart sped up when he saw she was staring at him.

"I was given the assignment to canvass the immediate neighborhood where the first girl was found. I interviewed approximately"—he paused and glanced at his open notebook—"thirty witnesses. Out of the thirty, fifteen saw or heard something that previous night." He glanced at the detectives, they all were taking notes, and Cam was still looking right at him. Mike was never going to believe this shit, he thought.

Clearing his throat, he began again. "All of the witnesses claim to hear moaning and screaming, but in that neighborhood, it is common. Three believed they had seen the victim in the neighborhood, around that particular alley, that night. They saw how she was dressed, so when they heard the moaning and screams, they assumed she was turning a trick."

Todd jumped in when Jonah paused. "Have any of the wits seen the victim in the area before?"

Jonah's nerves grated at the question. Did they think he was an idiot? He growled to himself. Not glancing at his notes, his ego answered for him. "Yes. Numerous witnesses had mentioned seeing someone matching the victim's description in the area turning tricks before." He wasn't one hundred percent sure of that, but he resented having his work questioned. He tried to work his temper down. *They called you, remember?* he asked himself. *They need your help. Screw them with their damn insinuations that you didn't ask the right questions.*

Reassured that he had this under control, he continued with his report. "Six of the witnesses reported seeing a tall white male in a dark suit walking away from the area where the victim was found." Before they could ask another stupid question he barreled on. "None could say, with one hundred percent certainty, that they saw his face. One of the wits said they saw the man had white hair. Another said it was blonde. A couple of them were sure the man had some weight to him. One compared it to a beer belly. But they were all positive on the suit and that the guy was white."

When he had finished he looked back around the room. Most of the guys were finishing up with their notes and talking theories. He risked another glance at Cam. She was finishing up her notes and he noticed she was glancing over at his notebook. Taking advantage of it, he slid his notebook around so she could see it full on.

"Thanks." She put her pen down and looked back at him. "Great job. I knew when I saw you that the witnesses would open up. It's your boyish good looks." She laughed and smiled.

Jonah had to stop himself from pumping his fist. When she had said that the first day, it pissed him off, but Mike had calmed him, saying, "She evidently saw something in you. Don't take it the wrong way." And that day, his relationship with Detective Cam O'Brien had been born. He had even found out that her family owned a pub in Fells Point. He was going to go there that night, but something had come up. But after today, he was definitely going to see her outside of work. He felt that she was just as interested. *Just look at her smiling and looking at me,* he thought. Yeah, the Irish dick screwed that up, and if Jonah saw him upsetting her again, he'd make sure his jaw was wired shut.

He realized she had said something when he felt her hand on his arm. "I'm sorry?" he asked. He blamed Finn for that too. If the fucker wouldn't be here, Jonah wouldn't be thinking about kicking his ass. He noticed her questioning glance and made an excuse. "Sorry I was thinking about the interviews again. Just mentally checking to see if I mentioned everything."

She waved it away. "No, it's fine. I was just thinking about maybe attaching you temporarily to this team. You do a great job with the witnesses and I think if we had the same officers interviewing them, we would notice any new or repeating information quicker."

She glance at Jimmy. "What do you think?"

Jimmy nodded. "I don't see a problem with that. Anytime we get a call, we will have dispatch get ahold of you. Now if you do this, you will be on call until we catch this bastard."

Not wanting to seem too eager, he jerked his shoulders. "If you could use my help, I would be happy to be a part of this." Mike was going to shit! *She needs my help,* he thought. Turning a smoldering gaze to Finn, he thought, *Watch out, fucker. She's mine.*

Finn noticed the look and made a mental note. He would keep his eye on the kid. He may be harmless, but a burning in his gut told him to watch out for him. Something wasn't right. And catching Jimmy's eye, he saw he wasn't the only one who thought so.

CHAPTER 15

It was quiet on the drive to the morgue. They were still in her Range Rover. Cam sat stoically in the front seat, trying to maintain an air of indifference. Maintenance said it would be two days for her department issue to be finished, but in a small way, Cam was grateful for the use of her SUV. There was more room so it decreased the chance that Finn would brush up against her. And she was desperate for him not to touch her. The razor thin thread she was dangling on couldn't hold much more.

Jimmy stayed back at the precinct to catch the captain up and to approve the temporary assignment for Jonah. He had left Cam and Finn, with Tom tagging along, to go and meet with Brooks at the morgue.

Tom had used the excuse of needing to stop by and brief his captain as the reason for him driving alone. One look and Tom knew he'd rather be in the middle of a fire fight than locked in the car with the two of them. Hell, even Jimmy had come up with a bullshit excuse to stay out of that car, he thought.

Finn was behind the wheel again. It had just dawned on Cam that he had had her keys the entire day. Her mind was scattered; images and conversations seemed to be swarming through her brain all at once. Normally she would pause and meditate for a moment, clearing the junk from her mind, especially during a case. She realized she was sheltering herself from the inevitable blow up, when she found herself taking refuge in the chaos.

There was only three men who had ever accepted her, all of her. Her grandfather, her father, and Jimmy. Every other man that she had let all the way in had broken her heart.

Glancing up to the rear view mirror, she was mortified to see the sheen of tears. She'd be damned if she'd shed another tear for this man. Who was he anyway? Just some dickhead Irishman who didn't know a damn thing about her. So what if they had spent the last evening having the best sex she had ever had. He wasn't the first man she'd ever had a casual relationship with.

She fought desperately to make herself see him as just another somebody. She hated herself for allowing this to happen. Hadn't she learned anything from Chad? Hadn't he said it best? *No one could ever love a freak like me?* The tears all but choked her now. But still she held them back. Until she saw Finn from the corner of her eye.

The emotions knocked her back. It shocked her to her core to discover just how much this man had come to mean to her. Just the thought of losing what they had last night was too much. She would rather take that day with Chad, over and over, than to have Finn look at her the same way. She wished she could blame Nina. Throw all of this on her, but Cam couldn't. She didn't have the heart to. When she had seen her there and saw the horror that flooded her face when she saw Brad there, Cam couldn't have ignored her. She just couldn't. Not even if it meant losing Finn. Because in that instant, Cam understood, she would be the same way if it was him on that ground.

And still it shocked her, to see his reaction. To see the look of betrayal and disgust in his eyes. But it rocked her more to realize the depth of her feelings. The amount of hurt. God, the unimaginable hurt her heart was feeling, to see that look on his face. And to know, with every fiber of her being, that she loved him. She loved him like she had loved no other.

She thought she finally understood why her grandmother had never remarried or went looking for love after her grandfather died. Once you had the love of your life, no other compared. It floored her to learn the depth of her feelings. She used to laugh and call her grandfather fanciful when he spoke of the love the Irish feel. He called them the truest romantics of the world. When the Irish love, they love with their body and soul, and no other could compare to the depth of an Irish soul. And now Cam finally understood what he meant by that.

She jumped when he broke the silence. "Are you going to tell me what's going on?"

Cam couldn't stop the tears that fell just hearing his voice. She took a deep breath and wiped her face. "What do you want to know?" she asked. She was staring out the passenger window. She was afraid of what she might see if she looked at him. Afraid of what that look would do to her. Closing her eyes, she waited for him to answer, swallowing the sob that threatened to come.

Finn drove quietly. His face was blank but his mind screamed with a million questions. What did he want to know? What did he want to know, she asked? Every goddamn thing! Calming himself, afraid he would lose control, he waited a minute before answering.

"What happened back there?" Stealing a glance her way, he tried his damnedest to ignore the tears. But it broke his heart and took all of his will not to pull the damn car over and gather her up. He knew the tears were because of him and it disgusted him. His mind screamed that it wasn't his fault. She's the one who kept him in the dark.

"I'm different," she began. "I'm different, and it pushes people away." She choked the last words out. She didn't care if he heard her sob. She didn't care anymore. The last of her will crumbled. Covering her face, she let the hurt rush out. She had lost too many people to this damn curse and now she was losing him, the one man she loved more than anyone else.

Angry at the gods above and everything else she punched the dashboard. "I fucking hate it!" she wailed. "But I can't stop it." Turning to face him, the anger rushed forth, the dam forever broken.

"I can't change it. It's who I am. The dead, they find me. Sometimes I find them. But they always come! They always fucking come!" Covering her face, she tried to calm herself. *Why? Why?* she thought. *Why me?*

Finn struggled to make sense of what was happening. Knowing if he pulled over, Tom would as well. It killed him to do so because he wanted nothing more than to gather up her broken pieces and put them back together.

Screw it, he thought and snatched up his phone. "Tom, we have to stop. We will meet you there. Give us ten minutes." He could tell Tom wanted to question him, but was thankful that he just agreed and hung up.

Finn turned the SUV into the next parking lot and whipped into an open space. Luckily no one ever parked at the end so they had the section to themselves. He got out and jerked her car door open. His arms wanted to immediately gather her up but he kept them on the car. He had to think rationally and he lost all sense when he was touching her.

He replayed the last thing she said to him. *I see dead people.* His mind was still processing that. The dead? She can see the dead? "You can see dead people? Real dead people? For how long?"

Cam was beginning to gain control of her emotions. She was calming the sobs, but the tears wouldn't stop. "My whole life. My whole damn life."

And then it struck him, like a damn bolt of lightning, something she had said, standing in her hallway. *My mother couldn't handle having a daughter like me.* Immediately he felt shame. They had begun to mean something to each other. More than that for him, he had tried to shy away from it, but he was falling in love with her, and fast. Hadn't last night proved that?

And at the first bump he had turned away from her. Now, this was one hell of a bump, he thought. But he had not given her the chance to explain. He had just turned away from her. Just as her mother had. Berating himself and thanking God his mother wasn't here, Finn tried to fix it.

"Cam. Cam?" He reached over and grabbed her chin, turning her eyes to his. "I'm sorry I screwed up. I'm sorry. I should have waited for you to explain. And yet I just turned away, and for that I am truly sorry. I know it is not an excuse, but I was shocked. If shocked even is the right word." He paused and moved closer to her. Cupping her face with his hands, he wiped the tears away and looked her straight in the eyes. "I am truly sorry—"

"You don't need to apologize," she interrupted. "But I'm sorry too. I should have told you, but I was scared. No one knows. No one except my family."

"Jimmy and Brooks too?" Although he already knew the answer.

"They're family." She took a full breath. And for the first time, she felt free. Freer than she had felt in a long time. "No one else does. Not anyone at the department or anyone else in my life."

She waited for him to answer. God, it felt like an eternity that she waited. Was he trying to find the words to end what was just beginning? she wondered. It was just beginning, but it was more than anything she had ever felt before.

Finn processed it all. Did it really matter? he asked. He knew the answer before he even asked. Nothing mattered but her. He stared at her, saw all of the misery and pain, and shame washed over him. My God, he thought, he put that misery there. The pain etched on her face was because of him. And immediately the shame he felt was overwhelming. His mother would beat him if she knew.

"Cam," he started. He reached out and gathered her to him. As he held her, he felt the sobs rock her body and he wished he had the power to change time. He gently pulled her back enough so he could look at her face. Her green eyes raged with emotion and hurt. Her face was splotchy, and his heart broke. "I'm sorry. I'm sorry for the way I reacted."

"I don't blame you for being shocked." She choked out a watery laugh. "Hell, I would be shocked too." She had to pause before continuing. Taking a cleansing breath she tried to finish. "But it was the look on your face. Something close to disgust. I saw it in your eyes. Please." She swallowed as more tears threatened. "Please don't look at me like that again. Please. I can take anything but that—" Her voice broke. She should have been mortified at the plea in her voice. But she could take anything, as long as he never looked at her like that again.

Finn's shame took his words. His arms tightened around her. He had always prided himself on his ability to accept people for what they are, and here, with the person who mattered the most, he failed. Emotion flooded his voice as he apologized. "God, Cam, I'm so sorry. I promise it wasn't intended. Oh, God, I'm sorry." He pressed his lips to her hair. He swore then and there, he would spend the rest of his life making that up to her.

She stayed pressed against him. For the first time, she was accepted for who she was. And for the first time, she thought she could be truly happy with who she was.

Finn cupped her face and wiped away the tears again. He spent a moment just looking and kissing her. He could tell that they had made it over this hurdle, but he knew he would never forgive himself for causing these tears. Just like he knew if another person knew about this, he wouldn't live to even think about this mistake again. "Um, I know this is probably not the best time, but um…do you think you can stop crying before Brooks kicks my ass?"

He smiled as he heard her laugh. She sat up and pulled down the visor, turning the lights on around the mirror hidden there. "Jesus, I look like hell." She reached into the console and pulled out some napkins. She tried blotting her face, to no avail. Then she remembered the bottle of water she always kept stashed in her glove box. Taking it out she wet a napkin and blotted her face with the cold water.

Finn watched her, amazement on his face. The redness started to disappear, and she replaced the cap on the water and put it in one of the cup holders. "You keep water in your glove box?"

She shrugged her shoulders. "You never know when you're going to need it. Or get thirsty." She smiled. He reached back over to take her hand and she knew there was one question he had, but he wouldn't or couldn't ask. "She comes to you sometimes."

Finn's throat closed. He had wanted to ask since this morning. He had begun to realize that part of his anger stemmed from jealousy. As much as it shocked and bothered him to admit it, he was. All he had wanted this past year was to see her smile one more time. To hear her laughter.

Cam understood. She realized how close they were the first time she saw her come to him. He had told her they were close, but until seeing the two of them, she hadn't understood. It was more than a man looking out for a friend. More than him mourning the loss of that friend. She was his. His child in every way but blood.

But for now, she wouldn't press. If he had questions she would do her best to answer, but if he didn't ask, she wasn't going to push it. He may not have realized it, but they both were in virgin territory. Never had a man accepted her for who and what she was. She was just as unsure about the situation as he was.

Tom watched Finn pull in next to his unmarked Crown Vic. Tom had always thought that he was lucky being issued one of the best-looking unmarked patrol cars, but seeing it next to Cam's SUV, he realized what a piece of shit it really was.

Most of the police cars were either Crown Vics or Impalas, and since Tom was taller than five foot seven and weighed over a hundred and fifty pounds, he passed on the brand-new Impala offered to him and stuck with a navy blue Crown Vic. All of the department cars came standard with no hub caps. Too many of them had come up "missing" and the department finally decided just to take them off. If the detective wanted tint on the windows, they had to pay for it, unless they were in Undercover Surveillance, then the city paid for it. It was unproductive if the suspect you are surveilling can see right through your window.

Tom loved his car, but still, it was rough to look at sitting next to Cam's Range Rover. Giving a low whistle of approval, he raised his eyebrows. "Nice ride." He left the unspoken hang in the air: How in the hell did a cop afford one of these? He knew he wasn't the first one to think it.

Cam ran a hand lovingly over the tailgate. "Thanks. She is my baby." She knew the question he was too polite to ask. Everyone had that question, which is why she hardly ever drove it around other cops. She rolled her eyes and added, "A present. For my thirtieth birthday from my father and my grandmother." Knowing the explanation wasn't needed, at least with Tom, it still irked her. The amount of crooked cops was rampant through any department.

Tom could see her bristle. "I wasn't trying to imply anything. Just curious." He knew if any cop was straight, it was Cam O'Brien.

But the real unspoken question he had was what happened to make the bad-ass Cam O'Brien cry? He glanced over at Finn and saw the slight shake of his head. OK, he thought, if he wants him to let it go, he'd do it. But he was sure of one thing–if the bastard made her cry again, his ass was toast.

Changing the subject, Tom pointed to the keys in Finn's hands. "She let you drive it?" He snorted a laugh. "She must really like you. I know if it was mine, you wrong way–driving sons a bitches wouldn't get near my keys."

Finn laughed and pocketed the keys. "Lucky for me then, it's hers." They began to walk to the door, and he added as an afterthought. "I guess I'm just that damn good in bed." Tom and Finn laughed as the flush crept up Cam's neck and face.

"Dumbasses." She threw over her shoulder, nearly running to get into the building.

Their laughter followed her in. Brooks heard the commotion and came out of her office. Seeing her friend red faced and nearly running she aimed her glare at the two men behind her.

Her stomach fluttered some seeing Tom. It was the first time she had seen him laugh. Hell, it was the first time she had seen him doing something other than brooding. And what a nice change it was.

Brooks ignored the fact that Cam looked as if she had been crying again. There was time for that later. Finn's shadowed eyes told Brooks who had caused those tears.

Cam stopped short, nearly plowing into Brooks. "Oh, sorry." Pointing over her shoulder, she continued. "Ignore the two idiots. They apparently think my sex life is funny."

Brooks feigned a hurt look. "Sex life? And no details? I'm appalled. I thought I meant more to you than that."

Cam fixed her with an icy glare. "Gee, I'm sorry, between the dead body and the fantastic meeting, it just slipped my mind. I know I should be ashamed of myself."

"Damn right. But you're forgiven." She dodged the swat Cam threw her way.

Cam saw the worry in her friend's eyes and knew her pathetic attempt at erasing the crying had failed. She subtly shook her head and Brooks let it go, but she would get her answers later.

Aiming a sultry smile and wave their way, Brooks stopped both men in their tracks. "What can I do for you fine men this morning?"

Finn smiled at all five feet five inches of her. She had changed into scrubs and she had piled her hair messily on top of her head. Most women would look, and feel, plain and ordinary, but Brooks's personality and beauty transcended all of that. He thoroughly believed if she dressed in a potato sack, she would make it beautiful because of who she was.

It amazed him that these two women were best friends. Polar opposites. Cam, who was beautiful and aloof, and Brooks, who was beautiful and charismatic. The two of them were so different, but so right together. They complemented one another perfectly.

He watched her stand there, one hand on her hip, eyes lit up, and a small pout on her mouth. On a whim, he strode up to her, put his arms around her, dipping her back and kissed her pouting mouth.

He laughed as he let her go and found her momentarily speechless.

Brooks fanned herself and turned to Cam. "No wonder you were so perky this morning."

Cam rolled her eyes and chuckled.

Brooks looked at Tom and raised an eyebrow. "Anything you want to add?" she asked playfully.

Tom slowly walked forward. He stopped as his body barely brushed hers and cupped her face in his hands, tipping it up. His lips stopped a hair above hers. "You're not ready to give what I want from you," he whispered softly, gently rubbing his thumbs across her cheekbones.

Desire burned low and hot in Brooks's belly. Her vision blurred and her knees went weak. Her vision blurry, she placed a hand on his chest to steady herself. She tried to think of a time when her body had this type of reaction to a man, and for the first time in her life, she couldn't get her brain to work.

Cam watched Tom slowly let go of her friend and was shocked to hear almost a whimper come from Brooks's lips.

Finn, blissfully unaware, started to pepper Brooks with questions about Brad Morris.

Brooks stuttered and stumbled her way back to reality and her brain finally clicked. "Um…Yes, he's on the table. This way." She pointed down the hall.

They all followed her down the hall, Tom bringing up the rear. His mind was on auto pilot. What started as an innocent play had his head spinning and his senses buzzing. He had only meant to joke around with the sexy ME, and boy, had that backfired. The moment he touched her, he knew he was in trouble. And by the lovely Brooks's reaction, he wasn't the only one.

But it all screeched to a halt when he heard Jimmy's voice behind him. Jesus, he tried to clear his head, then he turned and tried to erase the sexual buzz brought on by the man's daughter.

Brooks heard her dad and turned. "I thought you weren't going to make it?" She returned his peck and hug.

Jimmy shrugged. "Our meeting got cut short. The captain got a call from home. Something he had to go take care of."

He glanced around and paused a second on Tom, who was currently trying to do everything he could to avoid Jimmy's eyes. Interesting, he thought, slightly confused as to the reason. He glanced at Brooks. "Ready?"

Brooks nodded and folded the sheet down to Brad's waist. "Okay. Brad Morris. Six feet, one inch, one hundred and sixty pounds. Blonde hair, hazel eyes. Would you like a rundown of all of his previous injuries? Or do you just want the current ones?"

Tom wondered why the hell they needed old injuries. "Are they going to help solve the case?"

Brooks narrowed her eyes. "Do you want to know what his history was like? It may help you figure out what his life was like before and why he ended up the way he did."

Tom quieted, appropriately chastised. "Take it away, Doc."

"The victim has sustained numerous injuries throughout his life. In my opinion, he was abused. Broken wrist caused when someone grabs you and jerks and twists. Same with his shoulder. Ribs, fingers, nose. All seen in abuse cases."

She moved to stand at the top of the table. She moved her camera in and brought the picture up on the screen. Twisting his head to the left, she exposed the entry wound. Adjusting the camera again, she zoomed in. "There is stippling and burns on the surrounding skin. The gun was pressed directly to his head." Placing his head back on the table, she focused their attention to the exit wound. "The bullet traveled through his brain and exited out his left eye. Now the trajectory of the bullet mimics an execution type of kill."

Brooks waved Tom over. He moved around the table to stand in front of her. "Now, turn around and kneel in front of me."

"Yes, your majesty." But he did as she asked.

Smiling Brooks grabbed a blunt tool from her tray.

Tom heard it and swung around. "You are not touching me with something that has been in, or on a dead body."

Pushing him back around, Brooks rolled her eyes. "Stop being a pansy and let me finish. It's clean." Turning the tool in her hand, she added, "Mostly." And laughed when Tom grumbled.

"Anyway," she continued. "The victim was on his knees with his back to the assailant. He hung his head, knowing what was coming. The assailant then placed the barrel of the gun at the base of the victim's skull. And here's where it gets interesting." She stood behind Tom and mimicked the killer's action. "He must have been nervous or guilt ridden, because, instead of aiming straight, the gun moved slightly left, which is the reason the exit wound is in the eye."

Jimmy decided to play devil's advocate. "What makes you sure that the killer felt guilty or nervous? It could have just been that the victim jerked."

Brooks looked her father straight in the eyes. "Because I know my job. And I am damn good at it." She walked back to Brad's head. "Plus, there is evidence of a small, rounded bruise just above the entry wound. It looks as if the killer hesitated, then sucked it up and shoved the gun forcefully into the victim's skull and pulled the trigger. That evidence, along with the path the bullet took, tells me he didn't want to do this, but it was necessary."

Jimmy nodded and looked at the rest of the group. "Does her version sound plausible to you?"

Cam walked around and took a closer look at the screen. Finn followed her, pausing to give Tom a hand up. Together they scrutinized the wound. Brooks had shaved the hair three inches around the wound. Just above the center of the wound there was a faint outline of the gun's muzzle. The burns surrounding the opening showed the power and force of the bullet as it left the gun.

Cam then moved to the table and brought the camera to focus on the exit wound. The bullet exited just under his left lower eyelid. The wound was a smaller one, suggesting a smaller caliber bullet. Compared to the angle of the entry wound, Brooks's assessment made sense.

"What caliber would you say? We didn't find a casing at the scene, so we assumed it was a revolver or the shooter policed his brass." Only someone with experience or someone who was thinking clearly would pick up the casings.

Brooks grabbed up the file she had made some notes in. "My guess is a nine millimeter. Definitely nothing over a forty caliber. But my suspicion is a nine. Anything larger would have stayed inside, scrambling his brains more."

Finn, who was used to European laws, wondered about the accessibility of firearms. "How common is firearms here? Especially that caliber?"

Tom laughed. "It is the most common gun on the streets. The gun is widely available, cheap, and the ammo is the same way. Most gang bangers and thugs carry a nine or a forty. Hell, most suburban housewives carry those as well."

Jimmy moved in to check out the wound when Finn stepped away. "Nine times out of ten, the gun is untraceable. Serial numbers filed off. Gun was brought into the state from somewhere else and was never registered. The list goes on and on." He looked over his shoulder at Finn. "It's a bitch to work through. But sometimes we get lucky." Turning around he looked at the boy on the table. "But I don't think so on this one."

Brooks jumped in. "Find the gun and I can prove it."

"How?" Cam whipped around to look her friend in the eye, hope starting to build. They may be able to get this bastard. Although she had a feeling this was linked to the Flannery clan. "Most of the time the bullet can't be matched if it was mangled."

Brooks pointed to the screen that still showed the bullet wound. "When the trigger was pulled the gas seared the skin. Some of that skin fused to the muzzle. Now if he's smart, he cleaned it, but there is a lot of crevices in the muzzle of a gun. I doubt he got all of it. If it's there, the lab will find it. Plus I can match the muzzle to the bruising around the wound."

She turned off the monitor and camera. Cam and her merry men were finishing up their notes, and she decided to go ahead and put Brad back into the cooler. She zipped the body bag closed and double-checked the paperwork attached to the bag.

"Cam?" Brooks asked, Brad's paperwork in her hand.

Cam glanced up. "Huh?"

"When did Mr. Morris leave the city's fine hotel?" She was referring to the city jail.

Cam's forehead crinkled in concentration. She didn't have a damn clue.

Cam slapped her forehead. The sound echoed along the tiled walls. "Goddammit!"

She spun on Jimmy. "How in the hell did we miss that?"

Jimmy gave a quick shoulder jerk, but his face was already reaching a deep shade of red.

Finn just shrugged. "I just thought he was bailed out."

Cam flipped back through her mental files. What was he in for again? "Drugs," she blurted.

"Bubbles," Brooks quipped back.

"Smartass." Rolling her eyes, she glanced over at Finn. "No, he was arrested on drug charges. His third time in two months. Bail was denied."

"Then how in the hell was he out on the streets?" Finn queried. "I doubt he just up and walked out."

Jimmy had already pulled out his phone and was currently tearing the jail's captain a new asshole. "What do you mean you don't know? Do you not keep accurate records of your inmates over there? Or is it a come and go as you please type of joint? Who else have you morons let out in the past two days?"

He had begun to pace. His nostrils were flared and his head was an unnatural and alarming shade of red. Brooks was worried he was going to have a stroke. She had just started to walk his way when his explosion stopped her dead in her tracks.

"Are you fucking kidding me?" His voice brought the whole morgue to a halt. Heads started poking out of offices and rooms that lined the white tiled hallway. Cam, Finn, Tom, and Brooks were glued in place. "You jackwagons are the most incompetent ass clowns I have ever had to deal with! I am shocked that you bumbling idiots have kept control of the jail this long!"

Shock and awe was plastered on Tom's face. He had known Detective Jimmy Aaron for going on ten years and he had never heard the man yell, let alone shout and curse for an entire building to hear.

Jimmy was oblivious to the deafening silence that had descended on the morgue. Fury fueled his blood, pounding a storm through his ears and head. Of all the idiocy that he had heard through his career, what was being spoken on the other end of the line topped it all. His voice was ice as he spoke his parting words, "The commissioner will be in touch."

Cam opened her mouth to speak but the words had choked in her throat.

Jimmy, enraged, threw his phone across the room, shattering it against the far wall. He stalked off, pacing the length of the room, his hands scrubbing his face and hair.

Brooks made a move toward him and stopped at Cam's fierce look. She almost ignored her but Tom stepped in front of her. "Excuse me?" she hissed, her jaw clenched.

Tom didn't answer. But being a smart man, he prepared himself for a fight. And damn, he didn't want that. He didn't want to restrain the man's daughter, especially when the man was so completely pissed.

Finn, taking his life in his own hands, ignored the angry shake of Cam's head, and stepped in Jimmy's path. *Please God don't swing on me*, he pleaded.

Jimmy, oblivious, walked straight into Finn. He grabbed him by the sleeves of his jacket and tried to jerk the younger man to the side. But Finn stood his ground.

"Get the fuck out of my way, boy." Jimmy tried to get around him, but Finn was unmovable.

"No, sir." He placed his hands on Jimmy's shoulders. Trying to break through the fury consuming the older man.

Jimmy attempted to break free once again, but gave up when Tom came around and blocked him in. "So you going to tag team me?" he spat.

Tom shook his head. "No, sir. But you will calm your old ass down before you stroke out in front of your two girls."

Tom's calming tone was like acid to Jimmy; it irritated and burned him. He wanted to lash out at the two of them. They made themselves easy targets, but what he really wanted was to strangle the idiots at the city jail. He was flabbergasted. It was amazing that the place still stood with the amount of incompetency in the administration. And now he had these two morons standing on either side of him beating on their chests, telling him what to do.

He started to put his hands on Finn, when he heard a whimper behind him. He turned around and saw Brooks in Cam's arms, shaking and tears streaming down her cheeks. Instantly, all the mad left him, replaced with guilt.

Finn saw the change in Jimmy's eyes and he let him go. He watched as he gathered his daughter up and just held her. Finn searched Cam's face and was startled to see fear. Unsure of what to do, he watched her closely as Jimmy tried his best to calm Brooks down beside her.

"I'm sorry, baby. I'm sorry." Jimmy brushed his hand down his daughter's hair and kissed the top of her head. Shame enveloped him and he berated himself for losing it.

Cam finally found her voice. "What is going on?" Finn moved closer and placed his hand on the small of her back, although he wanted to gather her up as well. But he knew if he tried, she would just push him away.

Tom had moved to clean up Jimmy's shattered phone. He needed something to occupy his hands as he worked through the conflicting emotions washing over him. Seeing the fear and tears on Brooks's face, he found himself wanting to gather her up himself. And that knowledge unnerved him. A lot.

"I'm sorry…" Jimmy started. He held up his hand to cut off Cam's rebuke. "No. I need to apologize. So shut up and let me do it."

He turned to face them as one group, but he kept his arm on Brooks's shoulders. "Look," he began. "Normally I can keep my cool, but these asshat's at the jail have royally fucked us and I don't know what in the hell to do to fix it." He paused and looked down at the badge on his belt. He had a sickening feeling that this betrayal was going to hit close to home.

Cam watched Jimmy. Her nerves were shot and emotionally she was done. Reaching her limit she snapped. "For Christ's sake, what in the hell happened?" Her voice was beginning to pitch but she didn't give a rat's ass. She had just watched a man, whom she had known all of her life, turn into a raving lunatic. Jimmy was always the grounded one. The calm one. She searched back through her memory trying to remember a time she had seen him in the slightest lose control and she came up blank.

Jimmy took a deep breath and recounted his conversation. "According to the jail, Morris was released along with twenty-five other inmates." He had to stop when the three of them erupted. "Shut it and listen!" he yelled.

Cam immediately shut her mouth. Finn and Tom had a harder time than she did.

Jimmy's anger was rising again, just thinking about the shit-storm this was going to cause for the department. "According to the records for that day, twenty-five inmates were released due to the charges being dismissed. They were released at different times, so as not to draw any unwanted attention. The captain at the jail only caught it because I called and asked about Brad Morris. According to him, these inmates were all in on charges of narcotics, gangs, or prostitution." He tried to force the fury down. He could feel his face growing hot and his blood was pounding in his ears.

"There is no way in hell those men and women should have been released. They weren't in there for misdemeanors or first time offenses. Twenty-three of them were on their third strikes. The other two were on the second." Seeing the question on Cam's face, Jimmy held his hand up again. "Yes, the captain is compiling a list, along with mug shots and copies of the release forms so we can hopefully figure out what the hell happened and get these delinquents back in their cages."

Now it was finally time for Cam to lose it. "How in the fuck does this happen? And that is bull shit that no one caught on." Knowing a few of the detention officers personally, she knew that certain repeat offenders stuck with you. You knew them by name and sight. Actually, she amended, almost all of them do. And she voiced that to the group, who all agreed. Hell, it was the same on the street. You arrest the same person more than twice and generally you are on a first-name basis with them.

"Is there any way to trace where the release forms came from?" Finn hated to ask, but his next question was going to really get under a few people's skin. "And then my next question is, can these forms come from anywhere other than the department?"

Tom and Cam's loyalty quickly bristled. They both fought against the idea of a dirty cop, but Tom was the first to give in. Finn was right. The order had to come from inside the department. "It would come from the department, arresting officer, supervisor, or the DA's office." He thought of the district attorney's office and did not look forward to those interviews. Generally when they interviewed a suspect, they did their best to avoid lawyers. But here they would be interviewing the damn lawyers and that just made for a bad day.

Cam had to reluctantly agree. This case was turning into more than the death of three young prostitutes. This was turning into an all-out war—rival gangs, turf wars, mob ties, and now it looked like either the department or the DA's office, or both, had some kind of tie to all of this.

She was still trying to figure out if these murders were an isolated case of a murdering lunatic, or was this connected to Flannery clan. Or both? It was the last thought that scared her the most. She had seen the handiwork of the Flannery clan. Unfortunately those images would never leave her mind.

But something was telling her these cases were only related on the outskirts. The murders of the girls and the gang members and now these inmates being released, something was going on but she couldn't put it together. She could be wrong, but her gut was telling her she wasn't.

And by the looks on the faces of those around her, she wasn't the only one whose gut was rumbling.

CHAPTER 16

They received word that it was going to be the next day before they would receive the paperwork from the jail. Still Jimmy had spent the last three hours of that day in a closed door meeting with Captain Thems, Commissioner Donald Freeman, Jail Administrator Nick Patterson, and the Senior Officer Major Neal Simmons trying to figure out what the hell had happened earlier.

Cam and Finn caught up on paperwork and glanced at the captain's closed door with growing apprehension. Cam was still worried about Jimmy; his reaction from earlier in the day still on her mind. They could hear muffled yells and creative cursing occasionally come through the cracks, causing the bullpen to remain uncharacteristically quiet, trying to hear any tidbit of information. The department was in an uproar, and it had started four hours before in the conference room down the hall.

When the group, including Brooks who was afraid to leave her father, arrived back at the precinct, the rest of the team had been immediately called back in. They all were in various moods, depending on how their day of info gathering had been going. Officer Crabtree, joined the group. Jimmy felt he trust him to get the word back to Patrol to be on the lookout for any of the freed inmates.

Finn watched him walked in and grab a seat directly across from Cam. Something about the way the boy looked at her bothered the shit out of him. Jonah hadn't shown any obvious signs of obsession, but something in his eyes made Finn uneasy. He tried to ignore it, chalk it up to the stress of the case, but he couldn't turn it all the way off.

Jimmy stood up and filled the rest of the team in on what he had been told an hour before, and within two minutes, they were in an uproar. The Narcotics and the Gang-Task Force detectives were fuming. Some of the inmates who had been released were on the city's most wanted list. Jimmy gave the team an assignment—find out who was responsible. He knew they all feared that one of their own was involved in this and they all wanted blood. Cops lived by a code—blue blood is thicker than true blood. They were family. The tightest form of family. And now they had been betrayed by a member of that family.

Dismissing the team until oh nine hundred the next morning, Jimmy went straight from the conference room into the captain's office. For three hours, Brooks had been staring at the door, hearing her father's booming voice shake the windows. She feared that he was going to have a heart attack or stroke. Her foot tapped the floor nervously, as she grew increasingly anxious.

Cam had worked on paperwork and listened to every tap, huff, and hushed whimper Brooks made. When she pushed herself up to pace for the umpteenth time, Cam had had enough. "Honey," she said, reaching for Brooks's hand. Once she turned her face, Cam noticed the sheen of tears. "Sweetie, he's going to be okay. I promise." But the promise sounded hollow, even to Cam's ears. She was worried too. She had spent more time staring at the paperwork than finishing it, but she knew if Brooks saw her worry, it would probably cause her to have the heart attack.

Brooks was not pacified. She, just like Cam, could never remember seeing her father give an outburst like this. He had been worked up, sure, he had even hit a man, a bunch of them, but this? This was different. He'd never lost his cool. Never lost control.

Finn decided none of them were going to get any work done, so he stood up and closed the files on his desk and Cam's. Cam swatted at him and tried to take back her files, but he ignored her and shoved them into her bag. He slid the bag on his shoulder and held her coat out. She shoved her arms in and he walked over to Brooks and held her coat out. She didn't move. "Come on, fire faery, let's go." And like he intended, she couldn't hold back the chuckle.

"Fire faery?" she asked, sliding her arms in her jacket. She noticed she was still in her scrubs. In the midst of the chaos, she forgot to change. Oh well, she thought.

Cam asked the question on both of their minds. "Where are we going?"

Finn grabbed up Brooks's bags and started herding the women towards the door. "Home." Ignoring their protests, he kept at them. "Bloody hell! Shut it. I left a note for Jimmy, since he broke his phone during his temper tantrum, so he knows where we will be."

Cam reluctantly agreed. They were getting absolutely nothing done here, so they might as well take it home.

Brooks climbed in the backseat, sliding her butt to the middle. Cam automatically went to the passenger side and waited for Finn to open the door. After sliding in and buckling up she caught Brooks's eyes in the rear mirror. "What?"

Brooks had a smile plastered on her face. She couldn't believe what she had just seen. "Since when has that been going on?"

Cam scrunched her forehead. She was trying to figure out what she meant and it hit her as Finn slid in beside her and started the car.

Brooks, not missing a beat, slid forward on the seat closer to Finn. "So Finn," she began, "how do you like the car?"

Finn ran a hand along the wheel. "I love it."

Ignoring Cam, she fired off the next question. "As much as you love Cam?"

Not missing a beat, he answered smoothly, "Nope. Love the car more." Laughing, he tried to block the smack Cam hurled at him. "I was joking!" he pleaded.

Finn grinned as he pulled out. Thinking of Brooks's question, he realized one thing. Well, two, he thought. He loved the car, who wouldn't, but he loved the woman too. Glancing out the corner of his eye, he caught the smile on her face. Yeah, he thought. Definitely in love with the woman. And for the first time since coming here, Finn finally felt at home.

Pulling to the curb in front of Cam's building, Finn's stomach dropped. Sweeping the front stoop of the pub, Jack paused and watched Finnegan McDougal get out of the driver's seat of his daughter's prized SUV. His eyes narrowed and his father's instincts went on full alert. What was he doing driving that car? And then fear hit. Jogging to the passenger door he jerked it open and grabbed for his girl.

Startled, Cam yelped. "Dad! What the hell are you doing?"

Jack began to look over her. "Are you hurt? Are you okay?" Seeing Brooks, he noticed the blood on her scrubs. He rushed to the back door and nearly snatched her out.

"Jack!" she yelled. "Stop it! Calm down. Jesus. Cam! Tell him we're okay!"

Cam jumped out of the car and pulled on her father's arm. "Dad! Stop. We're fine. I promise. What the hell has gotten into you?"

Jack, whose heart was still frantically beating, tried to calm himself. "Well"—he pointed to Finn—"I saw him driving and then noticed that you weren't getting out and I panicked. Then I saw her in the back with blood on her. You fill in the damn blanks!" he said, pissed that he was worked up. And even more so that he was getting snapped at for being worried.

Finn came around the car and began to grab bags and closed the doors. "I'm sorry, Jack. We have had a rough day and I just stuck to driving."

Jack pointed at Finn and then to the pub. Finn, understanding, nodded. Handing the bags to Cam, he started toward the door. "You two go on and figure out dinner. I'm good with whatever. I'll be right up.

Cam looked at her father and narrowed her eyes. She then walked over to Finn and gave him a quick kiss. "Hurry up." She walked back by her father and stared hard.

Brooks walked over, reached up, and planted a kiss on Jack's cheek. "Go easy on him, old man." She sent Finn a wink and followed Cam up the stairs.

Finn walked on and entered the pub. A few bar stools were occupied by some of the regulars who stayed through most of every day. Jack entered after him and pointed to the booth in the corner next to the bar. Nodding, Finn walked over and sat.

Jack continued to the bar and pulled two Guinness. It was early in the evening but he thought the conversation called for it. His eyes tracked up and over toward Cam's apartment. He wondered how much this man knew about. Praying to the gods for wisdom, he carried the pints over and sat across from Finn.

Finn accepted the pint with a nod and a thanks. And then he waited. Jack seemed nervous and fidgety, something Finn had not seen.

A robust man, Jack's presence filled the room. The same way Cam's did, Finn thought. He had a hearty face, but kind and handsome. His hands were large and knew how to handle a tap, as well as a hammer. He was well over six feet, but Finn beat him by a hair. And considering the balding occurring on Jack's red head, it was literally a hair. His green eyes were as bright as a field in the spring sun, something else Cam inherited from her father. And his smile was as gentle as a babe's.

Jack cleared his throat and took a long drink. Turning his beer on the coaster, Jack got to it. "Look, um, I know that, um…you and Cam, um…"

Finn lowered his face to hide his grin. "Ah, yeah, He stuttered. This was a first, and Finn was sure it wasn't just his, the way Jack was stammering.

Jack's face turned pink. "Well, ah, just so you know. Ah, as her father I expect, ah, well…you know, I-ah, expect…Dammit." He took a longer drink this time. How in the hell was he supposed to sit here and do this? he thought.

Fionna had come out of the back at the same time Jack had sat down. She had been listening from the other side of a large beam that ran from the ceiling to the booth.

Men! she thought, shaking her head. All big and tough until you mention a little roll in the hay, they get all willy-nilly. Having heard enough stammering for a lifetime, she marched over and sat down beside Finn.

"What my bumbling son is trying to say is, what are your intentions with our Cam?"

It was Finn's turn to stumble. Leave it to a woman to stop pussy-footing around. Chuckling at this wonderful woman, he answered, "Well, I am in love with her."

Jack's head snapped up, but Fionna just reached over and patted his hand. Shaking her head at her son, she grasped Finn's hand across the table. "There's my boy." She smiled. "I knew it from the minute I saw you sing to her." Looking in Jack's direction, she wondered how much Cam's man knew. And hoping to get a sign from her son, she wondered just how much to tell him.

Seeing the worried glance between the two, Finn knew they were wondering if he knew. "I know. She told me everything."

And for the first time Jack relaxed. He couldn't take seeing his baby girl broken again. Like the last bastard had done.

Fionna squeezed her son's hand and smiled at Finn. "So then you know she is precious and special, in more ways than most." She decided to tell him. "The last man who sat here and told us he loved her left her broken and scarred. He couldn't accept her for who she was. Now, Finnegan," she began, her voice softening and hardening at once, in only the way a mother's can. "Finnegan, if you leave her broken and scarred, I will search the world over for your hide. And then I will skin it and send you home to your own Maimeo` and I know she will do the same."

"Yes, ma'am," he said seriously. "I understand, ma'am." And he did, there were two women he fearedand loved, his mother and his Maimeo`, his grandmother. A woman is a force you never want to battle, but a woman defending her brood? Well that, he thought, is a force that can rival a god's.

She patted her son's cheek and move to go. "Is there anything else you would like to say, dear?"

Jack, squared his shoulders and faced the man. "Don't disappoint me, son."

Finn understood. "Yes, sir. Ah, Jack?"

Jack stopped moving from the table and focused back on Finn. "Yes, son?"

Finn felt like a fool. Here he was, already sleeping with the man's daughter, and yet he was about to ask for his permission to date her. Jesus, he did this ass-backward. "Would you mind if I take your daughter out on a date?"

At that moment Jack knew this was the one. And with a sadness he wasn't expecting, he gave his blessing.

"Thank you, sir."

Jack touched Finn's arm to stop his escape. "Take care of her."

Finn turned and held out his hand. "With my life."

"I'm counting on it." Jack shook his hand and watched him walk away. He felt his mother slip her arm around his waist. "Do you think she'll be okay?"

Fionna laughed. "It's him I'd be worrying about."

Finn walked up the stairs toward the woman he loved. He thought back over the day's events and realized how many times he had caused her to cry. Bumbling idiot, he thought. He needed to make up for it. And by the time he reached her door, he had come up with a plan.

Brooks was sitting in the living room. Pajamas had replaced the bloody scrubs, but the worry and stress of the day was still etched on her face. Finn wasn't sure if she was even aware that he had walked in, and as he stood there watching her, he mentally changed his plans for the evening.

Walking back toward the bedroom, he hoped Cam would understand what he was about to do. He found her in the shower and had to fight the urge to undress and join her. God, she is beautiful, he thought. Sensations started surging and he did his best to refocus.

Cam was enjoying the warm water. Her attention was focused inward, reflecting on the day's events. Brooks was still worried about Jimmy and she had said nothing since they had walked in. *Hell, I'm worried*, Cam thought. She didn't think either of them had ever seen that side of Jimmy. Concerned she had placed a phone call to her nana, knowing that her father was tied up with Finn. Just thinking of that had her stomach in knots. But she had wanted to warn her father of what had happened with Jimmy. He was probably the only one on the planet who could get through to that stubborn-assed man.

She shut off the shower and opened the glass. The scream ripped from her before she even processed what was going on. She had not heard Finn come in and he scared the shit out of her, standing there holding a towel.

Brooks came barreling through the bathroom door. A wooden baseball bat in her hands. "What! What happened? Cam!" She stopped short seeing Finn standing there. "When did you get here?"

Finn's earlier plans were now sealed. "I came in about two minutes ago. You were on the couch, but I guess you didn't see me."

Rubbing a hand over his ear he pointed to Cam. "And she sure as hell didn't see me. Bloody hell, woman!"

Red faced, she snatched the towel he was holding. "You could have said something! Jesus Christ, I am going to have to get a bell for your goddamn neck!" Her hands were shaking as she tied the towel around her. "What do you expect when you scare the shit out of someone?"

Brooks backed out of the doorway. The two of them could work this out on their own. She tried to calm her heart as she made her way back to the living room.

Finn saw Brooks escaping from the corner of his eye. Chicken shit, he thought, while he stood there and listened as Cam finished her rant. "You knew I was coming up here. I'm sorry I startled you—"

"Startled me?! You think that was just startling me? You fucking scared the shit out of me!" She slapped at his arms as he wrapped them around her. Resting her wet head against his shoulder she allowed herself to finally calm down. She couldn't remember the last time someone had snuck up on her.

Finn ignored that her hair was soaking his jacket. This case was getting to all of them. "I'm sorry, babe. I really am. I thought you heard me."

She stood a moment longer in his arms, allowing herself the luxury of being taken care of and soothed. She pulled away and began to dry his jacket. "I'm sorry. I hope I didn't ruin it."

Finn brushed it off. "I don't care about the damn jacket. I care about you and that scared girl out in your living room." He took a deep breath and told her his plans. Hoping the finality of his tone didn't get her back up. "I need your keys so I can go get my stuff from the hotel. I am staying here, and so is she," he said, pointing toward the living room. "At least until Jimmy is home." He stood there waiting for the explosion of her temper. He knew he probably should have just asked, but the fact that he had walked past both women and neither knew he was there, firmed his mind on the fact that they were no longer staying alone.

Cam knew she should be pissed that he was telling her what was going to happen, but in reality she was relieved. After everything that had happened, she didn't want to be alone. Plus she be crazy to turn down the opportunity to have this man in her bed every night. "Okay."

"I don't care if you don't like it—" He stopped. "Okay?" He was fully expecting a fight. And it shocked him that she had so readily agreed. He placed his hands on her shoulders. "Okay."

She moved back into his arms and just basked in the security of them. She was never one to need a man or need one to protect her, but Finn was different, she realized. She wanted him there. Always.

Finn stood a moment longer, dumbfounded. He watched her walk to her closet to get her comfy clothes, as she called them. He followed her out, still unsure of the turn of events. "You're sure?" he asked again.

Cam smiled at his bewilderment. "Yes. I am sure. Besides I would be an idiot to turn down such an offer from a sexy man." She began to push some clothes aside on one of the racks. "Here, you can have this space." Then she walked over and grabbed her keys. Handing them to him, she began to laugh at the look on his face. "You better go before I change my mind."

Finn gave her a quick kiss and ran from the room. He heard her laugh follow him across the apartment and out the door.

Finn rushed through the packing up in his room. He caught a glance of himself in the mirror and paused to take a long look. His face had grown a beard in the past few days. He had dark circles under his eyes, but his eyes were clear and bright. His shirt was wrinkled from two days wear and his jacket had not yet dried from Cam's hair.

Thinking of her, his mind played back their short relationship. It still marveled him at the fierceness of his feelings for her. They had only known each other for a week, but it had felt comfortable. Right. Like it was fate. His chuckle echoed in the empty room. If only Cat could see me now, he thought. She had always been the dreamer. One day hoping for a love that would rock her all the way down to her core. A love that was fierce, yet gentle. Passionate, but still weather the simmer. A love that made you ache, but an ache that was comforting, welcoming. And it was then he realized, he had found that elusive kind of love. And he had found it with Cam.

He sat down on the bed and his heart broke a little for Cat. It seemed unfair that here he was, reveling in the very love that she had longed for. Had dreamt of.

He never thought he would be the one to find it. His parents had a lasting love, but he never thought that much about it. It wasn't in the cards for him, and he was good with that. He had a career he loved, friends to go to a pub with, and for a while he had Cat. But now, knowing what that love could bring, he couldn't live without it. He couldn't imagine living without Cam. And that brought up another dilemma. He thought of his family back home in Ireland. His sisters and nieces and nephews. His parents and grandparents. Could he trade his life there for one here with Cam? Shaking off the momentary soul searching, he finished throwing his crap in his bag. He glanced around the room and walked out.

Finn popped the latch on the lift gate and threw his bag in. A noise from his left had him spinning, his hand reaching for his weapon.

Officer Jonah Crabtree came slinking out of the shadows. He was dressed in all black. His weapon was clearly visible on his side, a method used to intimidate. He had been watching Finn since he left Cam's and had managed to control the fury at seeing him drive away in her car. He tailed him to this hotel and watched as he went inside. His anger reignited as he watched the fucker come back out with his bag and toss it in the trunk. His imagination ran wild at the thought of him and Cam together.

What the fuck does she see in him anyway? he thought angrily. Now here he was, standing face-to-face with the sonofabitch who was sleeping with his woman.

Finn dropped his hand and slammed the tail gate closed. "Bloody hell! Why are you here?" He had a bad feeling about this beat cop from the get-go, but he didn't think he would take it this far. He noticed the way he looked at Cam, with a feral hunger in his eyes. He tried to brush it off, saying it was just a one-sided infatuation, but looking at the fury on the young man's face, Finn now knew he had underestimated him. And the depth of his obsession with Cam.

Jonah balked at Finn's tone. *Who the fuck does he think he is?* Asking him that. It was his fucking city. He could be anywhere he damn well pleases. "Don't worry about why I am here. Why are you driving the detective's personal vehicle?"

Jonah paused and glanced around. "And without the owner present?" Moving one step closer, he baited him some more. "It appears to me that this vehicle is stolen."

Finn swallowed his anger. He wasn't going to let this fucker bait him. "I have the owner's consent, and you fucking know it. But, hey, call her if you like, she will validate my story. Or call it in. The vehicle is not reported as stolen. So you can't do dick."

Jonah smirked. "I will be the judge of that. It seems to me, you have the disadvantage here. Your badge and gun don't mean shit here, pretty boy. I am the law here. So I suggest you shove your attitude up your ass and shut your mouth." He smiled wide, thinking he had Finn cornered.

It was becoming harder and harder for Finn to hold his temper at bay. He saw through the kid's threats, but knew that he could and would ruin his next few hours as everything got sorted out. But he'd be damned if that shit was going to happen. So if the boy wanted to be all big and bad, well then he'd let him. "So, Officer, what can I do for you?"

Jonah ignored the sarcasm in, Finn's tone. The bastard thought he was better than him, just because he was fucking Cam. *Well*, he thought, *we will see who has the last laugh.* "Do you have proof that you are allowed to drive the Detective O'Brien's personal vehicle?"

"Other than the fact that she personally gave me the keys forty-five minutes ago?"

"How do I know that you are telling the truth?" Jonah took another step closer. "How do I know that Detective O'Brien is not tied up and gagged and you have not stolen her keys?"

Finn had enough. "Why don't you fucking call her? If you are so worried about her safety. Instead of standing here wasting my time."

Jonah bristled at Finn's anger; he wavered for just a moment. He changed his stance to a more aggressive one. Moving even closer, he stood face-to-face with him. "I am going to let you go with a warning. Watch your back, Danny boy."

It took all of Finn's control not to snap the finger pointed in his face.

Jonah continued, unaware of how dangerously close he was to snapping Finn's control. "She is too good for you. You and I both know it. I suggest that you stop fucking her and leave her the hell alone. It would be a shame if something were to happen while you are here." Jonah's eyes narrowed, challenging Finn. "It's bad enough you got your last girlfriend killed. I guess you were getting tired of sharing, huh? Did it piss you off that she had to go find real men to fuck because you weren't satisfying her? Is that why you sent her in there, knowing what would happen if she was caught?"

Finn had to clench his jaw and his fists. *He's just baiting me*, he thought. *Don't give in.* It is what he wants. Finn knew if he laid a hand on Jonah, he would be shipped back to Ireland. So Finn stared at him, hate and fury burning his eyes. "Fuck you."

Jonah stepped back and laughed. "Come on, pretty boy, what are you going to do? Oh, wait, that's right, you won't do shit." He stalked straight at Finn, stopping just mere inches from his face. "Leave Cam alone. She is not just another one of your toys that you can fuck and leave. She deserves a real man, someone who appreciates and understands her. You, on the other hand, are a fucking pussy. You couldn't protect her or love her the way she deserves. Just look at your goddamn track record. So here is your warning. Stay the fuck away from her. I am who she needs and who she wants. You are just a convenience and are expendable. Remember that, bitch. Like I said, it would be a shame if something happened to you while you were here."

Finn changed his tactic. He put an easy grin on his face and relaxed his stance. He knew that all Jonah wanted was for Finn to lose control, so he would do the opposite. But he promised himself one thing—before this was over he would personally break every bone in the little fuckers body, starting with his jaw.

He glanced back to the spot where Jonah had hidden. A dark-colored, four-door sedan was backed in to a corner spot. He had a full view of the parking garage. He noticed that the vehicle was identical to the police-issued detective's cars. So he could hide in plain sight, Finn thought. No one would question a police car sitting in the garage. And then Finn remembered something. He had seen the same type of car parked along Cam's street every night the past week.

Glancing back at Jonah's smirking face, Finn was filled with trepidation. He had chalked all of this up to a stubborn boy's crush on his boss. But now, seeing the car and then this whole scene, Finn realized this was more than that. Obsessed, Jonah was stalking Cam. That realization had Finn's easygoing smirk vanishing. He took a better look at Jonah. He was wearing head-to-toe black. He even had a black ball cap on his head. What appeared to be his service weapon was holstered to his side and a handcuff case was on his belt next to it. Jonah had black leather gloves on his hands and heavy-duty combat boots on his feet. This was more than a little dick-measuring contest. Finn knew if it had been later in the night, and less traffic, Jonah may have done something stupid. He also knew if Cam found out about this, it would shatter the small bit of control she still had left. This case had eaten away at her, and even if she didn't want to admit it, her resolve was barely hanging on. But there was one person who would hear about it, and together they would figure out what in the hell to do.

Finn decided that he had baited Jonah enough for one night. He left his last statement hanging in the air and turned to leave.

Jonah exploded. "Don't you fucking walk away from me you prick! I am not done with you." He grabbed Finn's arm and swung him around. "This is your last warning. Leave her alone or there will be hell to pay." He pushed Finn's arm back and strode away. *Who in the hell does that fucker think he is, turning his back to me?* Jonah growled as he stomped back to his car. He slid in the front seat and watched as the bastard drove away in Cam's SUV.

He put the car in drive and began to follow him, leaving enough distance so he wouldn't be made. Not that the idiot would notice him anyway. Besides he had been following the two of them all week and neither of them had noticed yet.

Hell, he had even been inside Cam's place. Touching her things, breathing in the scent of her. He had tested her bed, running his hands over her pillows and sheets. Imagining the feel of her under him, crying out for him to never stop, as he took her. He had thought about putting a camera in, but she was too smart. She might figure that out. So instead, he had pulled out some of her lingerie and laid it out on the bed. He tested the feel of it in his hands, on his face. Then he had taken a picture of it with his phone, so he could always see it and anticipate the next time, when he got to feel it. Only, the next time, it would be on her body.

The memory made him smile, and he pulled up the picture on his phone. He rubbed a finger over the screen, it wasn't the same as feeling the silk, but he had a great imagination.

Finn noticed the tail, but he had been looking for it. He picked up his phone and dialed Jimmy. Terrified for Cam's safety and knowing he couldn't deal with it on his own, Finn told him of Jonah's obsession and waited through the silence on Jimmy's end of the phone.

"Unfortunately," Jimmy finally began, "we have no solid proof that he is following you." Giving Finn no chance to reply, he continued quickly. "I know that he is following you now, but any mediocre judge or defense attorney could explain that away. What we need is solid proof. Something the bastard can't get out of." Raw fear was beginning to form a knot in Jimmy's stomach. There was enough shit going on. They didn't need this.

Finn slapped the steering wheel. He fucking hated that his hands were tied. "How do you propose we get this proof?" he asked angrily.

Jimmy took a deep breath and shook his head. "I guess we wait. We hope that he slips up and we can catch him. Look, it doesn't sit well with me either, but in order to put an end to this we have to be patient."

Finn asked the question that was on both of their minds. "What do we do with him in the mean time? Do we just play nice and leave him on the team or do we boot his ass out and lie to Cam and the others?" He already knew the answer, but if it came from Jimmy, Finn would have somewhere to vent his future frustrations.

"I guess we leave it how it is. But neither Cam nor Brooks is to be left alone."

"Do you think he would come after her, as well? He seems to only be focused on Cam."

Jimmy ran a hand through his hair. "If there is one thing everyone knows, it's if you want to get at Cam, grabbing or harming Brooks is the way and vice versa. It sickens me to say that, but it is the truth. So neither of them go anywhere alone."

Finn gripped the steering wheel; his knuckles glowed white. "Fine. But the minute he slips up, he is mine."

Jimmy understood. He would feel the same way if it was Brooks on the line. As it was he was struggling with the thought of using Cam as bait, but he knew that the only way to catch the bastard was to keep him close. "So tomorrow, you need to act like none of this happened. You are already weary of him, so that won't be a red flag to anyone. But I do believe that with enough rope, he will hang himself."

Finn hated it, but he knew the man was right. He hung up and punched the steering wheel. He glanced in the rear view mirror one last time, and it infuriated him that the bastard was still there, and there wasn't a damn thing he could do about it.

CHAPTER 17

Cam and Brooks waited in the living room for Finn. Cam's stomach was in knots as she told Brooks what was going on. "Do you think I am out of my mind?"

Brooks laughed for the first time in hours. God, she needed this. Just a little alone time with her best friend, a tall glass of wine, and dinner that was being delivered by a hot and sexy man. "No, I don't. Which is really odd. What I mean is, normally we both would be going crazy about this. Moving a man in this early in a relationship. I mean, is it a relationship? You can't say dating, because I don't think you two have even had one yet, have you?"

Cam feigned a hurt look. "What are you saying? That I am fast? Easy?" She laughed with Brooks. Some of the tension from earlier melted away. "I guess it is a relationship. No, we haven't gone on a date, but maybe that is where I have been screwing up. I am not meant to have a generic love life. Mine is abnormal. Hell, he asked my dad for permission to date me *after* we had sex. So I guess abnormal it is."

Her laughter faded into a lazy grin. And Brooks saw it written all over her face. "Oh my god! You are in love with him!" She leaned over and hugged her best friend.

Cam's blushed. A rarity with her, but she couldn't help it. She was right. She was stupid in love with him. "I know! It is way too fast but I can't help it. It just happened!"

She leaned back against the couch, a little drunk and feeling great. She listened as Brooks rambled on about life and love.

Finn walked in and saw the two of them sprawled over the couch. A bottle of wine sat on the coffee table and the soft glow of a buzz was on their faces. All thoughts of the earlier confrontation were pushed back when Cam turned around. She was glowing. Her face was lit up, full of laughter and wine. He green eyes sparkled in the light of the fire and there was an easygoing smile on her face. He thought she had never looked more beautiful. She was makeup free, in fleece pajama bottoms and a long-sleeved shirt. Thick socks covered her feet and her hair was left down to curl wild and free.

He remembered the bags in his hands and moved to the island that separated the dining room and kitchen. He was glad to see Brooks smiling and laughing. She, too, had changed into fleece bottoms and a long-sleeved shirt. Her face glowed from the wine. Which was good in his mind, she needed the color, after the day she had.

Cam stood and moved toward the wonderful smells coming from the carton Finn had just put down. "Oh, God that smells good. Please tell me that it is Chinese and my nose isn't playing tricks on me."

Finn laughed and walked around to get forks and plates. "I found the number on the speed dial in your car. Your car!" he said incredulously.

Cam just shrugged her shoulders. "Brooks and I live on pub food, pizza, and Chinese. What can I say?" She picked up the box of food and moved toward the living room. She placed it on the big leather ottoman that also served as a coffee table and started piling pillows on the floor.

Finn stood back and watched as she and Brooks did a kind of dance getting everything ready. It still boggled his mind that the two of them could do so much without having to speak a word. They worked and moved as one. He wondered if they even realized what they were doing. When it appeared that they were ready he moved to join them, carrying three beers and forks.

Brooks looked at the forks and laughed.

"What?" he asked.

"Only wimps eat Chinese with forks, just ask Cam." She laughed.

Cam's eyes narrowed at her and she snatched the fork Finn was holding out for her. "Not all of us are as awesome as you."

Brooks had an innocent grin on her face. "I know. And I am glad you have finally come to terms with my supreme awesomeness."

Finn watched the exchange and laughed. "I am completely in awe of your tremendous humility. It makes the nuns at my primary school look like complete egotistical maniacs."

"I am humble," she answered. Finn moved fast toward Cam.

Brooks jumped. "What?" she exclaimed, looking all around her.

"I realized I was too close." At her confused expression, he elaborated. "You know, too close for when God strikes you down for lying."

Brooks smacked his arm. "You're not funny. You scared the shit out of me."

"Then why are you laughing?"

Brooks rolled her eyes. "Ha-ha. You're lucky you're sexy and sleeping with my best friend. Otherwise I would have to humiliate you and whoop your ass in front of a pretty lady."

Cam laughed, finally the stress of the day completely gone. Looking over at Finn, she wondered how this all happened. He came here for help and found himself in the middle of a crazy group of people. But he fit. Clicked right into place, as if he'd been here all along. Which made her think of when he wouldn't be here. Try as she may, she couldn't help but fall for him. She was shocked at the well of emotion that choked her when she thought of him not being here. Going home to his family. She forced the thought from her mind, deciding to focus on the here and now.

Finn saw her staring. "What?" he asked. "Did I get the wrong thing? When I noticed the number on the speed dial, I called and asked if they knew what you liked. I guess they do since they called it the C & B special. So I just ordered two of them."

She shook her head. "No, this is fine. A piece of rice stuck in my throat," she lied and she quickly changed the subject. Pagoda An's is the best place in the city. And the C & B special was a weekly, sometimes more, meal for the two of them. House Fried Rice, Curry Chicken, Chicken and Broccoli, Beef Skewers, egg rolls, extra sauces, etc. The owners had been the same since Cam was a little girl. They had gone to school with the owners' daughters.

Stuffed to the gills, for the next two hours anyway, Cam dropped her fork in one of the empty cartons and fell backward in a huff. Groaning she rubbed her belly. "Why? Why do I always do that?" No matter how many times she suffered she didn't know when to stop.

Picking up the cartons, Brooks began to clean up. When Finn moved to help, she waved him back down. "No, sit. You bought so I'll clean. Anyway I need to move around so I don't roll down the stairs when I leave."

Finn stood anyway to help. "You don't have to leave. At least not because I am here. Why don't you stay?"

Brooks's heart warmed. He would definitely be good for Cam. If he decided to stay, that is. Because she knew Cam would never leave. Not for anything or anyone. "It's okay. My dad lives two houses down. My mom has already made my bed and I think Dad wants me to see that he is okay."

"And vice versa," Finn added, following her to the kitchen.

She smiled. Yeah, he is definitely good for her friend. "You're a good guy, Finn. I hope you know that." Pausing to see if Cam was near, she lowered her voice and continued. "The last guy she let get close crushed her and left her on the floor. He walked out because of who she is. He couldn't deal." She paused again. "If you do that to her, there will be no place on this earth that you can hide. I will hunt you down and flay you alive. Got me?"

Finn was a little shocked. He knew that she was fiercely loyal to Cam, but the seriousness of her threat, and tone, had him believing that she could and would make do on her promise. "Aye."

She smiled and nodded. "Good." She moved to go around him when he caught her arm.

She looked down at his hand and then back up to him. Getting the hint, he dropped his hand. "Now, my turn. She is never to be left alone. If I am not here, you stay, or she goes with you." Seeing the question in her eyes, he answered as well as he could in Cam's kitchen. "When you get to your dad's, which I will be walking you to, he will fill you in. You are not to fill Cam in. I will handle that. It won't be today or tomorrow. But I will. She doesn't need the added stress or distraction. Please put on your best poker face, because she does not know."

"Okay." She started back for the sink and he followed.

"The same goes for you. I don't want you alone either. Not until all of this is over." She saw the seriousness and finality in his eyes and nodded. If Cam trusted him, so did she.

"One more thing, does she like dogs?" Her surprise and laughter answered his question.

When he returned from walking Brooks down the stairs, Jimmy had met them at the front door, he found Cam dozing on the couch. He left her there for the moment and walked around, securing the doors and windows.

He stood over her, watching her sleep. The fatigue and stress, which seemed to live on her face the past few days, had melted away, leaving her soft and bare. His eyes traced every inch of her face. Her simple beauty took his breath away. Her long lashes rested against her cheeks. She had removed the little make-up that she wore during the day, not that she needed it. Her skin, whose color hovered between fair and a light rose-gold, was flawless, just a scatter of light freckles across her nose and cheeks. Her lashes were long and a dark auburn; they framed emerald green eyes under lightly arched eyebrows. She had a slender nose, slightly turned down at the end, almost pointing to her full lips below. She had a dark freckle on her bottom lip. He remembered the previous night and the soft nip he placed on that spot and another on the dark freckle right below on her chin.

Finn stood. He was struggling with his need to make love to her again. He probably should let her sleep. She was so exhausted, sleep was no longer peaceful. Nightmares plagued her, the murders just playing on repeat. And he thought with a pang of guilt, she was emotionally drained from their fight, or whatever it was, earlier this morning. He had planned on a romantic night tonight. A date. But the events of the afternoon curtailed those plans.

He thought back to the confrontation at the hotel and he crossed to the window to look for Jonah. He turned the lamp off, so his movement would be hidden. Pulling lightly on the blinds he peered out, searching the streets for any sign. Seeing nothing, he let go of the blinds and turned back to Cam. He was halfway around, when he squealed like a little girl.

"Jesus Christ, Cam!" He placed a hand over his heart.

Cam was bent over laughing. She had woken up when he switched off the lamp, and curiosity got the better of her. The look on his face was priceless. She was laughing hysterically and suddenly had to take off for the bathroom. "Holy shit!" she yelled running. She'd be damned if she was going to pee her pants.

It was Finn's turn to laugh. "Did you just pee your pants?" he yelled after her.

"Shut up, you ass!" She made it! She should be embarrassed but she felt they were now probably even.

He stood outside the door, taunting her some more. "Do you need another diaper—I mean panties?"

Flushing the toilet, she yanked open the door. "Ha-ha. I made it." His smile made her heart flutter. God, what was wrong with her. Here he was picking on her and just one smile made desire burn through her. Sticking her tongue out, she squirmed past him.

"What were you looking at?" she asked over her shoulder. She headed right for the fridge to indulge in a late-night soda. Her mouth was dry and she was in the beginnings of a headache. She took a long gulp and tried to pop her neck, hoping to loosen the tension.

Finn walked up behind her and began to knead her shoulders. He smiled at the slow moan that escaped her lips. "Just looking," he answered. He hated the white lie, but she didn't need any added stress. "The street life is different here than outside my flat in Dublin."

Sensing he was omitting the real truth, she played along. He would tell her when he was ready. "How so?"

He shrugged his shoulders. "Hard to explain. It's just different." He chided himself on his lack of imagination and hoped for a change in subject.

Cam took another swallow and turned to face him. God, he was beautiful, she thought. *How did I get so lucky?* She watched his eyes, a stormy blue now. And it looked like the storm was ready to blow.

He took the can from her and set it on the counter. His hands came up and framed her face. "You are so beautiful. So strong, yet so soft."

His lips came to within a breath of hers and paused. She yearned for him to close the gap. Desire roared through her, burning and singing where ever it touched. She closed her hands around his wrists, her eyes pleading for him to take. To quench the burn and bring it back. Stronger. Hotter. Faster. "Finn—" she started.

He placed his lips to hers to quiet her plea. And with great pain he pulled back a hair. Her fingers dug into his skin. Her eyes went a deep, dark green. He could see the want on her face; his was consuming him.

"Cam," he whispered. He didn't know if he should say what his heart was feeling. Did he want to believe it himself? He had never felt these feelings that were raging through him. Warring with his brain.

Her lips parted and a silent "please" breathed out. And it all clicked into place. He had told her it was different here. Different from his place in Dublin. And she was the difference. Because here was home. He had finally found his home.

She watched the emotions swirl in his eyes. A storm violently battled between his heart and his mind. She had learned his face so well this past week. She knew it better than her own. She struggled to keep the plea from her eyes. But she was losing that battle. She knew the love she felt was written all over her. Her need for him was winning over her pride. Her will. She swore she would never need or want a man so much. They always left. Always walked away. But with Finn, she knew if he walked away, he would take her heart with him. She had no claim to it anymore.

He watched the emotions play over her face. Her eyes. And he broke. He couldn't fight it anymore. "Cam," he began. His lips needed hers. He closed the gap, his need and love poured out.

"A'Ghra." *My love,* he whispered against her lips.

Her brain didn't want to believe it, protecting her heart. She pulled back and looked in his eyes. She poured every emotion into them. She wouldn't, couldn't say it. Please, her eyes begged, please say it.

He saw her need fighting against the fear. He knew what her heart had suffered. He knew her fears, just like he knew his own. And his melted away as a tear rolled down her cheek.

"Oh, Cam, love. Please, A'Ghra. Please don't." He brushed the tear with his thumb, and all his walls crumbled. "I love you. I don't know what happened. Or why so fast. But seeing you that first day, you took my breath away. My heart stopped and then started with your smile." He turned her so her back was to the counter. He needed her to stay and listen. He faltered as more tears streamed down her face.

No man had ever said those words to her and absolutely meant them. Her heart stuttered. Her mind still wanted to shut down, told her to ignore his lies. But his next words pushed aside all doubts and her heart took over.

"I said this place is different than Dublin. And it is. Because here, with you, I am home. There it wasn't. And now that I have found you, nowhere will ever be home without you. I need you, Cam. I need you like I need air to breathe."

He lifted her chin and made her look in his eyes. When the tears started, her instinct was to look down and hide her face. But she needed to look at him to hear the rest. Because it was a monumental thing for him to say, and dammit, he thought, she was going to be looking at him when he said it.

"Cam, please say you'll take me. We don't have to do anything rush right now. But please say you will have me for as long as you want me. I can't wake another day without you by my side. I need you. I want you. I love you."

Cam had to take a steadying breath. He had just ripped the rug out from under her, but to her shock, she wasn't falling. He was there, holding her and giving her everything she had ever wanted. Everything she didn't know she needed. She knew what he meant with his words. He loved her and wanted her. All of her. For now, they would see where that took them. And when she met his eyes, she realized he was home for her. She never realized she was lost until now. So she would see where this revelation went.

"I will. I love you, and I thought I knew what that meant before. But I realize I was wrong. We will take this road, and see where it leads us. I love you, Finn. All of you. Are you sure you can take all of me?" she asked. Every fiber of her being she was pleading for him to say yes.

He knew what her statement meant. All of her meant all of those who came with her. The dead. The living. He stepped back and scooped her up. Her breath caught, and the sound made him smile. So Camille O'Brien wanted romance after all.

He bent down and kissed her lips. He intended to make sweet love to her all night. But when he set her down on the bed, their lips met again and the fire exploded. Passion and need ignited the slow ember of their last kiss. Her arms wrapped tight around him, his closing around her.

Her hands moved up and her fingers tangled and fisted in his hair. Her body pressed against him. She was kneeling on the bed and he was still standing. Reaching down she yanked his shirt up and over his head. Her short nails scraping his skin.

Each scrape and squeeze of her hands, made his need for her grow. Her body rubbed against him and he groaned in pleasure. He returned the favor and her shirt went sailing across the room. He hissedwhenher hands moved to his belt, with one pull she had it gone.

She cried out as his lips closed over her breast. Her hands fisted in his hair again, pulling him further into her. The fire in her couldn't be controlled, it flashed and burned. Her need for him consumed her.

She fumbled with his jeans, desperate to have all of him, but he had other plans. In one move she was flat on her back and her pants were gone. She watched his eyes roam her body, need and raw desire plain on his face. It made her feel undeniably sexy. The power of it roared through her. She crawled back to her knees and beckoned him with the crook of a finger.

Bloody hell! he thought. The woman was amazing. He rid himself of his jeans, but he finally managed to be free of them, and he moved to her. His breath caught when she met him at the edge of the bed and he ended up flat on his back, her long legs straddling him.

The feel of him beneath her ignited her desire and she was desperate for control. She wanted to torture him, slowly. She laid over him and traced his jaw with her tongue, his low moan urged her on, and she began to move over him.

He struggled to control himself, but all coherent thoughts evaporated as he felt her hair begin a slow journey down his body.

She looked back up and watched his eyes as her mouth closed over him. Power coursed through her when he could no longer control the moans. Blinded by power, she moved back up his body, licking and nipping here and there, his moans and pleas making her drunk with power.

Unable to control it any longer, he flipped her under him and pressed himself to her. Her cry of pleasure nearly broke his control, but he held on. It was his turn to torture and smile when her breath quickened as his mouth began its journey down her body.

He nibbled on her earlobe and moved down her throat. She bucked, pressing against him and he bit back a moan. Her hands began to wildly roam his body. She was killing him. The need she brought out in him swamped him, leaving him senseless. Pinning her arms above her head, he tried to clear his head and regain control.

She bucked against him again, desperately wanting more.

His mouth began to journey again. Picking up around her collar bone and moving slowly, achingly slow, down her body. She was losing control. Sensations whipped through her body, blinding her, numbing her to everything but the feel of his mouth.

She arched and cried out as his mouth closed over her. The orgasm ripped through her fast, and hot, shattering what was left of her control. "Please," she begged. "Finn, please. I need you. I-I ne-need you n-now!"

Her desperate pleas broke him. He wanted to go slow, but he came into her fast and hard. When she cried out, it drove him faster, harder. The need for her burning in his veins.

She matched him. Thrust for thrust. Her legs wrapped around him, pinning him to her. When, finally, she crested again, he fell with her.

He could hear nothing but his heart rapidly beating in his chest. *Christ Almighty,* he thought. *What was that?* He was still on top of her, her legs locked tight around him. When he tried to move to get his weight off of her, she only tightened, something between a purr and a moan escaping her lips.

"Hmm," she purred. "Don't move. Not yet."

He smiled and kissed her flushed face, then her lips. He found the fire had simmered and tenderness had replaced it. Her hands moved up his back and framed his face. He was taken aback by the gesture. He propped up on his elbow and watched her eyes slowly open.

"Why'd you stop?" she asked sleepily. Her hands brushing his beautiful face.

He brought her left hand to his lips and kissed the pulse in her wrist, then her palm. He felt her heart skip a beat and smiled as her lips moved into a lazy grin. "Cam."

"Hmmm," she hummed.

He laughed. He leaned in and kissed her nose. "Cam, we have to move. I am crushing you." When he moved she tightened her hold. "Seriously!" He chuckled as he reached back and unhooked one of her legs. Grateful, because he was getting a cramp in his butt.

She laughed as he stood rubbing the spot.

He narrowed his eyes. "Haha. Laugh all you want."

"Not man enough to deal with a little twinge?"

He flipped her over and pinched her ass. "What? Not woman enough to deal with a little twinge?" He mocked as she yelped and rubbed her left ass cheek.

"Ass," she said smiling. Standing up she moved to him, placing her hands on either side of his face, and gently kissed him. She smiled against his lips when he wrapped her up tight and dipped her back.

He felt like a fool at the hitch it caused his heart. No woman had ever made him feel the way she did. It still boggled his mind when the intensity of what he felt for her washed over him.

She was laughing by the time he let her go. "Where are you going?" he asked as she headed down the hall—completely naked.

She paused and glanced seductively over her shoulder. "I am wanting something sweet. I'm thinking strawberries, chocolate sauce, and whip cream."

Her intentions became clear and he cleared his throat. "Are you sharing?" He was grateful that his voice didn't squeak.

* * * *

As they lay sleeping, tucked away under the down comforter, wrapped up in one another, he sat and watched. He saw the movement of the front blinds earlier, and the memory made him snort a laugh. Apparently the fucker thought he was an amateur. What did he expect? To see him sitting in plain sight in his car?

He looked around as he sat in one of his many hidey holes. He had been in an alley, tucked back in a niche when he had seen the Irishman look out the front window. Now he sat in another of his hideouts, watching the window to her bedroom.

The O'Brien's property backed to the harbor. When the front lights remained turned off, he had moved from the alley through a neighbor's yard and had made his way to the back of the building. He had sat and watched the silhouettes of Cam and Finn in the window. He saw how he had touched her and kissed her. They had "disappeared" from his view for a while and images flooded his mind of the things they were doing.

From his spot on the water, in a "borrowed" small boat, he sat and seethed. He knew he was fucking her. Touching her. Making her cry out. The rage burned hot through him, igniting a fury that consumed and twisted through him.

In his twisted mind, he saw himself up there, instead of the Irish dick. He was the one making her cry out. She was screaming his name and begging him for more.

He shook his head when he heard the loud blare of a boat's fog horn. He had to stay focused. He thought back to the confrontation he had earlier. Finn, or Irish Dick, as he thought of him now, had acted like he wasn't scared. But Jonah knew the truth. He knew that Finn was shaking in his boots when he watched him walk out of the shadows. Yeah, Jonah thought, the dick knew who was in charge. He knew who's city it was. Jonah's mind played back a twisted version of the events—one he truly believed had happened. He looked back up at the darkened window and his hands shook with rage. It should be him up there. He should have been the one to make her scream. His name should be the one on her lips. He should be the one sleeping beside her. Protecting her. Having her.

Camille O'Brien—no, he thought smiling, Camille Crabtree. Yeah. That's it. His hand went to his right hip. When his fingers closed over his weapon, a strange calm washed through him. He'd show that motherfucker. Show him what is going to happen if he touches his woman again. His property. Taking one last look, he turned to head back to shore.

Yeah, he thought. He'd show him. And then he'd show her.

CHAPTER 18

The ringing phone blasted through the room, ripping Cam from a peaceful sleep. She fought to free herself from the tangle of sheets and limbs and kneed Finn in the groin in the process. He moaned and squeaked as she fumbled for the phone.

"I'm so sorry!" she said as she answered the phone.

"Excuse me?" The nasal voice of the dispatcher screeched through the ear piece.

"What? Oh nothing. O'Brien," she finally said. She turned to look at the time. Her stomach dropped when she read the clock. Zero-four-eleven. Dread settled in her belly.

She listened as the dispatcher rattled off an address and then added, "Detective Aaron and the ME have already been notified."

"Ten-four, show myself and Detective McDougal en route," She responded.

She slapped the phone down and turned to Finn, who was curled in the fetal position. "Babe? Are you okay?" She assumed the groaning and Gaelic curses were meant as a no.

"Do you need ice?" She laughed at his horrified expression and rolled out of bed.

Finn finally found the gumption to sit up hissing and cursing the whole time. "Jesus, Mary, and Joseph. Are your legs made of iron, woman?" His accent thickened dramatically.

Luckily Cam was used to a thick Irish accent, especially a pissed off one. "I'm really sorry. The goddamn phone scared the shit out of me!"

Finn sat and watched her get ready. By the time he had the courage to stand up, she had already put on a bra and undies, literally hopped into her pants and was now tugging on boots, all the while her toothbrush was hanging out of her mouth.

When in the hell did she go in there? he thought, glancing toward the bathroom. Amazed at her speed and ability to multitask in a way the male species would never understand. He realized that he had to put aside his pain and get ready. He limped over to the closet to find clothes and barely registered the jeans being hurled at his face.

He turned in time to catch them before they hit his face. "Oops, I thought you heard me." She scrunched her nose, when she saw him wince and groan as he gingerly put them on.

He heard her open drawers and slam them shut. Apparently she was going to dress him, he thought. And when he took a painful step toward the closet, he was grateful. She really nailed him.

"Please," he begged. "Please don't throw my shoes at me. You've hurt me enough."

His eyes narrowed as she moved across the room to him. She rose on her toes and planted a kiss on his nose. Looking at him innocently she asked, "Do you want me to kiss your boo-boo and make it feel better?"

She yelped when he knocked her backward onto the bed. "Hey!"

"Kiss that," he hissed, limping to the bathroom and to brush his teeth.

He caught the scent of coffee on his way out and nearly cried with pleasure. He accepted the travel mug she offered and kissed her.

"Am I forgiven?"

He snatched the keys before she could and answered, "Now you are." And she followed him out the door.

Finn felt his eyes before he saw him. Officer Jonah Crabtree was manning the police tape as they drove up. It was hard to miss them in Cam's Range Rover. Her duty car was still in the shop.

Cam was oblivious to the tension boiling between the two men. And to the growing obsession Jonah had for her. She returned his smile as they approached the tape. "Good morning, Officer. Were you first on scene?"

Jonah couldn't hide his glee her warm welcome brought. He was momentarily sidetracked, but he quickly recovered. He dropped the tape before Finn could duck under. After a nasty glare, Jonah gave his full attention to Cam. "No, Detective O'Brien. I was off duty when the call came in from dispatch."

Cam nodded. "Okay. Detective McDougal and I need to meet up with Detective Aaron and the ME. Could you round up the first on scene?"

Jonah ignored her smooth dismissal. "I can fill you in. I interviewed both officers when I arrived." He noticed Cam's posture harden. "No disrespect. I wanted to make sure someone got it while it was fresh and so I could see if there was any new questions to ask any of the witnesses."

Cam rolled her shoulders. She understood the eagerness in the rookie's actions. The need to please superiors, but there was a reason detectives interviewed the first on scene. "I understand your eagerness with this case, but you need to remember a few protocols. Detectives need to interview the first on scene. We are trained to look for and pull out certain details others might overlook. And it helps keep the crime scene in order."

Jonah bristled and his face reddened. He knew the damn protocols, but should he be treated as if he were some damn rookie? Hadn't they requested for *him* to join the team? Which meant they needed him? Wasn't he in charge of interviewing witnesses? He was the one who could get the fuckers to talk, could they? He thought bitterly. He struggled to regain his focus.

He saw the slight upturn of the Dick's mouth and he had to dig his nails into his palms to keep him focused. He wanted nothing more than to rip his fucking face off. Stupid bastard. Jonah also didn't miss the fact that he got out of the driver's side of the car. He looked back at Cam. So if I fuck her, I get to play with her toys too. That lifted his spirits some.

After a quick internal war, Jonah nodded to Cam. "Yes, ma'am. I will remember that from now on."

Cam saw a flash of red and her attention was split. "Since you have the run down, why don't you fill us in as we walk?"

Finn recognized the look on her face. She saw something. He glanced over and didn't see anything, so he knew it was one of the girls.

Jonah was oblivious to her divided attention. Her request for him to personally fill her in settled his earlier anger. She knew that he was the best, he thought. She needed him. She just didn't know how much. His twisted mind kept spinning out of control.

They were in another alley, off Boston St., near Canton Waterfront Park. Close to the water again, she thought. But she was starting to really believe that these murders had nothing to do with the Flannery clan. Not directly. Some of the girls worked for them, and she had those other bodies tied to them, but the prostitute murders? She didn't think so. As they reached the body, she was certain, the Flannery clan had nothing to do with these murders.

People milled around. Standing on their steps, talking and gossiping about the redheaded, young prostitute lying dead in the alley. Cam ignored all the buzz and chatter and focused on the girl who was huddled in the corner shaking. She hadn't left, Cam thought incredulously. She stayed with her body. Cam searched and searched and finally saw the flash of red again.

Nina came and stood by Cam and followed her gaze to the scared girl in the corner. "She stayed?" she asked, bewildered. "Who the hell would stay and look at themselves dead on the street?"

Cam spoke with her eyes. Looking around at the people at the scene.

Nina's light bulb went off. "Oh, yeah. That's right, no one knows you're weird." She ignored Cam's roll of the eyes, but saw her next gesture. "Whoa! Wait, wait, wait. I didn't sign up for this shit. You go and talk to her."

Cam was ready to strangle her. Which gave her pause. Could you strangle a ghost? she asked herself. And if you could, would it be illegal?

Shaking her head, she got back to the issue at hand. She took a few steps forward, away from the group and spoke almost silently. "Dammit, Nina! Go and help her. I can't right now." She tried her best to ignore the teenage attitude. "Look. You know how she feels—I don't. Plus, think of it as penance."

"For what?"

"For being a brat! A smartass! And a royal pain in the ass. It appears that even death can't temper your freaking mouth! Shall I go on? " Cam turned on her heel and walked back to deal with the girl's body.

Brooks glanced up and saw her friend's face. She knew immediately what was going on, and by the exasperated expression, she guessed Nina was here too. It was actually fascinating, in a way. Cam had never had a spirit stay around this long. Brooks wondered what that meant, for Nina and Cam. Catching a glimpse of Finn's face, she was beginning to wonder if she was going to enjoy this show by herself.

Cam ignored the smirk on Brooks's face. She was used to that. What made her stumble was the amused look on Finn's face. "What?" she squeaked.

His face scrunched and he put a finger to his broken eardrum. "Jesus, Mary, and Joseph, woman. Are you trying to blow my ear out?" He continued quickly when her eyes narrowed. "Is everything all right, deary? You know, with that corner. Of that building, over there," he said, pointing toward Nina and the new girl.

She rolled her eyes. She knew he was baiting her because it was just the three of them there. Jimmy had a small group of detectives and officers pulled off and working on witness statements. So they were safe.

"Smartass." She smiled at him. It could be annoying, she thought, how easily he could bring a smile to her face. "Nina decided to show up this morning."

"Oh, that must have been the reason for you squeezing your hands together like you were wanting to choke someone." Finn chuckled as she stomped behind him to kneel next to the poor girl lying on the ground.

Never one to know when to shut up, as his sisters were always telling him, he knelt down beside her. "Does she not play nice with others, deary? 'Cause you know I know a great girl who plays nice and—" *Huummmff*! He went down on all fours. The punch to the gut had taken him by surprise. His brain registered a small amount of surprise. Not that he should be, he thought.

Taking a deep, painful breath, he slowly stood back up. He narrowed his eyes on her and began to move for her. He stopped when Jimmy started over. But he was going to remember that one. He owed her a big fat one.

Jimmy observed the whole exchange. He figured he should head back over before they had a knock-down-drag-out between the two of them, and he didn't think anyone would want to see that, he sure as hell didn't because it probably wouldn't end G-Rated. Jimmy went and stood near Cam and skillfully slapped the back of her head.

"Hey! What the hell was that for?" Jimmy laughed at her pathetic attempt at the puppy dog eyes and tears.

Finn couldn't help it and began to laugh.

"What's so funny?" she hissed.

Like a smart man, this time he said nothing. Just held up his hands, a sign of innocence and a plea for peace. He didn't think his abs could take another punch. But the look in Cam's eyes had him thinking a couch was definitely in his future.

Jimmy shook his head and muttered, "Sweet Jesus." Before turning to his daughter. "You have anything yet?"

Brooks wiped the smirk off her face. She had seen that look on her dad's face too many times. This time she was just grateful it wasn't because of her. "Female. Late teens, maybe twenty. Red hair. Blue eyes. Possibly a prostitute." She caught Cam's nod and amended her notes. "OK, definitely a prostitute. He beat the shit out of her." She paused and brushed the red hair away from her broken face. "He messed up this time. Went too far." She stood up and pulled off her gloves. "I'll know more when I get her on the table, but I would put money on your guy. He's escalating. Or he messed up bad."

Cam thought about what Brooks said. Looking at the broken and bruised body, pity filled her heart. She glanced over toward Nina. She was trying her best to calm the frightened girl. Cam was a little shocked. This was the first time she had seen this side of Nina, a softer, less self-absorbed side. Her killer didn't change his MO, his method of operation. No he was too careful for that, he planned too well.

Her mind drifted back to the nightmare she had the night before Nina showed up. Her system still jolted when she remembered his eyes. Something about them struck a primal fear in her, but it wasn't just that. Something else about them caused the fear, almost a recognition. But she couldn't be sure that she was the one recognizing them or if it was whomever she was in the dream. But the pale blue ice that stared down on her was dead-cold. The icy fingers of fear slowly crept up her neck. She could feel herself falling into sheer panic. She jumped a little when she felt Finn's arm on her shoulders, but that warm contact shattered the pale ice that bore down on her.

"He is losing control. He's not messing up. He didn't change. He can't control it." She didn't realize she had spoken aloud until Jimmy agreed.

"Then we need to find him. And fast." He stopped Brooks as she was raising the gurney with the girl's body. "Let us know immediately when you are ready."

"Of course." Brooks walked beside the body on the way to the van. She nodded her thanks to Jonah as he held the tape for her and noticed he wasn't even looking at her. Not that she was particularly vain, but hell, she wasn't horrible to look at. That's when she saw it—the crazy. It was saturating his eyes, and it was directed toward the group she just left, her friends, her family.

He sensed her eyes on him. He forced his rage down and turned. He saw the worry, laced with fear in her eyes. *Stupid bitch*, he thought. *She should know her place and do her job. Who the fuck does she think she is?*

But he shoved it down and smiled. "Do you need help?"

Brooks wiped all emotion from her face. She thought she saw rage following the crazy, but maybe she was just overanalyzing everything. She hadn't had a good night's sleep since Nina was found. Hell, none of them had. That had to be it. Shaking it off, she smiled at Jonah. "No thanks. Bud here is going to be doing all of the heavy lifting." Her assistant waved a hand toward the officer.

Jonah smiled back. "Have a good morning, ma'am." He dropped the tape and moved back to join the group.

Something bugged Brooks about the officer. She had noticed the attention and looks he had been giving Cam. Something about it wasn't right, but maybe she was just stirred up with this serial killer on the loose.

Jonah forgot all about the nosey ME as he walked back toward Cam. He smiled when she looked up at him and everyone dropped from his radar, but her. He swore she could stop his heart with one look. He remembered their first meeting and how much she'd pissed him off. He was ready to punch her, which had startled him because he had never had such strong emotions toward a woman. Sure, some had pissed him off, and maybe he had smacked one or two, but that was more like swatting at an irritating fly.

But it was full rage that morning, and it only grew as his dick-head partner ragged on him. He had to fight everything in him, so he wouldn't break the fuckers jaw.

Later that night, he thought about those feelings and he took all that energy to the gym. The power that came from him during that session shocked him. He remembered the feel of his knuckles busting on the punching bag. When his mind cleared he was almost horrified at the damage he had done. The side of the bag was smeared with his blood, his knuckles shredded. But another feeling began to sneak in—arousal. The feeling rocked him to the core and the face in his mind was Cam's. Every night he went back and every night it was the same. Bloodied knuckles, arousal, and Cam's face. Now, his knuckles hardly bled, but the arousal was uncontrollable, like a cancer feeding on his desire for her. He tried to release it with other women but none of them worked. He even paid for sex so he could get away with more. The feel of his fists hitting their flesh finally released an orgasm so intense he thought his head would explode. But the experience wasn't completely satisfying. He made sure the whore wouldn't call the police. Hell, he was the police, and she knew it. He made sure she did.

His memories broke at the sound of her voice. "I'm sorry. I didn't hear you." He mentally chastised himself. He almost blew it. He needed to stay focused if he wanted to stay near her.

Cam's forehead creased. "Are you okay, Officer?" He nodded so she continued. "I know all of us are dragging ass, but we need to be at our best to catch this bastard."

Jimmy interrupted. "Look we need to meet back at the conference room in one hour. If you need coffee or anything, get it done.

This is the last girl we are picking up, so get you heads on straight and get your ass to the station." He looked around the group, frustrated he lost it. "What the fuck are you doing standing here looking at me? Now!"

He watched as they scattered like roaches. He felt Cam's hand on his shoulder and had to physically stop himself from shoving it off. God, he swore, he just needed to fucking breathe. Why won't they just let him breathe? he pleaded.

"Jimmy?" She waited until he turned. She knew better than to push him now. "Give me your phone." She held her hand out. Instead of him making the call to every person on the team, she took his phone and sent a mass text. "There, the team is on their way. Why don't you ride back with us?" Not waiting for answer, she pulled an officer to the side and gave him instructions regarding Jimmy's car. She paused and rattled off more instructions to the crime scene techs and every other person under his command.

Finn stood back and waited with Jimmy. He knew the man was raging inside. He took responsibility for every girl they found dead or alive. Finn knew that feeling and was feeling it now. He still questioned why he couldn't catch the bastard before he jumped the pond, but he knew those questions were futile. They would do nothing but infuriate him and distract him.

He decided then and there, all of them had blamed themselves enough. Now it was time to start directing that into finding the sonofabitch who was doing this. He draped an arm around Jimmy's shoulders and began to guide the man toward the car. The ease of this made him realize not only was Jimmy mad, he was beaten. And it didn't do any cop any good, to work beaten. As he started the car, Finn made an executive decision, and he steered the car toward it.

CHAPTER 19

"Why are we here?" They had pulled up in front of O'Brien's Pub. Cam was confused; they were supposed to be heading toward the station. She looked back and Jimmy was staring off.

Finn got out and opened Jimmy's door. The noise seemed to wake him up and he looked at the pub and then back at Finn. "Does this look like the station to you, son?"

He ignored both of them and walked into the pub. Jack, of course, was already in. He and Fionna were both seated at the bar, drinking coffee and having breakfast.

"Well, morning to you all!" Jack's cheery voice rang out. Fionna moved to get three more plates and mugs for coffee. Cam walked around to help her, hoping Finn would explain himself soon.

"Morning, Jack." Finn sat down at the high top table behind the stools where Jack and Fionna were. "Is there any way we could bother you to get the file that we left in your safe?"

"Of course." His voice remained the same tone, but his eyes betrayed his worry. They hadn't left his friend's face and concern was beginning to eke in. "Jimmy? Would you mind helping me?"

Jimmy followed without a word.

Jack's office was up a small flight of stairs nest to the bar. Jack walked to his safe and began to turn the knob. His hand jerked when he heard the choked sob behind him. He turned to find his childhood friend, his brother, standing with his hands covering his face. Without a second thought, Jack moved around and took his brother in his arms and steered him to the sofa. Jack sat in front of him, perching on the coffee table. He knew his friend enough to let him work it out for a moment first. Just like he knew to get up and grab a sniffer and pour a generous Irish whiskey. He moved back and placed the sniffer in Jimmy's hands. And then he sat and waited.

He tried to think of the last time he had seen his friend this eaten up over a case. It had been a long time. He knew enough about a cop's mind to know that they had to train themselves to turn off the emotional part of their brains and work through the case. If they let emotions rule, there would be no more cops left to solve the unspeakable crimes of humanity. He knew they couldn't turn the emotions completely off, and he worried about the effect this had on his daughter and his friend. And seeing Jimmy like this, the worrying was justified in his mind.

Jimmy swallowed the whiskey in one gulp and focused on the slow burn in his gut. He couldn't bring himself to look at Jack yet. He knew that the worry would be there and he didn't know if he could handle it yet. He felt shame for losing it like this. The face of the young girl came flooding back. He blamed himself for her death. He should have caught the sonofabitch by now—

"Enough!" Jack's sharp bark, cut through his self-loathing and pity.

Jack shook his head. He saw the moment the shame and loathing came over his childhood friend. He knew Jimmy as well as he knew himself. The time for self-pity was done. "Suck it up, Danny boy."

Jimmy's lip curled slightly. He knew what Jack was doing. He hated that nickname. And Jack only used it to piss Jimmy off. He always had and always would. He finally glanced up at his friend. He saw the worry and he saw the anger. And he knew he had caused both.

"Thanks, Jack."

Jack jerked to his feet and began to pace. He shoved his hands in his pockets and glared at Jimmy. "What the hell is wrong with you? Coming in here and scaring an old man like that." He reached over and jerked the sniffer out of Jimmy's hand and marched to the whiskey. He poured a generous amount and knocked it back.

Jimmy saw the shake in his friend's hands as he set the sniffer back down. He got up and moved to Jack. He planted himself in his way to make the stubborn bastard stop. "Jesus Jack-"

"Jesus Jack? Jesus Jack! You have no right to 'Jesus Jack' me!" He started. "Bloody bastard. You came in here," he said, pointing. "You came in here and started losing it and you say 'Jesus Jack!' to me because I am pacing. Mind you I am pacing in my own damn place!"

Finn pushed back his stool when he heard the raised voices. Cam placed a hand on his arm and shook her head. "Leave them be. You were right. He needed my dad. Now let my dad take care of him."

Finn wasn't sure how this was helping but he decided to sit down and shut up.

Back in the office, Jimmy watched his friend go from pink to red. "Well if, you don't calm down you bloody bastard you are going to have a damn heart attack. Is that what you want, you crazy old coot!"

Jack stopped his pacing and stared at his friend. "Did you just call me a crazy old coot?"

Jimmy couldn't stop himself. He began to laugh crazily. Jack joined a minute later and that was how Fionna found them. Two crazy men chuckling in the middle of the office.

The clicking of heels filled the hall and then the doorway. Both men paused long enough to turn and face Jack's mother. "If you two asses are done, I have breakfast on the table for you." She stood a moment more, mostly to satisfy the need to be sure her boys were OK, before she turned around and left.

Jack placed a hand on his friend's shoulder and looked at him seriously. Knowing the question on his friend's mind, Jimmy nodded. "I'm good now. Thanks, Jack."

Jack nodded and moved back to the safe. He grabbed the file out and placed it in Jimmy's hands. "Thanks again, Jack. For just being there." And that, Jimmy thought, was just what he needed. Just someone to be there.

In the car, Cam turned to check on Jimmy. They had just received an urgent call from Brooks so breakfast had wrapped up fast.

Jimmy was in better spirits; the conversation with her dad seemed to help. The case file they had retrieved from her dad was open on the seat beside him. Cam wondered the reason Finn wanted it back.

"Why did you want the file?" she asked as she turned back around.

Finn tightened his hands on the wheel. He was hoping to have some more time to put together his thoughts before she asked. "Something didn't seem right this morning. I can't put my finger on it, but it just didn't feel right." He saw the question on her face. He didn't blame her; he couldn't believe it himself. This murder appeared no different than the others, other than the girl was dead upon their arrival. But that could have been due to a number of things.

"Why?" was all she asked. Cam was a little distracted at the scene. She was shocked to find the girl still there. And then Nina's arrival had taken her aback. She still hadn't made contact with Beverly, and she was beginning to think she wouldn't. Not all of the spirits came to her. Some just walked straight into the afterlife, skipping the meet and greet with her.

Finn took a deep breath. He didn't know why, so he was stalling. But he could feel her eyes on him. She wasn't going to let it go. "Gut feeling."

"Good enough for me," she said, turning back to face the front.

He was a little taken aback by her absolute faith in him. He wasn't used to it. Back home, he would have had a twenty-minute debate with his boss or team. Defending his position and reasoning, but not with Cam. She just took his word. He thought of her gift. He was taken aback at first, but it was just thrown in his face. He felt guilty in the way he had handled it, but he couldn't change it. But never once did he question it. He believed it and believed in her.

Brooks met them at the door. She had a crazed look in her eyes and Cam had to hold her arm to ground her. She rushed them to the back. Cam was shocked to find Tom waiting for them in the room. Brooks just waved a hand in his direction.

"I called him because he is the only other one I trust with this information," she said breathlessly.

Tom's eyes betrayed his poker face. Cam saw the shock come and go at Brooks's blind faith in him. She thought she saw something else too, but decided to let that go. Apparently they had bigger problems right now.

"Will you calm down a minute?" Cam planted her feet to get her to stop and take a breath.

Brooks did as she was told. She paused and took a deep breath. Then she immediately jumped into why she called. "So we are they only ones who know everything about this case, right?"

Cam looked up at Tom. Brooks noticed and huffed. "I filled him in. Look you can get pissed if you want, but I needed his help."

Cam just held up her hands. She knew when she was like this to just let her go. "Okay with me." She glanced at the other two men. "How about y'all?"

Finn and Jimmy looked at each other and then at Brooks. "Good with us."

Tom just nodded. He should have felt a little betrayed that a key piece of information was withheld, but he could understand their reasoning. They had no clue who was on the Flannery payroll and who wasn't. But Tom had come to the conclusion that the Flannerys had nothing to do with the girls' murders. But he was beginning to think that someone was trying hard to make it look like they were.

Brooks grabbed up her notes and moved the camera into position over the girl. "I ran her prints and her name is Stacy Lynn McCord. Eighteen. She has a couple of prior arrests for possession of marijuana and solicitation."

Cam was beginning to see the reason for her excitement. "She's not his type. She's too old. He has been methodical in his 'selection.' I don't think he would change now." She raised an eyebrow at Finn. "You saw it, didn't you?"

He nodded. "Something didn't fit. She looked too old. She didn't look like one of his girls. Also she was found dead. He has been very careful to leave them alive. Why would he change now?"

Brooks was grinning like a loon. "That's not all." She turned on the camera and started moving it over all of the bruises. Jimmy saw it first.

"There is no mark. Not anywhere."

Cam leaned forward. "Are you positive?" Her heart was pounding.

Brooks motioned to Tom. "When he got here, I had him look. I hadn't told him about it so he wouldn't have it on his mind. He didn't find anything."

Tom decided it was time to let them in on his theory. He didn't know how they were going to like it, but he needed to get it out. "This probably is going to cause you some—no, make that a lot, of anger, but I have a theory." He shifted his weight as they all focused on him. "I have been keeping up with the news feeds and all of the press releases. There are a few things that have purposely been left out. Some of the details detailing the types of injuries and, now that I am aware, this detail concerning this symbol that I assume is on a ring."

Cam had a ball of acid beginning in her stomach. She knew where this was going, but she still didn't want to believe it.

Tom saw the look of angst on her face. He ignored it and pushed on. He didn't like any more than she did. "None of us want to go down this avenue, but I think that we have no choice. This girl is a copycat kill. And I believe the copycat is a cop. And not just any cop, someone on our team."

When they exploded, he was taken aback, even though he had been expecting it. But what he wasn't expecting was the silence that came from Brooks. She was staring at him with tears in her eyes. He saw the slight nod of her head and he moved to her and placed an arm around her shoulders.

That was enough to cut Jimmy's protest off. He saw the look on his baby girl's face and he knew immediately that she had come to the same conclusion as Tom. He didn't know what bothered him more, the fact that she had thought of it, or the fact that it was Tom who was comforting her, instead of him.

Finn was calming down. He had grown to respect these men and to consider some to be friends. The thought of one of them betraying them, and the badge, sickened him. But he began to see that this was the only plausible explanation for the similarities. The only piece missing was the imprint of the ring, and they had purposefully kept that out of the report for this very reason. And in case if the suspect slipped up. He pictured every face of the team. His immediate thought went to Jonah. He knew he was probably projecting but the thought stuck in his mind. He did know one thing. He was keeping it to himself. He needed solid proof before he accused a fellow cop.

It was Cam who brought order to the group. The calm in her voice caught everyone's attention. "Okay. Okay." She lowered her voice and double-checked the door to the autopsy suite. She walked calmly back to the group. "So I know that this is an uncomfortable scenario, but before we go around pointing fingers and accusing, we have to be absolutely one thousand percent sure. The mere accusation could ruin a career. So"—she pointed to Tom—"since this is your parade, you get to lead. What do you want us to do?"

Tom shifted under the focus. Uncomfortable with the lead, he did his best to suck it up and deal with it. "Well, I guess we will finish hearing out the doc here and then decide, as a group," he stressed, "on where to go from here."

Brooks could feel the unease of being the leader coming off of him in waves. It struck her as odd, considering he seemed to be very confident and sure. She wondered what the story was, but decided that it could wait. Turning back to her notes she finished her assessment of the body.

"The victim was forcibly raped. There is considerable damage and tearing to her vaginal area. Bruising around her thighs indicates she fought her attacker, tried to keep her legs together. I did find bruising that I may be able to match to hand and fingerprints. No semen was found, so our boy suited up. Her body shows considerable bruising and swelling resulting from a horrific beating. He broke her jaw, left side. Her left cheekbone and orbital bone. I would say that he is right handed. He has considerable strength in his left hand as well, but I would definitely conclude he is right side dominant. He beat her about her torso as well. He ruptured her spleen and punctured a lung on the right side. She has a three mm tear in her liver. Six broken ribs and a dislocated right shoulder." She snapped her file closed and had to take a moment. Rage stormed in her, leaving her shaken and a little sick. It was bad enough they had one asshole out there doing this. Now there were two.

Tom watched her closely. The normally steady and ardent doctor was visibly shaken. He had to root himself to keep from gathering her up. He was shocked at the sheer will it took to keep him from doing just that.

Jimmy watched his daughter. His heart broke for her. He wanted to whisk her away from all of this, but knew if she even suspected that he was thinking it, she would have his ass in a sling. He never got used to the mix of sorrow and pride that coursed through him to see her doing this job. It took a special person to stand for the dead. And an even stronger one to catalogue and dissect it.

Cam broke the silence. She had placed the open file they had retrieved from her father down on the neighboring table. "Look, we know that even the thought of going down this road sickens all of us. But we have to put our big girl panties on and suck it up." She ignored the snort from Finn. She just narrowed her eyes in his direction.

"So," she started again. "Going over the file, the injuries match closely. They are not an exact match, but I think that would cause more of a stir."

"I agree." Brooks had finally swallowed down the tears and bile. "Every girl has had enough similar injuries for us to determine that they can be tied to the same guy. If this new killer had mirrored the injuries bruise for bruise, it would scream copycat." She paused and moved back to the girl on her table. Moving the camera back to Stacy's face, she began to adjust the position of the girl's head. She motioned for the others to come closer.

Tom, who stood at her right shoulder, began to see the injury she was trying to highlight. He glanced up at the screen, then back down. He reached up and adjusted the camera so the injury would be illuminated under the bright light of the overhead lamp and the camera's lens.

Jimmy tightened his jaw. The ease of the silent communication between his daughter and the moody detective was causing sensations he never expected to feel—apprehension and fear. He didn't dislike the detective, but he didn't know him, not well. He knew of his reputation and he knew what happened a year ago with his partner. Tom wasn't at fault for the kid's death, but Jimmy knew that he blamed himself. And since then he had become somewhat of a loose cannon. But beyond that, his feelings weren't a result of who Tom was, but what he was. A cop, through and through. Just like he was. He thought of his wife, the sacrifices she had made and the life she had lived. He wanted better for his daughter. He never wanted her to date or marry a cop. So far, she had stayed away, but something about Tom was different. And he didn't like it.

Brooks caught the expression on her father's face and her forehead creased in bewilderment. *What is wrong with him?* she wondered. She shrugged her shoulders and went back to examining Stacy.

Cam was the first to speak. "Is that what I think it is?"

Tom had seen the mark, but he was too stunned to speak. He wasn't expecting that.

Brooks nodded her head. "Yup." She glanced back at the monitor and zoomed the camera in. "I missed it the first time. The damage to the surrounding tissue was great. He seemed to focus a lot of his energy, and fists, to this area, in what I can only assume was an attempt to hide these marks."

Finn stared at the screen. Two small welts appeared. When a person is tased, there are two ways to do it. You can keep the cartridge on, and when the trigger is pulled two-pronged diodes shoot out, sticking to the person's skin, which then shocks the person. Or you can place the Taser in "drive stun." This happens when the cartridge containing the diodes is removed and the person is stunned using the arc of electricity, gun to skin. It appeared that Stacy was "drive stunned" under her left ear. Finn felt a bubble of anticipation building. "Could he have been that careless?"

Brooks grinned up at him. "I compared it to the city-issued Tasers and the distance between the marks matches." She moved Stacy's head back around to rest on the head support. "Now, don't get too excited. The Taser is a common weapon. Civilians can buy them from the company, so they are available to the public. But," she began, cutting through the muffled groans of the group. "But if you find that Taser, there should be trace DNA on it. He beat the shit out of her some, before he tased her."

Cam smiled. "She got away for a minute. She fought back."

Brooks nodded. "Yes, she did. But he did follow that part of the killer's MO. He scrubbed her hands clean. But he did vary just with one thing." She raised Stacy's arm and turned her head to look at Tom. "Smell."

Tom rolled his eyes, but complied. "Bleach?"

Jimmy moved in. He leaned down and sniffed her right hand. "That would be my guess."

Cam looked down at the open file. She skimmed through the Irish ME's report. "So the original killer used a mix of ammonia, alcohol, and peroxide." Her head snapped up. "I know that most of us have come to the conclusion that the gang deaths and these are not related." She paused to get everyone's consent on that. "Brooks, where is the files on those murders?"

She moved over to her laptop and logged in. She sent the data to the monitor above Stacy's head. Zooming in she highlighted the area she assumed Cam was interested in. "OK, so according to my results, the victims in this case had traces of ammonia, alcohol, and peroxide on their hands."

Finn stepped in. "Wait. I thought we were all on the same page concerning these murders? They were committed by the Flannery clan. So why are we trying to link these to our girls?"

"We're not," Cam replied. "But I believe the killer wants us too. Or he is doing a double fake. You know like in football? When the quarterback wants you to think he is doing a handoff, so he fakes a hand off, not once but twice before he throws. Or if he wants to throw, he will fake a throw and a handoff before he actually throws?" Closing the file she stood straight. "Hear me out." Brooks held up a hand and switched off the monitor and pulled her stool over. Jimmy leaned on the steel table behind him and Tom crossed his arms over his chest and stood just a step behind Brooks. Finn stood behind her. His hands were in his pockets and he was swaying slightly, shifting his weight from foot to foot.

Cam cleared her throat and began. "Now if you were a killer, your first priority, behind finding your victim, would be to cover your tracks. You know, if you like murder, you need to stay out of jail. So it appears that our killer thought all of this through before he made his first kill—well, the first one we know about. Anyway, getting back to the girls. The best way to stay off the radar is to follow two rules: Stay off of the suspect list and don't have any evidence point back to you." She paused to be sure they were staying with her. Satisfied, she carried on. "So if I were wanting to become a serial murder, I would do two things. Make sure I am nowhere near my stomping ground. And I would try to figure out how to keep the focus somewhere else and nowhere near me."

Jimmy nodded. "Makes sense. Easiest way to keep the attention somewhere else is to follow someone else."

"Sounds good. But here is the problem. We thought we were dealing with someone crazy and demented. But if what you say is true, then you need to add smart and cunning to the crazy. And in my opinion there are few things as dangerous as a crazy, smart man."

Finn nodded as dread filled his belly. Tom was right. They thought they were just dealing with a crazy killer. But it was a whole new ballgame when you add smart to it. But he was beginning to think that smart didn't even come close. This killer had fooled police in one country, and so far he had fooled them in this one as well. "I think smart is too simple a word." He didn't realize he had spoken aloud until Cam's eyes swung toward him.

"What do you mean?" she asked. But she had a feeling she already knew.

Finn pointed to Stacy's hand on the table. "He has researched common practices of local mobs and gangs. And probably even looked into other murders. I think he choose the Flannery's because he knew that they were hot in both places."

"But we didn't even know they were in both places!"

"Exactly." His simple statement made Cam's mouth go dry.

"Shit." Jimmy summed it up. They needed to call in the rest of the team. But one look at Stacy had him second guessing that.

Tom read him perfectly. "Who do you trust?"

"Who indeed?" Jimmy leaned back hard and scrubbed his hands down his face. He glanced at his surroundings. He never thought that he would be in this situation. Hell, he had never even thought of this situation. Settling the bile in his belly, he steeled himself. Glancing up he saw the whiteboard. Back to old school, he thought. "Honey, do you have some markers?"

He pushed off the table and walked to the board. He turned to face the eyes looking at him. But it was one set, the set who yearned for his daughter, he zeroed in on. "How much do you know about the ATF guy?"

Tom smiled and pulled out his phone. He had trusted the kid immediately.

CHAPTER 20

Matt Roberts whistled as he walked. Tall and lanky, he stood at six and half feet. His brown hair was short, a hairstyle he had since his days as a ranger in the army. He was the youngest on that team, and the skinniest. He had a variety of nicknames, most that shouldn't be said in polite company. He had hazel eyes and a long southern drawl.

Originally from a small town in the upstate of South Carolina, he joined the army as a way to get out and see the world, on the government's dime. What he hadn't expected was to fall in love with the rigid and structured atmosphere of the military. The instant brotherhood had sucked him in and had given him something that he hadn't realized he craved—belonging. He came from a tight family, but their life was very simple and safe. Church every Sunday and Wednesday, high school football on Fridays, and hanging out in an empty parking lots on Saturday nights.

His parents had been together since the ninth grade, and they married right out of high school. His sisters had followed suit, marrying their high school sweethearts and starting families nine months later. Their husbands all worked at the struggling mills, living paycheck to paycheck.

So after seeing a solider walking through the halls of his high school, he ignored the protests of his friends and immediately signed on the dotted line. After three tours in Afghanistan and seeing the world, he left that brotherhood and joined another.

Law enforcement was a lot like the military; the brotherhood was instant and infinite. There is a saying that every cop lives by: "Blue blood is thicker than true blood." And Matt was no different. In the army, he would have given his life for his battle buddy, or any other solider. The same is true for police. There isn't anything he wouldn't do or give for his fellow officer. When he was offered a job with the ATF, he jumped at it, much like he did with the Army.

But after two years, he was still trying to find his groove. His loyalty to his fellow agents was absolute, but he didn't feel like this was his place. He paused and looked at the sign above the door—City Morgue. He let out a short laugh. He never thought that he would be summoned to a meeting here, but he didn't hesitate to come. Because, unlike the ATF, he felt an instant sense of belonging when he walked into that first meeting. He had struck up a conversation with a moody and quiet detective who was attached to the Undercover Surveillance Division. But when he heard the details of the case, he was hooked. He didn't care if he had no claim to the case. When he heard what that monster had done to those girls, he had to help.

He had been keeping up with the day-to-day details with Tom. They both had an early feeling this had nothing to do with the Flannerys, but they both knew the clan wasn't completely innocent in their dealings. So Tom and Matt had started to quietly build a case against them. Finding hair-thin connections to the other gang murders, but none to the girls. So when Tom had to find someone he trusted, he didn't hesitate to call the kid in.

Matt paused and tapped on the doors leading in to the autopsy suite. He pushed through a second later and found himself in the middle of curious scene. Photographs were placed on all of the open autopsy tables. When he moved closer he noticed that they were laid out to reconstruct the bodies of the victims. He slid his bag off his shoulder and placed it near the doc's desk. Brooks looked over and smiled. "Hey, Slim, how have you been?"

Matt smiled back at the beautiful woman. "I am doing just fine, beautiful."

She swooned a little at the southern accent. She didn't know of a woman who wouldn't. The others were gathered around a table toward the back of the room, pictures of Nina's body spread before them. Brooks pointed to the table that still held Stacy's body. "She doesn't belong with them."

Matt couldn't hide the shock. He had heard what had happened and had assumed the murder was part of the ongoing investigation. "Copycat?" Walking over he began to examine the body. After a few moments he stood up. "Where's the mark?"

Cam's head snapped up. "What?" She quickly made her way over to him. "What did you just say?"

Matt was taken aback. He wasn't expecting her reaction, her heat. He held up his hands as a sign of peace. "Whoa! Sorry! Jesus." He took a moment to look to Tom. He tried to read the detective's face, but he found it curiously blank.

Brooks took pity on the boy. She stepped in front of him. She squared off, hands on her hips, preparing to take her friend on. "Goddammit Cam! Let the poor boy speak!"

Tom didn't know whether to be in awe or a little jealous. The mixed reaction startled him. God, she was sexy, was all his brain could think. Here she was, small and faery like, ready to take on one of the toughest cops he knew. And he bet she could hold her own. But another part of him was jealous. Jealous that she was defending the kid so fiercely; it placed a seed of doubt in his brain. Maybe these past few days of them dancing and flirting was all in his old brain.

He hadn't had a relationship since Mark died. Tom couldn't bring himself to make that emotional connection with another. Not at the risk of having it ripped away in an instant. But watching her defend Matt ignited a seed of jealousy. The reaction made him realize his old heart still had some life to it. But did he want it?

Finn glanced to Jimmy. Was he going to step in? He didn't think so. The old man had taken a step back and had a sudden interest in a spot on the floor. Finn prayed for divine help and stepped in between the two women. He felt safer turning his back on Brooks so he faced Cam. "Babe—," he began, but quickly regretted it the moment those eyes flashed to his. "Cam," he amended, "let the boy speak."

Matt, whose face reddened with every "boy" reference, risked speaking again. "I know it wasn't in the file, so I never said a word.

But I noticed the same mark on all of the bodies. It resembles a half cross. I recognized it so fast because it reminded me of the chaplin who was attached to my team in Afghanistan. He was raised Catholic and felt the call to become a chaplin in the military instead of the priesthood. His parents had a ring made for him when he was ordained and they had it blessed by the priest at his home church." He took a breath and forged on. He wanted to get it out as fast as he could so maybe she would cool down. "I only recognized it because one of our team was shot, and the dude took his ring and placed it on my buddy's finger. He then prayed and prayed with him. We all did, and miraculously he lived. When the chaplin's parents found out, they had another ring commissioned and they replaced it." He shifted when he saw the tears in Brooks's eyes. He didn't mean to tell the whole story, but it just came pouring out.

"Did the soldier and chaplin ever meet back up?"

Matt stared at her pretty blue eyes that were swimming in tears. If the story hadn't ended the way it did, he would have lied to keep those tears from spilling over. "Yeah, they did. My buddy knew when we were coming home so he met our plane on the airstrip. He was waiting with the chaplin's parents and he tried to give back the ring. He knew it meant a lot to him. But his parents had the other one waiting, so they told my buddy it was supposed to stay with him. He still wears it, every day." He hoped the emotion was staying out of his voice. He had seen a lot on that tour, but that one story still choked him up.

Brooks sniffed and blotted at her eyes. She turned a smoldering eye to Cam, and Cam quickly understood the meaning.

"I'm sorry." She narrowed her eyes as pure shock engulfed Matt's face. "Yes, I know how to apologize when I show my ass and I am in the wrong." She stuck her tongue out when Brooks moved out from between them.

"Shove it," Brooks said as she walked to the table the group had just left. "Okay, folks, gather around." Picking up the picture that showed a close up of the ring's indentation, she pointed to Matt.

"Have you ever seen another ring that could make this mark?"

He nodded. "The guy's parents had it designed after the rings some priests wear when they are in seminary. It is a gold, or silver, signet ring, that you can get customized any way you want. Any jeweler can make it."

Cam's heart sank. She had hoped that it would be a unique ring. One only a few jewelers could do. "Damn," she said, deflated.

Jimmy picked up on her train of thought. "Maybe not." Taking the picture from Brooks, he moved toward her camera, which hung above her main autopsy table. Turning back on the monitor, he moved it so it would enlarge the picture he placed on the tray. "Every jeweler has their own style. Some even 'sign' their work, using a mark or symbol in order to identify their pieces."

Finn jumped in, his heart beginning to race. "So maybe we can find the mark, which would hopefully identify the jeweler. They should have records of the ring, right?"

Jimmy nodded.

Tom moved closer to the screen. He noticed a small indentation, just a slight variation in the bruising. "Hold on," he said and moved to gather the other pictures showing the mark on the bodies. He came back with the stack. Before he changed the picture he pointed out the small mark to the others.

Brooks noticed it first. "I guess the only way to be sure is to see if it shows up on any of the other girls." She took the first photo Tom held out. Placing it on the tray she zoomed in two more times. "I'm not sure, but maybe here?" She pointed to a faint variation in coloring around the cross.

Tom switched to another photo. They all searched for a solid minute. Cam was starting to wonder if this was a solid lead, when Tom placed the next photo under the camera. She immediately saw it and hollered out and pointed. "Right there!" Pulling on Finn's sleeve she was nearly jumping. "Do you see it? Right there!"

Finn laughed. It was their first solid link to the killer. "Yes, I do. Can you put both photos up?"

Brooks nodded and moved to her laptop. Hitting a few keys she had both images side by side and centered on both marks. "I never noticed it." Her shoulders sank. She wondered if she had caught it before, would one of these girls still be alive?

Tom saw the thought written on her face. He placed a hand on her shoulder. "None of us saw it. Don't put this on you. Trust me."

His tone made her look at him and what she saw had her believing him. He knew from experience; the sadness still lingered in his eyes. She nodded weakly. She tried to shake it, but a part of her was laying the blame at her own feet.

Jimmy watched his daughter. He saw the blame she placed on herself, and he saw Tom trying to erase it. And as much as he hated it, his desire for his daughter to stay away from cops was quickly crumbling. Pushing that away, he focused back on the case. "So this still needs to stay here."

Matt had an idea. "We can do that and still search." He saw the doubt on Finn's face. "Hear me out, please?" He waited, giving him time to think. He hoped they would let him do what he was about to suggest. "I have been in the background this whole time. There is no reason for the ATF to still be actively involved in this part of the case, so let me do the leg work."

"Wouldn't your boss wonder why you are working this still?" Cam had her doubts too.

Matt struggled to hold back the plea. "No. They think I am working on the Flannery clan angle." He shrugged at Jimmy's incredulous look. "I may not have passed along all of the developments in the case. I know, I know," he pressed. "I should have told them, but you know, as well as I do, that these bastards are dirty. They may not have their fingers in this mess." He swept his hand around the room. "But you know the other murders are tied to them. So I have used that to stay on the case. I may have also downplayed the significance of the investigation, but I don't want this hijacked from me. And you know, as soon as they find out the significance of the coming bust, one of the fucktards above me is going to snatch this out from under me."

Tom laughed before he could stop himself. "The kid is right. And you know, just like he said, someone is going to hijack his case. Fucktards? Really?"

Matt laughed. "Well, they are. So…" He looked to Jimmy. "Can I work it?"

Jimmy rubbed his face. It gave him a minute to laugh himself. He had to admit, the kid had spirit. He tried to figure a way to keep him on the case and keep it out of the press whores every department had. "Who's your supervisor?"

Matt tried not to look deflated. "Dina Kellet."

Jimmy felt hope. He had met a wide range of law enforcement in his twenty plus years on the force. But he actually knew Dina. He had met her numerous times over the years and had even trained with her some in his younger days. "You're lucky, kid. I just happen to know Dina, so I will handle it."

Cam held on to this lead with both hands. It was the best thing they had so far. "Didn't witnesses say that they had seen a man in a dark suit around the time of the murders?" Her elation was turning to dread. "I hope this isn't going where I think it is going."

Finn agreed. That was the last thing they needed.

* * * *

The five of them arrived at the conference room twenty-five minutes late. Jimmy stood and began. "I apologize for the delay. We had an interesting development in the case." He took the laptop that his daughter had queued up for him. Pulling up a few of the photos of the crime scene, he put into motion the plan the six of them had come up with. He looked out at the team he had helped put together. Although the thought sickened him he wondered if one of them had betrayed them and the badge and took this girl's life. He shoved the rage and betrayal down, and focused on the case. "Stacy Lynn McCord. Red hair and blue eyes. We believe she belongs to our killer. She fits the description and the manner of killing is along the same lines. Only difference is she died at the scene. Other than that, she has the same types of injuries. She was raped and beaten."

Todd Smith, the detective from the Vice Unit, spoke first. "I just ran a quick check on the victim. She has priors for solicitation and a couple of drug possession charges."

"Anything on file about a pimp? Or a john that she had been busted with on more than a few occasions? A regular?"

Todd scrolled through the file on his phone. He couldn't find anything out of the ordinary, but he did notice that she had been busted with the same person four times. "Nothing really stands out, but I do see that she was busted with the same guy about four times. His name is Martin Foley. Aged thirty-six. White male. Five feet, eight inches and two hundred sixteen pounds." He forwarded the file and picture to the laptop, so Jimmy could put it up on the big screen.

Martin Foley was a nerdy and overweight middle-aged man. His hair was a mix of mousy brown and blonde that was thinning on top. His glasses were what most military guys called BCGs, or birth control glasses. They were oversized and unflattering. He had pale skin that was pockmarked and scared.

Cam understood why he turned to prostitutes. He wasn't a good-looking man, but what made him even more unappealing was the way he carried himself. His picture showed a man who was disgruntled and had a mix of resignation and anger on his face.

Although she probably had already guessed she asked where he lived. "According to one of the reports filed, he states that he lives with his mother." He knew what they all were thinking—the man lived in the basement, or depending on the house, the third floor attic. "He is employed as a janitor at one of the local office buildings downtown. It is the building that holds a local talent agency and sports agency."

Brooks almost felt sorry for the man. He already had a lot against him as far as the looks and the fact that he lived in his mama's attic space, but added to the fact that he had to look at all of the beautiful and successful young people every day as he walked around picking up their trash and cleaning their bathrooms. "No wonder he has to pay for it." She blushed when she heard Tom chuckle.

"But you are right." She faced Todd. He shrugged his shoulders; he had seen this many times before. "Think about it. Prostitutes aren't going to turn you away or say anything negative. They get paid to make you feel like you are the best thing that has ever happened to them. And if they want to stay successful, they need to make you believe it." Pointing to Martin's picture, he finished. "Working around all of those beautiful people had to make him feel inferior, not saying that he was, but you never know. Anyway, paying a woman to make you feel like you are a star was probably a no-brainer to this guy."

Cam ignored the conversation and snickers about the guy and focused on his face. He didn't look like a killer but not all of them did. "Is there anything in his past, or present, that shows a disposition to violence? Is there any reports that he liked to get rough or that he had gotten rough with any of them?"

Jimmy scrolled down. "Nothing here says that. Wait, his name does show up in another file." He paused while he read over it. "He may not have any record of violence but he does have an old acquaintance in prison. A friend he has had since childhood."

"Prison?" Finn sat forward. "For what?"

"Attempted murder. He caught his wife and his best friend in bed together. He beat the shit out of both of them, but the wife got help before he could kill the best friend. According to the file, he regularly beat the wife. She finally got the courage to leave and he didn't accept it. He still saw her as 'his wife and it was in his house' as he put it."

Cam was reading over Jimmy's shoulder. "There was a restraining order on file, but it was ignored. It is listed as being served three months before this incident. To surmise it, wife kicks the beating husband out and moves the best friend in. The husband, of course, doesn't accept it and comes back and beats them both. Almost killed the best friend. So the now ex-husband is in jail doing twenty-five to life on two attempted murder charges and various other things. And according to prison records, Martin Foley and the guy's mother visit every month."

"I think we need to pay a visit to the Foley residence. And then we may need to hit the friend's mother's house." Jimmy stood up and finished the meeting.

"Smith, I want you to go through all of the recent records and arrests dealing with Martin Foley. Then go have a chat with any of the prostitutes he likes to use. If he was caught four times with Stacy, I bet he uses their services on a very regular basis." Todd nodded.

"Crabtree, tag along with Smith. You have a way of getting the ladies to talk so you could be a great asset. Also help him go through and see if you can find any cases of violence, similar to the case, in any other files."

Finn saw Jonah clench his jaw when Jimmy gave his orders. He also saw the quick, but intense flick of the eyes toward Cam. "Yes, sir," he answered.

"Franks and Jones, I want you to look into another matter. Not only do we have the murders of the girls, we have three dead gang members down in the morgue. We have pretty much eliminated the Flannery clan as suspects in these murders, but they are still considered front and center on those gang murders. So use all of your resources and find me a connection to them. Since we had a small link between the two cases, I have been able to keep both cases with this team that we have formed." The two detectives from the Narcotics Unit nodded and left to get right to work. Jimmy hoped that the two of them could make some headway. So when this case was done, they could put an end to the Flannery clan and their multi-continent mob ring.

Looking around the room, there were five of them left. Cam, Finn, Tom, Brooks, and himself. Jimmy thought of Matt and hoped that he would have some news soon. But in the meantime, they had a family to interview.

CHAPTER 21

The Foley home was in a non-descript part of Baltimore. In the middle of Highlandtown, it was near the first crime scene, about five blocks west. A pale gray stone on the outside, the house blended in with the cement of the sidewalk. The row houses in this area are slender and tall, squished together to fit the maximum amount of tenants on one city block. Some of the houses boasted flower boxes and planters to brighten and add color to the cement and stone.

But the Foley house was plain and cold. All of the windows were covered with stark and colorless curtains, and the door was sealed tight. Finn knocked on the door after trying the broken doorbell. One minute later a stern woman opened the door, leaving the chain latched. Her voice was gravely and harsh. "Yes?"

Cam moved in and held up her badge. "Baltimore City Police. We need to speak with you and your son, Mrs. Foley."

A low whistle escaped her nose as she sharply exhaled. She closed the door with a snap and they heard the chain rattle as she removed it. Her voice pierced their eardrums as she called for her son to come downstairs. As Martin clomped down three flights of stairs, Mrs. Foley turned her sharply angled face back to them. Standing in the middle of the living room, Cam looked around the first floor. The walls were paneled in a dark wood and held no pictures. The room was sparsely furnished, with a seventies era dark green couch and a chocolate-colored vinyl chair. The two end tables held a lamp each and an old rotary phone on one. Still no pictures were anywhere to be found. The living room opened into a dining room. The old vinyl floor had yellowed in some places but still looked like it was in good condition. The table was plain and bare, which Cam decided was the theme of this house. Sterile and bare. No love, no emotion. No wonder Martin turned to prostitutes, although she was beginning to think he was paying more for the attention and the affection than he was for the sex.

"Ma!" Martin screeched, as he was coming down the stairs. "Ma! What do you want?" As soon as he turned the corner and saw Cam and Finn, he took off. Running through the narrow kitchen, he squeezed his round body through the back door and out through the concrete backyard.

"No fucking way." Cam breathed as she took off after him. For a fat fucker he can move, Cam thought, following him through the narrow galley kitchen and out the ancient metal screened door. As she turned to find him, she heard the grunting and wheezing of Martin Foley. Following the sound she found him desperately attempting, and miserably failing, to climb the fence. Cam stopped and caught her breath. Martin heard her chuckle and still he fought to get his ass over the gate.

"Really?" she asked incredulously. She only received a grunt in return as he was still scrambling. She knew she should go ahead and cuff him, but she didn't have the heart to stop him. She heard boots pounding the pavement from the direction of the alley and Tom appeared on the other side of the gate. He too paused to catch his breath and watch the poor bastard still trying to flee.

"Seriously?" he said. Pointing to Foley and cocking his head at Cam. She just threw up her hands in response. Tom watched him for another forty-five seconds before taking pity on him and walking up and unlatching the gate.

Martin's face fell in defeat. "It was unlocked?" he asked, wheezing and panting. His face an unnatural shade of red and purple.

Tom just shook his head and pulled out his cuffs. "Next time, look down."

Cam jumped as the screen door slammed open and Mrs. Foley started wailing. "Police brutality! Police brutality! Let my son go you bastards! Help! Help!"

Cam walked straight to her and got in her face. "Shut up! You know damn well there is no brutality happening, but I do see a textbook case of public disorderly conduct, interfering in a criminal investigation, assault on an officer, and felony stupid."

Mrs. Foley's mouth just hung open. Cam knew she probably went overboard, but goddamn, the woman's voice was like knives to the ears. As the older woman's face reddened, Cam knew another onslaught was coming.

"I have in no way broken the law!" she screeched. "And furthermore, I want the number to your supervisor, you rude little bitch. Never have I been insulted and accosted in this way." She defiantly stood her ground, her nose in the air, her breath whistling through it.

Cam's eardrums felt as if they were bleeding. "Coming out here screaming about police brutality and other lies is grounds for public disorderly conduct and gives way to interfering with my investigation. Be glad I didn't add trying to incite a riot." She took some satisfaction in the lowering of the woman's nose and the color draining from her cheeks.

"What about the other? I have in no way assaulted you or any other person here."

"Well, that may have been a stretch, but I could probably pass it due to my hearing being assaulted by your incessant and annoying screeching." Cam turned back to add, "And the felony stupid is a toss-up between you and your son."

Jimmy shook his head and watched her walk back through the house. But Mrs. Foley wasn't done. She started after Cam and started yelling again. "I want the name and number for your supervisor!"

Cam kept walking. "He's right behind you!"

Jimmy could have strangled her.

Finn and Brooks had already begun to look around the house. Jimmy had procured a warrant on the way over here, given the fact that Martin Foley had not only been a recurring customer with the last victim, they had found evidence that he had been with Beverly as well.

Finn glanced up as Cam came back through the narrow and dark kitchen and into the adjoining dining room. He cocked his head at her. "What?" she asked.

"I'm trying to figure out what you are doing?" She had come in rubbing both of her ears. She had a crazy face going as well, a cross between agony and ecstasy. At her blank look, he point to her hands.

She put one of her hands in front of her face and was still rubbing her right ear with her other hand. When he learned over to look at her ear, it finally clicked on what the hell he was talking about. "Oh," she said, with a sheepish grin. "The old woman screeched like a damn banshee." And right on cue, Jimmy came rushing through the kitchen with Mrs. Foley following in her house coat and slippers.

As they passed by Finn, she turned on him. "What the hell are you looking at, pretty boy? You all come in here and demand to see my son and then chase him through the house and neighborhood. And you haven't even said why you are here?"

Cam had slammed her hands back on her ears when she first leaned in. Of course the old hag was two feet in front of her, but Finn was unprepared, taking on the full brunt of the woman's yelling.

His ears ringing, Finn un-scrunched his face and turned to face the older woman. "No, ma'am. I am sorry that you feel that way, but we just wanted to ask a few question of your son, but now we have to take him in since he ran." He decided the only way to save any of their hearing, he would have to pour on the charm. So he reached down to hold her hands, and sympathy smoothed over his face.

Cam watched, mystified. She watched him as he patiently listened to her concerns and was amazed as Mrs. Foley's voice lowered and resembled something around normal. Of course he was laying it on thick, the Irish sang out, and she didn't know a woman alive who could resist a man with an accent. Especially when that man looked like Finnegan McDougal.

Cam realized they were talking about her, when Finn turned those gorgeous blue eyes on her. She saw it before he said it. There was no way in hell she was going to apologize to her. The woman threatened her, and her team, and then she assaulted the shit out of our eardrums, she thought. *I could take her in on that alone!* Okay, Okay. She knew the "felony stupid" was probably uncalled for, but in her mind they deserved it. Well, at least Martin deserved it; his mama deserved it for defending the bumbling idiot.

Her internal dialogue was interrupted, rudely she might add, when Finn cleared his throat. At her. *I'm still not apologizing to the old bat,* she thought as she crossed her arms and stood her ground. And ignored his stare. She glanced one more time at him, out of guilt, and found herself opening her mouth. "I do apologize, Mrs. Foley. I was out of line." When she finished she refused to meet Finn's gaze. But she saw Brooks standing behind him looking wildly around.

Finn moved off to the front room with a now calm, and polite, Mrs. Foley. Cam put her hands on her hips and glowered at Brooks. "What in the hell are you doing?"

Brooks paused for a moment. "Oh, me?" she said, resuming her search. "I was looking around to see if hell froze over."

Cam had to take a deep breath and unclench her fists. "Why, smartass?"

Brooks feigned a hurt look. "Don't turn on me now. I'll tell Finn that you were being mean to me. Do you think he will hold my hands and look deep into my eyes and make you apologize for insulting a fine woman, who was only scared for herself? I can't say 'and son,' well, because I don't have one."

Cam lunged for her and she squealed and ran into the wall. Brooks was expecting more of a reaction than that, so she was confused when Cam stopped and stared where she had bumped into the wall. Brooks scooted around and to take a peek herself. Her hands immediately flew to her mouth because she had knocked a hole in the wall. Part of her reverted back to the age of twelve and was worried her father would have her tail for the hole. She leaned over and was relieved to see him outside on the phone.

"Look what you made me do!" she said, swatting at Cam's arm.

Cam just huffed. "Shut up. Look at what you found."

They were in the dining room that was squished in between the living room, at the front of the house, and the kitchen which was at the end of the house, with a small full bathroom at the end. When they began their search, they moved the dining room table off to the side and back toward the kitchen. The yellowed linoleum ran the length of the room and into the kitchen and bathroom. The walls were wallpapered over a thin veneer paneling. About three feet from the ground, in the right corner was a small hole. She thought at first that Brooks had created the hole when she stumbled into it, but when she bent down and looked closer, Cam noticed that this piece had been made into a hidey hole of sorts.

Martin heard the bump and then the quiet and he started to sweat. His left leg began to bounce and shake, which caught Tom's attention. He followed the man's gaze and saw Cam and Brooks bent down in the corner. "Did they find your hidey hole?" He watched as the question sunk in. A bead of sweat bloomed on the man's lip and his eyes darted back and forth. "What's in there, Martin?" Tom pressed. He let out a low whistle and Cam leaned over from behind the wall. She saw Tom crouching in front of Martin and saw the man's eyes darting back between where she was and Tom.

"Anything you want to tell us before we tear out the wall?"

Mrs. Foley moved in the direction of the hole. "Who did that?" She swung around on all of them. "You're paying for this." Shaking the warrant in the air, she continued, steadily increasing her volume. "There is no reason to tear apart my house! This does not give you the right to tear down my house! Break holes in my walls!"

Finn moved back over to her. "Mrs. Foley—"

She shoved the paper in his face. "Don't you placate me, damn you! They are tearing apart my house! My *house*!" She stalked off down the galley kitchen. "I'm calling my lawyer! You have no right to do this!"

Finn glanced over to the visibly shaking Martin. "Do you want us to tear your mother's house apart? Brick by brick. Wall by wall. Floors, cabinets—do I need to continue?"

Martin shook his head. Sweat dripping and flying all around.

"We can't hear your head shaking, Marty," Cam coaxed. "Tell me what I need to know and where I need to find it." She waited for a minute. When he said nothing, she stood and moved to Jimmy. "Okay, boss, call in the wrecking crew. This place is coming apart—"

"Wait!" he croaked. Shaking like a chihuahua, he continued. "Just wait." He hung his head and began to cry. "I didn't kill her. I swear I didn't."

Cam moved in and leaned down to him. "You didn't kill who, Marty?" Her heart was pounding.

"I swear I didn't kill her. I found her. That's all."

"Who, goddammit! Who?"

He started to cry. Uncontrollable sobs. Cam opened her mouth, but he finally answered. "Nina."

Cam stood up, confused. "Nina?"

Marty's sobs got louder. "And Beverly and Stacy."

Cam was stunned. He had been with all three. "What do you mean 'found them'?"

Marty looked up at her. Snot and tears mixing on his face. "I got a phone call to meet them. When I got there, they were just laying there. Bruised and bloody. I called nine-one-one, every time. But I swear I found them like that."

"How, Marty?"

"Like I said, I got a call to meet them. I swear I didn't do it! They called me, told me where to meet them, and I went. But then when I would show up, they were dead. All of them were dead. So I called the police. And then the same thing happened to Beverly and Stacy. They were my girls. All of them. No one loved them like I did. I always called them. Only them. I didn't treat them like whores, or something I paid for. I was always gentle. Loving. I swear I didn't hurt them. I loved them. Stacey the best. I loved Stacey the best and she loved me too. Please you have to believe me. I wouldn't hurt them, not my girls!" His head dropped and he began to cry again. Loud body-rocking sobs.

Jimmy watched him. His mouth open. A stunned look on his face. He tried not to hope, but if what he was saying was true, someone was targeting Marty's girls. But in another part of his mind, he thought that Marty was still it. He could be making up the other man for many reasons. Two of them jumped out immediately. Either he was horrified at what he had done and he was projecting another scenario into his memories, or he wanted to throw them off track. But he knew, in his gut, that this was not their man. Marty was teetering on hysterical now. His face, a fire engine red, contorted into agony. Jimmy truly believed that Marty loved them, each one of them, in his own twisted way.

Cam tried to make sense of it all. Knowing she wouldn't get anything out of him now, she moved back to the hole. Pulling off the paneling, she reached in, unsure of what she would find. Finding the treasure, she pulled it back out for everyone to see.

As the gasps echoed around the room, Cam's knees went a little weak. In three, one gallon bags, were Marty's treasures. Polaroids of each of the girls. Alive and then dead, or he thought they were. All three bags contained hair, panties, and lipstick. And there was a white index card in the bags as well. Cam reached a gloved hand inside and let out a gasp as she pulled it out. On each card was a perfect impression, in lipstick, of each of their lips. But the most shocking, was that on the opposite side of the card was another set of lips. All with the same color. Cam looked over at the still sobbing Marty and held that card up. And sickness rolled in her belly. The other set of lips belonged to Martin Foley.

Marty, seeing the cards, wailed louder. Hysteria finally setting in. "It was all sent to me! I swear it. The cards, the lipstick, the panties. I swear I didn't take them. Someone sent them to me. But please, please don't take them! It's all I have left of them." His eyes searched wildly around the room. "Ma! Mama! Help me, Ma! Don't let them take my stuff! Ma!"

Mrs. Foley stood in the back corner of the dining room. Her face a stark white. Her eyes were wide with horror; her hands trembled in front of her mouth. "Please, God, no. God no," she whispered. She jerkily turned her head to face her son. "What have you done? What have you done? What have you *done*!" Her voice shrieked. Her legs gave out and Tom moved fast. He caught her before she hit the floor and Brooks helped move her to a chair. She darted into the kitchen and found a glass and filled it with water. Squatting in front of the older woman, she wrapped her shaky hands around the glass then covered those with her steady ones.

Brooks had to swallow and breathe before she could talk. This was the first time she had been involved in the apprehension of a suspect. And it damn sure wasn't like she thought it was going to be. Nothing about this case was what she thought it would be. *Why in the hell did I leave my ice box?* she thought, thinking of the morgue. *I know what to expect there*, she reasoned. Looking at the shaken and nearly hysterical woman, she thought of the dead she normally worked with. *I do better with them*, she scolded herself. *I stand for the dead. I don't work well with the living.* It was one of the reasons she left the hospital. The hysteria, the emotions, the drama, became too much, so she became the voice for those who had none. And she was damn good at it, she loved it. And she realized it was one of the reasons why she was here, trying to soothe a broken mother. She was standing for the dead, her dead. Those girls had brought here, so she better get off her pity boat and start finding answers for them.

Tom watched her internal struggle. He saw the panic in her eyes and wondered what brought it on. He knew some of her history, knew she worked with the living before transferring to the dead, so he wondered why the panic was there. What he had seen of hospitals and the chaos there, he just assumed she could deal with one hysterical woman. But as quick as the panic set in, he saw her push it back down and the resolve set back in.

Going on instinct Brooks decided to see what the woman knew. "Is there anything else I can get for you, Mrs. Foley?"

The older woman tried to focus on the pretty young woman at her feet. She seemed to just realize that she was there, and that she was holding her hands. "I'm not sure." Looking around, she took in the chaos of her normally rigid and ordered home. Her son was sobbing in the brown recliner. His hands cuffed behind him. Her eyes drifted to the red-haired woman kneeling in front of a hole in her wall, plastic bags strewn beside her. Snippets of conversations could be heard all around her and then more uniformed men and women came through the front door and began to move all about her home. They ran their hands over every surface and began to search through all of her possessions. She watched as two men moved her grandmother's hutch in the dining room, the plates teetering on the shelves. Tears began to gather in her eyes, shocking her. As did the torrent of emotions rolling around in her chest and stomach, finally tearing down the solid wall she had built to protect herself when her husband had walked out on her and her son. Unable to fight it any longer, she broke down and cried. Her slender body rocked back and forth.

Brooks was shocked to see the woman fall apart. She was so cold and rigid up to this point. The only emotion she had shown was shock, laced with fear. Unsure of what to do, she gathered the broken woman in her arms and held her as her world crumbled.

Neither of them noticed the complete silence that had come over the room. Those who had dealt with her before were startled to see this level of emotion from the woman.

Jimmy watched his daughter comfort the wailing woman. His eyes briefly met Cam's and he could see her thoughts matched his. He moved toward his daughter and lowered to her. Placing a hand on each of their backs he quietly asked his question. "Mrs. Foley, why don't we take you to our office so you don't have to watch this?" And he was shocked when she nodded her agreement. This was a total one-eighty from the stern woman he encountered earlier.

Knowing how her father and friend worked, Brooks held onto the woman as they walked to Cam's car. She got in the backseat with her, knowing they were going to ask her to be the one to talk to her. She knew that she shouldn't be bothered by it, but she felt as if Mrs. Foley had had enough for one day. The mother had just learned her son was possibly a sick and twisted killer and now her home was being violated. But she shoved that part of her heart away and thought back to the three girls in her morgue.

Back at the precinct, Martin Foley was left to himself in an interrogation room. Cam and Finn watched from the observation room, behind a one-way glass. The man had cried himself out on the way to the station and now had his head resting on the cold, steel table. He was handcuffed to the chair, which was bolted to the floor. Another chair was across the table and was a stark contrast to the one he was in. They had painted the steel a soft beige and had a plush cushion on the seat and arm rests. Another chair, of the same style was in the corner and allowed the prisoner a view of what they were lacking. The cinderblock walls were painted an ugly, harsh gray and met a concrete floor below and a tile ceiling above. The harsh florescent lights cast a yellowish and bright glow on the room.

The one-way glass showed a mirror in the room and occasionally Marty would glance over and mumble to his reflection. He shifted his plump frame in the chair and looked longingly at the plush one in the corner. His eyes were swollen and red from crying and his reddened nose stood out against the white pallor of his cheeks. Occasionally he would cry out for his mother, begging her to come. Then his tears would come when his calls were unanswered.

Down the hall, Mrs. Foley sat with Brooks, Jimmy, and Tom in a small conference room. Where Marty's setting was stark and cold, this room was warm and soft. It boasted a warm beige on the walls and a darker beige on the carpet. A worn, wooden table sat in the middle with six comfortable chairs around it. The chairs were a dark brown leather and were worn smooth by the countless number of people who had come in and out of there.

There was a small kitchenette in the back corner, which had a small compact fridge and a coffee pot sat on the counter. Cam, who had grown tired of the burnt coffee the old maker had produced, broke down and bought a new single serve maker. Next to it a rotating tower offered the user a variety of coffees and teas to choose from. Even though it was meant for visitors, most of the detectives had started to stock their favorites in here, so it had unofficially become the squad's go-to machine. And the fridge offered a bountiful selection of creamers as well.

The cabinets were stocked with tissues and snacks, and it was all offered to Mrs. Foley. Sensing her hesitation, Brooks had taken the decision out of her hands and made her a calming cup of tea and a plate of small cookies. And she was grateful to see some color finally returning to the older woman's face.

Jimmy had spoken to Brooks separately as Tom had been getting her settled in the room. "Honey, I know that this has been hard on you."

Brooks blinked the sheen of tears that had threatened and smiled at her father. "It's okay. You are right though. This has been rough." Curious she asked the question that had been in her head, "Are they all this intense?"

"No. Thank God." He glanced at the worn mother in the chair. "I never thought it would turn out this way," he said, remembering the verbal lashing he and Cam had received from her two hours ago. He took a deep breath and turned back to face his daughter. He wasn't keen on asking her his next question, but he pushed the dad part of him as far as he could and opened his mouth to ask.

"You don't have to ask. I know that you don't want to, but you need to. So I will save you the worry and just offer. I will talk to her." Looking at Mrs. Foley her resolve strengthened. "I think she needs to help as well."

Jimmy just stared at his daughter, amazed at the woman she had become. How had he gotten so lucky? he wondered. He just nodded his head and they headed back to the table.

Brooks focused and sat down across the grieving woman. Searching for the right way to begin, she reached across and placed her hand over hers. "Mrs. Foley," she began, "we need your help." She waited until the woman's eyes met hers. "I don't know what your son's involvement is, but I have three young ladies in my morgue and their families need answers, and so do we, before there is a fourth."

The woman squared her shoulders and nodded. Brooks smiled and nodded back. "Okay." Looking at her father she smiled. "We found three bags at your home, hidden in your dining room wall. Do you want to know what was in those bags?"

Steeling her resolve and pressing her lips together to stop the trembling, the older woman nodded once. She had to know.

"Okay, then we will tell you."

Jimmy pulled opened the file in front of him and placed three photos on the table. Each photo showed the contents of each of the bags laid out in a group and each bag had a name written on the outside in sloppy handwriting. He heard the sharp intake of her breath and he waited a moment before beginning. "The three names match the three girls. We are running DNA on the items to make sure that they match the girls and to see if your son's DNA is on any of the items." He laid another three photos out. Each eight-by-ten print contained two five-by-sevens of the cards with the lip impressions. One of each side of the cards. Jimmy placed the pictures so they corresponded with each of the girls. He hesitated before he pulled the other photos out, unsure of how far to push the woman.

Brooks asked the question that her father struggled with. "Would you like to see the three girls?"

At her nod, Jimmy took another set of photos out of the file. He didn't want to traumatize her, so he showed her the last photos of the girls alive. He placed each one above their other photos. He watched as the color faded from her face and he almost gathered them back up, fearing they had pushed her too far.

Mrs. Foley stared at the pictures. She stopped on the one of Stacy and hesitantly picked it up. Her voice shaky she began to tell them what she knew. "I have seen Marty with this girl. He brought her by the house and introduced her to me as one of his friends. I knew what she was the minute she walked in, but I couldn't bring myself to say anything. It is hard for him to make friends, and I don't think he has ever had a real girlfriend. It's my fault." She pressed a hand to her trembling mouth. Brooks squeezed her other hand.

"I'm sure it is not, Mrs. Foley."

She shook her head. "No, it is." She took a shaky breath before continuing. "When Marty's father left, I shut my heart down. It tore me to pieces and I just shut down to spare myself that pain. I didn't think I could live through it. I even shut out my own son!" A sob escaped before she could stop it. "What have I done?"

Brooks patted her hand as she watched her mourn for her son. For her mistakes. She glanced at her father and had to swallow the emotions that threatened to choke her. She couldn't imagine him ever leaving. And she couldn't imagine her mother shutting down, shutting her out if he did. Her heart broke for Martin Foley. How had he lived knowing his mother never showed him love? Or with the knowledge that his father had left without a word, never returning for his child? Thinking of it, she couldn't blame him for being messed up. But she still couldn't picture him beating the life out of a girl he liked enough to bring to his mother.

"I'm sorry," Mrs. Foley whispered. "This is my fault." She pointed to the girls. "They died because I couldn't love my son. I'm so sorry."

Tom had watched all of this quietly. His own childhood had come screaming back and he was afraid to speak. But he couldn't stay quiet any longer. He felt anger and something close to hate toward this woman, and the emotions stunned him. But he also felt pity, because even though she shut herself down, she still stayed to raise her son. So in some way, she showed him some care, some type of love. He slammed the door on his past and tried to calm the woman.

"Mrs. Foley. None of this is your fault. We all make our own decisions. You may not have shown him the love he craved, but you showed him love by staying with him. You didn't leave him, you stayed. But even without the love, every man makes his own choices. And he made his, not you."

Brooks was stunned. She had never seen him in this manner, and she had a feeling that he wasn't just telling her stuff. He was speaking from experience. And by the expression on Mrs. Foley's face, she was grateful for his words.

Mrs. Foley nodded. "Are you sure that he did this?" Tapping the picture of Nina, she continued. "Are you sure? I-I just can't see him doing this."

Brooks looked to her dad. She was no detective, but that same question had been nagging her since they showed up at the Foley house. Seeing Marty, and the way he reacted, had put a seed of doubt in her mind. She thought she saw the same doubt flash, if only briefly, in her father's eyes. Seeing that hardened Brooks's resolve. Even if it was just her, she would find a way to prove his innocence.

She was shocked by her father's answer. He looked directly into Mrs. Foley's eyes and answered without hesitation. "No. No, I don't."

Tom hissed and slapped the table, making the older woman beside him jump. "Thank, God!"

It was Brooks turn to jump. "What?" She was flabbergasted. What in the hell was going on? "I was sitting here trying to figure out how to convince the two of you to see my point of view," she exclaimed.

Mrs. Foley sat silently. Too afraid that she was imagining the whole scene. She didn't know how this had happened, but she swore to herself, if he was exonerated, she would do everything in her to repair the relationship with her son. The stress and emotions finally caught up and she covered her face with her hands and began to sob.

Before Brooks could turn to comfort the woman, Tom came around and knelt in front of her and gathered her up. "It's okay. It's okay to cry." He lightly pulled her hands from her face and waited until she looked at him. "But don't lose this chance. Trust me. If I had another chance, I would swallow my anger and try to fix it with my mom. I would give anything for that."

She nodded. "I'm just afraid that I am too late."

"It's never too late. Never."

She finally smiled, something they all thought hadn't happened in a really long time. "Young man, trust me, I have made too many mistakes but one thing I have never done is mince words. So believe me when I tell you, your mother would have been very proud of you. And I can guarantee, wherever she is, the pride for you is there."

Tom had to swallow the lump in his throat. Never would he have thought a kind word would have come from this woman's mouth. And definitely not directed toward him. "Thank you." He got Jimmy's nod before continuing. He stood up and brought his chair around so he could sit and face her. "We need your help. Can you do that?" She nodded. "We believe that Marty knows something about the murders. He may not know that but we need both of your help. Someone is doing everything they possibly can to frame your son for these murders. Every girl can be directly linked to your son. We found evidence in your house, although it looks like Marty did that one, unless someone did send him that stuff like he said." He thought of the lip prints on the cards. The lips on the other side definitely looked like they belonged to Marty. "But his name is linked to every girl. The murders took place all within a three-mile radius of your house. And I have a feeling when the crime scene guys are done with your house, we are going to find evidence linking him to these crimes."

Mrs. Foley's face lost all color. Her hands had begun to tremble, but her resolve held. They believed her son, and damnit, so did she. "I will do everything that I can. What do you need me to do?"

Jimmy smiled and told her what they needed.

Across the hall, Cam and Finn watched Marty Foley through the one-way glass. He had begun to softly snore; the emotional toll had finally exhausted him. His face rested on the cold steel table and he was still bound in chains.

Cam's brain had been on overdrive since they knocked on his door. His reaction to their presence screamed guilt, but everything about him suggested otherwise. She wasn't aware if anyone else shared her doubts, but with every passing moment, watching the poor man through the glass, seemed to add weight to her belief. Marty Foley was not their killer.

Finn was watching her think. Her mouth moving a mile a minute, working out whatever was on her brain. And he had a pretty good idea what she was working out. "He didn't do it. I don't think he did it. And I know that you don't think he did either."

She should have known. He could read her like a book. It still amazed her that they had only known each other for a little less than two weeks. It seemed like a lifetime. She turned to face him, leaning back against the glass. He took her breath away. The only word she could think to describe him was stunning. He was breathtakingly stunning. And she was learning that his mind worked similar to hers.

And that just added to his charm. "No, I don't think he did it. But he knows who did. He may not realize that he knows, but he does. It's somewhere in that brain of his." She had been in contact with the crime scene. They had found something significant. They had found a ring. A handmade, gold signet ring, with a cross carved into it. She was waiting on Jimmy to get out of the meeting with the mother so she could fill him in.

"Why do you think that someone would frame this guy? I mean why him? What is so special that he is targeted?" It was the one thing he couldn't figure out, and he couldn't put it aside to let it rest.

Cam turned back around to check on Marty. Her eyes widened at what she saw. Nina and Stacy were standing on either side of Marty. Both looked at him with sympathy, Stacy started to rub her hand over his bald head. Nina glanced up and looked directly at the spot where Cam was behind the mirror. She murmured something to Stacy and moved toward Cam.

Finn watched as Cam moved back. His brows bunched with concern. Cam must have sensed his concern because she said one word, "Nina."

"Oh. Can I stay?"

She grinned at the innocent question. It still boggled her that he was okay with what she was. "Yes, you can stay."

Nina overheard Cam's answer. "So hotness knows what you can do, yeah?" She smiled when Cam nodded. "Awesome."

Cam shook her head. It still boggled her mind that this was the girl she had met less than two weeks ago. Smart-assed and defiant. "Have you found Beverly yet?" Her heart sank some when Nina shook her head. "I guess she moved straight on."

Finn, who still struggled some to see her talk to what he saw as nothing, was wondering why Cam was so insistent on finding this other girl. "Why is it so important to find her?"

Nina had wondered too. Cam tried to figure out how to explain. "It can be complicated. Sometimes, when a person is violently killed, their spirit can become lost. Wandering around, confused and alone, not understanding what has happened."

"It's strange enough as it is. One minute you are alive, the next you are *poof!* somewhere else. Not knowing how you got there or what the hell is going on." Nina hadn't realized she had spoken aloud. She felt a blush steal across her cheeks when she felt Cam's eyes on her.

She turned to Finn and repeated what Nina had said. "She's right. But imagine that you can't find someone who can see you or hear you. That's what I am worried about with Beverly. Is she lost and wandering? Or is she already gone?"

Both Nina and Finn spoke at the same time. "Gone?"

Cam frowned. "Gone to…heaven, if you want to call it that. Wherever you go when you die." She struggled with that term her whole life. If there was a heaven, why did so many people get stuck in the in-between? Catholics would say it was purgatory, but Cam couldn't see it as that. She had seen too much to think that some were punished, banned from heaven, sentenced to wander around for a certain length of time. But she generally kept her views to herself. Too many arguments had gotten too heated and too many feelings were hurt when religion and politics were spoken between people. So she had learned to keep those views to herself. But if she was asked what she believed, she would have to answer that she believed in the soul. And just like you do in life, you choose where you go. You could stay here and watch over your family and friends or you could choose to go where all other souls go. Some call it heaven, some call it the afterlife, others would say it is another dimension, where you go to spend the rest of time, able to move between both places.

Finn nodded. He could agree with that synopsis. But he put that aside and nodded his head toward Marty and Stacy. "What is she doing in there?" He had been watching as the girl had been rubbing his head, petting him almost as if she was comforting.

Cam glanced to Nina and raised her eyebrows. Nina's face betrayed her. The normal nonchalant attitude gone, something akin to pity and sadness taking its place. "She loves him." She turned to look at the two of them. "I guess we all did to some degree. Although we never met each other, Marty would tell us how much we all meant to him, but when he would get to her, his face would betray him. Stacy was his real love, only he never knew that she felt the same way." She looked away and wiped at a tear.

Cam's eyes had filled. Finn wasn't sure what Nina was saying but he had the feeling that he knew what it was. Stacey was in love with Marty as well.

Cam asked Nina, "Why didn't she say anything?"

Nina shrugged. She remembered asking Marty that same question, but directed toward him. He had picked her up, but he had just wanted to talk this time. She knew that he had started to have feelings for someone because the last time they had been together, they had just talked as well. They had gone to the park and sat on a bench feeding the birds. A small part of her was hurt that he didn't have those feelings for her, but she had convinced herself long ago that Brad was it for her. He loved her and took care of her. But still, a small part of her heart longed for a man to look at her the way Marty looked when he spoke of Stacy. With his cheeks red and his voice low and stammering, he asked her if she thought he had a chance with Stacy. He looked so cute. Nina would have told him anything, but she knew that Stacy would be a fool if she didn't take that chance. And she told him just that. It was the last time she had sat next to him.

She smiled at the memory. "I guess he never got the chance to tell her. Neither of them did."

Cam was about to answer when Jimmy walked in the room. He had a grin on his face and hope had begun to bloom. He saw the tears before Cam could blink them away and his smile quickly turned to concern. "What happened?"

Cam swallowed and shook her head. "Nothing. Just getting filled in on something." She watched Marty again. Stacy had placed her cheek on Marty's head and had wrapped her arms around him. Seeing this, Cam walked out the door and into the room with Marty. Stacy jumped when the door snapped shut, and her eyes widened when Cam mouthed "sorry" to her. Cam nodded to the unspoken question and sat down across from Marty. He had woken up when Stacy had come in. Whether he knew she was there or not, Cam didn't know, but she knew that the tears had begun to silently fall again.

Cam turned to face the mirror and nodded to Jimmy. She knew that he would understand that this was to be a private conversation, and all recording equipment would be turned off. Finn must have told Jimmy that Nina was in the room because a minute later Nina came in and told Cam that he had shut everything down. She then moved to stand in one of the corners.

Cam reached out and placed her hand over Marty's. "Marty? Marty, my name is Cam. I want to let you know that right now, it is just you and me talking. Nothing is being recorded and nothing that you say right now will be used in any way against you."

Marty finally looked up. "I didn't do it. I swear, I didn't do anything. I-I love them. I couldn't hurt them."

Cam patted his hand. "I know. I know that you didn't do anything to the girls. Marty, I know that you loved them." She took a deep breath and looked at Nina out of the corner of her eye. Nina nodded, and Cam hoped that she was right and that she could trust this man.

"Marty, I am going to tell you something that no one else knows. I have been told that I can trust you. Can I trust you?"

Confusion and hesitation came and went on his face. He was unsure what to do, but he decided to trust the woman across from him. "Yes."

"I know that you didn't hurt those girls. You couldn't hurt them because you loved them."

He nodded. "I did. I did love them. They were my friends. They listened when no one else would. I couldn't hurt them. I couldn't."

"Marty, there are two other people in the room with us." She paused as his eyes roamed around the room, searching for the people he couldn't see. "Marty, you can't see them. But I promise they are here. Nina and Stacy."

"Stacy? Where? Where is she? She's not dead? Stacy!" Cam had to walk around and place her hands on his shoulders to keep him in his seat.

"Marty. Marty!" she snapped. "You have to sit. You have to be quiet. Please let me finish."

Tears flowed down his face. His eyes still roamed the room, searching for the woman he loved. Cam's heart broke. "Marty. Listen to me. Can you please look at me and listen?" She waited until his eyes focused back on her. "I'm sorry, but they are both dead. But I can see them." She pointed to the corner. "Nina is over there. She brought Stacy with her, so they could tell me that you could never hurt them. But they want me to tell you something else." She glanced up at Stacy before she continued. Her cheek still rested on Marty's head. Her hands rubbed up and down his arms. Tears silently flowed from her eyes, matching the streams that flowed down his cheeks.

"Stacy—" he choked. "Nina and Stacy? They're here?"

Cam blinked at the tears threatening in her eyes. This was all new territory for her and she wasn't sure if she was doing this right. "Yes. Like I said, Nina is in the corner. Stacy…Stacy is right behind you." She smiled as he spun quickly. "You can't see her, but she is there. She has been in here with you for a while, holding you close. Her cheek is on your head. Her hands are trying to comfort you. But what she really wants is to tell you that she is sorry."

"Sorry! Why is she sorry? She is—was, no is perfect! I'm the one who is sorry! I couldn't protect her!"

"Marty, it's not that. She wants you to stop blaming yourself. You couldn't have done anything. She doesn't blame you. She wants you to stop blaming yourself. But she wants to tell you something that she wished she would have told you before she died. She loves you Marty. She loves you the way you love her."

Marty put his head in his hands and cried. He kept saying a mix of "sorry" and "I love you too."

Cam patted his hand one more time and got up to leave. She needed a minute, and she needed it fast. Emotions swirled and threatened to choke her. When she turned the knob she heard him softly call her name. Swallowing the lump in her throat, she turned back. "Yes?"

His face still in his hands, he spoke. "I'll tell you everything I know. Everything I saw. I promise."

"Okay, Marty. That would help us. It would help us a lot." She turned the knob and opened the door. She needed that minute. God she needed it, she thought. But before she could walk out she heard Stacy's tears, heard her murmurs, her words of comfort to a man she thought she didn't deserve. She turned before she could stop herself. "Thank you. Thank you, Marty." And she closed the door.

CHAPTER 22

Finn found Cam in an empty holding room a few doors down. She was leaning against the wall, her face in her hands. She jumped when he closed the door behind him. Her face was splotchy and her eyes rimmed red, there were tears on her cheeks, and her shoulders betrayed the emotional toll the case had taken on her. He stood back a moment, taking her in. She had dressed this morning in a dark pair of jeans, a white T-shirt, an emerald green cardigan, and her trusty and worn brown boots. She hadn't bothered to pull her hair up and it was spilling over her shoulders and down her back. Her face was devoid of makeup, and in his opinion, she didn't need it anyway.

Without a word, he walked to her and wrapped his arms around her. Part of him was expecting her to resist the gesture, so he was surprised when she sank into him and wrapped her arms around him. And just as quickly, her control snapped and her body began to shake with her sobs. Finn just held her. He had an inclination that this was completely out of character for her. From what he had observed and what he had heard, she was very stoic and reserved when it came to a case. Never one to show her stress or emotions no matter the case. But something about this one had reached in and snatched her control. Her ability to separate herself from the case, a trait every good cop learned from early on. If not, this job would eat you alive inside of a month.

He held her and stroked her back until he felt her quiet. He pulled her back some so he could look at her, really look and see if there was another cause to worry. He cupped her face in his hands and quietly kissed her. Gentle and slow. And when he pulled back he smiled at the slow smile on her face.

"I'm sorry," she said. Pushing off the wall she shook her arms, willing the tears and emotions that threatened to choke her away. "I don't know what in the hell is wrong with me lately." She brushed her hair back with a jerk.

Finn smiled and took his first deep breath since she left that room. Here was his Cam. Pissed and irritated that the tears came and the emotions broke through. He would be far more concerned if she was still crying, but this Cam? This Cam he knew, and he knew how to deal with her. So he watched as the mad and the pissed came back and shoved those emotions away and scorched the tears from her eyes.

"I was beginning to worry. I almost sent Brooks in here." He smiled when her eyes narrowed to slits.

"You really would have had to worry then," she threatened. She loved her like a sister—hell, she was her sister. But she was not who she needed right then. Brooks had no issue with emotions. She lived in them, allowed them to lead her along. But that was great for her. It matched her body, mind, and spirit. It was one of the things Cam loved the most about her, and in some ways envied her for.

Cam became a total mess when her emotions broke through, blubbering and blundering around like a mindless ninny. Nope, she worked and lived better with that shit put away, she thought. But this case had brought them to the surface too many times.

Finn watched her, smiling. He loved to watch her think, mainly because he knew what she was thinking. He watched her lips move in a silent debate, her thoughts left as silent words across her lips.

"Stop it!" she exclaimed, still pacing, working her way through her thoughts.

He knew that she was aware that he watched her and followed her internal debate. It bugged the hell out of her, because she refused to accept that she did it, and it marveled him.

She finally stopped pacing. Her emotions and tears finally put away. She had mentally formed a list on what she needed from Marty. He knew who the killer was. She felt it in her bones. He may not know it now, but he would. And he would help put the killer away. Her thoughts betrayed her and jumped back to the image of Stacy and Marty. Her cheek resting on his balding head, her hands stroking his cheek. If they had been on the street, they would have made for an odd pair. Her youth and beauty clashing with his age and nerdy persona. But she saw something in that room. She truly loved him. And he the same. And unfortunately they were ripped from each other before either had the courage to speak their feelings.

Seeing it had broken her heart. And thinking of her own feelings, she had walked into that room, and for the second time that week, had revealed her secret.

Her eyes locked on Finn's. And in that moment she realized exactly why she had done it. Never had she had someone accept her for who and what she was, until now. And, she guessed, neither had Martin Foley. So that's why she did it. He needed to know it, and Stacey had needed to tell him.

"What is the smile for?"

She hadn't realized that she was. "I was thinking that these past two weeks have been the most emotional, yet satisfying of my life." She grinned at his puzzled look. "I never thought that I would tell my secret in this building, especially to a suspect."

"So why did you? If you are so worried about one of your colleagues finding out, why did you take the risk?" As he asked, he realized that he truly wanted to know. He knew that she held that secret close and very few were privy to it.

Cam took a moment to organize her thoughts. It bought her a minute to shake the nerves as well. This case was really doing a number on her mentally, emotionally, and physically. And with Finn thrown in too, her entire world shook to its foundation. Realizing she had nothing, she spoke and let the words come to her as they would.

"I'm not sure. This whole case has thrown my world upside down and shaken to the foundation. Never have I been so emotionally and mentally taxed by a case. I have had numerous cases that have hit me emotionally, but I still manage to keep them at arm length. They still never get close enough to do any damage." She paused. She had begun to pace without even realizing it. "This one… this one is shoved down my throat and I can't pull it back. I can't get this to back up. And some of it has to do with you—"

"What the hell did I do?" Finn hadn't meant to sound defensive, but he wasn't expecting to be lumped together with something she wanted shoved away from her.

She realized her error, as she heard his tone. She hadn't expressed herself right, but he was just going to have to deal with it, if he wanted to know what was going on. He was just going to have to shut his mouth and let her finish.

"Fine!" he snapped.

Cam hadn't realized she had spoken aloud. But she ignored him and finished. "Look, I understand this isn't coming through completely clear but just let me get it out. It will make sense as soon as you let me finish." And with his curt nod, she finished. "Until you showed up and opened up all these emotions inside of me, I could shove shit away. It was easy to. I hardly ever opened myself up that way so I never had this issue. And before you get your panties in a twist again, I am good with this. I like what you bring out in me. I'm just not used to it. I compartmentalize. And I do it for a reason. You know damn well that this job can chew you up and spit you out. You have to shove your emotions back. But this case happened to hit at the same time you did. So my efforts of compartmentalizing is going to shit. Plus Nina. Don't get me started on Nina! Her teenage attitude and frequent crying jags that swing straight into pissiness and bitching. I have been overloaded. And then today. Marty is in there, crying for Stacy and then *poof!* She's here. Crying for him and holding him, then apologizing to him for leaving him. I couldn't take it. I just couldn't watch it anymore. He had the right to know that at least one woman in his life loved him. And loved him for him. She didn't care if he was older, overweight, bald, and nerdy. No! She didn't care about that. She cared about him. She loved him for him. And he deserved to know."

Finn watched her. Arms flying around, her pacing back and forth, all the while trying to explain why one man's broken heart broke her own. And then getting pissed about it, before settling back into acceptance that she had emotions. And she had acted on those emotions. Was it any wonder why he loved this woman? And why the realization of this love was sudden or terrifying? But rather it was like coming home. He came to this big and noisy city, across the pond, and instead of just finding a killer, he had found his home. His home was a woman who baffled him. Infuriated him at times. But in all of that, his home held a love that he had never had for another, one that he had all but given up on. But even then this was a love that he had never thought he would find.

So here she was, defending her decision although there was no reason to defend, to tell a man that the woman he loved, loved him back. "Just like you deserve to know," he said. "You also, deserve that love. And you deserve to know that you have it. And you always will."

Cam's heart skipped. The tears she had so valiantly fought threatened to spill again. She smiled. "You have it too, always." She buried her face in his chest, praying that the tears would stay where they belonged.

After a moment, Finn asked if she was ready to find out what Martin Foley knew. He laughed as she nodded against his chest, and with one final squeeze, she let go.

"Let's go get this motherfucker," she said as they walked out the door.

Martin sat slumped back in his chair. His eyes darted back and forth, his right hand twitched nervously on the table while his left was grasped in his mother's. Five minutes earlier he jumped at the sound of the door creaking open, and he thought his mind had gone when his mother came walking through it. Her eyes were red rimmed and her nose a bright pink, and the moment she saw her son, she gave a small cry and rushed to him. The tears he had finally controlled spilled back over. He couldn't remember the last time he had seen tears in his mother's eye or felt her arms around him. He had long ago resigned himself to the fact that he would never be enough for his mother. He would never have any memories of a warm, loving home, fresh-baked cookies, or the comforting touch of her hand when he was sick or scared.

Martin had learned the reason of his mother's coldness one rainy morning when he was twenty. He had been helping clean out the attic so he could move his computer stuff into the space. There was an old trunk shoved tight into the far corner, and from the thick layer of dust, he surmised that it hadn't been touched since it was placed in here long ago. He had thought about mentioning the trunk to his mother, and he was on his way to when he thought of the contents. If the trunk was his mother's, he would never see the contents. And the curiosity was getting to him. If it turned out to be nothing, then he would go right back down and ask her what she wanted him to do with it, but what if something was in it? He knew nothing of family. It had just been the two of them since he could remember. He had asked his mother once before about his father and her parents or any other family, and she had coldly told him there was no one and he was never to bring it up or ask again. So an old discarded trunk was a definite curiosity, and he slowly and quietly backed up the stairs and walked to it. He knew he couldn't go through it now, so he placed a folded table in front of it and finished cleaning. He would go back to that trunk later on in the night.

After his mother had gone to bed that night, he had snuck back up the stairs and straight for the hidden trunk. He knelt in front of the clasp and reached for it. He chuckled to himself when he saw the trembling in his hand. "What the hell do I have to be nervous about?" But a ball of nerves had settled low in his gut. He took one final nervous glance behind him. Confident that his mother was fast asleep, he flipped open the lid.

He sucked in a breath and fell back on his ass. Pictures lined the lid. Black–and-white photos stared back at him. A smiling and happy woman held a tiny bundle. Clutching the chubby baby to her chest, his mother's head fell back in wide open joy. And with every fiber in his being, he knew that the tiny bundle, who brought his mother such joy, was not him. Another picture showed the same joyful woman, arms cradling her blooming belly, standing next to a tall, smartly dressed, attractive man. Martin stared at the photo in bewilderment. The man stood behind his mother, his arms encircling her belly as well. But this was not his father. No, not his father, but he was quite obviously the father of the child his mother had happily held. A baby who had brought her immeasurable joy. A baby who was so obviously not him.

He didn't notice the tears streaming down his cheeks. Rivers carrying hate, guilt, and shame. A slow burn of hate had built with every smiling picture he encountered, and the fast flood of guilt and shame followed. The child carried no ill will toward him, but he couldn't stop the jealous hate that engulfed him, knowing that his mother was joyous for that child, but had shown no joy toward the child she had raised.

Oblivious to the tears, he sat back up and began to pursue the contents of the trunk. Blankets and clothes had been lovingly folded and placed just right. A folded paper held the imprints of two tiny feet and two tiny hands. The ink had been smudges in places, small circles radiated out, and Martin was sure they were the result of his mother's tears. More photos were placed under the blankets. They were of the same man with his mother. As Martin was moving to place them aside, he noticed a feature that stopped him cold. In one photo, the man stood beside Martin's mother, they were looking into the others eyes, and their fingers barely touched. His mother was in a light dress and small heels. Her hair was curled and styled and she wore pearls at her ears and neck. She was carrying a white book, and a look of innocent love consumed her face. The man was standing in front of a platform that had three long steps joining it to the main floor. A tall stained glass window glowed in the midmorning sun, creating beautiful patterns on the floor below. The man was dressed in a dark suit and shirt. At his throat was the white card declaring him a priest.

Martin sat still. Shocked to the core. Questions screamed in his head. These pictures showed his mother, but she was a stranger. Never in his life had he remembered her smiling, let alone laughing. Obvious joy written on her face. But the one picture that cut him deep, down to his very soul, was the picture of absolute love as she stared down at the child in her arms. Furious and hurt he shoved the pictures aside and began a more thorough search of the trunk. There has to be something, he thought. Something that tells him who these people were. Who had brought his mother this joy? He had a brother, he thought, or a sister. How had he never known of this? How could she have never told him of this?

Buried at the bottom of the trunk was a leather book. Well worn. Well used. He opened the cover and saw his mother's neat and fancy script: Abigail Eleanor Matthews. Martin sighed, his mother's journal. *Hopefully it will tell me what I need to know*, he thought. He set the book aside and set everything back into the trunk. When he had it shoved back into the corner and his table covered it, he gathered up the journal and moved to the old plush chair he had salvaged. He sat for a moment, running his hands lightly over the old worn leather. He knew that the guilt should prevent him from intruding into his mother's personal thoughts, but the image of her smiling, happy face shoved the guilt aside and pushed him forward.

He opened the cover and ran a finger over his mother's name. He had never heard someone call her Abigail or Abby. She had always been Mother or Mrs. Foley. When his father left, she had never gone back to her maiden name. She had steadfastly held on to that one last piece of him. The image of her standing at the door, silent tears on her cheeks as she watched him drive away. Martin had stood on the step, crying for him, begging him to come back. Before he left, he had bent down and gathered his son up and held him tight. "I love you, buddy. But Daddy needs to go away for a while. You need to be strong for your mother. I will come get you in a few days. I promise." Martin had still begged and cried. He remembered begging his mother for her to make him come back. Three days later he was killed in an accident. And his mother had never spoken of him again.

Shaking off the memory, Martin turned to the next page. He began to read his mother's memories. Memories of dreams and fights with her sister. An argument with her mother because she couldn't go to the school dance with a boy, her father's insistence that she forgive her mother and move on. She wrote of how her father would sneak her books that her mother had forbidden, because they were inappropriate for a young woman. Another argument with her mother because she thought that Abigail was becoming to open minded and was moving away from the teachings of the church. She wrote of boys who were cute, who had smiled and waved, only to have her mother's disapproving look. Martin was fascinated. He had never known this person. Not a shred of this carefree and open-minded young woman had ever cracked his mother's cold, hard surface. Here, in these pages, lived a young woman who loved and hurt, who was carefree and smart, who flirted and giggled, who balked and rebelled against a narrow-minded and hard, cold mother, but reveled and basked in her father's love and pride. Nowhere in these pages was there even a hint that this bright and loving girl would turn into a stern, cold, and harsh woman.

Eager to discover what had caused it he read on. Well into the journal, he received his first revelation. A young seminary student had come to the church to study with the family priest. Father George, his mother wrote, was a handsome young man, with striking blue eyes and a captivating voice. He began to teach the youth and counsel them as they were transitioning into young adults. Admiring her intellect and love of reading, the young priest and Abigail had formed a friendship and had begun to correspond through letters. Abigail had written about how their letters had begun as common interests and talks of books and her future plans, and then evolved into personal dreams and a growing fondness for each other. Martin read as his mother talked of her secret dreams and her growing feelings for the young man. No longer did she refer to him as "Father George," but she began to call him only George, and a few more entries in he then became "my dearest, my darling, or my love."

Martin had to stop for a moment. The emotions swirling inside had begun to throb at his temples. His heart was beating fast and his fists had begun to clench. His whole world had been rocked and he was unsure of what he was going to do about it. His mind flashed to the picture of his mother and the man, cradling her growing belly. He found that now that he could put names to the faces, he struggled to do so. Abigail and George. He wanted to shut down, his body and mind begged for it, but he had to know. He had to know who the baby was and where did he/she and George go? How had his mother come to love and marry his father? These questions and more echoed through his mind. So he sat back down. He didn't remember getting up, but he sat back down and took a deep, calming breath and opened the journal again.

He read as Abigail and George fell in love and made plans for the future. Their dreams of marriage and a family, how George would leave the seminary and go back to school for teaching. Martin then read of a fateful encounter that had occurred one hot summer evening, and of the resulting pregnancy that changed their lives forever. When Abigail's mother, Helen, discovered what had happened, she immediately sent her to stay with relatives in a small town in western Maryland. He read of the heartache and anguish her mother felt as she was separated from George and her family. On three occasions, George had managed to sneak away and visit her. Their plans had held firm until the final visit and during that visit, she had gone into labor and given birth to a son. They had named him Timothy James. As George held his son, Helen and Abigail's father had arrived with the priest who was over George. Martin read as the two had been given only one option: George would go back to the seminary and have no contact with Abigail or their son. Abigail would be returning to her parent's home, but their son, Timothy, would not be. Helen had found a couple who would be adopting him, and Abigail would have no contact with him, nor would she know who would be raising her son. Martin read the hate-filled words his mother had written, as she had no choice but to go along with her mother's demands. Helen had threatened to bring charges against George, as he was ten years older than Abigail's sixteen years. Not only would George face possible criminal charges, but he would also face charges from the church. Abigail watched as George had no choice, but to turn his back on his love and his son and walk out the door. And then she watched as her mother looked at her daughter and her grandson with clear distain. She wrote of the harsh and hate-filled words her own mother had said to her. How Abigail had brought great shame to the family and to the church. How it was now her duty to return home and marry a man that her mother had found and to put this whole embarrassing and ugly blemish behind her. Helen had told her daughter that she should be grateful that she had found a man willing to marry her and accept this embarrassment. Someone willing to step up and bear the burden of marrying a harlot.

Martin snapped the journal shut. He was shocked as he felt pity for his mother. She had lost everything and then was forced into a marriage that she didn't want, to a man she didn't know. And she had to give up a child. A child that was conceived and born with love. Martin felt pity, but he also felt jealous. Jealous that he wasn't born into that, conceived into that. Unwilling and unable to read anymore, he silently walked back to the trunk and placed the journal back. He felt confused, but he also felt like he understood his mother. But he was also left with a million burning questions. As he looked at the closed trunk, he was resigned to the fact that he would most likely never learn the answer to a single one.

CHAPTER 23

"Martin?" Abigail Foley was certain that her son had gone into shock. Detective Jimmy Aaron had been waiting, silently, patiently, for her son to snap out of whatever had a hold of him. But Abigail was beginning to think that her son would never come out of what had a hold of him. When she had first walked in and saw him chained to a table and the floor, it had almost been too much. He had looked so lost. So tremendously sad and alone. And it was her fault, she knew. She had never been the mother he deserved or the mother he had needed.

Fear had choked the life from her when she discovered she was pregnant again. Memories of Timothy flooded her system. To protect the little sanity she had left, the little morsel of her soul that remained, she shut down. She remained emotionally distant from her child, her husband, and it had cost her dearly. Her husband had left when Martin was four and then was taken completely away when he was killed in an accident three days later. So she was left to raise a child she couldn't bring herself to love. It terrified her to even think of opening herself that way, and now she was realizing that she hadn't just lost her husband those many years ago. She had lost her child as well.

Martin blamed her for his father's death. She remembered when he was twenty and had moved his office upstairs. One day he was fine and the next he was spiteful and mean. It was the first time he had truly hurt her. He had come downstairs to breakfast and looked haggard and sick. She asked him for the reason and he had spit out, "Why do you care? I have never mattered to you. I could never be enough for you. Hell, Dad couldn't even stomach you, so he left. You are a cold-hearted bitch incapable of love and affection, even for your own child. It's your fault that he left. It's your fault he's dead." It was like a slap in the face. In that moment she realized what she had done. What her decision had truly cost her. What it had cost her son. Regret choked her, the weight crushing her chest. She looked at her son, unable to say anything. He was right. He was right.

Her soul withered at the hate his eyes held. "Martin—"

"Don't you fucking dare. Don't you say a goddamn thing to me." The ice in his voice froze her blood. She expected the heat and the yelling; instead, she got calm and ice. And somehow that hurt more. "You know what is ironic? You couldn't stand *her*. You hated her with every fiber in your being. And yet, here we are, and wouldn't you know it, you are just like her. You are just like her." She watched him shove from the table and leave. She didn't have to wonder any more. She knew exactly what had happened, and he was right. It was her fault. She pictured the trunk in the attic and the look on Martin's face confirmed her worst fears. He knew the truth. Just like she knew who he was comparing her to. Her mother.

Sitting here next to her son, Abigail would never forgive herself. Here, next to her, was a broken and defeated child. Her child. She knew and understood the emotions in his eyes. They were the same ones that had been in her eyes that day in the hospital. History does repeat itself, she thought bitterly. But there was one thing that would not be repeated. She wouldn't leave him. Like her mother did all those years before. No, she thought, heartbroken. *No, I am not my mother and it's about time I realized it.* Taking her son's hand in hers, she used her other to turn his face to her.

"Martin." Abigail heard her voice break but she didn't care. "Son, I am sorry." The tears began to fall when she saw the shock in his eyes. "I'm sorry. This is my fault. I was unable—" She stopped and closed her eyes. No excuses. Only the truth from now on. "I refused to love you. I told myself I couldn't bear to have my heart ripped out again. So instead of loving you, I selfishly chose to protect myself. And for that I can never forgive myself. But it stops now. I know that you know about my past. About your brother. I should have told you. I should have told you so much. But..." Her voice broke, the tears choking her. "I shut myself down. When he was taken from me, I thought that I could never love again. I couldn't risk it. Not even for you. I'm sorry. I'm so sorry. I know that can never fix what I did, but hopefully you can let me change your mind about the future."

Jimmy sat stunned. *What in the hell is happening?* he thought. *Another son?*

Cam and the rest were equally dumbfounded. *What the fuck is going on?* She jumped when she heard a voice over her shoulder. Turning she saw Stacy. Tears streaming, her eyes never left Martin.

"I knew. I knew about Timothy. Martin confided in me one night. He was thinking about finding him." She smiled at the memory. "He had wanted to do it for his mother. He thought if he brought Timothy home, she would love him. She would finally love him."

Cam's mouth hung open. Her mind was blown. Never would she have thought of this sharp turn of events. Everything about this case, everything they had thought that they knew, just exploded.

When they had first heard of Martin Foley, Cam's mind zeroed in on him. He fit. He fit perfectly. Loner. Older male. No real connections with anyone. He knew every one of the victims. Had interacted with all three on a weekly basis. They would trust him if he approached them. They wouldn't hesitate to go and spend alone time with him.

Finn watched Cam's face. The look on her face told him that one of the girls was here. One of them was talking. And with the information that they had just heard, he was leaning toward Stacy.

"Cam?" He had to say her name twice before she finally registered him. "The rest of us are not privy to the information that you are getting." He gestured to Tom and Brooks.

Cam's eyes widened at the sight of Tom, and Finn realized his mistake. *Dammit!* he cursed himself.

Tom watched her face. He had heard rumors that Cam O'Brien had a freak ability to put herself in the victim's head. A sixth sense.

He had been watching her through this whole case and he was sure that she did have that uncanny ability. One that most cops would ignore, but not her.

Now he stood here watching her and he realized it was more than a sixth sense. He had had a passing thought or two that she might be something more, but he just brushed those away. He didn't care what she could do, as long as she got the job done. But now, he saw it was more. And old Finny boy's slip-up confirmed it.

But something in her eyes had his smartass retort stuck in his throat. Fear. There was a genuine fear in her eyes. He wasn't sure why it was there, but he saw it. Raw and plain.

"Cam," he began.

"I can see them," she blurted out.

Shock emptied his mind of anything he was about to say. He wasn't expecting her to admit to anything. He was actually getting ready to give her an excuse. But what she just said erased it.

Cam took a deep breath and told her secret for the second time that day. "I can see them. The dead. I hear them. I talk to them." Anticipating his next question, she quickly continued. "No. No, they cannot tell me who killed them. It's like they don't remember that part, or whatever, but they can't tell me." She swallowed her pride and walked over to Tom and stood in front of them. She was about to beg for him to keep her secret and she hated to beg. She felt weak and pitiful when she had to beg.

Tom saw the plea in her eyes. But he also saw mad. "Cam, you don't have to ask. This is your deal, not mine. So it is not mine to tell. I won't say a word."

She took a deep breath. She could see that he was telling the truth. He wouldn't tell.

"But..." He placed a hand on her shoulder when she turned. He waited until she faced him again. "I only ask that if you get anything new, anything that would help, that you keep me in the loop."

She nodded. Cam could see in his eyes that he would tell no one of her secret.

She glanced at Tom one more time and swallowed her reservations. She wasn't used to informing other people what any of her dead, as she called them, said. "Stacy is here. She just told me that she knew about Timothy. Marty told her one night. And then he told her how he wanted to find him. And bring him home. He thought if he did that, his mother would finally love him. Finally want him."

Brooks's heart broke. Tears were streaming down her face. "That's so sad. How could a mother not love her own child?" She had seen in many times. Seen the aftermath of what parents could do to their own children. But this was new to her. She watched Martin try and try to reach his mother. Only to have him turned away.

But she also thought of the conversation that she had just had with Mrs. Foley. It was no excuse, but she saw a woman who was broken down. A woman who shut out her heart to protect herself. Only to realize, hopefully not too late, that not only had she lost one son, she had lost two. Brooks couldn't understand it. How could you turn away your own child?

She looked through the glass to her father. She couldn't comprehend the idea of her father, or mother, not loving her. Not showing her the love that she had grown up in.

Unaware of the revelations in the other room, Jimmy sat stunned, processing the revelations in this one. He looked over at Mrs. Foley and watched the tears slide silently down her cheeks. Her eyes hadn't left her son's tear-streaked face.

"Exactly who is this other child?" Jimmy asked.

Abigail Foley dabbed her cheeks with a tissue. She took a moment to still her trembling lips and had to squeeze her eyes shut for a moment when her son took her hand and held it firm.

Jimmy sat and listened as she told him the story of her first love and the child they created. How, on the day he was born, her mother came in and ordered the child to be removed and placed for adoption. How she was basically "sold off" for marriage to another man she did not know, or love.

Abigail reached down and bared her soul. She recounted the loveless marriage to Martin's father, and she struggled to hold her emotions when she told of the fear of being pregnant again. How she was determined to never allow herself to love this new child. Afraid that her heart would shatter completely if she did.

"I'm so sorry, Marty. I'm so sorry," she sobbed.

Even after all that she had done, her son still held her tight as she cried.

Jimmy left the room to give them and himself a moment. He walked into the observation room. He saw the tears on his daughter's face and gathered her in his arms.

"I don't understand it, Daddy. How could a parent do that? How can they do that?"

He shook his head silently. He didn't understand it either. He gave her back a final rub and let her go.

Cam was still turned toward the glass. She silently watched as Marty held his mother. Nina was in the corner of the room, watching the scene unfold. Regret was written all over her face, and Cam filed that away. They would discuss that later. Stacy still stood next to Cam, quietly watching and listening.

Finn was the first to break the silence. "Does Stacy know if Marty found him? Timothy?"

Cam hadn't thought to ask. She turned to Stacy, knowing she had heard the question.

Stacy shrugged her shoulders. "I'm not sure. He had said that he thought he had found him, but wanted to be sure before he said anything."

"Where is he?" Cam's brain focused sharply. "Did he say where he found him?"

Everyone watched Cam intently. Waiting for her to find the answers.

Stacy turned and began to pace. "I think he said he was still here. In Baltimore. He had said that he had found some records—" She stopped suddenly.

Cam realized how he had found the records. "Stacy, I don't give a flying fuck if he hacked into the state's records. I really don't. I need to know what he found. I need to know now."

"Okay. He said he had found some records that said that it was a local adoption. One that was handled privately between Abigail's mother and the family. But he knew that Timothy was still in Maryland. And he believed he was in Baltimore. But that is all I know. I swear."

Finn and the others were on pins and needles. Waiting, for what seemed like an eternity for Cam to share what Stacy was saying.

Finally she turned and relayed the information.

Tom spoke before Jimmy could. "How about I go and start researching this adoption. If you all get anything new, let me know."

Brooks held up her hand. "I am going to go help. It doesn't look like I am needed much more here so…"

Jimmy just nodded. He knew she just needed to get out. And he understood. He looked back through the glass. "That would be good. It doesn't look like we are going to get much from either of them for a little while anyway."

Back in the bullpen, Cam sat staring blankly at her computer. Finn watched her from across Jimmy's desk. She looked tired. Tired and emotionally drained. He wanted to take her out of here. Away. Far away.

He remembered the first time he saw her. Cool, yet fierce. A Celtic warrior. Her hair a warm red, it reminded him of a sunset he saw on the Cliffs of Moor. Her eyes, green and sharp. A cop's eyes. Her body was solid and slim. He had known many female cops in his time on the force, but never had one caught his eye. They were all just one of the guys. A badge and a gun. But Cam wasn't just one of the guys. It was like a sucker punch to the gut.

Picturing her then and her now, the fierce warrior was still there, but she was struggling to stay afloat in the battling sea of emotions and stress. And dammit, if he didn't know how to help her out. This case was going one way—straight toward those Flannery bastards. And now? Now it was going towards- towards- Where in the fuck was it going? He thought. They could have sworn Martin Foley was their guy. He fit the pattern. He knew all of the girls. Hell, they were all killed within a ten-block radius of his mom's house! But now, they were in search of a long-lost brother, and no one knew if this guy has anything to do with it.

And seeing the look on Cam's face, God, he wanted nothing more than for this damn case to be done.

It shocked him, that last thought. For so long, his only thoughts had been of finding the bastard so Cat could finally rest. That was his first and only thought, every day. But now, his first thought was of Cam. He wanted it over so he could see her smile. Really smile. To have the haunting look leave her eyes.

"What?" she asked.

Finn shrugged. "I was just thinking we need to get away. Far away."

Laughing, she began to brush off the thought, but it stuck. "That would be great." Looking at her board, all thoughts of warm beaches and coconut drinks evaporated.

Four faces stared back at her. And all she could do was stare back. It frustrated and ate at her that this bastard was still out there. And she was no closer to finding him. So she stared at the faces before her and thought of the bastard who was still wandering free.

Jimmy decided it was time to update the captain. He hated coming to him with nothing, but he was hoping that a fresh pair of eyes might be what they needed.

He knocked on the door jam and waited in the open doorway. He always liked the feel of this room. Some brass kept these rooms like a shrine to their glory days. Plaques and awards, medals and old sporting trophies would litter the walls and shelves, sucking up every available space. But not here. Not in this brass's office.

There were some awards and commendation's here and there. What swamped the captain's office were pictures. Pictures of family—kids, grandkids, and officers. Stuck in between pictures was various plaques and glass awards from fellow officers and some from his little league teams. Praising the man for dedication, hard work, and his selfless spirit. And all were surrounded by pictures of those who presented the awards.

Jimmy remembered a conversation they had had about why he kept all of this in here, instead of just the normal shit most brass keep in their offices. Captain Thems looked at him and said, "I'd rather be surrounded by the faces of those who really matter, those whose opinions I care about, instead of the politicians and bastards who could care less if I was here or not. Do you really think that the bureau commander and the police chief even know who I am? Hell no! So why do I want their fat asses standing next to mine, handing me a fucking award that they won't remember handing me twenty-four hours later? Fuck no, I'd rather have your ugly faces staring back at me. It reminds me of why I do the job. Why I go toe-to-toe with those jackasses downtown, to save one of your sorry asses." Smiling he walked in and sat down.

"Good news, I hope?" Captain Thems asked.

"What?" Jimmy realized he had mistaken the reason for the grin. "Ah, no, sir. Not yet. Sorry."

The captain's forehead crinkled.

"Sorry, sir. I was just recalling the first time I had asked you about your office style."

Captain Thems smiled himself. He looked over at his lieutenant and he was struck by how old he looked. This case was weighing heavy on him. He remembered that Jimmy always carried a case hard, until he solved it. But this one was different. His old partner looked ragged.

Sighing he stood up and walked over and closed his door. "Okay, cut the 'sir' shit and the 'oh, the case is progressing, sir' and break the fucker down for me."

Letting out a big breath, Jimmy realized why he needed to come in here. Not only did he need a fresh pair of eyes, but he needed his old partner for a bit. Thems and he had been partners for fifteen years before he took the captaincy and Cam came along. They held the record for the most arrests and convictions for the division. And Jimmy was hoping some of that would shine through to help with this fucking bitch of a case.

Jimmy sat in one of the visitors chairs that he had pulled up to the desk. The captain had just cleared everything from his desk and had sat down opposite of him.

Jimmy opened the file and spread it out before his old partner. "Okay sir—"

"How many times do I need to tell you to fucking stop with the 'sir' shit?"

Smiling, Jimmy apologized, and he began again. "Fine, dickie." He used the old nickname that bugged the shit out of Thems since their days at the academy.

"Fucktard." Thems hated that nickname "Dickie," but at least the "sir" shit had stopped.

Captain Richard Thems listened to his old partner run through the case. They really didn't have much. They didn't have shit. "Is that all?"

Jimmy didn't answer. He knew that he didn't have too.

"What about this mysterious 'brother'?" Thems asked. It seemed like a long shot but they had nothing else.

"I have Tom and Brooks looking into that. And the kid over at ATF is still pursuing any angle we can find on the Flannery clan. Although, we are all in agreement that they are just a patsy the perp is using. It threw us off for a day or two, but we can't find any solid evidence that would explain why they would be the ones behind this."

"I thought that you said the boyfriend of one of your victims is linked to them?"

Jimmy flipped back in the case file to Brad Morris's picture. "He is linked but we just don't see them killing the girls. Why kill your pay day? It doesn't make any sense."

Thems nodded. "I can see that. Have you thought of whether they were killed because they knew something?"

Jimmy shook his head. "No. This doesn't fit with that. And the way the clan works, no one really knows who the next one up is, so it would be extremely hard for anyone to turn evidence on them. Plus, they make sure everyone in the organization knows what happens to those who snitch on them."

Thems didn't need to revisit the photos from that murder to agree with Jimmy. That was an image that stuck with you.

"Okay. So that brings you back to Martin Foley. Why not him?" He shuffled back through the papers until he found the evidence log from earlier that day. "It looks like he has key evidence from all three murders, a personal connection to all of the girls. He seems like a solid suspect. Why is he not booked on the charges?"

Jimmy looked back over Martin Foley's sheet. He did fit. He fit solid and neat. But he knew in his gut that Martin had nothing to do with any of the murders, but his gut was also telling him that he was connected somehow.

Thems picked up Foley's mug shot and stared. A pasty, plump, and balding man stared back. His eyes were red rimmed and glassy, probably from crying. He had seen even the toughest of men start crying the minute the cuffs clicked around their wrists. It was pathetic really, the lengths a man would go to get out of a pair of those silver bracelets.

Focusing back on the photo, Thems's gut was telling him maybe Martin Foley needed another look. "Are you going to question him again?"

Jimmy nodded. "We let him go tonight, but he is supposed to be back in the morning."

"Why not leave him in lockup?"

"I think I will get more from him if I let him have his freedom. Lockup would not be beneficial. It would shut him down."

Thems wasn't so sure, but it was Jimmy's case. But if Martin Foley wasn't sitting in an interrogation room by morning, old partners or not, the captain's bars would come right back out. This was the one time he didn't agree with what Jimmy had done.

"Why are you so sure that he can give you what you need? You found evidence in his house for Christ sake!"

Jimmy was used to Thems disagreeing with his methods, so he took the disbelief in stride. "He is the key to it. That I am sure of." He had been toying with a theory, but he hadn't shared it yet. He knew that it would not be well received. It was a little too "daytime soapish," but the more he thought of it, the more it made sense. He had wanted to test it on Cam first, but since he had his old partner here, he decided to test the waters here.

"Okay, this theory is going to sound absolutely apeshit, but hear me out before you kick me out."

Captain Thems was used to Jimmy's hair-brain ideas, so he nodded and prepared himself for an interesting few minutes. "As long as it is sound enough and credible enough to warrant you letting a man go whom you had significant and sufficient evidence to hold for the foreseeable future, if not charge with the three, if not four, murders."

Jimmy understood the underlying tone to the statement. Thems was warring with the two sides of himself. The one side wanted to believe and back his partner, while the other, whose gold bars were weighing heavily on his shoulders, was ready to strangle his lead detective for letting a suspect walk out of the precinct.

"Foley mentioned a long-lost brother who was given away at birth. Well, what if that brother found out that dear old mommy had *and* kept another son? If he doesn't know the story behind the adoption, he may feel that he was just inferior and so he was given away at the first available opportunity. With this festering and eating at him, he struggles to cope with the anger." He paused because he could already see the doubt forming. "Remember daytime soap?"

Thems just nodded. He was beginning to wonder if Jimmy had cracked under this case.

"Anyway. Adopted brother finds out that his mother gave him away and then goes and has another new family. Then he thinks, 'Why is he so important? So special?' So he devises a plan to bring about the fall from grace for the other, so he can step in and be the prodigal son who returns home just when the other falls. Instead of killing and martyring the son she kept, let's completely ruin him and lock him away. Nothing is as mortifying as having a child who kills another. But he thinks, let me take it a step further. How about making it so revolting that she will never want to see the other son? How about he also sexually assaults younger girls and then kills them brutally? Not only will the other son be disgraced, he will be a monster that no mother would want. And here comes the long-lost son, just in time to fill the void left by the other."

Thems sat quiet for a long moment. Jimmy had always thought outside the box, following his gut and seeing things in ways that others never could. It was a trait that he admired very much. One that he always wished he had. But he was more of the practical and straightforward type, which is why they were successful as partners. One was grounded and kept everything in order, and the other wasn't afraid to look at and think of the abstract. Although this was beyond anything Thems had ever heard.

"So you think that there really is a long-lost son who is doing this to get the other out of the way?" he asked incredulously.

Jimmy knew he sounded nuts, but something was telling him that he was onto something. "I know it sounds nuts—"

"You think? It sounds fucking crazy!"

"Just let me work it for a bit. Try to see if I can get anywhere with it."

Thems knew what it took for Jimmy to ask. But he also knew what would happen if the fucking commander found out that he went along with it and they ended up with another body.

"Jimmy, you know that I would always follow you on any of your instincts, but—"

"Okay, so let me do it. If it goes south on me, it is on me. You knew nothing of it. Nothing. I will take the fall."

"Goddamn it! Don't you see I am trying to keep you from falling flat on your face? Is this really how you want to end your career?" He knew the answer before he even asked the question. Jimmy would do it in a heartbeat. Because that was the kind of cop he was. He didn't give a shit if anyone laughed or mocked him. If he thought it was a plausible theory he would follow it to the ends of the fucking earth if he needed to. And just like when they were partners, he would follow him. "Fuck me, Jimmy. If you are wrong and we fall on our faces, I'll fucking kill you myself."

Jimmy smiled. "I don't doubt it."

CHAPTER 24

Cam sat on her couch still thinking about Jimmy's hair-brained theory about Foley's long-lost brother. She would give him his day, without question, but after that day there may be a question or two. She believed him, without a doubt. If he said that his gut was leaning toward that, then she'd follow.

Finn asked her, on their way home, why she said yes right away.

And she told him the truth. "Never has he ever once doubted or questioned me. Never."

And was it any wonder why she loved this man, when all he did was look over and say, "Good enough for me."

So she would give him his day. No questions, no doubts, but they may only make it a day before questions starting creeping in. Picking up her wine she reran the theory threw her head. And not thirty seconds later, she screamed and almost threw her glass at the redhead behind her.

"Goddamn it! Put a fucking bell around your neck, would you!" she yelled as she stood and twirled around. Only to find Nina bent over laughing like a loon. "It's not fucking funny! You gave me a damn heart attack! Jesus!"

Nina stood and wiped her face. "I swear if I was still alive I would have pissed myself I was laughing so hard."

Cam just glared.

"Some medium you are. I thought you were supposed to know when my kind was around?"

"Shut up. What do you want?" Nina actually looked hurt, and Cam felt a moment of regret. But just a moment. Actually Cam didn't know what she felt about Nina. She had never had a spirit stay this long. This was a first.

There were a lot of firsts with Nina, the more Cam thought about. And it was really starting to unnerve her. What if they all started staying? Cam thought. What if they all started to be able to touch her, the way Nina could?

Looking around her condo, Cam had an overwhelming urge to just be alone. She had it for all of about ten minutes. Finn had an errand to take care of and Brooks was still off with Tom trying to find the brother. And Cam had finally given in and had a glass of wine and absolute quiet. Just quiet. And she found that she had missed it. And now here was Nina. Loud, demanding, flashy Nina.

"Well, you don't have to get bitchy." Nina pouted. She actually pouted, sticking her bottom lip out.

Jesus! Cam cringed. Do girls actually do that shit? Pout? She didn't think she had ever seen someone actually thrust their bottom lip out and pout.

Seeing that this was getting nowhere, she threw back her head and downed the rest of her wine. And then settled in for a long night.

Clearing her head of any nasty comments, she decided maybe the girl just needed to talk for a minute. So she swallowed her smartass retort and took a deep, calming breath. "I'm sorry, Nina. Is there something you needed?"

Thinking the pouting had actually worked, she bounced on her toes and smiled. Then, ignoring the cringe on Cam's face, she danced over to sit next to her on the couch.

"Where's McHottie?"

Cam rolled her eyes and shrugged. "He had an errand to run." Anticipating her next question she continued. "I have no clue where or when he will be back."

Nina huffed and nodded. "Okay."

"Why? Is there something you needed?"

Nina toyed with the necklace around her neck. And Cam noticed that she was no longer wearing the short, tight, red dress. She actually looked like a regular sixteen–year-old. She had on a gray cardigan sweater with white and pink circles, a white tank top with dainty lace trim, and dark boot cut jeans. She had traded her hooker heels for a pair of cute gray ballet flats. Her red hair was pulled up in a loose, messy ponytail, and cute little earrings winked at her ears.

Nina noticed Cam staring and blushed a little. "I finally figured out that I can change. All I really have to do is think, really hard, about what I want to look like and it's like *poof!* I'm wearing it."

"It looks good on you. And better. So much better."

Nina's blush deepened. "I saw this outfit in a store in the mall and I really loved it, but Brad said we didn't have the money. So when I figured out how to change, I thought of this."

Cam smiled and thanked God that she learned that trick. It was getting annoying seeing Nina dressed in the red hooker heels and dress. Especially after seeing a picture of her dressed like any other teenager. It was so much nicer seeing her this way. And it also seemed to change her attitude as well. Gone was the hard and bitchy brat, and here was a still sometimes bitchy, but softer teenage girl. Cam liked this Nina better.

"So what did you need?"

Nina shrugged. She wasn't sure. When she realized she could change her clothes the first person she thought of was Cam, so she came. It hurt a little that Cam seemed to only want to talk or see her when she could do something for her. And maybe that was her fault, she thought, remembering the nasty little witch she was the first few times they talked. But that wasn't really who she was. It was who she pretended to be when she was scared but didn't want to admit it. She fiddled with her necklace a while longer. If she had to admit it, this is what she wanted. Just sitting here, with someone who actually saw her, heard her, talked to her. She hated being alone. Hated it. And without Cam, that's what she was. Alone.

Sensing something else was going on, Cam just sat quietly and watched her twirl the necklace between her fingers. Seeing Nina like this made Cam realize just how young the girl was. She barely looked fourteen, let alone sixteen. And to go through death so young and alone.

And that's when it clicked. Like a light bulb switching on.

Cam shoved all other previous encounters, talks, and nasty chats out of her head and let this new version of Nina sink in.

"Nina?" She waited quietly until the girl met her eyes. "Where do you go when you aren't with me?"

Cam caught the sheen of tears before she could look back down. Nina held her lips firm until she was sure the trembling had stopped. "I don't know. Here and there."

Although she knew, Cam asked the question anyway. "And where is there?"

"Home." Nina tried to control the tremble in her voice, but it gave her away.

Empathy rolled through her body. No matter what their past was, Cam had to remember that Nina was just a child.

"Do you know if I am stuck here? Or will I get to leave?" The question was asked so quietly, Cam thought she had just imagined it. It wasn't until she saw a tear slide down her cheek that she realized Nina had actually spoken.

Cam reached over and grabbed Nina's hand. It still gave her a jolt to feel her. She wasn't as solid as the first time, but she was still there. Still solid enough for Cam to feel. "Sweetie, one thing that I have learned is that we all make that choice." Seeing the confusion she tried to explain.

"When we die, a million different things can happen. I don't know all of them, but I have found, through this gift that I have, that everyone has a choice. I have known some who just go straight to the afterlife. Whether it's heaven or hell, or to a new body or just disappearing, I don't know. But they just go. And then there are some, like you, who don't remember making the choice to stay, but you just 'woke up' and you were still here."

"I don't remember saying I wanted to stay, but like everyone else I was terrified of dying. Afraid of leaving. Why do you think I stayed?"

Cam sat back. She had never been asked this before. After a moment, she answered, "I think you stayed to help. Help me, yourself, but also to help the other girls who came after you. Do you remember when we found Stacy?"

Nina nodded and smiled. "She was scared shitless."

Cam chuckled. "Yeah, she was, but she wasn't after you went to her." She saw the doubt and then pride flash across her face. "You may not realize it, but because you stayed, she wasn't alone. And because you stayed, she has remembered stuff that has helped with the case."

"Because I stayed," she said quietly, smiling to herself.

Then just as quickly it was gone and her hand clamped like a vice around Cam's. It still shocked her, how real and solid Nina felt. Her face went white, her eyes darkened like a storm raging on the sea.

"Nina? Nina!" Cam had been saying her name over and over, but the look of pure terror never left Nina's face. She tried to pull her hand free but couldn't. With every tug, Nina clamped harder. So Cam tried the only other thing she could think of. Raising her left hand, she smacked Nina's right cheek.

She knew that she shouldn't have, but Cam was afraid she was going to break bones. Her hand was purple and painful. But she ignored that and focused on Nina. Her eyes were fixed and dark. Almost black. And she was pale. Very pale. Cam was lost. She didn't know what to do. A million questions flew through her mind. She was about to smack her one more time when she finally fell back.

"Nina! Nina, what's wrong? Please you have to talk to me."

Nina's head rolled back and she went still. After what seemed like an eternity, she slowly opened her eyes. Cam was leaning over her, gently rubbing her cheeks, forehead, and stroking down her hair. Nina saw the panic in Cam's eyes and felt guilty. She didn't know why but she hated that she had caused their nice time to go to chaos in an instant.

"Nina, please say something," Cam pleaded.

"I'm sorry. I'm sorry."

"For what? Why are you sorry? Just tell me what happened?"

Nina pushed herself up. She wasn't sure what happened. She remembered sitting here talking to Cam, and then all of a sudden…

"No, no, no! Don't you dare do that to me again!" Cam yelled.

"I remember. I remember him!" Nina's eyes widened. "I remember his face! Cam, I remember his face!"

Cam felt the color leech from her face. *What?* Her mind screamed. "How…h-how?"

Nina didn't notice Cam go pale. All she could think was *I remember the sonofabitch! His pale eyes, fleshy jowls, blonde, thinning hair.* She remembered the feel of his hot breath, panting over her as he forced himself into her. The pain that clawed through her stomach, starting low and moving up, forcing the bile up her throat. The feel of his hot, clammy hands groping and squeezing, painfully tight on her breasts, her ass, her thighs. The way his fingernails bit into her skin on her thighs, pulling them apart so he could reach her center. Pounding and punching her until the pain became too much and the merciful blackness to her down.

Unaware, Nina had dropped to the floor. She had always known what had happened to her, but the image of his face brought it all back in one rush. It was as if she had gone through it again. His face. His face had brought it back. His face had taken her back there. Back to the filthy, damp, and dark alley.

It was the rocking that brought her back. The gentle sway back and forth. She was cold, so cold. Shaking, she let herself sway. The gentle rocking slowly calmed her. Slowly closed the door, those glacier eyes tucked back in the dark.

The pounding in her ears finally ceased and she heard the gentle humming of Cam's voice. Finally she became aware of arms wrapped around her. When she hit the floor, Cam had rushed over and gathered her up.

"I'm sorry. I'm sorry," Nina whispered over and over.

"Shh. Shh." Cam gently rocked and petted. Her own heartbeat was fighting to slow. "Shush now. There is no need to be sorry."

Nina just allowed herself to be coddled and rocked. When she finally felt as if the memory wouldn't swamp her again, she began to tell her of what she remembered.

Cam listened and every few sentences she would ask a question or two. "Have you seen this man since then?" The nagging had come back. Lingering in the back of her mind. Trying to ignore it, she stood up and began to pace.

Nina shook her head. "Not that I remember." She sat up and moved so she could face Cam. "But it was for sure not Marty. I have always known it wasn't Marty, but now I am positive." Something still bugged her, ate at her. The eyes. Something about his eyes.

"What aren't you telling me?" Cam could see her holding back. Doubt lingered in her eyes. "Nina?"

Nina hesitated. "It wasn't Marty. I swear it wasn't Marty, but the eyes. Cam, they were Marty's eyes."

And then it clicked. The doors, that had closed that part of the dream, shut it up in the back of her brain, flung wide open and his face came into focus. Her knees gave out and she stumbled to the couch. Memories flooded her vision and the night of Cat's death came crashing down.

"Please! Please stop. Don't! Please!" she begged. Stars exploded as his fist slammed into her jaw. She gagged as vomit burned her throat. She struggled to roll over; panic flooded her mind as she struggled to breathe.

"P-Please." The words were like mush, her jaw wouldn't work right. Somewhere it registered that he had broken it when he hit her. Her mind struggled to figure out how this monster was the same man whom she had met earlier downtown.

He had approached her. Meek and timid, embarrassed that he had taken a wrong turn while he was walking back to his hotel. He was late for a dinner date with his wife. He had snuck away to buy her the flowers that were resting in his left arm.

"Of course, I'll help," she had agreed without hesitation. Just a harmless man turned around in the city he was visiting. So sweet and harmless, he looked like a kind father or grandfather.

"Which hotel?" she had asked.

"The Marker, over in the Docklands," he had replied. His voice was clearly American. From the accent, Cat placed him as an East Coast American. In her profession, she had had numerous interactions with tourists looking for a good time. Away from home, somewhere where they say magic still exists.

Her eyebrows immediately raised. "A beautiful and exotic new hotel. Are you enjoying it? I bet your wife is loving the beautiful and luxurious spa."

He smiled. "Her anniversary gift. She has always wanted to see where her family had come from."

So sweet, she thought. So sweet.

She was wrenched from the memory by his sweet breath. She felt his tongue on her skin and the bile slammed in her throat. She forced her eyes open and was shocked to see that they had come back to life. The ice blue gleamed with glee as she fought and struggled. His breath became ragged and his eyes darkened. She could feel him straining against her. Her mind told her to stop fighting, to lay still. Her struggling only seemed to excite him more. But her will shattered as he ripped her dress from her body. The fabric of her lace panties bit into her flesh as he tore them in half.

Her struggles made his erection harder. With each squirm and whimper, he strained harder and harder against the confines of his pants. Her skin was so soft and white. He ran his hands down the length of her, pinching and squeezing. Little bruises marked her body, like bread-crumbs for him to follow back to the start.

He saw when her will broke. Her struggles began to weaken and the fight was leaving her eyes. Infuriated, he used his fists to bring her back around. First he jammed his fingers hard and rough inside her. He almost came when she screamed. Next he punched and pummeled her, breasts and face. Body and hips.

Unable to control himself, he yanked his pants down and finally let himself take her. When she stopped fighting, he would punch and beat her, until he finally had his release.

Looking down on his work, he felt the confines of his life break free. The final piece of his plan clicked. He hadn't thought it would feel so good. He hadn't thought she would look so right. Just thinking of it had him hard again. But he ignored it. He had work to do. Taking a deep breath, he turned away.

As he began to walk away, he thought of his wife back at The Marker. Oh, that part was true, he thought with a chuckle. He wondered what she would think if she knew what he had done. She wouldn't understand. He paused and took one last look behind him. Smiling, he resumed his walk No, she wouldn't understand. No one would.

But he finally did. He finally understood what he was meant to do.

"Cam!" Nina shook her. *Jesus*! she thought. *Is it a competition now? Who can scare the other the most tonight?*

Cam screamed in her mind. She could taste the bile rising in her throat. *Please*, she begged. *Please don't be true.* "I know who it is. I know who it is," she cried. Her heart broke at the betrayal. Never, never in a million years would she have thought this was possible. Never.

"Who is it?" Nina struggled. Her emotions were on overdrive and Cam wasn't answering. "Dammit! I deserve to know! Cam! I deserve to know."

Not meaning to, Cam ignored the pleas of the girl beside her. She got up and moved to her bedroom. Her mind was too stunned to speak. Too hurt to explain her actions.

Nina's words fell on deaf ears. Hurt, she began to leave. She stopped in the living room to pout, thinking Cam would see and finally snap out of this…this…well, whatever the hell this was, she thought. She waited until Cam came back through the living room, and timing it perfectly, she planted herself in the way and tried to make Cam acknowledge her.

But something on Cam's face stopped her cold. Her eyes were dark, almost black. Her lips stood out against her pale, too pale skin. "Cam, wait," Nina tried. She reached out and tried to grab her arm. But she was too fast and she slipped past her and out the door.

Hurt, Nina stood at the door and tried to figure out what had just happened. Cam had remembered something. Something that had not only scared her, it frightened her down to the core. It tore at her resolve. Ate at her solid foundation. Nina struggled to figure out what could do that. What could shake the rigid and sturdy Cam? Something about Cam's appearance came back to her. Pale and shaken, Cam had fled the apartment. But she hadn't left empty handed. Searching her memory, Nina zeroed in on what was different. Two things: Cam had a gun out. And no badge.

CHAPTER 25

Cam stood at the corner of Martin Foley's street and watched the Foleys' darkened windows. Her eyes searched the streets for any sign of the killer's car. The lying, sick fucker was nowhere to be seen. She had wanted to be sure before she went knocking on the door. She needed to get the two of them out of there and to a safe location.

Her heart was pounding. Betrayal coursing through her in sickening waves. Cam thought back to the moment she had put two and two together. Her mind had recoiled in anger and disbelief. There was no way that this was true. None. She had known this man her entire life. She had trusted this man with her life. He had been in her home, her father's home. He wore a badge every day, just as she did. Just as everyone in their unit did. He had stood over dead bodies with her, including those on this case.

Cam had to put that away. File it away for now. Force down the bile that scorched her throat. She had other worries now.

Knowing she would be exposed in the front, she maneuvered her way down the alleys until she found herself in the tiny concrete backyard of the Foley home. Before knocking, she took a quick inventory of her situation. She had been so upset when she realized who the killer was, she had run out the door without any of her gear. Luckily she had her "rainy day" stash in the lock box in the trunk of her car.

She always kept a tactical, outer vest, to which she could attach other gear— handcuffs, OC spray, loaded magazines. She also had another patrol rifle and spare magazines. One thing she had been taught, and rigorously practiced, was you can never be too prepared. When she had been a rookie, only a year and a half out of the academy, she had been out with some friends when a gang turf fight had broken out. They had been pinned down behind her car and all she had was her off-duty weapon and the one magazine that was in the gun. From that day forward she had started to gather her own personal backup stash that was kept in a locked box bolted to the trunk of her car.

It was from that stash that she had armed herself tonight. And as she peered through the darkened downstairs windows, she was grateful she had learned her lesson all those years ago.

Something wasn't right. She could feel it in her gut, something else she had learned to trust. It was too dark. Too still. Checking the readout on her watch, the burning in her gut intensified. Eight o'clock. There should be movement or a light on somewhere in the house.

She heard the snap behind her a millisecond before she felt cold steel at the base of her skull. "How did you know I would be here?" she asked.

His laughter sickened her. "I trained you. I know everything there is to know about you."

He jerked her around, the bare skin on her forearms scraped painfully against the rough stone of the house. She was staring down the barrel of a Glock. The hand that held the gun was attached to Captain Dickie Thems. A man she had known her whole life. Who had been to every birthday party she had ever had. An honorary "uncle." And Jimmy's former partner.

She fought the urge to spit in his face. "Why?"

"Because I can." She heard a sickening crunch and then faded to black.

She tasted metal just a moment before the nauseating pain. A searing hot flash that screamed through her head. She swallowed back the bile and vomit. She wanted to open her eyes, but she fought the urge until the spots stopped dancing. So she decided to wait. Wait and plan.

She lay motionless, regulating her breathing to feign unconsciousness. The longer she could play possum, the longer she could recover and figure out a way out of here. Her wrists were cuffed behind her back, the cold steel bit painfully into her skin. She slowly worked her fingers back to feel that she was cuffed to more metal, and if her guess was correct, she was cuffed to a radiator. She swallowed the panic when she realized that the radiator was warm. She knew that it was only a matter of time before that heat transferred to the cuffs. She had seen the end result of this on another case, where the victims hands had been cuffed to a radiator and the heat had melted the skin around the steel of the cuffs. She fought desperately against the urge to panic. She needed to buy herself some time to get out of this.

Cam emptied her mind and calmed her breathing. She wondered where the Foleys were and resisted the urge to open her eyes. She wasn't sure where Dickie was, so she couldn't risk the peek. The thought of him brought on a new wave of anger and grief. Never would she understand why he betrayed them. Or betrayed the badge.

Memories flooded her mind. She couldn't remember the first time they had met. He had just always been there. Steadfast, like a rock, by Jimmy's side. When her mother had left, her father had sworn that she wouldn't leave her child. Jimmy and Dickie had been there, searching the streets for weeks, with her father and grandparents. The first time she had gotten her ass kicked in a fight, Dickie had taken her to the police gym and taught her how to fight. When she came home the next day, suspended for kicking the same girl's ass, he had taken her for celebratory ice cream. Up until she graduated the academy, he had been Uncle Dickie. But now he was a monster. A monster who raped and murdered four young girls. All the while playing the caring captain, urging his team to go and find the sick son of a bitch responsible.

Cam's thoughts then turned to Jimmy. The hurt and betrayal she felt would be nothing compared to his. Dickie was another brother. They had gone through high school and then the academy together. They had worked some as partners during their uniform days, and when both had made Homicide, they became partners again, until Dickie had made captain.

Cam struggled to make sense of it all. How could a man who was so dedicated to the service and protection of others throw it all away? How could he have done these terrible things? How? She struggled with the war of emotions tearing through her. He wasn't just her captain. He was her mentor. Her leader. Her friend.

Shoving it aside she began to formulate her plan. The cuffs were becoming uncomfortably warm. She resisted the urge to struggle, afraid he would realize she was awake.

She needed to get a visual of her surroundings. Ignoring the pain in her head, she slowly cracked her right eye open. She bit back a gasp and waited for her vision to clear. Realizing that it was as clear as it was going to get, she began to methodically access her situation.

Laying on her right side, she was chained in the corner of a room. There was dust and dirt caked on the old wood plank floor. She could see a faint light coming from a window somewhere on the far wall. The window was high up and the light was quickly fading, and Cam realized she had been unconscious for a while. Hope began to spring. Finn had to be looking for her. God, she prayed, she hoped that he was looking for her.

Her thoughts were interrupted by the heavy footsteps coming up the stairs. Her heart thudded with every approaching step. She quickly shut her eye again, not wanting to give him any indication that she was awake. The footsteps stopped somewhere just to the left of Cam. Fear bloomed fast and hard in her. Fear of the man who held her captive. He was a stranger to her, and she had no clue what he was capable of.

Shock echoed through the room along with the crack of a palm against skin. Cam braced herself for the wave of pain and was baffled when it never came.

The gasp of pain wasn't from her either. And one of Cam's fears was confirmed. She wasn't alone. He had someone else too. She recognized Abigail's voice as she pleaded with Dickie to stop.

"Stop? Why the fuck should I stop?" Dickie sneered.

Abigail's voice trembled with fear and pain. She understood why he hated her. Why he would do this to her, but Cam had done nothing. Neither had Marty. She stole a quick glance at Marty. He was strung up by his arms. His head hung limply against his chest and his toes barely brushed the ground. She had pleaded with Dickie to leave him out of this, but he had punched her and when she came too, her younger son was strung up. Dickie had bound his wrists and then thrown the rope up over a rafter and tightened it until Marty's toes barely touched the ground. His head had been drooped since she came to. He had been stripped to his boxers and she saw the bruises and blood that were scattered over his face and body.

"Why are you doing this? Why?" she asked again. She had asked this question repeatedly to no avail. "He hasn't done anything to you. Nothing."

She sickened when he sneered. "I know. But you have." He walked toward his brother. He kicked out, hitting him in the stomach. He laughed when he heard him groan and struggled with the urge to do it again when he heard his mother pleading for her son.

He reigned in his temper and warned himself about control. He needed that control if he wanted to truly make her suffer. That was a little side benefit he learned during his time with the girls. He learned to control his rage so he could prolong his time with them.

He glanced back at his mother. He saw the tears and pain on her face. Yes, he thought, he needed his control, because his mother was going to decide when it was time to let her baby go. Just like she let him go all those years ago.

He turned his attention to his other guest. She was currently unconscious, although he had a feeling she was faking, on the other side of the radiator. Dickie hesitated. She wasn't supposed to be here and he wondered how she had figured it out. He struggled with what to do with her. He tried to picture her not as Cam, but as another one of the whores he needed to punish. But memories kept creeping back in. Memories of a smiling, fresh-faced eight-year-old begging her Uncle Dickie for one more piggy back ride. One more push on the swing.

He turned his back to her. He wasn't ready. He just wasn't ready to deal with her yet. He walked back to his brother and took it out on him. Each kick and punch carried fury. He was furious with his own weakness. His mother's screams intensified the fury raging through him. He beat and kicked and tortured his brother until his hands bled. Finally, winded and trembling, he stopped. He stepped back and admired his work.

Marty's bare chest was mottled with red, purple, and black spots. His face was a bloody, swollen mess. And joy flowed through Dickie's veins. He could hear his mother's gasping sobs, and the ecstasy was like a drug, drowning the hurt and abandonment he still felt. It carried it deep and locked it away.

He turned and faced the bitch who caused all of this. "Stop your screaming and crying. You're the cause of all of this." He knelt in front of her and gathered his hands gently in his. "The day you and my father turned your back on me, discarding me like a piece of trash, was the day this all started." He saw the agony and hurt on her face. All for his precious brother. The one she decided to keep. *Where is the agony and the hurt for him?* he thought. Disgusted, he gave her hands one last squeeze and fled the room, unaware that he had snapped three of her fingers.

Cam heard the bones snap and the sharp cry of pain that followed. She waited until she was sure Dickie was gone and she struggled to sit up. She slowly opened her eyes and breathed deep until the nausea subsided. Turning as far as the cuffs would allow, she tried to calm Abigail. "Mrs. Foley..."

Abigail jumped at the sound of Cam's voice. "Detective? Oh, Detective! I'm so sorry that I caused all of this. I'm so sorry—"

"Mrs. Foley! Mrs. Foley, Abigail, stop!" Cam snapped. She was afraid that Abigail was beginning to go into shock.

Abigail jumped a little at the harshness in Cam's voice. "I-I-I'm sorry."

"Stop saying sorry! None of this is your fault so get that shit out of your mind." Pausing she glanced at Marty. She held her breath and listened; she let out a sigh when she finally heard a shallow, ragged breath. She didn't think Marty had much time left. He was hanging limply, his arms were the only thing holding him up. She could see that Dickie had strung him up, leaving him with only the tips of his toes to take his weight. She had seen this before. It was a method of torture. One ties the victim's hands above their heads and pulls the rope tight until their toes barley touch the ground. It leaves tremendous pressure on the shoulder sockets, but it also hinders their ability to take in air. To add to the strain, the victim is beaten about their torso, making even shallow breathing hard and excruciatingly painful, until the body goes into shock and breathing is impossible, resulting in a slow and painful suffocation. And Marty's coloring was not good. She could see the skin around his neck turning a reddish purple, and that told her that he was beginning to suffocate.

"Marty!" she hissed, glancing toward the stairs. Cam didn't know where Dickie was and she needed him to stay away long enough for her to, at least, get Marty conscious. If she could wake him up, she may be able to buy him some more time. "Marty! You have to wake up and breathe. Marty please! If you don't wake up, you are going to die!"

Panicked, she searched around her. She needed to get her hands free. She had to wake him up. She tried to ignore Abigail's hysterics; she didn't need that shit right now. "Goddammit Abigail, shut up! That is not helping anything right now."

Abigail's mouth hung open. She had never been talked to like that, and this woman, whom she had begun to respect, had been the one to do it. But she couldn't control the hysteria that was building.

Cam whipped back around to face the older woman. "Because hysteria and crying are not going to fucking help right now. Does crying wake him up? Does hysteria make him breathe? Fuck no! So shove it all down and put your big girl panties on and fucking help me save your son!"

Stunned, Abigail's mouth hung open. But somewhere deep down, a voice told her that Cam was right. This was no time for hysteria. Not time for tears and fear, she needed to save her son. Steeling her resolve and ignoring the searing pain in her hands, she began to work at the cuffs securing her wrists, all the while staring at her son, willing him to stay with her and breathe.

Cam's search was turning up nothing and she was beginning to lose her battle with pain. The cuffs were becoming hot, fast, and the metal was cooking her skin. She glanced up at the window and noticed that the sun was gone. Darkness blacked the window. She wondered how long she had been gone. Two, three, four hours? Was anyone looking for her? Had they noticed she was gone? Had Finn come home to find her gone? Would he know where? *Nina! Shit*, Cam thought. How had she forgotten about Nina?

Heart racing, she began to frantically call out to Nina. She didn't know if she would even hear her, but Cam had no other choice. When she was younger, she had experimented with different ways to connect to the spirits who came to her. Her gift had intrigued her back then, and she had been curious on whether or not spirits could tune into her mind. Or her soul. Could they talk spirit to spirit? So one day she tried it. She opened herself up for communication and began to call out with her own spirit, trying to find one that would answer. And to her astonishment, three had. Within ten minutes, she had three spirits in her room. They had all heard her. After that experience, she had never done it again. It had frightened her to the core. She had never really had any issues with any of the spirits she had come into contact with, until that experiment. When a medium opens themselves up, if they are not careful, they can open themselves too much and then a spirit can "jump" them, meaning, the spirit can enter the medium's body and begin to take over. And that happened that day, and Cam almost lost that fight. And she had never done it again.

But now she had no choice. She just prayed and crossed her fingers that only Nina answered. So she concentrated and opened and called. After ten minutes, Cam heard nothing. And then she heard footsteps, heavy and fast, so fast Cam couldn't react. And in a matter of seconds she was face-to-face with Dickie Thems.

He dropped to his knees so he could look straight into her eyes. "I knew you were faking." He saw the lie form before she could speak it. As soon as she opened her mouth to speak it, his hand whipped out and smacked it from her mouth. He watched as the shock registered and then the pain.

"Don't lie. I can see it before you even open your mouth." He noticed a small line of blood start to trickle from the corner of her mouth. He cupped her face, ignoring the jerk of her head, and wiped it with his thumb. He hadn't been this close to her since she was a child.

He held her face firm in his hands and stared at the woman she had become. Her eyes were green glass. Her skin was flawless, although she had a few freckles scattered here and there. He hadn't noticed those before. He saw her every day, how beautiful she had become. Of course, until today, she had always just been Jack's girl and Jimmy's partner. Another one of his cops. How many times had she sat across his desk and he all he could think of was her beauty? he asked himself. A slow burn began deep and low in his belly. He began to rethink his plans for her. He may keep her around a bit longer.

Cam sat frozen. Dickie had never raised a hand to her. Hell, she thought, he hardly ever raised his voice to her. She had thought another was coming when he cupped her face in his hands. She had begun to hope that he was changing his mind about her, until she saw his eyes change. She knew what that look meant, and bile rose in her throat. As his eyes darkened, he began to absently rub his thumb along her jaw. Cam sat perfectly still and kept all emotion from her eyes. At first she wanted to cringe away, but she realized that this may buy her some time. The whole time she never moved. Never flinched. Never stopped calling to Nina.

Dickie wondered what she was thinking. He had seen the way she looked at Finn. Just as he noticed the way Finn looked at her. He also was aware that he was staying in her condo. He wondered how close they were. They couldn't be that strong yet, he thought. The Irishman had only come to town about two weeks ago. Then he thought of how she came here alone. Where was Finn? Where was Jimmy? It gave him confidence that he would have a while with Cam. They would have time to really get to know one another.

He had to turn away from her. The burn was raging through his belly, turning him hard fast. But he had other business to finish before he could enjoy his new-found plans with Cam.

Cam let out a ragged breath when Dickie finally turned away from her. Bile was beginning to choke her. She saw the unmistakable desire in his eyes, and fear ripped through her. She had seen what became of those he desired. She tried desperately to calm herself, but she was losing, and losing fast.

Dickie had moved to Abigail. When Cam heard a bone crunch and Abigail scream, she opened herself up completely and screamed for Nina.

CHAPTER 26

The ATF building in downtown Baltimore was in a nondescript building. It blended in with the other brownstone buildings that surrounded it on all sides. The underground garage was accessible through the back alley. Finn passed through a guard station, showing his badge and credentials, before continuing through what appeared to be a simple mechanical arm that blocked entry to the garage. He thought it looked a little lacking until he inspected the contraption closer. Hidden in the concrete floor were four ten-inch solid steel pillars that would raise automatically a sensor was not deactivated by the guard. The "simple" mechanical arm was made from titanium and could stop a car traveling at high speeds. As he searched for his assigned spot, he noticed the armed tactical officers positioned in various spots around the garage. He had to show his credentials again at another guarded post, and was finally let into the elevator. The elevator had no buttons; the floor was selected by the guard.

After a brief ride, the doors opened to a nearly deserted office area. Cubicle walls sectioned the large room off into about forty different work areas. Small "hallways" ran a maze through the cubicles. Unsure where Matt was, Finn hollered out his name. Finn was reminded of the "whack a mole" game when Matt's head shot up. He waved Finn over then sat back down, disappearing behind one of the walls. He was back in the far left corner, in the center of a cluster of six cubicles. A couple of other agents were scattered here and there and had also looked up when Finn hollered out. Some had the look of annoyance on their faces, but most were just curious.

Matt heard Finn approaching so he marked the file he was reading and stood up. "Detective McDougal."

"Matt," Finn said, smiling. "And please. Just call me Finn."

Matt ducked his head and nodded. He noticed the curious glances that were thrown his way. He tried to ignore them, but his chest did puff out some. Rookies didn't get many visitors, especially international ones. He knew that his meeting with Finn was going to circulate through the ranks fast.

Finn noticed Matt's reaction to the curious onlookers and decided to throw the kid a bone. So he spoke a little louder than normal. "Did you find the brother? Cam said that is the key to this whole mess."

Hearing the name Cam, Matt seemed to notice for the first time that she wasn't here. "Where is Detective O'Brien? Sorry, ah, the brother, um…" He shuffled through the files again, trying to find the right one. Putting his hands on it, he pulled it to the top and showed Finn what he discovered. "I searched through all the adoptions in the city for that month and came up blank. So I decided to expand outward toward the surrounding counties and again I came up blank."

Finn listened while he read over the file. The names on the file made no sense to him. They didn't match any of the names that they had on their list. "Why are you showing me this file?"

"OK, I am getting to that," Matt said. "Sorry—"

"Stop saying sorry. It makes you sound as if you don't have any faith in yourself."

Matt stopped himself before he said it again. "Okay. After my first search came up empty I went back through who all was involved in Abigail's life during that time, and I got a hit. Kathleen Smith."

"Kathleen Smith?"

Matt flipped to another page in the file. A list of names was neatly written and Kathleen Smith was circled with a question mark. "According to what Martin Foley said was written in his mother's diary, Abigail was sent to live with relatives in the western part of the state as soon as her mother found out about the affair and pregnancy. Well, the aunt's name was Kathleen Foggerty."

Finn caught on. "Let me guess. Her maiden name was Smith?"

"You would be correct, sir." He flipped the file back to the birth certificate. "And one Kathleen Smith, age eighteen, gave birth to one healthy baby boy on March 18, 1957. And that baby was given up for immediate adoption. The father was listed as unknown."

Finn thought it could work. "Did Kathleen Smith have any other children after 1957?"

Matt grinned and shook his head. "Kathleen Smith doesn't show up anywhere else in the database, from that day on."

Before Finn congratulated the kid, he asked one final question. "Do you know where that baby boy went from there?"

Matt nodded. But Finn noticed the enthusiasm leave his face. "What?" A ball of dread knotted in his stomach. His famous gut instinct.

"The child was adopted through a closed adoption, meaning no contact or information would be shared between either party."

"So how did you find him?"

Matt leaned heavily on his desk. When he found out where Timothy went and what had happened, he had double and triple checked all of the data before he called Finn. For once in his career he wished to be wrong. Dead wrong. "Timothy was adopted by an established couple who lived in the area, but made the move to a Baltimore suburb in the sixties. The couple only had their one son, a little boy they named Richard—Richard Anthony Thems."

Finn went white. He thought he might be sick. Now he understood the hesitation the kid had about the news. "Are you sure? You said it was a closed adoption." But he knew the kid would be sure before accusing another cop of this, which is why he already was dialing Cam's number. He waited for her to pick up and half listened to how Matt found the information to start with.

"I only found the information, because someone else already requested the closed file. Someone with high-enough clearance to throw their weight around and get the damn file." He grabbed another sheet and handed it over.

Finn looked at the signature on the sheet and heard Cam's phone go straight to voicemail.

Before Matt could blink, Finn turned and took off across the office floor heading for the bank of elevators. "Shit!" he muttered as he grabbed his coat and took off after him. He caught up with him at the elevator doors and grabbed him and pulled him to the staircase. "This way is faster."

Finn had already redialed Cam twice and had gotten her voicemail twice. He tried to think rationally, but fear ate at his belly. He burst through the door straight into the garage, Matt close on his heels. Matt went straight to his car, and Finn followed.

Finn spat out Cam's address and dialed Jimmy, praying the entire time that Cam hadn't decided to take on this bastard herself.

Ten minutes later, Matt screeched to a halt in the middle of Cam's street. The noise and bustle from the pub couldn't drown out the commotion of the team as they all flooded in to find Cam.

Finn threw open the car door and bounded up the stairs to Cam's third-floor condo. He heard the boom of Jack's voice before he hit the second-floor landing, and Jimmy's not far behind. Two uniforms attempted to stop him before he could enter, but he pushed them aside. They caught up to him before he could make it to the living room.

"I fucking live here! Let me go! Cam! Cam! Goddammit let go of me before I shove that baton up your ass!" Jimmy heard the threats and Irish curses and rushed in before Finn could make do on any of them.

"Let him go!" Jimmy rushed to stand in between Finn and the two officers. "He's with us."

Finn yanked his arm out of the hold of the taller officers and shoved him back. He ignored the yell from Jimmy and fled into the living room and straight into a broken down Jack. "Jack? Cam?" Finn's stomach dropped. *Please, God, don't tell me I am too late*, he prayed.

Jimmy came back in and saw Finn knelt in front of Jack, a look of pure anguish on the kid's face. "Finn, we can't find her." His voice cracked.

Matt walked in with the rest of the team and Brooks immediately ran to her father. "Where is she?" Tears streamed down her face.

Jimmy just hung his head. "I don't know, baby. I just don't know."

Unsure of what to do, Matt looked around. The team stood in the open room; some milled around the dining room table and others had taken up stations around the living room. He began to wander, taking in the comfortable room, with its large plush sofa and leather coffee table. The huge fireplace dominated the far wall, and its wide plank mantle held photos and trinkets. While the others tried to calm their fears, he made his way down the hall and wandered into Cam's bedroom. A king-size bed filled the space with its pillows and throws. An eclectic array of antique and second-hand furniture made up the rest of the space and Matt could tell that love and talent had gone into restoring them.

He walked back to the door and turned to face the room again. He pushed all worry from his mind and pictured Cam. Everything he knew about her and what he had observed all told him that she was organized and methodical. Independent and strong. Canny and smart. Loyal and honorable. He wouldn't be surprised if she had gone after this guy herself.

But he was trying to get a feel for how she thought. How she lived. So he thought of how he was when he came home from work. First thing is drop your keys, and he remembered a crystal bowl on the counter in the kitchen. Slip your jacket off and throw it on a chair. Walk to your room so you can remove your gear, stow your weapon—*Safe?* he thought. And he moved to the closet to check for a gun safe. He noticed a floor safe, about five feet tall, and more than likely bolted to the floor. He thought of his routine and began to look for another bowl or basket or something that she would store her badge, holster, or whatever else in. On top of the safe, tucked in the back, was a wicker basket, and seeing it, Matt pulled it to him. Sitting in the basket was Cam's badge and credentials. Unsure if she had more than one set, he hollered for Finn and Jimmy.

He stuck his head out of the doorway of the closet. "In here."

"What? What did you find?" Finn couldn't hide the panic building in his voice. His mind had played out so many different scenarios that Cam could be facing. And none of them ended well.

Matt tried to ignore the plea in his friend's voice. "I started going through my routine of what I do when I come home, and I found this basket tucked back in the far corner. It has her badge and ID in it. Does she have another set?"

Finn blanked for a moment. He could smell her in here. Her soft and subtle scent filled him and he could think of nothing else for a moment.

Jimmy tried to think through the raging panic. He could not say for certain if she did have another set. He would bet that she did, but he wasn't certain.

"She does," Jack said from behind them. He reached a hand out and Matt placed his daughter's badge in his hand. He caressed the cool metal and thought of his only child.

Unsure of what to say, Matt stumbled. "Sir…I, um, I only worked with Detect—Cam, for about two weeks, but sir, um, if anyone can take care of themselves, it would be her, sir."

Jack smiled. "Yes. Yes, she would." But fear and fury rolled and mixed like fire and ice in his belly. He was unsure if he could trust his judgment anymore. Hell, just twenty minutes ago, he found out that a man he thought he knew he could trust was a coldblooded killer. No, just a killer but a monster. Could he really trust what he thought he knew?

Jimmy could read the thoughts on Jack's face as easily as if he would have spoken them aloud. "Don't go there, Jack. Don't. She's smart. She's tough. She wouldn't have gone after him if she wouldn't have thought she could take him."

Jack nodded; his friend was right. His daughter was tough. She was smart. So she would come home. "Okay. But if he hurts her, I swear I'll kill him myself."

"I'll hold your coat, sir," Matt said. And Jack smiled for the first time since he had heard the news.

Jack put his daughter's badge in his pocket. "She has another set in her car. In her console." He thought back to the conversation they had about it, the night she got caught in the crossfire of a gang turf war.

"She had it made up when she put the trunk safe in. And she went and bought up all new back-up gear. Vest, shotgun, rifle, Glock, ammo, handcuffs, etc."

Finn mentally slapped himself. The car! Her fucking car! "Fuck me! Her car has GPS on it!"

Before they could have someone check it out, one of the uniforms came in. "Sir," Officer Adams stepped in front of Jimmy. "The

BOLO has come back on Detective O'Brien's car. We have it located. It is in the Patterson Park area."

"That's where Martin Foley's house is." Jimmy started barking orders. "Get me the officers who spotted her car now! Tom, I need you and Matt to head that way now. Get eyes on that house. No one moves until we are ready. If any officer tries to take that house before we get there, they will have to deal with me."

He turned and looked Jack in the eye. "Jack, I need you to stay here—"

"The fuck you do! That's my daughter in there!"

Jimmy swallowed the anger. He didn't need this right now, but he sure as hell didn't need Jack anywhere near that house. Or Dickie. "Jack! Jack, shut up and listen to me!" he snapped. "Please trust me. I can't get her back if I am busy worrying about you going in there and doing something stupid. You have to trust me."

Jack paused. He knew Jimmy was right, but that was his daughter. His baby. "Jimmy...," he started. He had to pause and swallow the tears that were lumped in his throat, before he could start again. "Please don't make me wait here. Please. I have never once interfered in one of yours or Cam's investigations. I am not going to start now. But goddammit he has my daughter! Don't make me sit here and wait by the damn phone."

Jimmy had never heard Jack beg. Until now. The plea was on his face and ringing through his voice. He hung his head, regretting his next words before he had even said them. "Fine. But Jack, I swear, if you get in the way, at all, I will put cuffs on you and put you in the back of a car. Understand?"

Jack nodded. Relief and terror warred on his face.

Jimmy looked at Finn next. "Before you say anything, you better listen. She means a lot to all of us. But I swear, if you do anything, anything that in anyway jeopardizes us getting her back or anything that jeopardizes another officer in order to get to her, I'll take you down myself. I swear I will."

Finn nodded. He would have agreed to anything as long as Jimmy didn't try to keep him away.

"Say it."

"Yes, sir. I understand."

"Good." Now that that was done, he could focus on getting his partner back. "All right, folks," he said, addressing the rest of the team that was gathered in the living room. "Joe, I need you and Blake to go in the back. The Foley house will be the fifth house down on the right if you are coming in from the Pratt Street entrance."

Blake Rogers voiced something that he and his partner had discussed on the ride here. "Sir, just one thing..." He paused. He was hesitant to bring it up, but he knew he had to voice his concern. "Are we sure that it is the captain? I mean we have been working the Flannery Gang connection and that seems like a sure thing. How did we get around to the captain?" Blake hated to ask, but it was a huge thing going after another cop, not to mention that it wasn't just any cop. It was the goddamn cop in charge!

Jimmy had to pause. He didn't have time to fucking explain this right now, but he knew if he was asking these guys to go and hunt down one of their own, they were going to need a damn good reason for doing it.

So he laid it all out. From the connection to Martin Foley to the "coincidence" in Ireland. The fact that Dickie was Martin Foley's older brother, but had hid this fact from all of them, added credence to their side. "Once Capt—" He stopped. No, he thought, no he didn't deserve that respect now. "Once Richard Thems found out about the investigation heading toward the Flannery Gang, he took advantage of it. He even tried to get me to go back to them, when our investigation turned toward Martin Foley's unknown older brother." And God, that stung. He had laid out the whole fucking case for him. The whole goddamn thing.

The look on Jimmy's face had the rest of the questions stuck in Blake's throat. He glanced over at Joe. He could read the worry and doubt written on his partner's face. Neither wanted to believe that Captain Thems was guilty of any of it, but the truth of the evidence was hard to ignore.

CHAPTER 27

The Foley house was quiet and dark. Blake and Joe hid in the cover of darkness and watched for any sign of movement. The back alley stank of trash and piss, and they had to carefully move through the mounds of clutter and trash that littered the cracked concrete.

Even though the evening air had chilled when the sun set, sweat rolled down Blake's back under the weight of the bullet-proof vest. He had his service weapon strapped to his thigh in his tactical drop holster and his patrol rifle slung across his chest. The weight of his badge was heavy on the chain around his neck.

"So do you think it was the captain?" Doubt still laced his voice and his partner picked up on it.

Joe shrugged his shoulders, adjusting his vest. "The evidence is strong. And our job is based on evidence."

"Yeah, but what does your gut say?"

"My gut is telling me that it is him." He rushed to continue before his young partner could resume his doubting. "No cop wants to be where we are now. Waiting to arrest one of our own, especially one so respected and loved. Not to mention the goddamn crimes that he is accused of."

Blake sat quietly, digesting what Joe had said. Never would he admit the fears he also had with arresting a commanding officer. What if they were wrong? Where would that leave all of them? Arresting a decorated and well-loved member of the force, the backlash would be horrendous. Shaking off the doubt and concern, Blake radioed in a "Go" for their position.

Blake and Joe weren't the only ones struggling with doubt. Detective Todd Smith, a Vice cop, was currently in a heated debate with Jimmy in the command vehicle. "What the hell are you thinking, Jimmy?" Disbelief rang through the veteran cop's voice. "Are you nuts? How could you possibly believe that he did this? You were his partner for fifteen goddamn years!"

"Don't you think I know that?" Jimmy exploded. "Don't you think I have questioned this myself?" He turned on Todd, all of his hurt and anger unleashing in one explosive breath. "I know goddamn well what this means. What it is going to cause. Don't you dare question my resolve with this. That man is like my brother, my goddamn family, and I have enough to deal with without you throwing it back in my face!"

You could hear a pin drop. Never before had anyone seen Jimmy explode the way he just had, not even Jack. And he sat stunned, his mouth gaping open. Sure, they had had their fair share of scuffles and fights, but Jimmy was always one who kept his anger in check. Never exploding, he always managed to keep his calm façade in place.

Todd was shocked. But somehow Jimmy's outburst confirmed his worst fears—the captain was guilty. He had seen Jimmy take down hardened killers, mob bosses, and infuriating gangsters, all with a cool and calm façade. But this killer was different; it was someone close. Someone he thought he could always trust. And now, it seemed, as if he crossed another line. A line that never should be crossed—he took another officer. It was akin to taking and hurting someone whose blood runs in your veins.

"Okay," Todd spoke softly, as if the words would crack the very foundation that all of them stood on. "Okay."

Jimmy's head was spinning. He had to sit a moment to gather himself. He wasn't sure he could trust himself to speak yet, so he nodded to Todd and the detective walked out to take up his post out front. Jimmy closed his eyes and dropped his head into his hands. His heart was still pounding and his head was roaring.

Jack watched his oldest friend deal with a broken heart. Others may only see a man who has been betrayed by his former partner, but Jack saw past that to what that betrayal caused. And to add to the hurt and betrayal, the same man had kidnapped a woman who was more than a partner, more than a friend. She was like another daughter. And Jack understood that pain. And he understood what Jimmy was feeling at the very bottom of the pile—guilt.

"Don't you dare blame yourself." Jack stood up in the command RV and stood in front of his friend. "You didn't cause any of this, and there is no way in hell you could have anticipated this."

Jimmy heard the words, but he struggled to accept them. He had to fix this. And he had to fix it now.

It took all Jack had to remain inside when Jimmy got up without a word and walked out. He knew that Jimmy blamed himself for Cam and Dickie both. And he was scared that it was going to be a heavy distraction when he knew his friend needs to be calm and clear.

Jimmy gathered around the corner from the Foley house. He was gathered with Brad Franks and Donnie Jones, the two detectives from Narcotics who were brought in during the beginning of the investigation. Once they realized that the Flannery gang was not involved in the murders, the investigation shifted and the gang and narcotics units took over and began to investigate the Flannery gang for other crimes.

Although they were no longer working the same case, they all gathered to help when Jimmy called in the kidnapping of an officer. So standing around the corner from the house, Jimmy brought all of them up to speed on the layout of the house and the plan for entry.

Speaking to the team in front of him as well as to the other two teams listening in on the mics he laid out the entry plan. "Okay, Franks and Jones, you will enter first. Head straight to the second floor and clear. Joe and Blake, you two have five seconds to move in and clear the backyard. At the count of one, you must breech the back door and we will simultaneously breech the front. Finn and I will take the third floor. Tom and Matt, you two will take sentry point and watch for any suspicious activity on the street."

Jimmy waited for confirmation from all of the team members before he began his countdown. "Five…four…three…two…"

* * * *

Cam was desperate to reach Nina. Unfortunately she had never had to do this before. The spirits and dead always came to her, never the opposite. But she tried anyway. She opened herself completely, not caring who came, just as long as someone did. She didn't know how they would help, but trying was better than giving up. And she damn well would try and fight until he choked the very last breath from her body.

Nina! her mind screamed. *Nina, please God help! Nina, please! I need you!* Cam's mind repeated the plea over and over.

Abigail's screams and pleas became hysterical. Cam's concentration broke, with a sickening crunch. She looked over and saw that Dickie had stomped on Abigail's right knee cap. The pain must have been too much because the older woman's head was sagging to her chest. The look on Dickie's face had Cam fighting the bile rising in her throat.

She looked past Dickie and noticed the tears on Marty's face. His eyes were fixed on his mother's slouched form. Rage, pain, and guilt warred on his swollen and bloodied face. Cam tried not to let Dickie see the concern on her face, so he would hopefully believe that Marty was still unconscious.

She was still open, calling for Nina, when Dickie turned back to her. She tried and failed to hide the fear and pain, but looking at his face, she realized that she was failing. The cuffs were starting to really burn. The radiator had had time to really start to warm and that heat was transferring to her cuffs.

Cam struggled to ignore the look of want and desire that was in Dickie's eyes, afraid her reaction would either excite or anger him. She refused to let him see her fear, see her pain, see her terror. She watched as he knelt in front of her and began to run his hands over her ankles and calves. It took all of her strength to keep her instinctive jerk from happening. She was shocked to realize just how much willpower that it actually took. Without thinking she raised her eyes to Marty and saw pure rage darkening his face. She watched as he struggled with his bindings, trying to break free.

Dickie noticed that he had lost her attention, and he pinched her calf painfully. He smiled as a cry of pain broke through her lips. "So strong, yet so soft," he crooned.

Defiance screamed through her, and before she could think it through, she spit at him. "Fuck. You."

Shocked, he ran his fingers across his cheek, wiping the spit away. And like a whip, his hand flicked out and a backhand split her lip deep. She couldn't stop the tears that flooded her eyes. The force of the slap had spots dancing before her eyes. She could feel the blood running down her chin, mortified when she could no longer hold back the tears.

Instinctively Marty yelled out for his brother to stop. Dickie spun around, surprised to hear his brother's voice. Cam opened her mouth, ready to bring the conversation back to her, but shut her mouth at the slight shake of Marty's head.

She hung her head, ashamed of the tears, but mostly because she allowed the focus to stay on Marty. She was beginning to lose hope, afraid of what would happen to her father. To Jimmy. To Brooks. To Finn. Would Dickie continue with his pattern and leave her death to her family? Or would he finish the job this time?

She was so lost in herself that she didn't hear her name being spoken. She refused to allow him to see any more reactions from her. So she tried to retreat deeper. And then she felt it. Deep and warm. A tingling. Something tugged in her mind. She struggled to remember what the tingling meant.

Cam? Cam? Please, Cam... She knew that voice. Who had that voice? She struggled to come back, something was dragging her down. Down deep, so she wouldn't feel. Wouldn't remember. But she fought. She reached and fought and finally she broke the surface.

"Cam? Cam!" The voice was panicked. Hysterical. Annoying. Nina struggled to bring her back. Cam, powerful and strong, had begun to retreat. She had started to hide, and when Nina got a good glimpse of her face, she could understand why. Bruises littered her face, dried blood dotted and mingled with her freckles. She had a line of caked blood coming from her left ear, and a trail of bruises going down her neck to her chest. The bastard had ripped her clothes, tearing her shirt in half. Her bra was still in place but blackish bruises peeked out from behind the lacey fabric. Her stomach was an unnatural shade of plum, and Nina worried about internal injuries.

Nina forced her eyes to ignore the bruising and focus back on Cam's face, only to see that her left eye was blood red. He had hit her so hard the blood vessels in her eyes burst. "Cam, please come back to me," she begged.

Cam was struggling to stay afloat. The darkness beckoned her back, promising bliss without the feeling of pain. Cam focused on Nina's face, and finally she could vaguely hear the words that she was saying.

"Cam!" Nina was scared she had retreated too far. She knew that she was open, so Nina went on instinct. She jumped in.

The pain blinded her. Nina gasped and the sound escaped Cam's lips. She fought to ignore the pain and find Cam. She could feel her. She was slipping into the dark and Nina was scared that she wouldn't be able to come back. Unable to get her to respond, Nina did the last thing that she wanted to do. She took over and jerked Cam's arms hard against the hot steel surrounding her wrists. Cam screamed in her head and the sound startled Nina so much she lost her connection and was thrown from Cam's body.

Cam's first coherent thought was of the immense pain in her left wrist. She thought she felt the bone snap, and she held on to the pain as a lifeline. As long as she held onto it, she couldn't fall back down the rabbit hole. She glanced to her right when she heard her name. And relief poured through her when she saw Nina crouched beside her. She glanced around and searched for Dickie.

"Don't worry. He's downstairs."

Cam focused all of her energy on clearing her head. "Why? Why did he go?"

Nina shrugged. "There was a loud crash and yelling."

Cam's hope rose. "Jimmy?"

Nina rose and walked to the high window. "I see flashing lights! They are down the street! It looks like they are at Marty's house."

Cam thought she heard her wrong. "But we are at Marty's house."

Nina glanced behind her. "No. No, we are down the block."

"No, no, no..." Cam trailed off. Hope quickly vanished.

Nina watched as the strongest woman she had ever known broke in front of her. Panic rose in her, but to her surprise she squelched it.

Determined, she began to figure out how to get Cam to realize that this wasn't the end. Her end. But she didn't know how.

"Cam," Marty's voice was soft and full of pain. He struggled to hold his head up so he could look at her. "He moved us before you showed up."

"Why—?" Cam stopped herself before she finished. She knew why. Marty's house would be the first place they would go, and the flashing lights outside proved her point. But where in the hell were they? she wondered.

"Where are we?"

Marty slowly glanced around. His left eye was swollen shut and his right wasn't much better. His jaw was broken so he slowly and quietly talked, each syllable painful and pure agony, but he wanted to live. He needed to live. He glanced at his mother; he had been avoiding this look because he was afraid she was dead. He hadn't heard her voice in a while, and fear raced through him. A sob choked him and he struggled to keep it in.

Cam heard as Marty tried to regain his control and looked up. She saw that he was staring at his mother. She turned, painfully, and tried to access the older woman's situation. Her right leg was bent at an unnatural angle and her knee was a black and purple and a swollen mess. Her face had a scattering of bruises, and she could see the same pinch marks all over her arms and legs. But she was breathing. Slow and shallow, but at least she was breathing.

Marty sagged in relief. "I just don't understand why he is doing this. I just don't know why."

"Well, then let me enlighten you." They both jumped at the sound of Dickie's voice. Neither had heard him come up the stairs.

Dickie pulled a chair from a back corner and sat down in the middle of all three of them. He glanced between the two, crossing his legs and folding his hands on his knees. "Now where do I begin? Hmm…Oh, I got it.

"Once upon a time, there was a young girl who loved the church dearly. God and family were her only ambitions, the only things she wanted or cared about in life. One day, during service, a new young seminary student comes to intern at her church. He is tall and thin, someone nice and faithful she thinks to herself. But one day, this young girl finds herself alone in the sanctuary, sitting in the front pew talking theology with young new priest.

"So wrapped up in the moment, sharing their faith and dreams, neither hears the sharp clicking of expensive heels, coming down the aisle. So both were startled to hear a shrill voice echo though the sanctuary. 'Abigail! Enough of your dilly-dallying. There are more important things this young man has to do than to waste time talking to you.' The woman's words deflated the young girl's growing hope. Never had another boy shown interest in her. Why would they? Abigail thought. She wasn't beautiful. She was told so every day. She wasn't smart enough. Her parents told her that too."

Cam watched the glee in Dickie's eyes as he recounted the story. She stole a glance at Abigail, the older woman's head hung, her chin brushing her chest. Tears dripped from her cheeks, dotting her dirty and ripped shirt. Cam wondered how this man she had looked up to her entire life could sit and recount this heart-wrenching story as if it was a comedy. No sympathy could be seen anywhere on his face. And Cam guessed there was none in his heart, not even for his mother.

Dickie had carried on, unaware or not caring, of the effect it was having on his mother. "Unbeknownst to Abigail's mother, the young priest sought out Abigail. Stealing away whatever time he could with her, using counseling and spiritual advisement as his cover. The two became close, falling in love and stealing any time that they could away from the watchful eyes of the church. At the end of the summer the love that had blossomed between the two of them had created new life. A child. A child neither was prepared for and one neither of them wanted. George, afraid of losing his position in the church, left Abigail, alone and pregnant. Left with no choice she ran back to her mother, so she could fix everything. Her mother sent her to live with an aunt in the country, so Abigail's reputation could remain intact.

"The day of the birth, Abigail's mother had already found a place for the unwanted child, a boy, with a family who lived away from the city. So there would be less chance of gossip. The family who adopted the boy were made to sign a contract, one that said they were to never tell the truth, they were never allowed to tell the child where he came from."

Dickie jerked up and began to pace, anger swamping the room. "Can you believe that? My parents were threatened with jail and financial ruin if they told. Helen Matthews, a conniving and wretched old hag, swatted away her own flesh and blood as if he was a gnat. An inconvenience, a piece of trash to throw out."

He stopped in front of Abigail and kicked her hard. He smiled when she cried out. "So how does it feel to have that piece of trash come back? Never once did you try to find me! You just turned your back and left me with strangers! Your own child! While you went and had"—he turned away and charged Martin—"another child!" He ended with his fist slamming into his brother's face.

Abigail screamed for him to stop. "Stop! Please. He had nothing to do with it! Dammit *stop*!"

Dickie turned. "See she even cries for him! Did you cry for me, you bitch? No, no, you didn't. You just gave me away! And never looked back."

Cam spoke up. "You're wrong. You're dead wrong."

Dickie spun on Cam. "What would you know about it? You and your perfect life. You have a family who loves you, who would fight for you, who would never let you go."

"She never let you go. She was sixteen and had no choice. Her mother took you from her. And the church took George."

Dickie was seething. "Lies! All lies to save her other son!"

Abigail finally spoke up. "I cried for you. I begged for you. My mother married me off to another. I mourned for you so much, I wasn't there for the son I did have. I ignored him and pushed him away because he wasn't you! He wasn't the little boy my heart longed for. It wasn't until a few days ago that I realized that in mourning for you I lost another. I had robbed myself of two children."

Dickie looked momentarily confused. He shook his head. "No. No. I know the truth. I know the real story. You never wanted me. And neither did my father. I lived every day dreaming that you both would come and take me home. But you never did. Do you know what I lived in? Do you know who you gave me to? The bastard who raised me?"

Cam was shocked. She had always thought Dickie had a happy childhood. A family who adored him. "You always spoke of your parents with love."

Dickie chuckled. "A mirage. A fantasy. My father was a bastard. My mother was no better. They beat me and would lock me away.

I was an abomination to them. They were happy at first to have a child. But then the real story of my birth was revealed to them and I then became a burden. A sin from God. My father was a minister in a small town, and he couldn't have it come out that the child whom they had was actually the result of a wayward priest and the whore who seduced him."

Then it clicked. Cam finally found how all of the pieces fit together. "The cross and the whore."

Dickie laughed. "Took you long enough."

All of the girls were whores, prostitutes who sell themselves to whomever is willing to pay. The mark: the cross left on all of the girls. It had to symbolize the fact that his mother seduced a man of the cloth. And now he used it to beat back the whore, marking them with the sign of the church. Cam remembered the picture she had seen of a younger Abigail, red haired and blue eyes. All of the girls represented his mother.

"But where does Cat fit in?" she wondered aloud.

"Ah, the first to die," he remembered fondly. "I had never killed before. I had used prostitutes numerous times. If they weren't red haired, I would have a wig. And at the same time I was in costume myself—a man of God. At first it started as rough sex. Doing little things first. A pinch here, a smack there. But I paid for them so it was okay. They became my whores. As time went on, I found that it excited me to hear their cries of pain. Hearing them beg for me to stop. I was beginning to get bored, the pleas and tears becoming old." He sat back down in front of Cam, back in story mode. "So one night, while I was in Ireland, I was out for a walk, looking for another girl and I see Cat. She is standing next to an old church, working the street. I took it as a sign from God. It was time to move forward with a deep, dark desire that had been consuming me."

Cam tried not to get sick. The look of pure desire and delight on her former captain's face was pure evil.

CHAPTER 28

Jimmy and Finn burst through the broken door, moving methodically and stealthily through the dark and quiet house. Finn had a sickening feeling that something was wrong. His gut told him this was wrong. But he pushed it aside and continued through the house.

Jimmy noticed the quiet. It was too quiet. He tapped Finn twice on the shoulder, a silent signal to begin their move to the second floor. Jimmy ordered complete silence, not wanting to give Dickie any opportunity to shoot or hurt Cam or the Foleys. He also wanted to lessen the opportunity for Dickie to use one of them as a shield.

Finn moved silently up the stairs, his rifle at the ready. He was prepared to take a life to save the one he loved. But it was too quiet. Dead quiet. Ignoring the plan, Finn silently moved to the third floor. Jimmy followed, both eager to find Cam.

When they reached the third floor landing, it became apparent that no one was here. "Goddammit!" Finn kicked a chair across the floor. He could see blood and scuff marks scattered over the dusty floor. "They were here. They were fucking here!"

Jimmy called an "all clear" across the radio. "Dammit." He heard Jack rush through the door, yelling up the stairs. "Cam! Cam! Jimmy! Jimmy, do you have her?" He watched with a heavy heart as his friend rushed in the small attic area and his face fell as he saw the empty room.

Jimmy rushed over when Jack's eyes found the scuff marks and blood. "No! Jimmy, where is she? Where is my girl?" Jimmy held his friend as he shook.

Finn was suffocating. He rushed down the stairs and out the front door. He ignored the questions and looks and walked to clear his head. He knew he couldn't leave the scene, but dammit he needed air and quiet. He just needed to think. He needed to breathe.

Where are you, Cam? he thought. Emotions threatened to swamp him. *Where are you?*

And then he heard it. A clicking. It encircled him. Searching the evening, he tried to see what could make that noise but there was nothing. But still the *click, click, click* continued.

Nina had watched with a heavy heart as the men stormed the wrong house. She couldn't do anything about it. She kept going back and forth between the scene outside and Cam inside. Frustrated with her limitations, she was seething.

She watched as Finn burst through the front door and began to walk by himself. And then an idea struck her. Switching back to her hooker heels, she rushed to where the heartbroken man stood and began to test her theory. Walking around him she tried to make noise. She screamed at him and shouted. She whispered in his ear and stood face-to-face with him. All the while moving, trying to get him to hear her.

She had about given up. She had already stopped yelling and shouting. And now, with tears on her cheeks she tried walking around one more time, begging him, in her mind, to please hear her. She almost missed it at first. The look of bewilderment that crossed his face. But she saw the slight jerk of his head and hope bloomed bright.

She began to walk faster, with more excitement, but he looked doubtful. And she realized he couldn't hear her anymore. So she desperately tried to remember what caused him to hear in the first place. She had about given up hope and emotions surged through her—that was it! she thought. Emotions. Drawing everything she had, she etched Cam's face in her mind and let all of the emotions and feeling she had for her swamp her. And it worked.

Finn was struggling to figure out where the clicking was coming from. He radioed for Jimmy and the team and prepared to be heckled. Here they were looking for Cam, and he was about to ask about "clicking," but they had nothing else, and the clicking was tugging at something in his brain.

Jimmy and the team rushed over. "What? What is it? Have you found something?"

Finn shrugged. "I don't know. But I walked over here to get calmed, and I started hearing clicking."

Jimmy started to get pissed, when all of a sudden he heard it. He held up a hand for silence and listened closely. He faintly heard a *click, click, click. Footsteps?* he thought.

"Heels!" Jimmy and Finn turned around and found Brooks. "It's heels." To prove her point, she walked around Finn in her pointy-heeled boots. "Heels."

Finn slapped his forehead. He was a fucking idiot. Of course Cam would call for the only person who could hear her—Nina. "Shut up!" He snapped and then closed his eyes. "OK, where is she?" It took a few moments, and he thought he had lost his mind, but slowly the clicking moved away from the Foley house. And he began to follow.

A block down the street the clicking abruptly stopped at a house that had been ravaged by a fire. The first two floors were blackened around the windows and doors, but the third floor looked untouched. Finn had motioned for everyone to stay back, so he moved silently back to them. They had positioned themselves around the corner, ten houses to the south.

Matt and Tom looked a little doubtful, but Jimmy and Brooks were willing to give this plan a little bit of faith. "It had been gutted by a fire, but the third floor looks OK. I am not sure what the rest of the house looks like but he had to have found a way in and up."

Jimmy listened. He began to try and think like his old partner so maybe he could figure this out. "Matt and Tom, move to the rear of the house. See if you can see anything useful from back there. Finn, you and I are going to take the front. We need to see if there is a way in there."

Finn thought about it for a moment. "Jimmy, the rear seems like the best entry. I say we all take the back. Matt and Tom can cover and you and I will breech. Brooks, slowly walk back to the Foley house and get the rest of the team. Tell them to regroup here. Give us thirty seconds and then take the front. They need to hug the stone of the building so it lessens the chance of him seeing their approach."

He watched her walk back to the Foley house and began to move to the back. They were all on radio silence, because they knew Dickie probably had his on.

Finn and Jimmy counted to thirty and then, trusting their back up, made entry. The blackened walls stretched from the back of the house to the front. The silently made their way through the kitchen and into the dining room. This house seemed to mirror the layout of the Foley house, so they navigated their way using that specific layout.

As they reached the stairs, they could see a faint flickering, causing shadows to dance along the walls. Silently they began to slowly make their way up the charred and brittle stairs. Finn had to fight the urge to rush, knowing that his actions could cost Cam and/or the Foleys their lives.

A low voice started to rumble down the stairs. A deep, almost amused sing-song voice that sent chills down Finn's spine. He felt Jimmy tense and knew that they finally had their man.

Finn paused when he heard Cam's voice. "...Cat fit in?"

His heart tripped to hear that name. Rage began to build up and he readied himself for a fight. Betrayal and disgust churned in his belly and he fought with everything to keep his head straight.

The closer they got to the landing, the more and more Finn's control slipped. He heard the older man begin to recount that fateful encounter.

"She deserved what I gave her," he heard Dickie say. "She was a whore prostituting at a church! A church! God will bless me for that one."

Cam had tears running down her cheeks. "No one deserves what you did. No one."

She flinched when he bounded up and moved in closer to hit her again."

"Move one fucking inch and I swear I will put a bullet in your forehead."

Cam's head jerked up just as fast as Dickie's did. "Finn!"

Dickie began to raise his hands, when lightning fast he brought up his weapon. Cam seized the momentary distraction and scissor kicked out and swept Dickie onto his ass.

Finn kept his weapon on Dickie, but focused on Cam. Dickie, in turn, reached for a small caliber handgun tucked in his jacket. The deafening boom echoed through the small, empty space. They both watched in horror as Dickie screamed and fell, holding his right shoulder in place.

"You bastard! You shot me! You fucking bastard," Dickie wailed.

Finn rushed to Cam and took inventory of her injuries. When he got to her writs, he yelled for Jimmy. "Call an ambulance! And get me a fucking cuff key!" He ran his hands over her face and checked her for any other injuries.

Jimmy radioed the dispatcher to get the ambulance on the way and to get the other two victims, as well.

He moved over to check on his former friend. "Why?" He needed to know that answer. Just that one answer.

Shock and anger raged through him at his answer. "Why not?"

Finn was just a bit faster than Jimmy as his fist slammed into Dickie.

Jack rode in the ambulance with his daughter. Holding her hand and stroking her hair. Showing her love and support, all the while chewing her ass out. "Why? Why did you go alone? You stubborn as a mule girl!"

Finn followed in Cam's vehicle and Jimmy sat beside him. They had left the rest of the team to clean up the scene and canvass the area. Abigail and Martin Foley were in two other ambulances.

Jimmy's emotions warred between rage and hurt. He had trusted this man with his life, only to learn that it was all a lie. He struggled to understand what caused it. Cam had told both of them what had happened and what he had said to her, but none of them could fathom what made him snap.

Finn left all of the paperwork to Jimmy and focused on Cam. He stayed by her side as she was examined and released. She had refused to remain in the hospital for observation. She wanted the comfort of her own home. Finn promised the doctor that she would follow all of his orders and just rest for a day or two.

Later that night, they sat on the plush sofa in front of a roaring fire. Finn tried to ignore the stab of guilt and anger that he felt every time he saw the white bandages around her wrists. They had checked on the Foleys before they had headed home. Martin was in ICU, in a medically induced coma. He was expected to make a full recovery, minus a spleen and gall bladder. He had numerous cracked ribs and one that was precariously close to puncturing his lung. His jaw was shattered and so was his left cheekbone. His left orbital bone was cracked, but he should still be able to see with no issues.

Abigail suffered a broken knee and a fractured shin bone. She was bruised and swollen on her face, but no bones were broken there.

Cam ended up with a mild concussion and second-degree burns on her wrist. She had a busted lip and bruises, but nothing too serious.

Cam saw the guilt on Finn's face and rushed to reassure him. "I'm fine. I promise. And that bastard can never hurt anyone again." She turned, taking his face in her hands. "Besides, Jimmy shot his good arm."

Finn had to laugh. And Cam smiled at the sound. She had had enough crying and anger for one day. "How do you think Martin Foley and his mother are going to deal with all of this?"

Cam shrugged. She remembered the guilt that had made a permanent home on Martin's face. Even through the beatings. "He has to remember that he isn't his brother's keeper. Dickie did all of this on his own. None of it had to do with Martin. He will probably always feel guilty but at least now he has his mother to lean on."

Finn nodded. Looking down, he swallowed the lump in his throat.

"Hey?" she quizzed, taking his chin in her hand and turning him towards her. "We know the answers. We know why he did it. I know it won't bring her back, but at least we know."

"Cam," he started. Where did he start? he thought. How did he begin to tell her what she meant to him? How she had become his whole world in just two weeks.

Cam watched the emotions run across his face. She saw everything she needed to see and more. She saw her future. She saw her life. She saw him. "I know, Finn. I know."

He scooped her up and carried her to the bedroom. All the while he smiled, as he held his world in his hands.

EPILOGUE

He hadn't been there to save her. Goddamn Jimmy never called him. "Motherfucker. Stupid motherfucker," He mumbled drunkenly. He stumbled down the semi-deserted street in a seedy part of the city.

He had showed up when the ambulances did and he watched as the fucking Irishman carried his woman to the waiting paramedics. "It should have been me," He yelled. "It should have been *me*!"

He tried to remember where he was going and took a swig of whiskey to help clear his mind. He was going somewhere important, he remembered. He had a purpose.

He saw the blue sign up ahead and smiled. Now he remembered. *See*, he told himself, *I knew where the fuck I was going.*

The inside of the building was loud and hot. Sweaty bodies bumped and grinded on the dance floor, and others danced in cages lining the whole building. The woman in the cages were slowly stripping, erotically showing the consumers what their money could buy. Of course if the police raided, this was just your average strip club. Unbeknownst to them, that all of the dancing was just a sampling to see if you liked it before you bought it. The cops would also never know that the ones in the cages were more money, because they were young and fresh. The forbidden fruit—underage girls. He only knew this because he had been here before. He had sampled some of the fruit.

He sat down shakily on a bar stool, looking around deciding on what he wanted to do, when a firm hand clamped on his shoulder. He turned and stared into the smiling face attached to the hand. "Uncle Duke," he said with a slur.

Duke Green, owner of the Faery Hill, smiled tightly at his nephew. He was beginning to tire of him coming in here drunkenly, disrupting the flow of the club. "Let's go take a walk, Jonah."

Jonah jerked his shoulder free and stood and followed his uncle toward the back. He smiled cockily at the line of bodyguards that followed his uncle around like punks.

Duke stepped into the small hallway that ran between two cage areas. He spun on his nephew and slapped his face.

Jonah hollered and was shocked sober. "What the fuck, man?"

Duke shook his head and put his hand up to shoo away the guards. "Haven't I told you to stop coming in here drunk?"

Jonah's face reddened. "I had a bad night. Jesus!"

Duke shook his head and started to motion for his guys to take Jonah out. But Jonah's words stopped him.

"They got the killer, my team. I was on a call when the call came in, but they went in and got him anyway. He almost killed Ca—Detective O'Brien."

Duke paused. This killer had been hell for his business. If his idiot nephew hadn't been feeding him intel, he could have really screwed up. He already had Sean on his back about staying off the radar. The last thing he needed was his idiot cousin taking over his part of the family business. He needed that pompous ass to stay the hell over in Ireland. It would ruin everything if he came over here, if he thought Duke couldn't handle the situation. And from their last conversation he already had one foot on the damn plane.

But now he saw an opportunity. He knew that his nephew had it hard for this Cam O'Brien. Just as he knew that Finnegan McDougal, the thorn in his cousin's side, was now staying with this Cam. So now an opportunity had just presented itself.

Looking at his nephew, he decided to make a bargain. "What would you say if I told you that I could get the Irishman out of your way?"

Jonah looked up eager. "Are you serious?" His insatiable need for Cam slammed into him. "What do you want?"

Duke smiled. "An inside man."

ABOUT THE AUTHOR

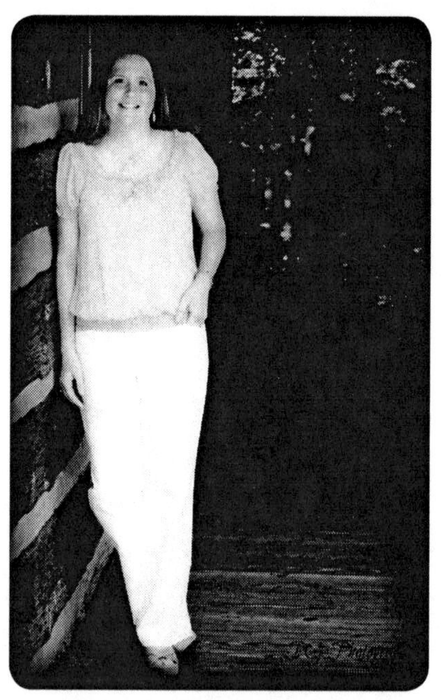

Photo by Pam Gravley with PG Photography

Kimberly Blair's debut novel, *His Brother's Keeper*, is the fulfillment of a life-long dream. Kimberly is married to her high school sweetheart, Josh, who is a police officer in a neighboring town. Kimberly and Josh have two children and live in upstate South Carolina. Kimberly is a dog and cat groomer, as well as an author. *His Brother's Keeper* is the first novel in The Cam O'Brien Series.

CPSIA information can be obtained
at www.ICGtesting.com
Printed in the USA
LVOW12s1455240816
501678LV00003B/500/P

9 781681 398